THE FALLEN ODYSSEY

COREY McCULLOUGH

THE FALLEN ODYSSEY

2nd Paperback Edition

ISBN: 978-0-9966902-1-8

First printed in the United States of America in 2013

10 9 8 7 6 5 4 3 2

For Mom and Dad,
Who have always believed.

PROLOGUE

As I begin this volume, I can't help but think back to my earlier writings, when I was still convinced this was all a nightmare or a fantasy. For a while, I thought it was purgatory, and at times, it has come close to a kind of hell. Back then, all I wanted was to return to Earth. I spent a long time thinking it was all a dream, praying I would wake up. I wondered if I had gone insane and was trapped in my imagination. Eventually, I realized that this place was real. As real as Earth itself. If I hadn't come to that realization, I surely never would have discovered that there is a way home.

Why do I write this? I think it is to help maintain my sanity, because even after I accepted my reality, my fate was not so easy to reconcile. Often, I wondered if I would ever see my family again. Was I destined to die here, in this alternate world so far from my home that the distance could not be measured in miles?

I don't know how I got here, and I certainly never expected to become the man I am today. I never would have thought, in my lifetime, that I would need to raise a weapon to defend myself . . . let alone to take so many lives.

I may have discovered the way home, but leaving is no easy matter. Every day, I wake up and wonder, is my time in this world of swords, shields, magic, and monsters finally nearing its end?

Will I ever see my family again? Or will I die here, farther from home than any map can measure?

Part I

YOUR MOVE

CHAPTER 1

Justin leaned forward and tightened his grip on the wheel. The little pickup usually did well in the snow, but the plows hadn't been out yet. Several inches coated the roads, and it was still coming down hard. There were no tire tracks. Even the tracks Justin had left fifteen minutes ago driving down Allegheny Hill were already filled in. But he hadn't been thinking about the conditions of the road when he'd left the house. All he'd been thinking about was going somewhere, anywhere, to get the hell away from his dad.

Justin flicked the wipers to the highest setting as he felt his phone vibrate in his pocket again. Probably Dad asking where he was.

Justin, you colossal idiot, he thought. *You shouldn't be on the road right now.*

Lighten up, another part of him responded. *It'll be fine. You'll make it home. You're a good driver—you've got this!*

"Sure," he whispered. "Everything will be all right."

He hated when he had to tell himself that.

He was halfway up the hill when a gust of wind buffeted the pickup and sent loose snow swirling in updrafts, creating a whiteout in front of the windshield. He felt the uncomfortable lightness of his tires losing traction, and as the truck's back end fish-tailed, the whiteout cleared long enough for him to see that he had drifted over the center line. He was in the opposite lane, sliding toward a van parked on the side of the street.

Holding his breath, Justin steered into the skid. The tires found purchase on some tightly packed snow, giving him just enough control to ease back toward the center of the road. He passed the van with about a foot to spare between it and the truck's grill, and he reached the top of the hill.

He pulled into the driveway of the small, white house—one of the few in sight without Christmas lights hanging from the gutters. He parked in front of the attached garage and let out a long, deep breath he hadn't realized he'd been holding.

"See? Told you everything would be all right," he whispered in the cold stillness of the truck. But he'd gotten lucky that time, and he knew it.

He pulled out his phone. The message, to his surprise, hadn't been from Dad after all. It was from Kate.

"*Hey. Merry Christmas. Missing you today.*"

"*Missing you, too,*" he typed, then deleted it. "*Merry Christmas,*" he typed, then deleted that, too. His thumbs hovered over the screen. Without sending a reply, he slid the phone back into his pocket.

He got out of the truck just as a slate-gray SUV rolled up the street, its tires producing hollow crunching sounds in the snow as it passed the Holmes mailbox and pulled in next door. The rear doors slid open, and two boys and two girls, ages three to twelve, jumped out and chased each other into the house carrying toys, clothes, books, and other Christmas plunder. The youngest of the four children, a small girl, brought up the rear of the procession carrying two stuffed Curious Georges and a baby doll while she sang in a tiny voice, "Let it 'no, let it 'no, let it 'no." Cecelia Emerson exited the front passenger door, snuck up behind her singing daughter, and scooped her up in her arms. The girl squealed and laughed, and they finished the chorus together on their way into the house.

Jeff Emerson stepped out of the driver's side door. He wore no coat, only a long-sleeved button-up shirt and a stocking cap. He had walked to the rear of the SUV and opened the trunk before he noticed Justin standing in the next driveway. He smiled broadly as he called out in a deep voice, "Well, Merry Christmas, Mr. Holmes!"

Justin's tongue turned to sandpaper. Suddenly, he couldn't get the image out of his head: Jeff driving with the kids singing in the back, getting through the whiteout on the hill just in time to see Justin's pickup turned sideways in the road—too late for Jeff to stop. . . .

"Merry Christmas," Justin finally managed.

Jeff tromped through the snow and leaned against the chest-high picket fence that separated their properties. Snow stuck in his neatly trimmed black beard. "What the heck you doing here?" he said. "I thought you and your dad were visiting your gram'pa today. You're not letting some slippy roads stop you."

Jeff was Justin's current science teacher, and his family had lived next door for as long as Justin could remember. Mr. Emerson was a favorite among students at the high school, due mostly to his ripe-for-parody manner of speech. Like many locals, Jeff didn't "wash" the car; he "wa*r*shed" it. And the roads didn't get "slippery"; they got "slippy." His heavy "Pittsburghese" vernacular resulted in quotable classroom expressions like, "You kids, quit jaggin' aroun'," and, "I'm telling you, yinz gotta know this stuff." Everyone's favorite, "Time's up, pencils *dahn*," had attained almost catchphrase level status among Justin's classmates.

"For once, we're the ones staying home," Justin said. "Grandpa and Uncle Paul are coming over here for dinner. That means I have some shoveling to do, though."

Jeff looked Justin up and down. "You ever gonna stop growing? What're you up to now? Six-four?"

"Six-five."

"*Jeez,*" said Jeff. "No wonder the basketball team stinks so bad without you."

"Yeah, I watched the first few games," said Justin. He decided to leave it at that.

Jeff was not the only one to lament Justin's departure from the team. He'd been the leading scorer last year, and there was not one class photo all the way back to kindergarten when he hadn't been the tallest in the grade. He wasn't *good* tall, unfortunately, but awkward tall. He'd hit six-foot-five by fourteen years old and then, mercifully, stopped. He was almost eighteen now, and over the past few years, he had bumped his head against so many different things in so many different ways that he'd developed a sort of sixth sense about it. He tended to walk permanently slouched. It was the best defense.

"Want any help clearing the driveway?" asked Jeff.

"I can handle it," said Justin.

"That's not what I asked," Jeff said. "Why don't you tell your dad to get his lazy ass out here and do it himself?"

"He doesn't work on holidays," said Justin.

"Government worker, huh?" Jeff said with a smile. "We'll be stopping by sometime this evening, probably, if that's all right. We'll call first. Wouldn't want to be *those* neighbors."

"Dad has a couple gifts for the kids, I think," said Justin.

Jeff looked away. He hesitated, then took off his hat and ran a hand through his black hair before blurting out, "How's your dad doing? Really doing, I mean."

"Fine," said Justin. He said it the way he always did—quick and a little higher-pitched than normal. "He's fine."

"I know he is," said Jeff, "but, you know. I hope. . . . What about you?"

"Hey, a lot of people out there are worse off than us, right?" said Justin.

"Okay," said Jeff. "Well, good enough, Justin. I guess we'll see yinz tonight." He started back toward his driveway and held one hand up in a wave, calling over his shoulder, "Try to stay warm!"

Jeff grabbed some boxes from the trunk of the SUV and walked to the house. Christmas music floated across the lawn when he opened the door. When it closed behind him, all was silent again.

CHAPTER 2

"Dad?" Justin called as he stepped through the front door, trying, as usual, not to look at the coat rack.

"Living room!"

Justin left his boots on and walked to the living room, which was also the dining room, depending on the time of day. Benjamin Holmes sat at the table. His glasses were perched at the end of his rather large nose, and he turned to look at Justin not through the glasses but over them. There was a chip in the left lens that had been there so long Justin doubted Ben even noticed it anymore.

"She'll be seaworthy by dinner," Ben said, showing off the hollow piece of plastic in his hands—the hull of the model ship Justin had given him as a Christmas gift that morning.

Justin looked at it and made an acknowledging sort of noise in his throat that was not quite a confirmation, not quite a sigh. It came out as a dull, noncommital, "Hmm."

Ben craned his neck to look through his glasses and used a tiny brush to apply some glue to the crow's nest. He looked so *stupid* doing that. . . . Why didn't he just push his glasses up so he could see through them like a normal person?

"I'm thinking of calling her the *Maine*," he said. "Remember the *Maine*."

"Not really," said Justin.

"It wasn't a question," Ben said. "Remember the *Maine*. The Spanish–American War. Don't they teach history anymore?"

Justin looked around the table at the scattered bags of tiny plastic pieces and paints. "Where are the instructions?"

"'Remember the *Maine*! To hell with Spain!'" said Ben. "It was a battle cry. The sinking of the *Maine* is what sparked the war, but, to this day, nobody knows if Spain had anything to do with the *Maine* going down."

"Hmm," Justin said again, same inflection.

Silence.

"Did the Lewises lend you the salt?" Ben said.

Justin looked away. He had almost forgotten the pretense he had invented to leave the house. "It's Christmas," he said with a shrug. "How could they say no?"

"Good," said Ben. "Wouldn't want Uncle Paul and Grandpa getting stuck in the driveway again."

"Maybe they should just stay home," said Justin. "The plows haven't been out at all, and I think it's supposed to get even worse."

"I doubt that'll stop them," said Ben. "Uncle Paul said Grandpa really wanted to see you today."

"I guess I'd better clear the driveway, then," said Justin.

Without waiting for a response, he walked back out to the front door. He felt a pang of guilt for lying to his dad about where he'd been, but it would pass.

As he grabbed a pair of gloves from the closet, his eyes went automatically to the coat rack and the green jacket. It had hung there, unmoved and untouched, for almost a year. Exactly where his mother had left it.

From the garage, Justin grabbed a plastic shovel with a metal edge and a bag of rock salt left over from the previous winter, with an old Pittsburgh Pirates souvenir cup inside as the scoop. His breath showed in puffs of vapor as he got to work. The scrape of the metal edge against the ice echoed up and down Main Street Extension. Each time he cleared a row, he dipped the Pirates cup into the bag, pulled out a scoop of salt, and spread it over the concrete. The irony was that after a few rows, he actually *was* running low on salt. Hopefully Jeff had some.

As Justin turned toward the Emersons' house, a small brown object half-buried in the snow along their sidewalk caught his eye. He squinted and recognized it. He speared his shovel into the snow to stand it up, then walked to the waist-high picket fence separating the Holmes and Emerson properties.

Justin braced himself against the top of the fence. He did a few warm-up motions—he hadn't done this since he was a kid—and boosted himself up and over the fence to the Emersons' side. He crossed the driveway, walked to the sidewalk, and stooped to pick up the brown object: one of two stuffed Curious Georges.

Brushing the snow from its head, he carried it to the front door. He raised his hand to ring the doorbell but, on second thought, came up short. Instead, he tilted back the lid of the old-fashioned letter box mounted on the wall by the door. He placed George standing in the box. Then he rang the doorbell, turned, and ran.

This time, Justin took the fence in a leap, no warm-ups. He lost his footing when he landed on the other side and fell flat on his rear end. He started to stand but heard the Emersons' front door open, so he ducked low to stay hidden.

A pause.

"Well, look who's here!" Jeff announced, chuckling. "Come and see who's at the door!"

A moment later, a little girl's giggle floated across the frozen lawn.

"Must've hitched a ride on Santa's sleigh," said Jeff. His voice shifted, directed toward the Holmes house, and he added, "Thank you, Santa, for giving Georgie-boy a ride home!"

Justin cupped his gloved hands over his mouth. *"Ho, ho, ho!"* he bellowed.

When the Emersons' door swung shut again, Justin stood back up and brushed himself off.

Justin's gaze wandered to the basketball hoop mounted on the garage. Bending over, he scooped up a handful of snow, smashed it into a tight ball, and took a jump-shot. The snowball sailed in an arc, came down through the rim, and broke into a white cloud against the frozen net. As he turned, he realized he was being watched from his dining room window.

Ben Holmes, perched forward a bit in his wheelchair, raised both hands, pantomiming the referee signaling that the three-pointer was good. Justin tried not to smile but couldn't help it. He grabbed the shovel and returned to the half-cleaned driveway.

CHAPTER 3

Justin adjusted his necktie in the mirror. He hated wearing a tie, but for as long as he could remember, it had been an unspoken tradition that everyone dressed up for the Holmes family's Christmas dinner.

He crossed his bedroom to his window. The sun had set, and the street was lit up by Christmas lights in addition to the usual, dirty glow of the streetlights. One of those streetlights was situated directly outside the window of his second-floor bedroom. It sometimes flickered weirdly, and it buzzed so loudly at night that you could hear it from inside, even through double-paned glass.

Justin's grandpa had once told him that the houses in this neighborhood had all been built by an old, rich guy who had predicted the hilltop's valuable access to the businesses on Main Street. That seemed like a funny concept these days, given Main Street's empty storefronts and revolving door of tenants. Grandpa Holmes called it a "rust belt" town. Or he had, anyway. He couldn't talk much since the stroke.

Justin turned back from the window. He looked around his bedroom, at the bed and the nightstand with his old-fashioned clock radio—always better at waking him up than his phone's alarm. At his TV and his PlayStation on his dresser. At his iPad on his desk and his backpack beside it. At the posters on his wall, the push-pinned yearbook photos of his friends, and the taped newspaper cuttings from some of his highest-scoring basketball games.

He looked at it all, and without warning, something deep inside rose up and said, *You should just tear it all down. Put it in the trash where it belongs.*

No, he thought. *That's crazy. This is my life. My memories. It's all. . . .*

Pointless. All of it. It's all pointless.

He tried to squash the feeling, but the best he could do was relocate it. He looked at his phone again, at the message from Kate: "*Hey. Merry Christmas. Missing you today.*" What was he supposed to say to something like that?

He tossed his phone onto the bed and looked at his reflection again. The tie and dress clothes felt all wrong. It felt like make-believe. Like polishing a cheap knockoff. Their Christmases had always been good. Truly good. How could he even pretend that today compared, after everything that had happened?

He loosened the tie and ripped it from his neck. His fingers couldn't unbutton the shirt fast enough. He threw it over his head. When his belt got stuck in the belt loops, he yanked it out and flung it across the room into the corner, and the buckle gouged the drywall. Angrily, he grabbed the jeans and T-shirt he'd been wearing earlier and changed back into them.

"Justin?"

Zipping up his jeans, Justin craned his neck toward the bedroom doorway where he had a clear view down the stairs to the first floor of the house. At the bottom of the stairs, his father sat in his chair. He wore a sweater vest and tie. His hair was perfect.

"You . . . all right?" Ben asked.

"Fine," Justin said.

Ben's glasses were halfway down his nose again. This time, he pushed them up to the bridge to look at Justin through them. "Uncle Paul just called," he said. "They're on their way, but they'll be a little late. Wanna help me finish that model ship?"

Justin shook his head. "If they're going to be late, I'd better give the driveway another once-over," he said.

"Nah, the driveway's fine," said Ben. "You don't have to—"

"I know that," Justin cut in, still riding the wave of frustration. "But if I don't do it, it's not like anybody else is going to. . . ."

Ben's nostrils flared a little. He leaned forward in his chair.

"That's not what I . . ." Justin said. "You know I didn't mean it like—"

"I know things have not been easy, Justin," said his father.

"Dad, you know I didn't—"

"No," Ben said with uncharacteristic sternness. "That's enough. I know things are hard right now, so I've done my best to try to be understanding about the occasional slamming door. I've tried to keep my mouth shut about all these drives you take in the truck that you won't tell me about, because I know you need your space to deal with what happened in your own way. But you *can't. Keep. Doing* this."

"Dad, listen—"

"*You* listen. If you're pissed at me about something, we can argue—we can have a fight. Stay here, and we'll fight. If you need to yell at me, stay here, and let's have a yelling match for God's sake, but you don't get to just storm out of the house and leave me here every time something makes you a little upset. Problems aren't solved like that. Running away won't work the way you think it will. You're not a child. Your actions have consequences—"

"I *know that*!" Justin snapped.

It came out much more loudly than he'd meant to, and Ben drew back a bit. Soberly, Justin realized a threshold had just been crossed. He had never yelled at his dad like that before. But instead of getting angry, Ben smirked a little.

"Good," Ben said evenly. "Now we're getting somewhere." The oven timer went off in the kitchen, and Ben pivoted his wheelchair. "Come downstairs when you're ready," he said. "I'll be in the kitchen. I will listen to you yell at me for as long as you want. Anything, if it will keep you here."

Justin opened his mouth to say something, but he wasn't sure what to say as Ben used his hands to wheel himself back through the living room, which was currently the dining room. Then Justin put his phone into his pocket and headed down the stairs.

He hesitated. For a moment, he just stood there, looking down the hallway, listening to the clatter of pots and pans as his dad finished up dinner. Then he turned, and he walked toward the front door.

Quietly, he pulled his boots on, wrenching hard on the laces to tie them and clenching his teeth, already angry at himself for his decision. And angry at his dad for always being right. And angry at Uncle Paul for being dumb enough to bring Grandpa over in this weather just because it was Christmas. Angry at the whole world for reasons he couldn't decide on right now.

He grabbed his coat and pulled it on. He gripped the doorknob, looking at his mother's green jacket on the coat rack for about the thousandth time. He always tried not to look at it. But he always looked. And it made his stomach hurt every time. He balled his hands into fists. Now *there* was a reason to be angry if there ever was one.

He opened the door and stepped outside. At the sound of the door, his father yelled down the hallway, "Justin? Wait, Jus—!"

Justin slammed the door behind him and marched out into the snow.

CHAPTER 4

Justin woke with a gasp of panic and sat straight up in bed.

His heart was racing. His breath came in quivering, shallow inhales. He took a deep, slow breath in through his nostrils and out through his mouth to try to calm down from whatever had woken him with such a start.

Must have been a nightmare, he thought with a sigh. *The kind you don't remember.* He had been having a lot of those recently.

He blinked hard, trying to force his eyes to adjust to the darkness around him. He rubbed his eyes with his knuckles but still couldn't see anything. No light—not even any from the streetlight outside his window. No sound, either.

Power outage, he thought. *From all the snow, I guess.*

He turned and groped in the darkness for his phone on the nightstand but couldn't seem to reach it. He stretched farther. Then he felt his phone in his pants pocket and realized he was fully dressed and lying on top of the covers. His phone, wallet, and keys were all in the pockets of his jeans. He couldn't remember why he had gone to bed without bothering to get undressed first—couldn't remember going to bed at all, for that matter. Even his boots were still on. The last thing he seemed to be able to remember was storming out of the house, but that felt like a long time ago, for some reason.

As Justin wondered about this, it suddenly dawned on him that the bedspread beneath him was not his thick, downy comforter. It was a thin, rough quilt.

"This isn't my bed," he realized aloud, and his voice sounded strangely hollow in the darkness.

He struggled to pull his phone from his pocket and turn on its flashlight. The LED bulb shone unfocused and white. His nightstand should have been to his left, beside the bed, with his clock radio and a pile of loose change that clanged like a cymbal if he missed when karate-chopping the snooze button. But it wasn't there. His TV, his dresser, and his desk should have been at the far end of the room. Those were missing, too. So were his posters and his pictures of his friends—even his window was missing. The walls were bare timber. There were no windows at all and only a single door. The air smelled like sawdust.

A chill grew in Justin's stomach and worked its way outward, making him shiver.

"This isn't my bedroom," he whispered.

Scanning with his flashlight, Justin saw nothing he recognized except his winter coat hanging by its hood on the bedpost. He wiped a trickle of sweat from his brow, and it occurred to him that the room was stiflingly hot—a strange way to wake up on the day after Christmas.

He swung his legs over the side of the bed, and his boots touched a floor made of unfinished planks. He tried to swallow, but his mouth was dry. Grabbing his coat from the bedpost, he reached into the inner pocket and pulled out his asthma inhaler; he always kept it in his coat, just in case. Usually, he only needed it during conditioning drills at basketball practice, but his breathing was currently rapid and painful, so he took a quick medicated puff.

Calm down, he told himself. *This is not the time to freak out. Everything will be all right, everything will be all right.*

He really, really hated when he had to tell himself that.

The bed and the floor both creaked as he stood. Using his phone as a lantern, he crossed the room toward the door.

What happened last night? he thought. *Can't remember anything.*

"I must be at a friend's house," he whispered. He looked at the timber walls and the bare floor. More like a shack, really.

The bedroom door made hardly a sound as he pushed it open. The ceiling was unusually low, and he had to duck a little so as not to bump his head on the doorframe as he stepped out. He squinted. The room outside the bedroom was just as dark as inside. He raised his phone for a better look and saw a round wooden table, a set of big game antlers on the wall, and, at the far end of the room, a small, diamond-shaped window set in what appeared to be the front door. In the opposite direction was a short hallway with a couple of other doors, but no lights appeared to be on anywhere. With each passing second, Justin grew increasingly certain that he must have done something immensely stupid after storming out of the house the night before.

Did I get drunk or something? he wondered. *Maybe there was some sort of party.*

That had to be it. It wasn't really like him, but what other explanation could there be? This house must have belonged to one of his friends' parents. Which meant his friends were somewhere in here, too. It didn't appear that anyone was awake, though. He checked his phone, searching for messages from the night before to jump-start his memory, but there were none. The last one was the one from Kate. He blinked in surprise, realizing his phone had no signal. Worse still, it was almost dead.

Justin approached the front door, shut off the light on his phone, and cupped his hand to the glass to look out, but he couldn't see anything. He opened it as quietly as he could. To his astonishment, the air felt warm and humid, and he heard the high-pitched peeping of frogs.

Justin stepped outside, and instead of a foot of snow, there was springy, dew-slick grass under his feet. There were no streetlights—no lights whatsoever that he could see. Only a lopsided crescent moon in the sky peeking through thin snakes of gray clouds. Rolling plains stretched out before him, and there were no roads or even a driveway in sight. He checked his phone and confirmed the date. It was Wednesday, December 26. But it felt like it was 70 degrees out here. It was also uncommonly quiet. Even in his small town, day or night, you could always hear vehicle engines in the distance. Or planes passing overhead. Or the garbage truck. Or somebody's pool pump. Or an old lady's TV turned up too loud. Or . . . *something*. But out here, Justin could hear nothing but peeping frogs, the whistle of the breeze, and—

A sudden thud made Justin jump. He turned and realized a moment too late that the breeze had blown the house door shut behind him. He grabbed the knob and tried to turn it. It wouldn't budge.

"Really?" said Justin. He jiggled the doorknob, tugged on it, but it was no good. "Eff. . . ."

He backed away from the house, hoping to see a side door somewhere, but the place was just a tiny hut, probably no bigger than three or four rooms. There were no other houses in view, and he still couldn't see a road anywhere.

"Well, look on the bright side," he whispered. "At least you're not freezing. Couldn't ask for a nicer night to get locked out, really. A nice, warm . . . December night."

Justin cleared his throat. He tried the door again. If there really had been a party here last night, the parents weren't likely to be home, but if they were, pounding on the door in the middle of the night would not go over well. Never mind that this did not look like any front door he had ever seen before and there was no house number in sight. But that was too much to think about right now.

He had almost decided to pound on the door in spite of his reservations when he looked up from his phone and saw something he hadn't noticed at first. At the top of a nearby hill, about two hundred yards away, the black of night was broken by an orange flicker. Then he heard someone yelling.

Justin shoved his phone back into his pocket and moved cautiously through some ankle-high grass. He reached the hill and moved up the incline to get a better look. The yelling, wherever it was, was getting louder.

At the top of the hill, Justin looked down and saw what he thought at first was a massive bonfire. Then he noticed a group of men and women assembled in a line, passing buckets in a relay. They were tossing water into the raging flames one small pail at a time. Within the flames, Justin saw the outline of four walls, a chimney, and a glowing front door.

My God, thought Justin.

It was not a bonfire. It was someone's house.

CHAPTER 5

Men and women rushed toward the fire, some joining the relay and others circling the building. A snapping sound erupted somewhere nearby, and Justin turned to see a wooden fence being pushed down by a herd of cattle panicked by the flames. The animals broke free from their pasture and stampeded past the fire, casting larger-than-life shadows over the ground as they fled into the night.

He heard rapid footsteps behind him, and a tall man in dark clothing suddenly materialized out of the shadows. The man raced past Justin and ran down the hill in long-legged strides. When he reached the site of the fire, he grabbed a member of the bucket relay by the collar and appeared to shake him for information. Then he dropped the poor fellow and sprinted straight at the burning house. He lowered his shoulder and broke through the front door, disappearing into a wall of fire. Men and women shouted in horror at the sight.

A few people tried to follow after the tall man but came up short of the door, shielding their faces. Justin watched from a distance, feeling his blood pulsating through his head like bass notes through a subwoofer.

"Justin!" someone yelled.

Justin turned. An elderly man was shuffling toward him. He had a long, thick white beard and wore black robes like a monk. He approached Justin and grabbed his shoulder in a bony grip.

"Where is he?" the old man said in alarm.

"The guy who just ran past?" said Justin. "He—he went into the building." Justin trailed off, pulling away from the old man's hand. "How do you know my—?"

But the old man was already hustling down the hill toward the fire. Justin followed.

As they neared the house, the sweat on Justin's forehead turned searing hot, and he wondered how the people with the buckets could stand to be so close to the fire. A flaming joist toppled outward, and the man at the front of the relay team dropped his bucket in surprise and stumbled backward, barely avoiding the falling wreckage as it slammed into the ground, spitting sparks and red coals. The rest of the line of people backed away, too, apparently recognizing that it was a losing battle.

The old man got closer to the fire, but Justin had to stop. The heat sucked the air from his lungs, hurt his skin, and made his eyes feel like they would melt like wax in their sockets. Flames fluttered from the windows. Whole sections of the roof had been eaten through. And the doorway where the tall man had disappeared was solid flame.

A shadow appeared in the doorway. A figure stepped out. It was the tall man—with a limp body slung over his shoulder.

As the tall man stepped forward, a support beam gave way with an ear-splitting snap. The roof caved in behind him. Fire reared up from the collapsed foyer in orange and yellow spectral arms, and the tall man dropped to his knees with the body still over his shoulder. Rescuers rushed forward and bludgeoned the flames riding his back as he laid the body on the ground: a young man in scorched clothing.

The young man lay unmoving for a few frightening seconds. Then his chest convulsed. He hacked out smoke, blinking rapidly.

The tall man sat down in the grass, coughing hard as everyone in the crowd tried to speak to him at once. But the old monk with the white beard elbowed his way to the front and shooed the rest away, barking, "Give him some room to breathe, would you?"

Justin looked at the tall man, and the tall man looked right back at Justin. The whites of his eyes looked bright against his face, which had turned licorice black either from soot or charred flesh—Justin couldn't tell which.

"Are you okay?" Justin asked.

The tall man gestured with his chin toward the burning building behind him. Fingers of smoke trailed from the edges of his charred hair. He coughed and said in a strained, hoarse voice: "My house."

"What—?" said Justin.

He meant to ask "what happened," but the words caught in his throat before he could finish the sentence. Something in the sky had caught his eye. The wind had pushed away the clouds, and the blue-gray moon shone in a crescent. And higher still, previously hidden by cloud cover, was a second crescent moon, bronze, craggy, mountainous, and several times larger than the first.

CHAPTER 6

Justin didn't remember falling over, but his legs must have given out. He sat flat on his backside in the grass, dew soaking through his jeans as he stared up at the two moons. For a long time, he and the tall man sat on the ground across from one another. Neither said a word.

It's a dream, Justin realized. *Of course it is.*

It was borderline pathetic that it had taken him this long to figure that out. His dreams did tend to be funny like that, though. He never thought to question the reality of a dream while he was in one. It was usually only after waking up that the signs became obvious—sometimes comically so.

The people around him watched with regret in their eyes as the tall man's house burned down. The sky now glowed with the coming dawn, and Justin noticed in the light of morning what he hadn't seen in the dark. These people were all dressed in earth-toned clothes hanging with sashes and sheaths. Many wore hooded cloaks. Some had leather armor, metal helmets, and swords.

Yep, thought Justin. *Definitely a dream.*

He also saw that they were on the outskirts of an archaic-looking, stone-built town with thatched roofs, windmills, fields of grain, and a lack of familiar fixtures such as paved roads or power lines. No traffic lights. Not a single car. And the fire department, if there was one, never showed up. The person the tall man had saved from the house appeared to be a first responder who had entered looking for occupants to rescue, only to end up needing rescued himself.

Some of the onlookers tried to offer words of comfort to the tall man who'd lost his house, but his only replies were intermittent fits of hard coughing. No one spoke to Justin, though their gazes did sometimes wander suspiciously to his T-shirt and jeans. Meanwhile, the old monk who had called Justin by name just stood quietly off to the side.

Dawn revealed sprawling grasslands. Far off in the distance, a rocky range of gray mountains encompassed half the horizon, cradling green steppes. Their peaks were jagged razors overlapping and resting against one another. It was like the jawbone of a fossilized titan laid to rest with its snow-capped fangs eternally bared. The sun turned the summits white long before it ever broke the horizon.

Justin heard a whinnying sort of sound and saw a farmer on horseback wrangling some of the cattle that had broken loose in the night. But a second glance proved the farmer was not on horseback at all. The four-legged mammal he rode *looked* like a horse but had an elephant-like trunk hanging from its face.

Must've hit my head, Justin thought as he watched the horse that wasn't a horse reach down with its trunk, rip up a wad of grass, and lift it to its mouth. *Slipped on the ice while I was shoveling the driveway and cracked my head. Maybe this'll convince Dad to get the old snowblower fixed.*

He grabbed a pinch of the small hairs on the back of his own neck with his thumb and forefinger, got a tight grip, and yanked. He hoped no one heard his resulting yelp.

Well, that didn't work, thought Justin, rubbing his fingers together to let the hairs fall in the grass. *Devil's advocate: Let's pretend for a second that this is actually real. Are there any other possible explanations?*

"Renaissance fair, maybe?" he muttered under his breath.

He looked up at the two moons in the sky, now fading to white with the dawn.

"They really went all out for it," he said, grinning. But his grin didn't last. He felt a little sick.

The assemblage dispersed as the flames died down, and the men with swords began poking in the wreckage. The tall man didn't join them but instead got up and started scanning the mountainous horizon with a spyglass. His chestnut hair hung shoulder-length, and his rigid features were weathered by many scars—tiny, hairless lines in the stubble coating his jaw. Only now did Justin gain a true appreciation for the man's stature; he was lean with corded muscle and must have stood seven feet tall, which made this one of the rare instances when Justin wasn't the tallest person present.

Justin looked over his shoulder, back up the hill he had come from, but he couldn't see the hut from here. He started to walk away, but the old, bearded monk turned and fixed his gaze sternly on him, raising one bushy eyebrow as if to ask where he thought he was going, so Justin decided to wait a minute longer.

The tall man lowered the spyglass. He approached the monk and grumbled something in a foreign language. His voice was rough from the smoke. Then he walked away.

Justin walked hesitantly to the old man. "Uh, sorry to bother you, Father," said Justin, "but did everyone make it out of the house? No one was hurt, or. . . ?"

The expression on the monk's whiskered face in response to Justin's words was one of such severe disapproval that Justin thought the old man was either about to scold him or smack him.

"Young man, I am no Father," the monk said in an accent was hard to place.

"Oh, sorry," said Justin. "I guess priests are the ones you're supposed to call Father. What do I call you? Brother?"

"Zechariah," said the old man.

"Oh," said Justin. "Okay."

"Follow me," said Zechariah. "We've little time to pack."

"Follow you where—wait, did you just say 'pack'?" said Justin. "Pack for what?"

"We have an errand to run."

Justin opened his mouth to respond, but the old man named Zechariah was already walking away. He hustled up the hill after him.

In the daylight, the empty plains were not so empty. Livestock in the pastures surrounding the town included black-furred bison, long-horned red cattle, and more of those elephant-trunked horses. In small pens beside farmhouses, flightless ring-necked birds pecked the ground and squawked as children gathered eggs.

"I suppose summer had to end sometime," said Zechariah wistfully as they passed an oxen-hitched plow tilling a field.

"Huh?" said Justin.

"When the Gravelands' farmers start planting the last of the late-season seeds and preparing other pasturages to fallow, it means autumn is upon us."

"Gravelands?" said Justin, but Zechariah offered no explanation.

At the top of the hill, Justin saw that the grasslands stretched out like an ocean in every direction. The town, it seemed, was an island in the middle. And he still didn't see any roads. He took out his phone to check for a signal again, but the screen was black. He tried to turn it on. Nothing happened.

Dead.

His hand trembled a bit as he slipped the phone back into his pocket. It hadn't occurred to him to turn it off.

It's okay, he thought. *It'll be okay, you'll see. Everything will be all right.*

"It is just a dream," he reminded himself.

"Hmm?" said the old man ahead of him without turning around.

"Nothing," said Justin. "Just a. . . ."

He paused, feeling dizzy. His chest jumped with his heartbeat. He sucked in a deep breath, but it wasn't enough. He blinked rapidly and tried to take another breath, but it felt like his lungs were empty. He thought of his inhaler, still in that strange bedroom in his coat pocket, just as his legs turned to rubber.

"A—dream . . ." he gasped.

His vision had already gone black by the time he felt his body hit the ground.

"Justin?" he heard the old man say. "Justin!"

CHAPTER 7

Justin's eyes snapped open. He sat up in bed, breathing heavily and clutching his chest in the dark.

See? he thought. *A dream. I knew it was all just a—*

He looked around the room. He lay on top of a quilted bedspread with his clothes and shoes still on. This time, an old-fashioned oil lantern in the corner glowed brightly, illuminating the glaring lack of decor.

"Ah, hell," said Justin.

He stood from the bed, checking his pockets. His keys, wallet, and phone were still there. His winter coat was no longer hanging from the bedpost, though. Instead, there was some sort of gray garment or blanket. He crossed the room, paused to shake away some lingering dizziness, and opened the door.

In the adjoining room, sunlight streaming through the diamond-shaped pane in the front door revealed further oddities: no wallpaper, no carpet, no appliances, and no electrical outlets. Not far from the antlers on the wall was a pendulum clock bearing symbols he did not recognize. He counted the runic figures and realized it was a quarter past seven—on a clock that measured time in eighteen-hour increments.

He turned at the sound of footsteps. The old monk named Zechariah emerged from around a corner and did a double take upon seeing Justin. "Oh, good, you're up," he said with a diplomatic smile. He wore pale gray robes now instead of black ones. "You're about my size. Put these on, won't you? Quickly, please." And he tossed something at Justin.

Justin barely got his hands up in time to catch it. "What are you—?" he started to ask, but Zechariah turned back down the hallway. Justin unfolded the bundle in his hands. It was a pair of tan, woolen pants, a brown shirt, a linen undershirt, and a brown jacket as coarse as burlap.

Zechariah returned with an ancient-looking book in one hand and a pair of boots in the other. The only furniture in the room was a small, round table with only one chair. He dropped the book on the table with a thud. He traced its parchment with a finger, his beard bobbing up and down as he mouthed the words.

"So," said Justin. "This is your house."

"What a bright lad you are," Zechariah said without looking up. Whether the remark was supposed to be condescending or sarcastic, Justin couldn't tell, but he thought it was certainly one of the two. It was hard to catch the subtleties in the old man's lilting accent. His voice reminded Justin of a church song: pleasant on the surface but with an underlying vigor that seemed poised to erupt any second. "A heavy lad, too." The old man stretched his spine with an audible pop. "Next time, please pass out a little closer to the house, won't you? Oh, and this fell out of your coat."

With a flourish, Zechariah pulled Justin's inhaler from one of the sleeves of his robes and held it toward him upside-down. Cautiously, Justin took it.

"Thanks," Justin said, putting it in his pocket. "I, uh, play on the basketball team. Or I used to, anyway. I have exercise-induced bronchoconstriction."

The old man looked at him strangely.

"Asthma," said Justin. "Well, not technically asthma, but kind of. I usually don't need the inhaler, but every once in a while—"

"Tell me, Justin," Zechariah cut in, "what languages do you speak?"

Justin scrunched up his face. "How do you know my name?"

"What about your letters?" said Zechariah. "Can you read and write?"

"I don't remember telling you my name," said Justin. "Do I know you from somewhere? Or did you. . . ? You didn't, like, go through my wallet or anything, did you?"

Zechariah ignored this and turned the book in his hands around to face Justin. "What does it say here?" he asked.

Justin sighed. He leaned forward and opened his mouth to read, only to realize that, like the clock on the wall, the letters of whatever language this book was written in were foreign to him. Just lines upon lines of unfamiliar symbols.

"What is this?" he said.

Zechariah made an appraising sort of noise in his throat, then shoved the boots at Justin. "Go on, then. Get dressed."

"In *this*?" said Justin. He held up the shirt. It had laces instead of buttons, no pockets or collar, and was as brown as a turd. "I'll look like a jackass in this."

"You look like a jackass now," said Zechariah. He pointed at the bedroom door. "Try the gray cloak I left in there, too. With a little luck, you may pass for almost normal. Now, hurry. We must get moving." He closed the book and abruptly left the room again, muttering, "If I just had some more time."

"Get moving where, exactly?" Justin called but got no reply. He grumbled as he balled up the clothes and went back into the bedroom.

The gray fabric draped over the bedpost turned out to be a cloak, though he had little idea of what to do with it. He dug his keys and wallet out of his jeans and sat them beside his inhaler on the bed. Hoping against logic for a miraculous recovery, he tried to power on his phone. The screen stayed black.

He tossed his phone onto the bed. This wasn't funny anymore.

He grabbed the new clothes and changed, if only to distract himself. There was no mirror to confirm it, but he must have looked ridiculous. His comfortable jeans were exchanged for rigid trousers that rubbed roughly against his skin. His nicely broken-in tennis shoes were replaced with stiff, unpadded boots half a size too large. Instead of the linen shirt, he decided to keep his T-shirt, over which went the brown lace-up shirt. Over that went a brown jacket with forearm-length sleeves, buttoned up the front. And over it all went the gray, hooded cloak, which fastened by way of a brooch at the neck. By the time he had figured all this out, Zechariah was pounding on the door.

"I'm coming!" Justin said.

He slid his belongings into the pockets of his new jacket. Giving his jeans and tennis shoes one last look, he left the bedroom to find Zechariah standing in front of ten books stacked high on the table. Several packs were slung over his shoulders, but despite his haste, he was still taking the time to read.

"Jeez," Justin said, looking at the stack of books.

"Research," said Zechariah without looking up. "A pity I can take so few, but I wouldn't want you to hurt yourself."

"I need to talk to you about this errand," said Justin. "I don't know where you're going, but I'm not. . . . Did you just say 'hurt yourself'? As in, *myself*?"

Zechariah stared at him, looking almost hurt by the remark. "You mean you would force a frail, old man to carry such a load?"

"Well—"

"There's a good lad."

For being so "frail," Zechariah didn't seem to have any trouble loading the hardcover monsters three and four at a time into a sturdy satchel.

"What sort of research—?" But Justin slapped his forehead in mid-thought. "Research, what am I saying? Forget that! You need to tell me right now what the hell's going on. I'm not going anywhere with you! Not until I know who you are. . . . And how I got here."

The old man shot Justin a look that made him feel very small. For the second time, he thought he might be scolded or struck for his callousness. It also occurred to him that he had momentarily forgotten that this was a dream. Usually, by this point in a dream, he would have woken up. Either that, or any logical sequence of events would have come to a grinding halt, and dream-Justin would have looked down and suddenly realized he wasn't wearing any pants.

Justin looked down. His new pants were still on. And they still looked ugly as sin.

"I am a scholar and scribe named Zechariah," the old man answered. "And what *the hell* is going on is that a man's house burned down last night—just after something very valuable was stolen from it. That fire was no accident. The culprits were covering their tracks. But don't blame yourself for Ahlund's misfortune. I'm sure you'll make it up to him in time."

CHAPTER 8

Justin made a face. "Don't blame myself? For the fire? Um. Okay. Done. Why would I blame myself for the fire?"

Zechariah squinted at Justin sourly. "Because," he said slowly, "if Ahlund hadn't been here with me last night trying to decide what to do with you, this all might have been avoided."

"He was here?" said Justin.

"Of course he was here!" said Zechariah. "We were downstairs in the cellar when you ran off. I won't even ask what you were hoping to achieve with that stunt. That is the least of my questions for you, young man. I wasn't overly surprised when Ahlund brought you to my doorstep, but by now he is probably wishing he'd left you to the buzzards."

"Wait," said Justin. "You're saying that the guy whose house burned down—Ahlund—he brought me here?"

Zechariah closed his book deliberately. He looked Justin up and down and seemed to consider him for a moment. Finally, he asked, "What is your name?"

"Justin Holmes," said Justin.

"You really don't know what is happening?" said Zechariah.

Justin's cheek twitched in annoyance. "No. I do not."

"You don't *seem* like a simpleton. . . ."

Justin sucked his teeth. "High praise. So, it's been real nice, but it doesn't look like you have a phone here, and I kind of need to find someone who does." He shook his head, realizing he was forgetting again that this was a dream. "Anyway, thanks for the clothes, I guess. I'll, uh, return them the very first chance I get."

Justin turned and started for the front door.

"A young lady is in trouble, Justin," Zechariah said loudly. "I told you, that fire was no accident! Someone—an individual or a group of people, I'm not sure—burned down Ahlund's home and stole something valuable: a person who was secretly living with him under his protection. She was hiding from some bad people, and last night, evidently, they found her. She wasn't in the home when Ahlund entered last night searching for her, and thankfully no bodies were found in the wreckage. That means they took her. And I do not know what they want with her."

"You're saying this happened while Ahlund was here?" said Justin.

"While we were all here, yes," said Zechariah. "Ahlund brought you here late last night. He said he found you lying alone out on the Gravelands. You were unconscious, so we put you in the bedroom and went down to the cellar to get a drink and decide what to do with you. When we came back up, you were gone, and when we went out to search for you, we saw the fire. Ahlund knew at once what had happened. He entered the home to search for the young lady, but all he found was a hapless town guard. This morning, he spotted a group of riders on steedback heading north. He suspects they are the kidnappers, and he plans to leave at once to follow them. He could be killed if he goes alone, so I convinced him to wait for us. But we have to hurry because he'll leave without us just the same if we keep him waiting, and each *agonizing* moment I take to spell this all out in terms you can understand puts us at an increasing disadvantage. So I suggest we stop talking about it and move our feet."

"So, you want me to hunt down kidnappers with you?" said Justin.

"Ahlund needs our help," said Zechariah. "More importantly, that young lady needs our help. I'm sure you have plenty of your own pressing personal matters to attend to. So do I! But sometimes, a man must forget himself. And if it is within our power to assist someone in need, don't you think we owe them as much?"

Justin hesitated. "Not really. I mean, call the police, right? Or the . . . knights, or something. Whatever you people have here—"

Without warning, Zechariah slammed the satchel of books down violently on the table. It shook the room, producing a rattle of crockery from the kitchen cupboards and making Justin flinch.

"Fine," Zechariah said with an edge to his voice. "Then get out of my bloody way."

Zechariah left the bag of the books sitting on the table and crossed the room, tightening his robe around his shoulders as he went. Justin stepped aside to let the old man pass.

"Stay here, for all I care, and best of luck to you!" said Zechariah as he opened the door. He slammed it shut behind him.

Justin stood alone in the old man's kitchen. The only sound was the clock on the wall—a clock with eighteen strange symbols on its face. Each swing of the pendulum produced a dull *tock*.

He reached into his pocket and pulled out his phone almost automatically. He tried to power it on again. Still nothing, of course.

His gaze wandered to the bag of books. Then to the front door.

It's a dream, remember? said a voice in his head. *None of this is real. Just wait here until you wake up.*

"Still," muttered Justin, "a person's been kidnapped, and all I can think about is myself and my own problems. Even in a dream, that's pretty sucky. What would Mom say?"

CHAPTER 9

Do your best and don't look back, thought Justin as he ran, struggling under the weight of the heavy satchel slung over his shoulder. *That's what Mom would say. She would say, do your best and don't look back!*

With every step, Justin felt as if he were about to collapse. The bag of books over his shoulder probably weighed sixty pounds, and his new outfit was oversized and unwieldy. He must have been a pitiable sight, running up the hill from Zechariah's hut to try to catch up with the old man, tripping over his too-large boots while his cloak dragged behind him.

At the top of the hill, he saw Zechariah already at the bottom on the other side, walking toward the burned house. A ghostly vapor of stale smoke hung over the wreckage, blurring an otherwise cloudless sky.

"Wait!" Justin shouted. "Zechariah!"

"Hurry up then, if you're coming, you damn fool!" Zechariah barked over his shoulder without even turning around.

Justin growled in annoyance and adjusted the satchel as he ran. He nearly fell several times, and he was gasping for breath by the time he caught up with the old man. "You, uh, really like to read, huh?" he said, hefting the pack of books a little higher on his shoulder.

Zechariah overlooked the comment. "Before we join Ahlund, there are a few things you should know," he said in a low voice. "First off, the young woman who's been kidnapped is the daughter of the king of Nolia."

"The king?" Justin said. "Of this place?"

"No," said Zechariah. "This town is called Deen. It is an independent municipality. Nolia is a nation to the west beyond the Gravelands. A few weeks ago, the king of Nolia and his family were killed. He, the queen, his sons, his siblings, and every other known successor to the throne were *all* murdered. The entire royal bloodline was severed in a single evening—almost, anyway. Somehow, the king's only daughter survived the regicide."

Zechariah stopped talking as they passed an adolescent boy mending a part of the fence the cattle had broken the night before. The boy barely even looked up from his work except to wipe the sweat from beneath his straw hat, but Zechariah remained silent all the same until they were out of earshot.

"It's possible that the coup originated from inside the Nolian government," Zechariah continued under his breath, "so the princess quietly relocated to Deen, bringing only one bodyguard so as not to draw unwanted attention."

"Ahlund," said Justin. He tried to pronounce it the way Zechariah did—*Ahl* as in "all" and *und* as in "under"—but it felt awkward on his tongue.

"Yes, Ahlund," said Zechariah. "The fugitive princess has been living secretly under his protection. The Nolian public believe she died with the rest of her family, and the people of Deen think Ahlund's just a wealthy rancher from inner Darvelle here to stake a claim on some land. But, apparently, someone learned the truth. And last night, they acted."

"Seems risky," said Justin. "Having only one soldier to keep her safe, I mean."

"Well, Ahlund is no soldier. He is a sword-for-hire. A mercenary under contract with the government, and a very dangerous man. At any rate, now you understand why we must help him. I don't know who took the princess, but I suspect that with the potential of a royal ransom to be made, almost anyone would be interested in her capture. A word to the wise, though: I wouldn't mention any of this in front of Ahlund. He would not be pleased to know I had told you."

Justin looked ahead at the wreckage of Ahlund's house. There were no visible flames at this point, but the blackened pile still smoked like a chimney. Nearby stood the very tall man called Ahlund.

"So, how do *you* know all this?" whispered Justin.

"Pardon me?" said Zechariah.

"The stuff you just told me is supposed to be top-secret, right? What makes you the exception?"

"You're rather forward, aren't you?" whispered Zechariah.

Justin shrugged.

"Ahlund and I are acquaintances," Zechariah said.

"You?" said Justin. "You're friends with a mercenary?"

"Acquaintances, I said," said Zechariah.

Justin considered for a moment. "Hold on," he said. "You told me that Ahlund found me out on the plains. What was he doing out there if he was supposed to be protecting a princess?"

"I have been wondering the same thing," said Zechariah. "Maybe you can ask him, at a more opportune moment."

Ahead, Ahlund as watching them as they approached. He had replaced his burned clothes with fresh ones and now wore a cloak of forest green with the hood pulled over his head. One gloved hand rested on the hilt of a longsword sheathed at his side.

If he's the one who found me and brought me here, thought Justin, *maybe he can help me find my way home.*

"Dream," he whispered. "Don't forget. *Not real.* A dream. . . ."

Three horses-that-weren't-horses were tethered nearby. The animals had muscular bodies with short, umber-brown hair, hooves, and wiry tails. Their long faces had the pronounced brow ridges of a camel, and their snouts were elephant-like trunks that hung halfway to the ground. To Justin, they looked like the kind of bizarre extinct species you might see painted on a museum wall—an ice-age precursor to modern mammals. All three had saddles on their backs.

Ahlund said something to Zechariah in words Justin couldn't understand. His voice was deep and sounded painfully hoarse from the smoke inhalation. As Zechariah rattled off a reply, Justin took pleasure in dropping the heavy pack to the ground beside him. He glared at it as he massaged his aching shoulder. It hadn't occurred to him until now to wonder why the old man needed books for a search and rescue mission.

When the men's conversation appeared to be over, Justin stepped forward.

"Ahlund?" he said.

Ahlund looked at him. Justin hesitated, feeling very small beneath his gaze.

"So, I don't really know what's happening right now," said Justin, "but Zechariah told me about what happened last night, and I guess that's sort of the reason you weren't here when whatever happened, happened. So, if I screwed things up for you and made what happened, uh, happen, then I wanted to say, I really didn't mean for anything like this to . . . occur. And I'm really—"

Ahlund turned and walked away.

"Sorry," Justin finished a moment later, now speaking to no one.

Ahlund approached one of the three not-horses, pulled himself up and into the saddle, and growled a few words at Zechariah. Then he gave a command, and his mount reared. Its hooves beat the ground as he rode off onto the grassland in the direction of the mountains. He did not look back.

Justin looked at Zechariah. "What'd he say?"

"He told us not to follow him," said Zechariah, "unless we wish to die today."

"Is that advice or a threat?" said Justin.

Zechariah didn't answer.

"It doesn't really seem like he wants our help," said Justin.

"Read between the lines, young man," Zechariah said as he slung his packs over one of the not-horses. "He took the time to saddle these steeds for us, didn't he? Besides, I never said he wanted our help, I said he needed it."

The third animal seemed to be watching Justin, and Justin wondered what kind of teeth were under its elephant-like trunk. Imitating Zechariah, he placed the satchel of books over the animal's back. He must have done something wrong, though, because it shifted its weight and let out an annoyed half-whinny, half-trumpet sound that made Justin jump.

"What are these things?" Justin said.

Zechariah cleared his throat and moved to assist. "This," he said, placing a hand on the animal's neck, "is a steed. They are for riding. To get on, put your foot in the stirrup here, grab the pommel there, pull up, and swing your leg over to the other stirrup."

"Okay," said Justin, "but I don't know how to ride—"

"They are smarter than they look," said Zechariah impatiently. "Yours will follow mine. All you have to do is not fall off."

Justin gave the animal another look, then grabbed the saddle and tried to do as Zechariah had instructed. He did a few warm-up motions—as if preparing to jump Jeff Emerson's fence—and hopped up. His stomach made it into the saddle, but the rest of him was stuck hanging there. He tried to work his body like a lever but only managed to wobble obscenely. The steed huffed and stomped its hooves in irritation. When Justin attempted to swing his leg over, his oversized boot got caught, and he promptly lost his grip, dropped like a stone, and hit the ground, producing a thoroughly indignant, "*Oomph!*"

The old man and the animals looked down at Justin. Even the steeds seemed embarrassed for him. He stood, brushing himself off.

"Foot got caught," Justin said, "and I couldn't. . . . Well, it's trickier than it looks."

He tried again. This time, he almost made it but had to give up when things went awry. The steed shuffled anxiously. On the third try, Justin made it into the saddle. He shot Zechariah a proud smile. The old man did not congratulate him, though. He just bunched up his robes in one hand and hopped onto his steed with such ease that Justin's satisfaction vanished.

Zechariah tugged at his steed's reins, and the animal started moving. He clucked his tongue, and Justin's steed followed.

Justin's body seized up with the movement, fighting gravity that seemed to tug at him first from one side, then the other. It reminded him of the first time he'd tried to balance on a skateboard; he seemed to be using all the wrong muscles.

The steeds' walk sped to a canter, and as the canter became a run, Justin gave up on sitting straight and just grabbed the edges of the saddle with white knuckles, leaned against the animal's neck, and hoped for the best. His rear end bounced so hard against the saddle that it rattled his teeth. He was wondering if it was too late to jump off and run back to the house when he looked forward and saw something he hadn't noticed before. Hanging from Zechariah's side, previously hidden under his robes, was a scabbard holding the bronze hilt of a sword.

CHAPTER 10

They had been riding for what felt like hours when Ahlund finally let them stop to rest.

When the steed came to a halt, Justin tried to lift his leg over its back to get out of the saddle but discovered too late that it was cramped into position, and he shrieked some choice words as he fell off.

He landed on his back with a thud, half-buried in the high grass. He didn't bother trying to get up.

Ahlund had led them across the grasslands in winding, zigzagging, illogical routes, which had not been easy on an inexperienced rider. Justin had wondered why Ahlund didn't just ride straight. Eventually, he had realized that Ahlund was intentionally avoiding high ground, cutting between hilltops and sticking to the low country whenever possible to avoid being seen.

Their rest stop was in the shadow of an old, stone tower whose top half had collapsed untold years ago and now lay beside its foundation like a fallen tree. In its heyday, the tower must have been the size of a lighthouse. Stone blocks as big as hay bales were scattered all around like the disassembled bones of a scavenged carcass. The structure was overgrown with thick moss and creepers. Nearby, Zechariah and Ahlund conversed in that foreign language again, and since Justin didn't feel much like talking—and since his legs were probably too numb to stand anyway—he just lay there.

Come on, Justin, he thought. *Wake up, already. This is getting ridiculous.*

Zechariah and Ahlund were raising their voices, now. Justin craned his neck to look at them, upside-down. Their conversation seemed to have escalated into an argument. He closed his eyes and tried to ignore them. He hadn't seen any kidnappers yet, or anyone else, for that matter. All he had seen were some predatory birds riding the currents above and some brown spots on the plains that turned out to be wild bison.

He put an arm over his head and tried to tune everything out. Maybe if he fell asleep in the dream, he would wake up in his bed. No matter how hard he tried, the last thing he could remember was storming out of the house into the cold, then waking up in a bed that wasn't his own. But if he could fall back asleep, maybe—

"Get up," said Zechariah.

Justin looked up. The old man stood over him.

"You can't just lie there resting while your steed is still burdened," said Zechariah. "Remove that load or he'll get saddle sores."

"I'm the one with saddle sores," said Justin. "Are we getting close?"

"We will know in a moment," said Zechariah. "Ahlund's climbing the remains of the watchtower to have a look."

Justin sighed. "Any idea how long this is going to take? Will we be back by dark?"

"It will take as long as it takes."

Justin glanced up at the tower. "What is this place, anyway?"

"An old kingdom once had a citadel in the mountains and used watchtowers like this one to relay information across the Gravelands. There used to be many, but most have been pulled apart and looted for the stone. And please, by all means, let me know if you have any more idle inquiries, as I do live to serve your curiosity, Master Holmes."

Justin sat up and was about to make a smart comment when Zechariah's gaze shifted behind him. Ahlund stood there quietly.

"Any change?" said Zechariah.

"You shouldn't have followed me," Ahlund said with a voice like the crunch of gravel underfoot.

"I think we're past that, now," said Zechariah.

Ahlund took a drink from a leather wineskin-like container. "We're gaining ground," he said. "Twelve of them. Still heading toward the mountains. It doesn't seem like they have spotted us yet. We may catch them within the day."

"Any idea where they're going?" said Zechariah. "One of the hamlets at the feet of the mountains, maybe?"

"My guess is they plan to rendezvous with a larger group," said Ahlund. "As long as I intercept them before then, it won't be a problem."

"Be encouraged," said Zechariah. "If they haven't killed the princess by now, then that is probably not their intention."

Ahlund scowled at Zechariah. Then he gave Justin the same look. Had Justin been standing, that look would have been enough to sit him down.

"Don't get indignant," said Zechariah. "Yes, I told Justin about the princess. What are you worried about? Who's he going to tell?"

Ahlund pointed at Zechariah. "You know you shouldn't be here." His gray eyes flashed at Justin. "And neither should you."

You're telling me, thought Justin.

As Ahlund walked away, Zechariah nudged Justin with his boot and hissed, "Get up, already!"

It was a painful endeavor, but Justin managed to stand, albeit bow-legged. He had clung to the steed so tightly with his legs for fear of toppling that it felt as if they were now permanently locked in that position.

"That guy's a regular ray of sunshine," whispered Justin.

"I pray I'm half as sunny the day I lose my home and everything in it," said Zechariah.

"Noted," said Justin. He raised his arms over his head to stretch and looked back over the plains in the direction they had come. It was unnerving—more unnerving than he might have expected—to realize that the hilltop town called Deen was no longer visible.

It's not a town, though, he reminded himself. *Because it's not real, remember? None of this is real.*

It also unnerved him how increasingly difficult it was becoming to convince himself of that.

"So, what's going to happen when we find these guys?" said Justin.

Zechariah, rifling through his saddlebag with his back to Justin, answered, "We take back Princess Anavion, of course."

"Uh-huh."

"And I don't suspect they will part with her willingly."

"Uh-huh."

Zechariah turned around and presented an object to Justin. It was a sword.

Justin hesitated at first but then held out his hands, and Zechariah balanced the object on his palms. It was a short sword, about the length of Justin's forearm, currently sheathed in a leather scabbard, with a knobby handle made of polished black wood.

"Do you know how to use one?" asked Zechariah.

"Absolutely not," said Justin.

Zechariah took the weapon back. He bent down and tied the scabbard to Justin's lower right leg. "If you need it," he said, "you can draw it easily on steedback. And if you're standing, you just stoop a bit to draw it. Let me see it a moment."

Justin gripped the black handle and pulled. The scabbard stayed where it was, on his leg, and the weapon slid out in his fist. For some stupid reason, he expected the steel to ring as it was drawn, but there was only a dull sliding sound.

Zechariah took the weapon and ran his hand along one edge of the blade. It should have cut him, but when he presented his palm, there wasn't a mark. "This is the dull side," he said. He flipped it over. "This is not. Very important to remember which is which. A dirk has only one cutting edge, like a knife. See how the tip is sharply pointed? It's meant for thrusting and stabbing, not for slashing. Hold it like this for defense."

Zechariah held it pointed forward, wrist bent.

"It isn't a strong blade, and it has no crossguard, so blocking should be a last resort. But, if you have no choice, do this."

Zechariah held the handle with both hands—the left cupping the right—and planted his feet as if bracing for impact.

"When attacking, use quick thrusts only. Never swing it wide like a sword, and never fully extend your arm, or else you leave yourself open."

Zechariah stabbed at the air in a flourish of lightning-quick jabs.

"A dirk is for self-defense," he said. "It's meant to disable and discourage your foe. However, a well-placed cut to the throat." His wrist spun with a slash at the air. "Or a careful stab." He threw his body forward, leading with the blade's tip. "Can kill a man. Both options bring you quite close to your target, however, which I would not recommend. The most important thing to remember is that a dead person can still kill you. Even a perfect lethal strike never kills instantly. It can take minutes or hours, and a man in his death throes can kill you just as easily as a healthy one. Sometimes, far more easily. After all, what has he got to lose?"

Zechariah held the weapon by the dull edge of the blade with the handle presented to Justin and added, "Not a very thorough lesson, but it will have to do for now."

"Uh, thanks," Justin said numbly. He took the dirk and replaced it in the scabbard at his calf, just trying not to cut himself.

"If all else fails," said Zechariah, "just treat it like normal, old fisticuffs. There's more at stake, but the same rules apply."

"Okay," said Justin.

He decided not to bring up the fact that he had never been in a single fistfight in his life. He couldn't even remember a time when he'd felt enough aggression toward another person to merit physical action, except for maybe playing some extra-tight defense in a few basketball games against players who had ticked him off. But he'd never fought anybody before. The idea of fighting to the death, *today*, made this mouth dry.

Maybe you're already dead, said a voice in his head. *Maybe this isn't a dream after all. Maybe you died, and this is some kind of purgatory, and. . . .*

He shut his eyes hard and shook his head. *No! Don't think like that. It's only a dream! A really long dream but a dream all the same. And anyway, when you die in a dream, you always wake up in bed. Pretty soon, my alarm will go off, it will be the day after Christmas, and I'll still have almost a whole week before I have to go back to school. So, really, there's nothing to worry about. Nothing at all.*

He frowned, thinking about how he'd left the house—choosing to run off instead of talking with his dad.

But what had happened after that? And why couldn't he remember it?

CHAPTER 11

Justin woke with a start. His alarm hadn't gone off, for some reason. He was going to be late for—

The toe of a boot spurred the vulnerable spot between his ribs and pelvis.

"Ow!" he yelped, sitting up.

"On your feet!" barked Zechariah. "Never have I met someone who spent so much time on the ground!" He reared back to kick Justin again, and Justin scrambled, fleeing from the boot.

"Hey, I'm up!" he shouted. "What's the rush?"

"They have stopped to rest," growled Ahlund. He was on his steed. His face was blank. Emotionless. "And they still don't know they are being followed. If we ride hard, we'll catch them within the hour."

Within the hour? thought Justin.

He hurried to his steed while Zechariah mounted up. Again, Ahlund did not wait for them. He set his steed galloping over the grasslands.

"Is he going to fight them?" said Justin as he climbed into the saddle.

"No," said Zechariah. "*We* are going to fight them."

Justin tried to wet his lips, but his mouth was sticky and dry again. "Can't I stay here?" he asked. "You guys can come back for me when it's over."

"For your sake, I'm going to pretend I didn't hear that," said Zechariah with a frown. "Have some honor, boy. Show a little backbone! Are you ready?"

"No!" said Justin.

But Zechariah tugged on the reins, and his steed took off. When the old man made the clucking noise in his cheek, Justin's steed followed. Justin nearly fell off the animal's back at the change in momentum.

"No, wait—turn around!" Justin pleaded with the animal. "Whoa, pony, whoa! Halt. Stop. Slow down, Seabiscuit! Um . . . about-face? Please?"

He looked over the side of the steed and considered abandoning ship, but they were already moving so fast that the ground whizzed beneath him like rushing water. He dared not jump.

His heart was in his throat, beating nearly as quickly as the steeds' hooves. His mind replayed Zechariah's little stabbing motions with the dirk, his imagination adding blood-spurts with every thrust.

"It's just a dream," he told himself. "Wake up!"

It seemed like only minutes had passed when they rode over a small rise, and Justin gasped at the sight of the enemy camp less than five hundred yards away. Suddenly, battle was no longer an idea. It was a reality.

Men scrambled for their weapons and rushed to their steeds at the sight of Ahlund's approach. He was halfway there before any of them managed to get on steedback. At the far side of the camp, a woman was pushed onto the back of a steed, and its rider took off with her. The rest mounted up and charged at Ahlund with blades drawn. The tall mercenary drew his longsword, and a moment later, Justin heard his bellowing war cry.

Ahlund never slowed. Like barreling into the burning building the night before, he plunged headlong into the enemy.

The first rider brought his sword down at Ahlund in a lumberjack chop. Ahlund dodged it casually. Their steeds grazed shoulders as he passed. Two more riders closed in on him from either side. Steel reflected summer sun as one swung his sword and the other stabbed. Ahlund jerked with a wicked block and knocked the first attacker from his steed to hit the ground in a bone-snapping roll. Before the second enemy's blade could land, Ahlund slashed him across the chest. The rider dropped his weapon and slouched in the saddle.

The rider carrying the woman hazarded a look back, and Ahlund's hand whipped forward. A hunting knife pinwheeled through the air and found its mark with a *thump* in the soft tissue between the rider's neck and shoulder. His body tensed, and he tumbled from the saddle, leaving the woman alone on the steed.

Justin couldn't breathe. He was so close now that he could see the riders' faces—the colors of their eyes, the plaque on their teeth, the tangles in their beards, the blood spilling from the man Ahlund had slashed with his sword. Half of the remaining riders pursued Ahlund. The other half faced Zechariah and Justin. Some wore faces contorted with fury. Others appeared relaxed, almost businesslike.

Zechariah drew his sword and charged at them. Justin, out of no desire of his own, followed right behind him. Intelligent thought escaped him, replaced by pure, crystalline terror.

"It's a dream, wake up," he heard himself repeating, almost shouting, as vomit bubbled at the back of his throat. "It's a dream! Wake up!"

An enemy rider closed in on Justin from the side. The man raised his sword, taking aim—as if he were a major-league batter sizing up a pitch and Justin's head was a juicy, hanging curveball.

Zechariah flew in, catching the attacker off balance. Faster than a man of his years should have been able, Zechariah redirected the man's strike and stabbed him below his collarbone. The man dropped his weapon and retreated, clutching the wound. Another rider came at Zechariah. The old man dodged a potential killing blow, then cracked the rider in the face with the butt of his sword's hilt, stunning the man enough to knock him out of his saddle.

A rider advanced on Justin from the opposite side. Justin turned away out of reflex. In the process, he inadvertently tugged on the reins in his hands. His steed stepped sideways in response, and a stab from the enemy's blade glanced off the animal's hindquarters instead of hitting Justin.

The steed reared. Justin lost his grip, and he fell from the saddle.

He hit the ground amid stamping hooves. A few more enemy riders fell beneath Ahlund and Zechariah's blades, and the cries of the wounded and the dying hurt Justin's ears as he struggled to his feet. Soldiers surrounded Zechariah, now. A blade caught the old man in the shoulder with a splash of red. He retaliated by burying his sword halfway to the hilt in the rider's midsection and twisting upward. The rider fell, gargling.

"It's a dream," Justin said. "It's a dream." His heart now pounded in his chest so hard he thought it would split like overripe fruit.

Zechariah's eyes found Justin. "Behind you!" he shouted.

Justin turned on weak legs. An unseated rider—the man Zechariah had cracked in the face—was coming at him. Blood from a broken nose soaked his mustache. He raised his sword as he ran at Justin.

It wasn't like the movies. There was no slow motion, no out-of-body experience—hardly enough time for Justin to think, let alone for his life to flash before his eyes. He raised his hands to surrender, but the man just smirked a little in amusement, then bared his teeth and lifted his broadsword like a butcher's cleaver. Justin tried to run, but he couldn't move.

It's . . . not a dream, he thought.

Suddenly, Justin saw Ahlund leap from his steed. He was too far away to make it to Justin in time, but he stabbed his sword forward in midair. The weapon flashed, and yellow and orange flames exploded from the blade.

Raging fire rolled over itself and flowed from Ahlund's sword in a blazing cloud. The man in front of Justin disappeared in the billowing flames without so much as a scream, and the wall of heat knocked Justin off his feet. He landed hard on his back.

For a long time, Justin did not move. He lay on his back, the wind knocked out of him, wheezing and staring up at the sky. Dark clouds were rolling in overhead. He was vaguely aware of some fighting still going on, but his head was somehow both hot and cold at once, his senses somehow heightened and dulled at the same time, and his body an empty, quivering husk.

The ringing of steel gradually ceased. The clomping of hooves faded. There were a few more painful, wet yells, but soon, the voices were silenced forever.

Zechariah approached and stood over Justin. There was a rip in his robes at the shoulder, and his sleeve was soaked reddish black. He offered Justin a hand. Justin did not take it. He sat up on his own, refusing to look at the old man. Zechariah walked away.

There were tears on Justin's face that he didn't remember crying. Riderless steeds milled about, munching the grass. A dead man was still slumped in the saddle of one of them. Bodies littered the ground. For some reason, all Justin could think about was how fast it had all been. So brief. A few short minutes was all it had taken for these people, brought from birth along decades-spanning, lifelong journeys, to die.

The napalm-like cloud of fire that Justin had almost dismissed as an illusion had apparently been real. Ash still floated in the air, and a sharp, pungent aroma stung his nostrils. The earth was scorched black. Smoke rose in ribbons from the grass. He tried not to look, but he couldn't avoid seeing the body. It was half intact. The part hit by Ahlund's fire was obliterated; there was no skin, only slippery-looking muscle charred jet-black. Half the face was gone. An empty eye socket stared at Justin.

Justin leaned away and emptied his stomach into the grass. His body trembled as he retched. When it was over, he closed his eyes, trying to shut everything out. Never had life seemed so cold. Never had he felt so alone. So lost.

PART II

CLOSE TO THE EDGE

CHAPTER 12

Justin jammed the blade into the earth and threw another scoop over his shoulder. He paused to wipe the sweat from his brow. It was late afternoon, but dark clouds dimmed the sun. They carried the promise of rain.

The shovel in his hands had been procured from the supplies of dead men. Zechariah had told him they had probably brought it to dig lightning shelters in the event of a dangerous storm on the open grasslands. Presently, Justin used it for a very different purpose. Digging graves. Ahlund had said every man who fell in combat, friend or foe, deserved a proper burial. Zechariah had said smugly that it was good for the soil.

Justin, in shock over all that had happened, had said nothing. He just did as he was told, since he didn't know what else to do.

His arms burned. The wooden handle dug into his palms where loose skin was starting to rub with blisters. The ground was hard, and the roots of the grass were thick, making digging the first six inches surprisingly arduous work. After that, the soil was a silty loam he could push through furiously, easily clearing a trench the length and breadth of a man.

After the battle, Justin had found one of the enemy riders lying in the grass, still alive, clutching his side and trying to hold something in that shouldn't have been out. With every beat of his heart, rivulets of lifeblood had escaped through his fingers. This had been no man, but a teenager. A boy younger than Justin.

"Help," the boy had said. "I don't want to die."

Before Justin could say anything, Ahlund had stepped past him and was kneeling beside the boy.

"Bless you," the boy had said. "Thank—"

Then Justin had heard a crunch, and Ahlund had stood, wiping his knife clean. The dead boy's face was left frozen in his final emotion: agony-stricken hope.

"You killed him!" Justin had yelled—almost screamed. "We could have helped him!"

"He was dead," Ahlund had growled.

"No, he wasn't!"

"He was."

"You son of a—"

"Nothing could have saved him," Ahlund had said. "Out here, a mortally wounded man and a dead man are one and the same."

"That wasn't a man," Justin had growled through clenched teeth. "That was a kid!"

Ahlund had walked away.

At present, Justin blinked against tears and squeezed his fingers tightly around the shovel's handle. His anger overrode his other emotions for a moment, so he embraced it. He twisted his hands against the grain of the wood just to force his blisters to break.

At least anger made sense. It was pure and easy. But no amount of wrath could block out the way those men had gargled as they died. The way they had writhed in pain. The way the boy had asked for help, only to receive his final reward.

Justin squeezed his eyes shut. It didn't make sense that someone's entire existence—their past, their present, and all the potential futures that might have been—could be snuffed out so quickly just for being on the losing side of one small conflict. No motive, prize, or purpose could justify what these men had done to each other here.

"Good enough," said Zechariah.

Justin turned to scowl at the old man, angry at being interrupted, angry for being brought here, angry for everything.

Zechariah tossed him a canteen. While Justin grudgingly took a drink, Zechariah dragged four bodies across the grass one by one and dropped them into the trench. Try as he might to hide it, Justin felt his whole body flinch each time a corpse thudded home. When they lay piled to the surface, Zechariah nodded.

"Filling it up is easier," he said, almost cheerfully.

Justin wanted to tell the old man to do it himself, but he couldn't look away from the grave. The teenaged soldier was on top. His eyes were still open, and the expression on his pale, dead face had gone slack. He looked bored.

"He would have died all the same, you know," Zechariah said. "If anything, Ahlund showed mercy."

Justin pursed his lips. "He was defenseless, and Ahlund killed him. That's not mercy. It's called murder."

"If your roles had been reversed," said Zechariah, "and you had been the one lying wounded, that boy would have killed you instead."

"That's for him to decide," Justin said. "I wouldn't. The fight was over. He wasn't a threat anymore. And Ahlund wasn't even sorry. He had no remorse for executing a helpless kid."

Zechariah sighed. "Sometimes, wounds can be healed. But some things just cannot be undone. A wounded person may live for days, or even weeks, enduring a living hell of agony, infection, disease, horror, and madness. Then he dies. Warriors like Ahlund know the sight of a wound that is beyond healing. Better to show mercy than to condemn a man to unnecessary suffering. Do not doubt that he would have done the same to me—or you. I am sure he has had to before."

Justin's voice was a mutter. "That's terrible."

"That's war," said Zechariah. "And it is terrible. And some people choose to live through it so that others may enjoy lives free from it."

Silence settled over them for a time. The talk of wounds reminded Justin that Zechariah's shoulder had been cut in battle. He must have treated it, though, because his sleeve was mostly washed clean, and he showed no discomfort.

The freed prisoner was cleaning a gash across Ahlund's back, who, judging by the abundance of long-healed scars coating his torso like tattoos, had chosen to live through quite a bit of war in his time. The woman—a princess, if Zechariah was to be believed—took a roll of dressings from a pack to bandage the wound. Justin had yet to see her face clearly, but her hands, red with Ahlund's drying blood, worked with the expeditious mastery of seasoned practice.

"Better keep at it," said Zechariah, "before these clouds let loose."

"What's her name?" said Justin.

"Of all the questions you could ask, why that one?"

Justin shrugged.

"Leah Anavion," Zechariah said. "You should feel proud for helping her."

"Proud," said Justin sickly. "Right."

The old man gave him a strange look. He started to turn away, but, at that moment, Justin lost control, and everything spilled out.

"I'm lost, Zechariah," Justin blurted. "Really lost. The place I'm from doesn't have princesses or swords or even steeds. We worry about things like politics and bills and football scores, not kidnappers. It's a whole different world, and I'm . . . I'm just some kid. I have to get home! I have to—"

He paused, choking on his words, hating the way his lower lip quivered. He was seventeen. Almost a man. But suddenly, he was nine years old again and had just struck out in Little League—old enough that he didn't want to cry, old enough to know he wasn't supposed to cry, but not old enough not to.

"My dad," Justin said. "He needs me. I have to get home to him. He can't take care of himself."

Zechariah squinted, chewing on his tongue a bit. "What's the matter with him?"

"He just . . . he needs help with everyday things, and Mom—" The words caught in Justin's throat again, and he shook his head. "Mom's dead. That means it's up to me. Dad was in an accident, and he needs me. I *can't be* here—I can't leave him alone. I have to get home. He doesn't have anyone else to. . . !"

But Justin was breathing too quickly for his words to keep up, and the only sound his mouth could make after that was a wet, bubbly sort of moan as he tried not to cry and failed miserably. The tears slipped past his nose and mingled with leaking snot. He wanted to wipe his face, but to do so would have been to acknowledge and therefore admit that he was crying, so he just looked at the ground and let it dribble.

"It's all right, Justin," he heard Zechariah say softly. "Why don't you take a break? We'll finish digging after dinner. You'll feel better with a full stomach. Come on."

Zechariah walked away, but Justin didn't follow. He took his phone out of his pocket. With a sense of detachment, he realized he must have landed on it when he'd fallen off his steed. It was smashed.

Justin tossed it. He didn't even bother watching to see where it landed in the tall grass.

CHAPTER 13

Justin tried not to look at the faces as the earth showered over them. They had already been dead for hours, he knew, but there was a terrible finality about covering them with dirt.

The last corpse was the man Ahlund had killed with fire. With a final scoop of dirt, the half-missing face was covered, but Justin knew the image would never again be far from his thoughts. He pounded the blunt end of his shovel against the mound, and finally, his work complete, let out a long sigh.

Zechariah approached. The princess was off with the animals, bandaging the spot where Justin's steed had been cut during battle. Ahlund sat sharpening his sword by the fire, where a pot bubbled.

"Have you noticed the change in temperature?" asked Zechariah.

Justin looked up at the gray clouds. "Colder," he said. "Probably because it's going to rain."

"I believe you're right about the rain," said Zechariah, "but the reason it's colder is that we're in the cradle of the mountains. The warm west winds are blocked. The ancient Elleneans called these mountains Thucymoroi, which translates, 'the mountains that shift.' Long ago, there was a kingdom in the Shifting Mountains, and its people had a legend about these grasslands. It is an epic poem that takes days to recite in its entirety. The story goes that the world was once controlled by two powerful empires. One ruled the east, and one ruled the west. Border skirmishes broke out between the two, leading to full-scale war. There are many heroes and heroines in the tale, many great deeds of valor on the war front. But meanwhile, the warriors' homelands were falling apart. All resources went to the war. The people became poor and hungry, and the empires crumbled.

"Legend says that the war ended here, on these grasslands. The final battle of the divided planet. The two largest armies ever assembled clashed, and, one by one, their soldiers fell. There was no surrender, no retreat, no mercy. After weeks of fighting, all were killed except one man on each side, and they faced each other in single combat. Finally, a mortal blow was struck to each, and both fell. In their dying moments, the two warriors surveyed the battlefield and saw that it had become a land of open graves, with not a victor in sight. No one left standing, no one to bury the dead, no one to mourn them. Only buzzards to tend to the carrion. Their grief for the dead united these two warriors in their final moments, and as they died, together they drove a sword into the ground as a solitary memorial to remind the world what terrors can be wrought by war and human ambition."

"The Tale of the United Planet."

Justin turned. Standing behind him was the princess, and he could now see her clearly for the first time. He didn't know what he'd been expecting, but this wasn't it.

She looked only a few years older than him, with green eyes and messy, straight black hair worn tied back. The word "princess" evoked in his mind images of a tall, fair-skinned lady with striking features, probably in a flowing dress, maybe on a white pony, or wearing a funny, pointed hat, at least. But this woman was not tall—she had a small build and stood at least twelve inches shorter than Justin. Instead of a flowing dress, she wore dirty traveling clothes similar to Ahlund's. And instead of fair skin, her skin was several shades darker than Justin's. Ahlund's dried blood was still nestled in the knuckle lines on her hands and caked beneath her short nails. Her face was dirty, and her features were not striking but plain.

"I haven't heard that story since I was a little girl," she said. "Bards used to recite it during festivals."

"Why's it called the Tale of the *United* Planet?" said Justin.

"With their armies destroyed and all power lost," continued Zechariah, "the two great empires fell into chaos. Famine and disease ravaged their cities, barbarians destroyed their citadels, and their lands splintered into squabbling cities and states. The world entered an age of darkness that lasted for centuries. As for the two warriors, they were only united after they lost everything. In that brief minute, when they drove the sword into the ground before their deaths, the planet was united. The moral is: The only true peace is that of shared sorrow and defeat. The only way people will put everything aside is when they have already lost it."

"Well, that's uplifting," said Justin. "Is it true? The story, I mean, not the moral."

Zechariah shrugged. "There are many legends in this part of the world. Some folks pass the tale off as pure fiction. Others claim that the battle really did take place, and further, that the Sword of the United Planet still exists somewhere, powered by ancient magic and having survived through the eons." He smiled and laughed. "Probably just a wonderful story. A little rational thinking is all it takes to poke holes in it. After all, if the two men were the last of their armies, and they died together, who told their story? It does make you wonder, though, why the grass on the Gravelands grows so green."

Zechariah paused and looked at Justin. His tone became quite serious. "You should be proud of what you have done. Not all soldiers are so blessed as to rest in proper graves. The men you buried are at peace now. And in good company."

Justin looked at the mounds. He would never have admitted it, but it actually did make him feel a little better.

"Pardon my manners, my lady," said Zechariah. "I am called Zechariah, a humble scholar and scribe."

"And a storyteller," she said. Her speech, unlike Zechariah and Ahlund's, had little accent to Justin's ears. "Please, just call me Leah." She looked up at Justin expectantly.

Justin hesitated. He had never been very comfortable with his stature. In a weird way, people of below-average height sometimes intimidated him—especially girls. Looking down on them made him feel like a lanky, goofy giant. Like Lennie from *Of Mice and Men*. This rather small woman was no exception. It felt so wrong, in fact, to be looking down on royalty that he bowed a little just to try to even the playing field, but it probably looked as awkward as it felt. "I'm Justin," he said.

Leah grinned unsurely at his bow and offered her hand. For a second, Justin was terrified that he might be expected to kiss it or something, but when he took it, she casually shook his hand.

"A pleasure, Justin," she said. "Where do you hail from?"

"Hail from?" Justin said. "Why, uh, the County of Venango in the modest Commonwealth of Pennsylvania."

Leah cocked her head. "I'm not familiar with that province."

"Not many people know of it. Are you—are you all right? They didn't hurt you or anything?"

"They did nothing to harm me," she said.

Her smile became a sad, forced one, and Justin wondered if he had just said something wrong.

"I think dinner is about ready," said Zechariah.

Leah nodded and went to the fire. Zechariah started after her, but Justin grabbed him by the sleeve.

"Wait," he said. "I have to know. How did Ahlund do that, with the fire?"

"Never seen someone cook a stew before?" said Zechariah.

"You know what I mean. His sword. He shot fire from it—!"

"Maybe that's better explained some other time, Master Holmes. I could eat a dinoth."

Zechariah turned and strode off. Justin sighed. It was not the first time Zechariah had called him "Master Holmes." He got the impression it was meant to be ironic.

He flexed his raw hands, grimacing at the tender, pink flesh where flaps of skin hung from his dirt-encrusted blisters, and walked to the fire. Ahlund eyed him as he approached. Zechariah had warned him that Ahlund was a dangerous man. It seemed he hadn't been exaggerating.

CHAPTER 14

Justin was in desperate need of a bathroom.

It was an unexpected dilemma. If there had been any cover—a tree, some shrubbery—he would have just removed himself from the group, walked around the other side, and done the deed. But they were in the middle of a flat stretch of open grasslands, where there was no such cover to hide his shame. Had he been among males only, he might have simply turned his back and answered nature's call, but now, a lady was with them. A lady he had only just met. Even that embarrassment might have been dismissible, had the lady in question not happened to be royalty.

I need a crash course in wilderness social graces, he thought, shifting in his cross-legged position on the ground. *Taking a leak in front of a princess might be one you don't come back from.*

The sun had gone down, and with the moon and starts clouded, the only light came from the campfire. The stew was a salted broth of sliced potatoes, dried meat, and what Justin assumed were carrots until he bit into one. The broth was bland, the potatoes were crunchy, the meat was tough and gamy, and the unknown, carrot-like vegetables were sour. On any other day, it would have been the worst meal of his life. Today, it was the best. He ate four bowls and drank a whole canteen of water, which had only made his bathroom situation more dire.

As the sun set, Justin found that a full stomach did wonders to mend his sores and his spirits. It also made him sleepier than he could remember ever being in his life.

"I understand, Ahlund," Zechariah said, picking his teeth, "that you managed to question one of the kidnappers before he died."

Mention of the afternoon's altercation brought Justin's dinner to the top of his throat. He managed through willpower alone to keep it there but couldn't hold back the belch that came with it. He covered his mouth and stared at the ground, afraid to see if the princess had noticed.

On the other side of the fire, Ahlund added a stick to the flames. Without looking at Zechariah, he said, "I did."

A long pause followed.

"They did not look like independent agents," Zechariah pressed. "They looked more like soldiers. Uniformed, but without insignias or heraldry."

Ahlund remained silent. Justin looked at Leah, sitting beside Ahlund. Her face was pale, her lips drawn into a tight line. Zechariah opened his mouth to continue, but he was cut off.

"I will not discuss the agenda of dead men tonight," said Ahlund. "Not when we are scarcely out of earshot of their graves."

"Just when I thought I would sleep," said Justin as he peered over his shoulder at the mounds not far from where the steeds were tied.

"If you will excuse me," said Leah as she stood. "I am exhausted."

"My lady," said Zechariah, nodding.

Leah removed herself from the fireside, unrolled a stuffed mat, and lay down.

"The rain may hold off until morning," said Zechariah. "Where do we go from there?"

"There is no we," said Ahlund. "Your part in this is over. Tomorrow, the lady and I return to Deen. You two can do as you like. Separately."

There was no passion in his voice. It was simply a statement. He did not wait for a response. He left the fireside and made his bed.

Justin watched the tall mercenary lay down. He was having a hard time remembering why it had been so important to follow him out here. When Justin had made the decision to follow Zechariah, he had still been operating under the assumption that he was dreaming and would wake up at any moment. That no longer seemed likely to happen anytime soon. Zechariah had said the venture was an "errand" to help Ahlund, but the idea that this mercenary needed anyone's help seemed laughable, now, given what Justin had seen him do with that sword. . . .

"Zechariah," said Justin, louder than he meant to. He lowered his voice to a whisper. "How did he do that thing with his sword? The fire."

CHAPTER 15

Zechariah squinted slightly. "You really don't know?"

Justin shook his head.

"You really are lost, aren't you?"

"What, you didn't believe me?"

Zechariah waved his hand dismissively. "It's nothing personal; the only way to know truth is to entertain doubt. Tell me about your father. You said he couldn't take care of himself?"

Justin smirked. "You're very good at avoiding questions."

Zechariah snorted a small laugh. "Forgive me—you asked about the fire. Yes. Well." He cleared his throat. "What do you think it was?"

Justin shrugged. "Magic?"

"Magic!" Zechariah laughed. "Magic is just a word people use for things they either do not understand or are incapable of doing themselves—outside the realm of what they consider possible. I suppose you could be forgiven for thinking aurym is magic."

"Aurym?" said Justin, trying to pronounce it the way Zechariah had: *ORE-im*. "What is that?"

A sprinkling rain had begun to fall and hiss in the fire. Zechariah pulled up the hood of his cloak. After a few tries, Justin got his up, too.

"In a way, seeing it firsthand is better than any explanation," said Zechariah. "To understand aurym, you must first ask yourself: What is a person? Is a person his body? Is he his brain? Is he his bones, blood, muscles, and organs? The answer, of course, is no. The parts do not make the person. The person is what drives the parts. Some call it the consciousness or the mind. Others call it the spirit or the soul. Either way, it's what makes a human an individual, and it exists in a not-so-easily defined state."

"But you can make fire with it?"

"Patience, young man. Similarly, the physical world is built of measurable parts. Rocks, soils, plants, animals, air, and a billion parts within those parts. Through it all flows aurym, the essence of life. It is nowhere and everywhere at once, individual to everything. Apart from them, yet connecting them all. The spark in us—the human spirit—is made of aurym, and there is a bit of it in everyone, though the amount differs from person to person for reasons we don't quite understand. A stronger spirit means greater potential for aurym power, and the opposite is true also."

Justin hoped his face didn't betray his thoughts. His mother had taught him that you didn't have to agree with people's beliefs, but that you should always be polite to them.

Especially to the crazy ones.

"We are all born with a spark already in us," Zechariah went on. "As we grow, live, learn, and love, our spirits flower and bloom, and the power grows stronger. While a person's body reaches its zenith after adolescence and then deteriorates over time, a person's spirit can grow stronger throughout his or her entire life. . . . Or it can fade. As we stray from our principles, make compromises, become embittered by woes, and lose sight of goodness and wonder, the power of the spirit can shrivel, die, and be lost forever.

"Aurym, Justin, is the measure of a person's inner strength. Their will, their faith, their compassion. If a person can tune in to his own aurym, he can learn to listen to the aurym around him. And feel it. But aurym is still more than that. It is an energy source. If one can learn to use it, it can do powerful things."

"Like make fire?"

"Like make fire. Aurym does not take physical form spontaneously, however. There must be a conduit. One must channel aurym through minerals called aurstones. What you saw Ahlund do today was release an active form of aurym energy through aurstones forged in the blade of his sword. He fed his spirit power through the stones, and his aurym took the form of fire."

"So, why didn't any of the soldiers today shoot fire back?" said Justin.

"Aurym ability is a rare gift," said Zechariah. "Few people have the spirit strong enough to manifest its energy. Far fewer have the discipline to sharpen and hone the talent. The form that aurym takes depends on two aspects: the wielder and the stone. Some people have great aurym power. Others have none. Different types of aurstones can unlock different potential powers. As for the wielder, it varies from person to person, just as any talent will. Some aurym ability comes with training, but a great part of it is as natural as eyesight or hearing. Even properly trained, I could never produce fire from Ahlund's sword. If someone else could, their manifestation might be some variation, or a different effect like steam or a wave of heat. Or, more likely, nothing at all. It is a great mystery. Even those who can use aurym may never come to realize their potential. The chance of a wielder finding a stone compatible with his or her spirit is slim."

"What about you?" asked Justin.

"The power I wield is a far cry from what you saw Ahlund do today. As opposed to willing a large amount of energy through the conduit all at once, I am constantly feeding a small amount of aurym through my stone, and it gives me a constant result."

"Which is?"

"Among other things: enhanced physical prowess, heightened strength and reflexes, and longevity."

"Longevity? Like, you'll live longer than somebody else your age?"

"Yes."

"How old are you?"

"Always so forward! Let me put it this way. I was already at an age most men never reach when I mastered an aurstone ability that made me feel like a young man again. Since then, I haven't aged a day for the last twelve centuries."

Justin realized an instant too late that his mouth had fallen open. He hastily clamped it shut.

"Give or take a few years," Zechariah added.

"Are you. . . ?" Justin said.

A slow smile crept across Zechariah's face. The twinkle in his eye reminded Justin of the look his grandfather used to get when he was telling a tall tale.

"Oh. I get it," said Justin. "Very funny. Mess with the new guy. I see."

"What! You don't believe me?" Zechariah said, a look of feigned insult on his face. "Why, of all the—"

"Right, sure," Justin said flatly.

Zechariah chuckled.

The rain was falling harder, and Justin, more than ready for bed now, got up and rummaged through the supplies.

"Bad news," he said. "Looks like there's only one more sleeping mat."

"You take it," Zechariah said. "I prefer to sleep sitting, anyway."

The only items of clothing Justin bothered to remove were his jacket and his boots. He sat the boots upside-down to keep the rain from getting in and laid out the straw-stuffed sleeping mat on the grass. It was hardly comfortable, but it was better than the ground. He lay down and draped a blanket over himself. The sky was shrouded in clouds, mercifully hiding the double moons, so he found himself staring at the dying fire instead, thinking about the flames Ahlund had unleashed to kill that man to save Justin's life. It seemed impossible. But in a world where two moons hung in the sky, impossible was a relative term.

He glanced at the princess and her bodyguard, making sure they were both asleep.

Finally! he thought.

He scrambled from the mat and tiptoed barefoot over the wet grass, away from camp. He stopped some distance from the steeds, pulled down the bulky trousers to conduct biology's demands, and sighed in relief.

"I better not be dreaming," he whispered, "cause if I am, I just pissed the bed. At seventeen years old."

He returned to camp feeling like a new man and was about to lie back down when he tripped over his jacket and heard made a familiar metallic jingle. His keys. He reached into the jacket pocket and took out his keys and wallet. Opening his wallet, he discovered that the otherwise ordinary contents suddenly carried disproportionately sentimental value. The precious artifacts included a bank card, twenty-three dollars in tens and crumpled ones, some faded gas station receipts—he didn't know why he kept them—a coupon for one free coffee that had expired, not that it mattered, and, set behind a piece of transparent plastic, his driver's license.

Justin lay down and looked at his license through the plastic.

Pennsylvania Driver's License. Justin C Holmes. Organ Donor. Sex: M. Class: C. Eyes: BLU. Height: 6'04". Main Street Extension. Oil City PA.

He ran his thumb over the sixteen-year-old version of himself in the photo. His hair had been longer back then, and it had flopped against his forehead when he ran. Part of the logo on his Pittsburgh Panthers T-shirt was visible at the bottom, and there was a dumb, crooked smile on his face; he had just gotten his license, after all.

As Justin wiggled the license free, something fell out from behind it. He picked it up. It was Kate's yearbook photo. He thought he had thrown it away. Her brown hair was pulled back, her smile was casual, and her cheeks were dimpled. She was tall and athletic, but while Justin's starting spot on the varsity team was owed mostly to his stature, her place on the girls' team was justified by her raw talent and hard work. Over the course of the ten months they'd dated, they had played one-on-one after school several times a week. She rarely missed from the top of the key.

He wondered what time it was back on Earth. The girls' team sometimes had tournament games on the days after Christmas, but he wasn't sure if there were any scheduled for this year. Maybe she was getting ready to take the court for the second half. Meanwhile, he was out here, just trying to survive.

If it's not a dream, then what happened to me? he thought. *How did I get here?*

Turning the photo over, he smiled at her signature on the back. *Katie*, with a heart over the *i*. Despite an effort to remain friends, they hadn't really spoken since before Thanksgiving, well over a month ago. It had been even longer since he'd played one-on-one with her—or with anyone, for that matter. On the very same day he had broken up with her, he'd also quit the basketball team. It had made for one heck of a Friday.

He would never forget the guilt he felt that day, knowing that he was the source of Kate's tears. Nor would he ever forget his coach's parting words as Justin collected his things from the locker room: "A quitter. What would your mother say?"

Justin put his license back in the plastic sleeve, slid Kate's picture behind it, and put the wallet and keys in his jacket pocket.

I got here somehow, so there must be a way back, thought Justin. *I've got to get Ahlund talking. If I can figure out where he found me, I can go back there, with or without help, and maybe find some answers.*

He rolled over to see Zechariah sitting cross-legged with arms drawn into his cloak and head tucked to his chest. He looked like a big bird nestled up for warmth. The bag of books lay beside him.

Look at that. He didn't even open a single stupid book.

It was Justin's last thought before he fell asleep.

CHAPTER 16

Justin went from dead asleep to wide awake in about half a second.

He had rolled over in his sleep, and the cover of the blanket had fallen off, allowing the rain to hit him full in the face like a garden hose. He wiped himself off in surprise. The light sprinkle was now a downpour, and distant thunder rumbled. It was morning, but he could hardly tell, through the darkness of the clouds. He was about to get up when he heard a pair of hushed, frantic voices.

He turned his stiff neck. Leah was still sleeping with blankets pulled over her head, but Zechariah and Ahlund stood near the doused fire. Both had their hoods up, hiding their faces, and both spoke rapidly. Mid-sentence, as he said something emphatic in a foreign language, Zechariah's arm flung up to point a finger at Justin.

They're talking about me, realized Justin.

He had resolved to continue faking sleep, to see where this heated exchange led, when Leah stirred. Ahlund and Zechariah noticed and quickly separated. By the time she got up, they were making a convincing show of ignoring each other while packing up camp, as if their conversation had never happened.

Justin stood and groaned. His thighs were so sore from riding that he regretted getting up. His hands were bubbled with blisters, and there was a sharp pain in his back from falling off his steed yesterday—multiple times. All he wanted to do was lie back down, but the ground was so uncomfortable that sleeping on it any longer would have only made things worse. Even putting on his boots was painful.

Zechariah marched over to him. "Something has come up," he said.

Justin was about to ask what he meant when he heard Ahlund telling Leah: "We cannot go back to Deen, my lady."

"Because of the house?" she asked. "Surely we can find somewhere else to stay until we move on. Perhaps Zechariah wouldn't mind if we—"

"It's a bit more serious than that," Ahlund said. "Zechariah and I woke in the night. Both of us felt a dark presence."

Leah hesitated. "What do you mean?"

"From the southeast," said Zechariah, stepping in. "An entity shrouded in shadow." He shook his head as if trying to clear a foggy mind. "I can feel it heading for Deen. With malevolent intent."

"You can *feel* it?" said Justin.

"Yes," Zechariah said. "Aurym."

Leah looked up at Ahlund. The difference in height between the princess and the nearly seven-foot-tall mercenary was almost comical.

"I don't know what it is," Ahlund said, answering her unspoken question.

She set her jaw. "All the more reason to avoid it, I suppose. What do you suggest?"

"Our options are limited here, within the Thucymoroi cradle," Ahlund said. "We can wait and hope it passes us by, or we can head toward one of the towns in the mountain foothills."

"The fortifications of the Ancients run the length of the mountains," said Zechariah, "but there are gates that lead through the walls if the need calls for it. The village of Irth is closest. It is situated just outside one such gate."

"I would rather try that," said Leah, "than be without shelter in the storm."

A loud boom of thunder rolled across the Gravelands, and the wind seemed to pick up in response.

"If we leave now, we could be there by this afternoon," said Zechariah.

"We'll have to move quickly," Ahlund said. "The people of the foothill towns do not admit travelers after dusk."

Justin was amazed. Only last night, Ahlund had wanted nothing to do with Zechariah or Justin. Now, he and the old man were working together. It made Justin wonder what sort of "presence" was enough to rile them like this.

"Are the Irth people superstitious?" said Leah. "Fear of the dark is no reason to turn away travelers."

"There is no superstition involved," said Zechariah. "They sleep at the feet of the Thucymoroi. And there is a reason their town is built outside the walls rather than within. Remember, my lady, Nolia is only one small corner of the world. Things are different in the wilds."

Leah shifted uncomfortably beneath Zechariah's gaze. "Fine," she said. "Anything's better than waiting for trouble to come to us."

Ahlund and Zechariah set about packing up the camp, throwing supplies into bags and loading up the animals. They had commandeered a small herd of steeds from the enemy soldiers and had planned to take them back to Deen. Instead, Zechariah separated their three, found a fourth for Leah, and smacked the rest hard on the rears, freeing them to run wild. Justin, meanwhile, tried to figure out how to re-fit his sleeping mat into the bag he'd taken it from.

"Justin."

He turned. Ahlund looked down at him. He held a broadsword with a three-foot blade in a reddish-brown, wooden sheath. The hilt was encased in a metal basket, a sphere of protective steel forged to cover the wielder's hand.

Ahlund pulled the sword from its sheath a bit, just enough to show Justin some blackened patches on its otherwise shining, steel blade. Scorch marks.

The sword that almost killed me, thought Justin.

Ahlund held it out to him.

"I don't. . . ." said Justin. "I don't want to fight anybody."

"But you will have to," Ahlund said.

Reluctantly, Justin took it. It was so surprisingly heavy that he nearly dropped it when Ahlund let go. The mercenary strode off without waiting for a response.

Justin slipped his hand under the basket-hilt and gripped the handhold. He pulled the blade out a bit and looked again at the black stains on the blade like oil in water. The last man to wield this sword had tried to kill him with it. Instead, he had been swallowed up by Ahlund's fire. It made Justin sick to think what had happened to that man just so he could survive.

What makes me any different from him? Justin thought, staring at the blade. *Why am I here and he's not? Chance? Luck?*

He had to believe it was more than that. More than a flip of a coin or a roll of the dice. This time, he had lived, but for that to happen—for the scales to tip in his favor—the man who'd carried this sword had to die. That made life a gift, bought and paid for. Silently, Justin promised never to forget that. Never to forget the soldiers in those graves he'd dug. Or the man who had burned in Ahlund's fire. Or the boy who had begged for help as he lay dying. All so that Justin could keep living a while longer.

"Ah!" said Zechariah. Justin jumped. He hadn't heard the old man's approach. "The dirk I gave you will still come in handy, no doubt, but this is much more practical. Allow me." Zechariah eased the sword from Justin's grip and kneeled beside him. "Is this your good hand? Okay, then you put it on the opposite side so you can reach naturally across your body to draw it. Like so." He attached the sheath to Justin's belt on his left side. "There you are. Like the dirk, it's got a single cutting edge, so when slashing—oh, never mind. I'll explain later."

Zechariah departed to finish packing, leaving Justin alone in the rain. The sword hung heavy at his side, interfering with his center of balance. He looked down at the metal-woven basket-hilt on one side and the dirk's knobby handle on the other. Days ago, the thought of carrying a sword and a knife might have sounded exciting. Now, they just made him feel dirty.

Out of the corner of his eye, he saw a bright flash. Half a minute later, the rumble of thunder reached his ears. He tightened the hood over his head.

When everything was packed, with nothing left but a circle of charcoal where their fire had been, the four travelers mounted their steeds. Justin grimaced as the pains of yesterday rubbed against the saddle.

Ahlund looked at Leah. She nodded, and Ahlund rode forward. Leah and Zechariah did likewise, and Justin's steed obediently followed.

It didn't take long before Justin was cold, wet, and miserable. As their pace quickened, the rain came at Justin from above and in front. It found ways to splash into his face and run down the front of his shirt. The mounds marking the graves of the enemy soldiers disappeared behind them as the world grew darker.

CHAPTER 17

The sun's position was hidden behind the clouds, and time seemed an endless circuit of grassland flowing beneath and rain falling above. The only change came from behind, as the ocean of black clouds drew ever nearer. Never had Justin faced such a storm out of doors. After a while, he dared not look back to see how close the lightning struck, and the thunder was so loud it hurt his ears. Curtains of rain and cloud veiled the path ahead. Lightning sparked horizontally in the clouds above.

Ahlund raised his hand and began to slow down. The others followed his example.

Looking over his shoulder, Justin saw the blackness behind illuminated by a bolt of lightning that sizzled from the sky like a crack through an eggshell. An explosion of thunder rocked him not ten seconds later, setting his heart racing. The storm was moving faster than they were. He didn't want to stop. He didn't want to give it a single moment's advantage. The crazy idea came to him of whipping the reins of his steed and rushing past the others to make a break for it alone.

Get a hold of yourself.

They came to a stop and, still on steedback, crowded into a tight circle. The steeds sucked in air through their trunks and shook water from their long faces.

"Irth is close," said Zechariah. "But we will not be safe there."

"We won't?" Justin blurted. "What do you mean?"

"The gate is our only chance," Ahlund said, ignoring Justin. "It's the only pass for a hundred miles in either direction, right?"

"Right," said Zechariah.

"What's going on?" Leah said, yelling to be heard over the storm. In her barely disguised fear, it came out closer to a demand than a question.

"They are following us, my lady," Ahlund said.

"They?" Leah said.

"The dark presence," said Zechariah. "It is black aurym, belonging to multiple beings. They're coming this direction. They use the storm as cover."

Justin swallowed hard as thunder crashed like a timpani.

"Irth," Leah said. "They will have a town guard. If we alert them to the danger—"

"No militia could hold back the things hunting us," said Ahlund. "We must reach the mountain gate and shut ourselves off from them. My lady, I swore to protect you with my life. This is our only choice."

At the word "hunting," a shiver ran up Justin's spine that had nothing to do with the cold or the rain.

After a moment's consideration, Leah nodded. Ahlund looked at Zechariah and said something in that strange language. Then he yelled and slapped his steed. The animal started galloping. The rest followed, this time with Justin and Leah in the middle and Zechariah at the rear.

Justin held tightly to the reins, trying to keep his hands from shaking. He had seen these men kill without mercy. He had seen Ahlund charge into a burning building. He had seen Zechariah get cut by an enemy blade without making a sound. Together, they were a force to be reckoned with—yesterday's massacre of a dozen enemy soldiers could attest to that. What could make these two retreat?

Justin could hardly see anything. The rain fell in stinging sheets. The sounds of thunder exploded at almost the same instant as the lightning flashes now, shaking the ground beneath him, making him flinch and wonder each time if the next would be his last. It was all he could do to keep an eye on the shadowy figures of Leah and Ahlund ahead of him and, if he looked over his shoulder, Zechariah close behind. Justin's fear was steadily transforming into something more: a cold sickness in the pit of his stomach. It felt like doom. Unnatural. Ethereal. Hanging in the air.

Am I feeling it? he thought. *The dark presence?*

A shout from behind brought Justin's attention around.

"Faster!" came Zechariah's voice on the wind. "They're right behind—!"

The rest of his words were cut off by the snap-boom of electrical impact as lightning struck, and the world around the old man became momentarily illuminated. Burned into Justin's retinas for a split second was a jagged line of light drawn from the blackened sky to the ground less than fifty yards behind Zechariah.

And in the aftermath, he saw them.

CHAPTER 18

Now that he knew where to look, they were visible through the storm. If not for Zechariah's urgency, Justin might have passed off the sight as an anomaly, a mirage, or an optical illusion. The darkness behind Zechariah was caving in on itself. Light fell inward as if caught in a vortex. And at the center of that vortex were huge figures.

Something shot from the heart of it. A dark ball of energy sizzled over Zechariah's head as fast as a javelin.

The projectile missed Zechariah and flew past Justin. A rushing, sucking noise filled the air. The driving rain fell in a parabolic pattern to meet the dark, globular thing, as if drawn in by superior, artificial gravity. The projectile hit the ground at Ahlund's flank and exploded upon impact in an inferno of concentrated night. Darkness expanded outward and upward in a blooming spheroid of energy. Veins of indigo electricity crackled and sizzled around its edges, and all light seemed to warp inward, as if the world were being viewed through a concave lens—a terrestrial black hole.

Thankfully, Justin's steed had the presence of mind to swerve around the explosion's sputtering aftermath. Even through the pouring rain, Justin could smell ozone and charred earth. The blast zone was a blackened, smoking crater.

He looked over his shoulder and immediately regretted it. Now, not far behind Zechariah, their hunters had gained form and substance. Four were visible through the haze: dark, humanoid figures twice the height of a man and as wide at the shoulders as Justin was tall. They rode strange, giant mounts. Details were dulled by the rain and darkness, but Justin saw the monster in front raise its arm above its head. Another ball of darkness appeared within its bony hand.

"Watch out!" Justin screamed.

The monster brought its arm down. Zechariah veered his steed sideways as the projectile flew toward him. The ground where he had been an instant before erupted in blackness and sizzling effervescence. Everything it touched was engulfed.

Zechariah's cloak billowed from the blast. His steed tossed its head in fear.

Peripheral movement caught Justin's eye. Turning, he saw that Ahlund had dropped back and was riding beside him. Ahlund gestured forward at something, then dropped his steed still farther back. Ahead, Justin saw that Leah was leading the way toward what looked like a dead end. Rain battered vertical, stone walls that must have been five hundred feet high. They were trapped.

But no. There, at the base of the wall, was the village. Wood and sod buildings sat clustered around a semicircular opening in the wall that looked no greater than a mouse hole against the enormity of the fortifications.

The gate!

Ahlund dropped back past Zechariah, closing the distance between him and the monstrous riders. Holding the reins with one hand, he drew his longsword and brandished it above his head. Flames erupted from the white-hot blade. A fireball leaped from his sword and rocketed toward the silhouettes of their pursuers.

The flames hit true—a full-impact shot to the front-most of the riders.

To Justin's horror, the fireball shattered into pieces. Its flames were doused. The creatures rode on, unscathed.

The pulsating panic in Justin's stomach was creeping into his chest, holding him frozen in the saddle. He tried to focus on the gate ahead and the shape of Leah racing toward it on steedback, but the fear weighed on him like a physical ailment. The buildings of Irth became clearer. He saw windows alight from hearth-fires within. A bolt of lightning hit the wall with a deafening explosion. Justin shut his eyes in fright. More explosions rang out behind him, but they weren't thunder. They were the sounds of powerful battle between Ahlund and the monsters.

The hole in the wall grew larger, and finally, they reached the gate. Leah disappeared within it. Justin followed, and the gate swallowed him up into darkness.

After long hours of rain falling heavily upon his back, the abrupt relief of cover was like a change in gravity. He was nearly thrown to the ground as his steed skidded to a halt beside Leah. It was more like a railroad tunnel than a gate—tall, wide, and at least a hundred yards long. It was empty, save the frame of a large winch system made of metal gears, wood, and cables.

Zechariah came racing through the curtain of water at the gate. Behind him, a few hundred yards past the town of Irth, battle raged in flaming flashes and spots of concentrated blackness.

The old man leaped from his steed before it even came to a stop. He rushed to the winch and grabbed the enormous lever with both hands. His long, white beard was soaked and plastered against his chest, and his gritted teeth gave him a wild appearance.

"Help me!" he shouted, pointing above their heads.

Justin followed the gesture. The gears of the winch controlled a great coil of metal cables running to the tunnel ceiling, connected to a multiple-pulley system suspending a massive block of stone above the entryway. A door.

Leah and Justin dismounted and sprinted to Zechariah's side.

"We must shut the gate!" he said.

"What about the town?" Leah shouted.

"It's us they're after, not the town!" Zechariah shouted. "Those things will be right behind Ahlund. We've got to cut them off! Ready: one, two, *pull*!"

At his order, the three pulled on the lever. It didn't budge.

"It's stuck!" said Leah.

"Again," said Zechariah. "One, two, *pull*!"

The metal cut into Justin's hands, breaking all the blisters of yesterday and coating his palms with watery fluid. His boots slipped on the stone floor. His arms burned with the effort. He thought he felt the lever move slightly, but it wasn't enough.

Justin felt dizzy. The flashes of battle were drawing nearer, and the seizing panic had climbed up his spine and was clawing at the top of his throat. His insides felt frozen. It was like succumbing to hypothermia from the inside out. Black tendrils crept into the corners of his vision. It suddenly dawned on him that he was about to black out.

Ahlund was nearly there, but the monsters were right with him. A dark projectile missed Ahlund and struck a house. In an instant, the building floated off its foundations, fragmented, and exploded outward in a shower of support beams, window glass, furniture, and human screams.

"No!" Justin shouted.

Zechariah backed away from the lever and drew his sword. He raised it high and brought it down with a mighty swing at the cable supporting the door. A spark and a pitiful clang resounded as his blade bounced away. He raised his sword and struck again and again, but the cable held firm.

"Justin, Leah," he said. "Ride hard! We'll hold them off as long as we can!"

Leah's voice was shrill as she shouted, "But, we can't—!"

"Now!" said Zechariah.

Between the blasts of thunder and battle, Justin heard the people of Irth screaming. With what little sense he had left, he grabbed Leah's arm, pulling her toward the steeds. They mounted up and rode down the tunnel.

Justin tried to adjust his weight and realized a moment too late that his left foot wasn't secured in the stirrup. He tried to compensate by grabbing the pommel, but his hand missed. His body weight pulled him sideways, and he hit the floor on his hip and rolled. Looking up, he watched as Leah and his steed galloped down the tunnel, leaving him behind.

Suddenly, Zechariah yelled, "Get down!" The old man dove sidelong, throwing himself to the ground.

Justin, already on the floor, could only watch in shock as a comet of fire came raging through the gate and into the tunnel, trailing the steam of boiled rain.

The fireball collided with the winch system and exploded with a blinding light. The force lifted Justin back up off the ground and tossed him like a plaything. Deafening noise ravaged his ears as he bounced off a stone wall and landed amid a hailstorm of flaming wooden pieces and half-molten gears. Cables formerly bearing thousands of pounds of force broke free and whipped wildly. One whizzed past Justin and cracked like a bullwhip against the wall, digging a gouge into the stone as cleanly as a spade through fertile soil. The stone block of the door was released all at once and crashed down.

The sound of the door hitting home, the grating thud of stone against stone, was the final noise. It echoed down the tunnel for what seemed like hours as Justin lay on the ground with smoke stinging his sinuses. The battle, the rain, the thunder—everything was muted. But for the dancing flames of burning winch pieces and the shadows they cast, all was still. The door was seamless. They had been cut off.

Zechariah got gingerly to his feet. He stumbled toward the door like a sleepwalker. Tiny flames rode the edges of his robes. He stopped before the door, ran his palm over the surface, and pressed his ear against it.

Justin stood. The feeling of doom was gone. The unnatural, nearly blinding panic that, only moments before, had threatened to suck him into the depths of unconsciousness, had been muted along with the sounds.

Leah dismounted her steed and came sprinting back. She slowed to a jog as she passed Justin, and she stopped behind Zechariah.

"Ahlund," was all she said. Whether it was a question or something else, Justin could not tell.

Zechariah did not look at her.

After what seemed like a long time, Zechariah pressed his palm flat against the stone, bowed his head, and began to utter the words of another language. Leah drew her hands into fists and looked at the floor. Her shoulder twitched.

The old man's prayer reverberated through the tunnel, producing mournful, ghostly harmonics. Justin did not know the words, but the meaning was clear. The danger was gone. And Ahlund with it.

CHAPTER 19

Silently, Zechariah leaned several wooden and metal pieces against the gate door, piling them up into a crude memorial. One by one, he leaned the pieces against one another. Though the arrangement was random, its meaning was clear.

"Ahlund was a Ru'Onora," said Zechariah, and though his voice was but a whisper, the tunnel amplified his words to rich volumes. "We cannot lay his body to rest, but Ru'Onorath tradition gives the utmost honor to heroes who die nobly in combat."

He retrieved two sacks from the saddlebags of his steed and returned to the door.

"Today, Ahlund sacrificed himself to save the lives of others, and there is no deed nobler than that. And so, we offer provisions for his journey." Zechariah opened the sacks. "Salt, to flavor the meat of his game." He scooped a handful from the sack and let it fall across the threshold. "And coin to pay the ferrymen for his journeys ahead." He opened the second sack and let the contents fall. Small, metal pieces clanged and jingled against the tunnel floor—silver coins and tiny bars of bronze.

Zechariah dropped to one knee. "Farewell, Ahlund Sims, Ru'Onora. May you find peace and fellowship among your ancestors."

The three were silent for a moment. Justin waited until Zechariah stood back up to speak.

"He. . . ." said Justin. "He did that on purpose, didn't he? He meant to shut the gate."

Zechariah nodded.

"Why?" Leah said. "He could have made it through." She cleared her throat. "Are you sure he—?"

"After the gate shut, I could no longer sense him," said Zechariah. "He sacrificed himself so that we might survive."

"But, all those people!" Leah shouted, making Justin jump. "Out there in the village! What about all of them? That was not his sacrifice to make!"

"He swore to protect you," said Zechariah. "He did it the only way he could."

"What about those things out there?" said Justin.

Zechariah only looked at him.

"Won't they get through?" Justin said, his voice cracking a little. "I mean, this door won't hold them for long. They blew up that house like it was nothing."

Leah turned away.

"These walls are stronger than the stone they're built with," said Zechariah. "They are unlikely to be broken and even unlikelier to be scaled, and it's a two-day ride to the next pass. We are safe. For the moment."

"Don't get me wrong, that's reassuring," Justin said, "but shouldn't we still get out of here as quick as we can, just in case—?"

"Justin," said Zechariah. "If they do break through, our steeds are too tired to get us far enough away in time, so there's no use worrying about it. I don't *think* they can break through. I can't make any promises beyond that."

Justin didn't care for that answer, but he could think of nothing else to say except, "What were those things?"

Zechariah seemed to consider a moment, then said, "I do not know."

Justin shivered. Somehow, it was the worst answer the old man could have given.

Zechariah walked to Leah. He drew his sword. Laying it upon his outstretched palms, he kneeled before her.

"A fighting man of Ahlund's caliber could never be replaced," he said. "But I humbly offer my services in his stead, for as long as her highness should have need of them."

Zechariah had lowered his eyes in reverence, but he glanced up long enough to shoot a meaningful look at Justin. Justin hastily did his best to pantomime the ritual. He pulled his new sword from its sheath and held it out as he kneeled.

"Stop," said Leah. "Stand up. Both of you."

Justin quickly got to his feet, feeling like he was in the middle of a botched marriage proposal or something. But somehow, a man like Zechariah could maintain an air of dignity even on bended knee. He stood slowly, looking at Leah.

"Thank you for everything you've done," said Leah. "I would probably still be a prisoner if not for you two. But you're not soldiers, and you aren't my subjects. I can't accept that kind of pledge." She paused. "I would, of course, appreciate your help—in an unofficial capacity. But no oaths of fealty to 'her highness' or any of that nonsense. Just help. Normal people helping another normal person. Please."

Zechariah smiled. "As you wish."

Leah looked at Justin. It took him a second to realize she was waiting for him to say something. He nodded and said, "Okay."

Leah grinned. It was refreshing to see her smile.

Zechariah grabbed the steeds by the reins and led them down the tunnel, toward the semicircle of light that marked their exit point. Leah gave the gate door one last look, then followed.

Justin lingered behind at the memorial. It seemed a sad thing for a man's life to be reduced to: a salty pile of coins and garbage. He was a mercenary, so maybe the coins were fitting, but still.

That's twice you saved my life, he thought. *Wish I'd had the chance to repay you.*

What a strange concept, *his life*. What did it even mean anymore? What had it become? The worries and woes of Earth, where his life did not hang in the balance at every moment, seemed petty and childish by comparison.

If I ever see home again, he thought. *I'll never take it for granted. I'll never take a bed, a warm meal, running water, safety, or peace of mind for granted ever again. I'll never take Dad for granted again, either.*

Justin hung his head.

Apathy and depression had him dragging his feet as he left Ahlund's memorial behind and followed Zechariah and Leah. Moments later, he stood at the end of the tunnel beside them. Rain and twilight blurred the country outside. A distant echo of thunder rolled. The storm was passing.

"Were they coblyns?" Leah asked.

"No," Zechariah said. "These things were far too powerful to be coblyns."

"And they were after me," she whispered.

"Focus ahead, my lady. We don't have enough supplies to stay here long. We could try to make it to another gate and back out to the Gravelands, but that may put us at risk of another encounter with those things. Our other option is to climb. I know of a nearby village about a day's ride up the mountain path where we can find food and shelter. I'm afraid it is only a temporary solution, but we may find sanctuary among them for a time, at least."

Leah said nothing, but Justin thought he saw her nod.

"Best to rest, now," Zechariah said. "We can spend the night in here, where there's dry ground, and be on the move in the morning. We need to get a fire going, to dry us out and keep unsavory creatures away. You two wait here. Hopefully, there's some dry wood to be found."

He passed through the curtain of falling water and was gone.

Justin and Leah did not even attempt conversation. They sat on opposite sides of the tunnel, alone with their thoughts.

CHAPTER 20

After a meal of dried meat and half-stale bread, Justin, Leah, and Zechariah sat around a fire. Cloaks, jackets, boots, sleeping mats, and the like were arranged around the flames for drying. Justin was in his T-shirt and brown pants, Zechariah was in a wool shirt and trousers, and the princess was dressed similar to the men.

The tunnel was roomy—big enough to have comfortably fit a tractor trailer. Justin remembered the sight of the walls from outside, vertical stone faces, five hundred feet tall if they were an inch, and wondered what kind of civilization had built such a marvel. Without power tools.

"Were these walls built before or after that story?" asked Justin. At the strange looks he got from Zechariah and Leah, he added, "The one about the armies fighting on the Gravelands."

"Ah," said Zechariah. "Supposedly, these walls were actually built thousands of years prior to that. The men who fought in the War of the United Planet were said to be descendants of the Ancients. All that remains of those ages are these walls and the abandoned cities beneath the mountains."

"Beneath the mountains?" said Justin.

Zechariah nodded. "Cities, palaces, and citadels under the stone, some discovered and long raided, but others, surely, that no human has entered since the fall of the Ancients. Think of what treasures might remain there!"

"Do people live there now?" Justin asked.

"I don't think so. There are things in this world that crave dark places. The abandoned cities are breeding grounds for coblyns and worse."

"What are those?" asked Justin. Again, the looks from his comrades indicated he needed to explain himself. "Sorry. You mentioned it before. Breeding grounds for, what was it?"

"You've never heard of coblyns?" asked Leah.

"Coblyns are a kind of demon," said Zechariah, before Justin could answer. "Remnants of a darker age. They are creatures absent of spirit. Soulless. They must feed on the life force of other things to survive."

"Life force," said Justin. "You mean aurym?"

Zechariah nodded. "They need it to survive, so they forage for it. They hunt in packs, feeding on unlucky creatures, but what they really crave is human flesh. No place is aurym riper or sweeter than in a person. But dead meat is useless to them. Since they can only gain nourishment from living aurym, only *living* prey can sustain them."

Zechariah looked at the ground, and though his thoughts turned inward as if he were reliving a memory, his voice sounded matter-of-fact, almost chipper.

"To be killed by a coblyn is to be fed upon while still alive. Since their prey must be living to provide nourishment, coblyns will quickly tear a person open to feed on the still-living entrails before he or she can expire. Once the prey is dead, it provides no further nutrients, so the corpse is abandoned. The aftermath of a coblyn raid is as gruesome a sight as you may ever see. Bodies torn open. Hollowed out for as long as the victim could cling to life. The rest stays to rot, a mutilated, festering heap for carrion beasts and maggots."

Justin gulped, thankful that Zechariah had waited until after dinner to share this.

"There are coblyns in the Borderwoods north of Nolia," said Leah. "Soldiers are sometimes sent to hunt them, and the heads are brought back as trophies. But I've never heard them described so . . . eloquently. You've really never heard of them, Justin?"

Justin shook his head.

"You know the language of Nolia and speak like a westerner," said Leah. "But you seem little-versed in the knowledge of the country."

Little-versed, thought Justin. *Sister, you could fill a book with the things I don't know. Heck, make it a whole sack of books.*

"What do coblyns look like?" Justin asked, eager to change the subject. "I want to know when to start running if I see one."

"Start running?" Leah said. "You certainly didn't run today. I thought you were right beside me, but the next thing I knew, I turned and realized you weren't on your steed. I couldn't believe you had gone back with Zechariah to face those things."

Justin blushed a little. She clearly hadn't seen the full version of the event. "It, uh, felt like I almost didn't have a choice in the matter," he said.

"Coblyns are humanoid," said Zechariah. "About the size of a child, with arms nearly twice as long as their legs. They knuckle-walk and lope about. Hairless, with tough, pitch-black hide, beady eyes, fangs, and long claws. They despise the sun, which makes the underground caverns ideal. That, and the black aurym."

Leah leaned forward. "You've said that twice now. I am a graduate of the Cervice Academy, and we were taught that black aurym was only folklore."

"*Only* folklore?" said Zechariah. "My dear, just because something is folklore doesn't make it untrue. If you traveled the old roads or delved into the forest where axe has never cut, you would find that much folklore and legend is based strongly in reality. As for black aurym, it is a phenomenon not easily described. The proper word for it is *daemyn*. Daemyn is evil. But I would clarify this; the word is not quite right. Saying that something is 'evil' generally implies that it possesses evil qualities. Daemyn is evil—incarnate. The heart of darkness."

"We were taught," said Leah, "that daemyn was the imaginary tool of sorcerers and necromancers, like witchcraft and magic spells. You speak of it like it's a living thing."

"Daemyn is the equal and exact opposite of aurym, and it is anything but imaginary. There are places in the world that are thick with daemyn. Places that give you the feeling of evil right down to your bones, as if something were trying to turn your blood to stone and suck the life out of you. It smells like death and sickness. Aurym-sensitive individuals know it for what it is, but nearly everyone can sense it in some form, whether a chill up your spine, the feeling of somebody watching you, or the conviction of sharing a room with an apparition. These sensations are not baseless. Few sensations ever are."

Justin stared at the ground, thinking about their flight through the gate. He remembered the fear, the feeling of his heart racing and his blood turning cold. The way his vision had started to falter, as if he were about to black out.

"Those monsters," said Justin. "Were they daemyn?" The word came out clumsily, but he tried to pronounce it the way Zechariah had: *DAY-min*.

Zechariah nodded without breaking eye contact. "Very perceptive, Justin. Daemyn hung on them like sopping wet garments. It is how Ahlund and I sensed them from so far away."

It wasn't the storm I was afraid of after all, thought Justin, *or even the monsters themselves. It was their daemyn. I felt it.*

"I *think*," said Zechariah, as his gaze narrowed to squint into the fire, "that they may have been cythraul. Another kind of demon. But the implications would be. . . ."

Whatever other thoughts he had on the matter, he left them unspoken, and neither Justin nor Leah pressed him further.

CHAPTER 21

The fire died down to embers. Leah lay near the fire in her sleeping mat. Like the night before, Zechariah opted to sleep sitting, facing the tunnel exit as if looking out into the night. Before settling down himself, Justin ventured outside the tunnel to use the bathroom. Harrowing circumstances notwithstanding, the body's processes didn't stop. Another thing the movies tended to get wrong.

The rain had become a sprinkle. The surrounding countryside was dark, and the air was thick and heavy with moisture from the bygone storm. Stumbling over uneven terrain, Justin went only far enough from the tunnel to ensure his privacy. Somewhere in the distance, rainwater rushed down the slopes.

The deed was done, and he was turning back toward the tunnel when he heard a noise behind him.

Justin froze. It could have been anything, but it had sounded too abrupt to be a branch falling or some underbrush settling. In the moment he'd heard it, he would have sworn it was a twig breaking under someone's foot.

Someone's foot? Or some . . . thing?

"Who's there?" he said into the darkness.

Nothing answered.

After a few seconds of listening to the blood pumping in his ears and imagining monsters eating people's guts, he backpedaled toward the tunnel, keeping an eye on the underbrush.

Settle down, he told himself. *Even if all those stories are true and there really are demon monsters, there are also animals. Perfectly normal animals. It was a squirrel. Or a deer or maybe a bear or something. . . . Never thought I'd be* hoping *that what I heard in the woods was a bear. At least that would kill me before it started eating—*

Justin's foot caught the rock lip of the tunnel. He had retreated a step too far and stumbled backward. He braced himself for a hard fall. Instead, a pair of hands grasped his shoulders and lowered him to a less painful landing.

"What in the world are you doing?" Zechariah demanded.

"I thought I heard something," said Justin, standing and dusting himself off. "I mean, I did hear something."

"I'm sure you did. Get some sleep, Master Holmes."

Justin shook his head at being called "Master Holmes" again and mumbled, "Like I'm going to get any sleep tonight."

He walked to his bedroll, was grateful to find it dry, and pulled a blanket over himself.

Zechariah, in his sitting position, looked over his shoulder and said, "You can rest easy. We're safe here. I didn't mean to frighten you about the—"

"No," said Justin. "Not because of that. I meant because of what happened today. You know. To Ahlund."

"Ah."

"You said the two of you were acquaintances. Not friends, then?"

"That's a long story and one I will not tell at such an hour of the night, but suffice it to say that I knew of him, and he knew of me. We had a few correspondences when he first came to Deen, and he eventually told me about the princess. I promised to help by increasing my normal watch over the town. I suppose we were associates."

"It's crazy," said Justin. "I mean, just yesterday he killed all those men in the blink of an eye. I never thought that, in the blink of an eye, he'd be gone, too."

"He died with honor. Someday, I'll tell you how he lived."

"I just . . . can't believe it."

"I know very little about death," said Zechariah. "As I told you, I've gone to great lengths to distance myself from it, and I've succeeded for a very long time."

"Right. I forgot. You just had your millionth birthday."

Zechariah ignored the sarcasm. "A side effect of avoiding death for so long is that you see quite a lot of it. It is never far from anyone. Those who live dangerously—like Ahlund—are at greater peril. However, if there is one thing I've learned, it's this: Something has a hand in this world. Something influences what happens and what doesn't."

"You mean like God?"

"Call it God if you like. I call it a plan. I've seen the plan at work, and I've seen people become part of it. Sometimes, that means living. Other times, it means dying. Do yourself a favor, Justin, and try not to think too much about it. Lives are decided quickly, yes, and in ways we can't understand—sometimes in ways that seem unfair, illogical, or cruel. But everything happens for a reason."

Justin made a face. He couldn't count the number of times people had told him that after the accident. In the hospital. At the funeral. Everywhere. People always said it in this saintly, all-knowing sort of voice, like it was supposed to comfort you. But the truth was, it was exactly the kind of B.S. a person could say with impunity, because no one could refute it or prove it. By the time Justin's mother was in the ground, those words, "everything happens for a reason," and the closely related, "it's all part of a plan," meant less than nothing to him.

"Do you actually believe that?" said Justin. "I mean, really believe it?"

"Yes," said Zechariah. "Get some sleep. Let's try not to do anything stupid—at least until it stops raining. I'm sick of the rain."

"Zechariah," Justin said. "Who the hell are you?"

The old man made a surprised noise in his throat.

"Seriously," said Justin. "And don't say 'a scholar and a scribe,' or I swear—"

"That's one too many questions for today," said Zechariah. "Go to bed." And the old man turned his back to him.

CHAPTER 22

A cold breeze woke Justin. It was dawn, and the dry, frigid breath of the mountains swept down, howling into the tunnel.

He pulled his blanket tighter and shivered. He'd been having that dream again. The one he never remembered. The one that always left him feeling the same way he'd felt in the hospital after the accident. Although he couldn't remember the dream exactly this time, for some reason he was thinking about his father's record player. The one in his office that sat on a small shelf lined with vinyl albums.

A few years ago, Justin's mother had given Benjamin that record player, along with a high-quality surround sound system, for his birthday so he could play his old record collection. That collection was a curiosity to Justin. He didn't know what he'd expected his father's music to sound like—maybe like those cheesy hair-metal songs that played on the classic rock radio station. He did have some of that. But most of Ben's records were, to put it lightly, just weird. He had a love for the progressive rock acts of the 1970s—albums with intricate, otherworldly covers and ten-plus-minute-long songs about things like magic, mythology, science fiction, and . . . trees. It was music that, Justin speculated, must have enjoyed a fanbase comprised exclusively of nerdy white guys. Nerdy white guys who had grown up to become nerdy white dads. More like granddads, really; most of the music was from before Ben's time, but for some reason, he loved the stuff. And most dads listened to their music on earbuds. Not on high-quality sound systems that could be heard from halfway up the street as the school bus made the turn onto Main Street Extension.

Through prolonged exposure, Justin had gained an appreciation for the musicianship—when it wasn't overly self-indulgent—but he still didn't quite get the appeal. One of those long, intricate songs from Ben's collection was stuck firmly in Justin's head now as he looked up at the jagged peaks outside the stone tunnel. The mountains reached up into a sky that was as clear blue as a tropical sea. The lower slopes looked as if they were overgrown with moss. But it wasn't moss. It was miles upon miles of unbroken, evergreen forest trekking up the mountainsides.

He sat up. The breeze coaxed spirals of smoke from the campfire's coals. An old man sat in front of it with his head tucked down and his hood drawn over his face. Nearby, a young woman lay sleeping.

Zechariah's hooded head shifted to face Justin.

"Don't you ever sleep?" Justin said.

"No."

The answer caught Justin off guard. "No?"

"No, I do not sleep. An additional benefit of my aurym abilities. Longevity, heightened senses, quick reflexes, and energy. Lots of energy. Pent-up energy that does not need to be replenished on a regular basis through sleep."

"You're not joking, are you?" said Justin.

"Hmm?" said Zechariah.

"You really think you're hundreds of years old."

Zechariah pulled his hood back. "*Think* it? Yes. In the same way I think water flows downhill. I normally keep the not sleeping part to myself, though."

"So you just fake it every night?"

"The look on your face is exactly why I don't tell people. It makes them uncomfortable." He closed a book in his lap that Justin hadn't noticed until now. Maybe he had been reading them after all. "You're up early. I had planned on letting the two of you get a little extra sleep this morning, considering the circumstances."

"I had a dream," said Justin.

"Ah, dreams," said Zechariah. "Now there is something I miss about being mortal."

Justin felt a shiver run down his spine. Zechariah seemed to bounce from one extreme to the other. One moment, wise and capable. The next, senile—if not just plain crazy. It was rather worrying to think that Justin and Leah's lives rested in his arthritic and possibly demented hands.

"This dream was more like a memory," Justin said. "A memory from home."

"And where did you say that was, again?"

Justin sighed. After a moment's thought, he stood and picked up a burned twig that had escaped the fire. He crouched beside Zechariah and swiped at the tunnel floor, cleaning it until it was a bare, stone surface. With the twig held like a pencil, Justin began to draw.

The charred end of the stick left black lines as he outlined shapes from memory. The continents took crude form under his hand. The amorphous blob of Asia, the puzzle-piece looking coast of Africa, Europe's jagged edges, Australia, and the others. For reason of familiarity, North America was the most accurate reproduction. When the map was complete, it was little better than a child's rendering. Justin had never been much of an artist. He estimated about where the state of Pennsylvania would be, in the eastern corner of his home continent, and drew a tiny *X*.

"Home," he said. He held the twig out to Zechariah. "So, where are we now?"

For a long time, Zechariah would not take it. He just stroked his beard and studied the map. Finally, he lowered his hand as if to point at something, flattened his palm against the stone, and erased Justin's lines. He rubbed them out until his hands were black with soot, and the stone was a blank canvas again.

There was a lump in Justin's throat as Zechariah took the twig. He held it like a paintbrush, and with intricate strokes and gentle curves, he began to draw a map of his own.

Moments later, Justin was studying a new charcoal drawing on the ground. By comparison, its detail made his amateurish sketch of Earth look like the kind of randomly squiggled borders you'd find in the front pages of a fantasy novel. Its closely packed continents, to his dismay, bore not even a passing resemblance to anyplace he recognized.

Zechariah made a graceful *X* at the center of a small continent in the western half of his map, separated from the surrounding landforms by narrow seas and bordered to the north by a series of islands.

"Here," he answered.

Justin stared at it.

"There's more to the world than this, of course," Zechariah said, almost apologetically. "This is just the inhabited, human world. The Ancients named it the Oikoumene. Beyond it are unknown, wild lands populated by barbarians, demons, cyclopes, and other forms of humans." He pointed to his *X*. "The continent we are on is called Athacea. The country of Nolia, where the princess is from, would be on the. . . ."

Zechariah trailed off. Justin had been perched on his heels, but now he fell flat on his butt. His face was white. He swallowed hard against the taste of bile.

"I, uh," said Justin. "I think I need to sit down for a while."

Zechariah chewed on his tongue a moment, then said, "Fair enough."

"I'm starting to think I've gone certifiably nuts," said Justin. "Maybe I'm locked up somewhere right now, bouncing off rubber walls, and this is all in my head."

"And that would make me a figment of your imagination?" said Zechariah.

"Maybe."

"It's not a bad theory," said Zechariah. "I certainly can't disprove it. Who's to say we aren't all just figments of someone else's imagination?"

"Very deep."

"I'm serious," said Zechariah. "Are there many religions where you come from?"

"Several that I can think of."

"And do the tenets of those religions involve a god who created the world?"

"Most of them, I think."

"Then, in essence, isn't your world, and everyone and everything in it, no more than a figment of that god's imagination?"

"Come again?"

"Well. Most monotheistic religions of the Oikoumene believe their god is an all-knowing, all-powerful creator. All that exists, exists because he thought it into being. If we accept this as truth, then reality becomes quite relative. The creator's *thoughts* determine what is real and what isn't. And if we also accept that he is all-powerful, then he has no limits. He can, by definition, do anything—including changing his mind about what is real and what is not. Couldn't it then be said that everything that exists is nothing but a thought—a figment of the supreme imagination of the creator?"

"Um. . . ."

"And why stop there? If we accept that god is real, and that he is supreme and all-powerful, and that nothing is beyond his ability, then we obviously cannot impose human limitations on him. Could he not, therefore, have more than one imagination? More than one reality? More than one world?"

"I don't know," said Justin wearily.

Zechariah shrugged. "Just a thought."

"I shouldn't have come with you," Justin said. He gestured down the dark tunnel, toward its impassable dead end. "Now, I'm trapped out here. If I had just stayed in Deen, I could have looked for the way home. Instead, I was nearly killed, and I've been no good to anyone. I've only slowed you guys down. And it was my fault Ahlund was away from his house in the first place. If he'd been there, maybe none of you would be in this mess right now, and Ahlund would still be alive—"

"That's enough," said Zechariah. "I won't abide that sort of talk. You're upset. That is understandable. Grief is healthy, but regret is not. And self-pity is worse. You think you don't belong here, but I believe you do."

"Why?"

"I told you why! Because everything is part of a plan. If you arrived in this world spontaneously, as you say, of no will of your own, then something else brought you here. Whatever the case, it happened for a reason."

Justin gave him a look and asked him for the second time, "Do you actually believe that?"

"I believe in aurym," said Zechariah. "The living spirit in all of us. That's what I believe. And I think aurym had a part in your arrival here."

There was a noise from behind them. Leah had gotten up from her sleeping mat. She was looking out of the tunnel, at the dawn on the mountain peaks, and seemed not to have heard their conversation.

Zechariah leaned in and reiterated in a whisper, "You're here for a reason, Justin."

CHAPTER 23

"The walls really go all the way along the mountains?" said Justin.

"Why is it, Master Holmes, that you never believe anything I have to say?" said Zechariah, busy saddling the steeds.

Justin shrugged. "It's just hard to imagine, that's all."

Sheer faces rose straight up. The walls looked too natural to be manmade yet too perfect to be natural. Nearby, a massive stairway carved into the wall led all the way up to the top, but it had been worn so smooth by the hand of time that the steps were just a rutty, stone slope without handholds of any kind. Justin wouldn't have braved such a climb for all the money in this world or any other. Besides—he didn't want to see what had become of the village of Irth on the other side.

As impressive as the manmade wonders were, the mountains outshone them. It had been too dark to see anything during the storm, but today, dawn broke with sapphire skies brushed with white. Traveling through the walls was like entering another realm. It was a vast, monumental landscape of ridges, valleys, hillocks, peaks, cliffs, and escarpments. Evergreen forests—thick bands of the greenest green—enveloped the hilltops. Morning fog wafted across ridgelines and whirled down into deep, pitted hollows. To Justin, it evoked a kind of geomorphic mystery. Every valley could hide a village. Every wooded slope, a sanctuary of otherworldly creatures. Every ridge, a ruined fortress of the Ancients.

Above those foothills loomed masses of gray stone. Intermittent green havens of high-altitude forests dotted the gray. Sunlight glimmered from a waterfall emerging from a rocky canyon, visible many hundreds of feet above. Farther up, the world was locked in everlasting winter, with glaciers and moraines taking the place of forests, and ice encasing the jagged summits. These elements were repeated, similar yet unique, as far as the eye could see.

Justin tightened his cloak against the chill in the air. A well-worn path, starting at the tunnel, led up into the mountains. It wended its way out of the rocky valley and soon became shrouded by pine boughs in a nook between ridges. Justin thought a person could probably wander in that wilderness for a lifetime and never see the same tree twice. And they were going into it.

Everything happens for a reason, huh, Zechariah? he thought. *That's good. Tell me another one.*

"The shutting of that door could be problematic for Nolia," Leah said, looking back at the tunnel. "Traders and Nolian patrols sometimes use these gates on their travels."

"Can't somebody bust a hole through it or something?" Justin said.

"Not an easy task," said Zechariah. "As I said yesterday, these walls are stronger than the stone they're built with. The fortifications are protected by the magic of the Ancients."

"Magic?" said Justin. "Wait. I thought you said magic was just what people called things they didn't understand."

"My definition holds true," said Zechariah. "The engineering knowledge was lost long ago. Somehow, aurym protects the walls, and when the gates are closed, they are said to be impenetrable. The Ancients had great expertise in aurstones and were able to incorporate them in metallurgy, or even build with them."

"You mean," said Justin, "these walls are aurstones?"

"Heavens, no," Zechariah said. "But I suspect that aurstones may be built into the walls at strategic waypoints to generate their protective power. It's been said that when the gates close, nothing can pass through."

"What about climbing over?" said Justin. "Or, like, tunneling underneath?"

Zechariah shot him an irritated look. "Unless you have, in your pockets, the equipment for three people to scale and descend a five-hundred-foot wall, or you boast the tenure of a seasoned miner, then it does not much matter, does it?"

Justin frowned. "I mean other people. People who need to use the gate."

Zechariah grunted. "It's likelier that travelers will circumnavigate to the next nearest gate, several days out of the way. The people of Irth will have to. . . ."

But Zechariah looked away in mid-sentence. The silence that followed chilled Justin more than the mountain breeze as he thought back to the house in Irth being destroyed. The panic. The screams. Zechariah wore a strange face. Leah was studying the ground. Justin wondered if they were thinking the same thing he was: Were there any people of Irth left?

And it's our fault, thought Justin. *We brought that evil right to their doorstep.*

The old man cleared his throat. "Local herding tribes also depend heavily on this gate. They spend the summer months in the mountain valleys and winter on the Gravelands. We'll have to inform them of the mishap when we arrive."

"When we arrive?" said Leah.

"That's the village I mentioned," said Zechariah. "They'll provide us with shelter, we can barter for supplies, and the food is always good."

A pained smile crossed Leah's face. Clearly, she had not known the details of Zechariah's chosen destination. Justin felt sorry for her. Sleeping on the ground and begging for a meal may not have been royal treatment, but she was making an admirable go of it.

CHAPTER 24

Justin had never ridden a horse in his life. Not long ago, he would have laughed at the idea. Now, here he was, astride a prehistoric beast halfway between camel and elephant, and riding it like some sort of alien cowboy. Ever since the name had popped into his frantic pleadings the day before, he had begun referring to his furry new friend as Seabiscuit.

Zechariah had taken a few minutes to instruct him on how to control his steed—to press his legs inward against the animal's ribs to move forward, to apply pressure to either side of the reins to steer, and to pull back on the reins to stop. It was easier on the body, now that he'd learned to sit perched on his pelvis instead of on his rear, and to distribute his weight evenly to avoid bouncing up and down so much.

But riding uphill, he soon learned, was a treacherous balancing act. He often pulled the reins when he didn't mean to, causing abrupt changes in direction, and his steed's hooves slipped on loose stones, sometimes causing the world to drop out from under him for a frightening second before the animal regained its footing. He would have almost preferred walking; it would have been easier on the nerves.

Their road left the valley and entered the forest, where evergreens lent generous shade. Looking back down, Justin saw the top of the walls: a causeway a hundred yards wide, snaking along the base of the mountains. He imagined military encampments on the tops of the walls—catapults, archers, soldiers sharpening their blades, blacksmiths forging arrowheads, and watchers standing guard against invaders.

Having grown up in a small town surrounded by rural areas, Justin had spent many weekends of his youth outdoors, sometimes camping or fishing, but never in his life had he seen woods like this. The forest grew tall and thick with stands of hemlock and pine bigger than any he had ever seen. Two-hundred-foot monsters were the standard, with canopies so thick as to nearly blot out the sun. Branches, leaves, and needles encompassed all experience.

From Science class, Justin knew that this must have been an old-growth forest—uncut, unlogged, and undisturbed by human hands. Trees never stopped growing, and they could live for a very long time, when given the opportunity. On Earth, there were few places left where such opportunities existed. But here, this forest had been left to its own devices for countless hundreds of years, to thrive in its unspoiled, natural form. A four-hundred-year-old tree was a juvenile. The oldest ones, if they had existed in Justin's world, would have been around to witness the fall of the Roman Empire.

Justin stopped to gaze in astonishment as they passed a giant, fallen hemlock, blanketed in moss and spongy lichens. His entire childhood home would have fit within the diameter of its massive trunk.

It was late morning when Zechariah dropped back to ride alongside Justin.

"I want to show you something," he said.

He reined his steed to a stop, and Justin did the same. The old man held out his hand. Resting on his palm was a semi-translucent rock.

"You're clearly a skeptical young man," said Zechariah. "Bordering on cynical, if you ask me. So, maybe you'll respond better to demonstrations than explanations."

"What are you. . . ?"

The stone in Zechariah's hand began to radiate a soft, blue glow. At first, it looked like a tiny flame, like a pilot light in the center of the stone, but soon, the light enveloped the rock, burning as brightly as a welder's torch.

Justin shielded his eyes. The swirling blue light reflected on the old man's face.

"It that one of those aurym-stone things?" Justin said.

"This little rock," said Zechariah, "is what the Ancients called *y'thri'ra*, which means, in the common tongue, 'keystone.' Among aurym-users, it is better known as a 'gauge.' Unlike most aurstones, gauges can be used by almost anyone with the gift. With a bit of spirit fed through it, the stone will light up. Aurym-users sometimes use these instead of torches in dark places, but, beyond that, gauges have been used for millennia to test and measure aurym ability. If someone has the gift, these little tools are good for teaching them to channel their power—without any dangerous surprises."

He held his hand out toward Justin, and just as quickly as it had appeared, the light was extinguished. It was a plain, old rock again.

"Try it," Zechariah said.

"Me?" said Justin. "I can't do that."

Zechariah was undeterred. He dropped the rock into Justin's palm. Without the blue light, it was a very unremarkable-looking thing. Just a milky, quartz-like pebble.

"Try it," Zechariah said, again.

"How?"

"Aurym is a process. You must reach deep down within yourself for the spark of the spirit. You will feel peace and calm that surpasses understanding. Feel the rock, feel your spirit, and connect them. Impart yourself into the stone."

Justin laughed a little. "I don't know about this."

"Knowing is most of the battle."

Justin looked at the rock in his hand. He studied its features—every little crest and divot on its semi-translucent surface—and tried to picture it glowing the way it had for Zechariah. It looked no different than any of the rocks he used to throw from riverbanks as a child back home.

He tried to search himself for something to "impart" into the stone. There was no spark; he'd known there wouldn't be. All he found deep within himself was that he was hungry, and he wondered how much longer it would be until lunch was imparted into him.

He shut his eyes and tried to focus. He imagined the stone bright and brilliant, and he concentrated on that image.

He peeked one eyelid open. The stone was dull and normal.

"Did it do anything?" Justin said.

Zechariah shook his head. "It comes with practice. We will try again some other time."

Justin shrugged and handed the stone back. Leah was a good ways ahead of them by now, and Zechariah made a clucking noise in his cheek, commanding his steed to hurry.

And suddenly, Justin was on the ground.

The wind was knocked out of him, and he was so dazed that he barely heard Seabiscuit's frightened whinny. For a moment, he thought he had fallen off. Then he realized somebody was on top of him, yelling, but he couldn't tell who it was or what they were saying.

Everything sounded like it was underwater. Stars floated across his vision like drunken, gilded butterflies. The world tilted as he was hauled roughly to his feet. His arm was pinned behind his back, with his own hand mashed painfully between his shoulder blades. Something was being pressed under his chin.

As his vision righted itself, he saw Zechariah and Leah a few yards away. Leah sat on steedback, looking alarmed. Zechariah had dismounted, and he stood stock-still, face as hard as steel.

A gruff voice spoke so close to Justin's ear that it hurt.

"A slip of the wrist, and he's dead."

The torque on his arm increased, and Justin grunted in pain. He was being pulled away from the others, heels dragging in the dirt of the mountain path.

"Not a step closer," said the man who held him. The stubble of the assailant's cheek scraped against his face. "Throw down your sword, old man."

"Of course," said Zechariah. "But think this through a minute—"

"Do I look like a man to be reasoned with?" shouted the voice, making Justin's ears ring. "Care to see *how* unreasonable I am?"

Justin felt the thing under his chin shift a little. A sharp edge dug into his skin.

A blade.

"All right," Zechariah said, with a voice calmer than the look on his face.

Leah had her hands over her mouth. Her face was pale. Zechariah reached under his robes and undid his belt. His sheathed sword hit the ground with a thud.

"What do you want?" Zechariah said. "Money? We have little of—"

"No money," the man said. "Just the girl."

Part III

TIME AND MAN ALONE

CHAPTER 25

"We can all get out of this alive," said Zechariah. "Clearly, you two know what you want, but I'm sure we can work out some sort of—"

"Shut up."

Zechariah's hand was under his robe, and his face was scrunched up in a weird expression.

Justin could feel his every heartbeat as his blood pumped against the blade at his throat. Twenty minutes ago, he had been looking down at the Ancients' walls. Five minutes ago, he'd been admiring the forest. One minute ago, he'd been trying to make a stone glow. And now, he was trying not to crap his pants.

Justin tried to pull away, but his arm was wrenched more tightly against his back. He yelped as tendons in his shoulder stretched nearly to the breaking point.

"Don't be a fool, boy," the man whispered in his ear. "There's no need for you to die, but that's never stopped me before. We just want the girl."

Justin's frantic eyes found Zechariah, but there was no help there. The old man just kept staring, face still strangely contorted, as if he were thinking intently about something. Maybe he was going to use some kind of aurym power, the way Ahlund had. Or maybe he was sizing up the opponent for a weakness.

Then Justin remembered the hunting knife the old man carried. He had his hand hidden beneath his robes, at the spot where he kept it. And suddenly, Justin recognized that facial expression.

Aiming, thought Justin. *He's aiming! He's going to throw the knife!*

Justin's tall body was ample cover for this smaller aggressor. The only target would have been the man's face, inches from Justin's own—a wildly minuscule margin for error.

"We don't negotiate with kidnappers," said the man holding Justin. "Let her go, you old billy goat. I'll take the steeds and your weapons, too."

Justin's heart skipped a beat. "Let her go—?" he started to say.

Before he could finish, the knife tightened against his throat, and coherent thought was wrung from his head like a rag.

"*Last* warning!" the attacker shouted in Justin's ear. "Keep your mouth shut, and I might keep your throat shut."

"Olorus," said Leah. "Is that you?"

"Yes, my lady," the man said. "Do not be afraid!"

"Wait!" Leah said. "Olorus, stop! Let him go!"

"What?" the attacker said.

That was when Zechariah acted. His arm shot forth from his robes, and sunlight glinted against a rotating object as it was flung from his hand, straight at Justin and his captor.

Justin heard Leah yell. He braced himself for the impact of the knife.

In a blur of motion, a second man jumped in front of them. Justin heard a gong-like clang and saw Zechariah's knife hit the ground. Then another blur as the figure spun toward the unarmed Zechariah. He held a machete-like blade in his hand, raised high and ready to strike.

"Stop!" screamed Leah, throwing herself in front of Zechariah.

The second figure, a long-haired man clad in armor, halted in his tracks and slowly lowered his weapon. Justin now realized why Zechariah's knife had done him no damage. Strapped to this man's back was a huge, metal shield. He had thrown himself, back-first, into the path of the projectile to block it.

"These people aren't kidnappers!" Leah said. "They are my friends."

"Friends?" said the man holding Justin. "But, your highness—"

"Friends, Olorus," she said. "Allies. Put away your weapons. And let him go."

Justin hit the ground again. He rolled sideways, looking toward Zechariah. The old man stood still, leaned slightly toward his sword belt. Justin nearly jumped out of his skin when he felt hands on him again, but this time they meant no harm. It was the second man, the one with the long hair. He had sheathed his sword and was wordlessly helping Justin to his feet. His dark hair was bound by a piece of cloth tied around his forehead. Despite having put away his weapon, his calculating gaze bounced suspiciously from Justin to Zechariah.

The other one was an older man, stocky, with short, reddish-blonde hair. Little scars marred his face, and an orange bristle of facial hair covered his rounded chin. He was currently sliding his knife into a scabbard at his belt—moments ago, that knife had been at Justin's throat. Both men wore leather armor dotted with metal plates. They wore no helmets, but strapped upon their backs were kite-shaped shields of blackened steel. Their short swords were shaped like machetes with crossguards.

"Friends," the red-haired man said. "We assumed. . . . My apologies."

"Leah," said Zechariah. "You know these men?"

"Yes," said Leah. "They're Nolian soldiers."

"I am Lieutenant Olorus Antony of the High Nolian Guard," said the red-haired man. "And this is Sergeant Hook Bard." He gestured to his partner, and the dark-haired man bowed without a word.

"I am Zechariah," Zechariah said, eyes still sharp, body still tense. "You've already met my young friend, Justin Holmes, on more intimate terms."

Olorus's face flushed almost as red as his hair.

"Olorus," said Leah. "What are you doing here?"

Olorus saluted. "Your highness. Sergeant Bard and I have been here for several days, waiting to rescue you."

"Rescue me," Leah repeated, with an edge to her voice. "The same way I was rescued from Deen? Abducted in the night?"

"That," said Olorus Antony, "is what we meant to rescue you *from*, Princess Anavion."

For a long time, no one spoke. It was Zechariah who finally broke the silence.

"Well, then," he said. "If you've been here so long, you must be well-supplied. Run and fetch us some food. And if you've any tea, make it strong."

Olorus sneered at Zechariah. "Sergeant Bard," he said, "find something to eat for the princess. And some hay for this billy goat."

The younger, dark-haired soldier turned and strode into the woods. The kite-shaped shield on his back covered him from knee to neck. A few twigs snapped underfoot as he went, and Justin couldn't help but think about the noise he had heard in the woods the night before, so close to their camp.

"Leah," said Zechariah, "are you certain these men can be trusted?"

Olorus glared. "I was about to ask the same thing."

Leah looked from one to the other. "I. . . . I'm not certain of anything, anymore."

CHAPTER 26

Minutes later, the five of them sat under a large pine. Day-old rainwater dripped from needle and branch. Fog rolled through the evergreens. Or perhaps it was a cloud. After all the climbing, it certainly seemed to Justin as if they were high enough to be in the clouds.

Justin eyed the soldiers. The dark-haired one hadn't brought any tea—or hay—only a bag of supplies, some dried, salted meat for Leah, which she hadn't touched, and a pair of barb-tipped spears longer than the soldiers were tall.

And Justin had noticed something else. They were dressed an awful lot like the soldiers he'd buried.

"I am very sorry that you were abducted, my lady," said Olorus. "I had hoped that the Guardian, Sir Ahlund, would have been able to protect you."

"Ahlund is dead," Leah snapped.

Olorus's eyes widened. He exhaled wearily through his nostrils and closed his eyes. "I mourn his loss. But how did you escape? What about the men who kidnapped you?"

"They are in the ground," said Zechariah. "We saw to that."

Olorus's shoulders slumped. "Then I mourn the loss of my countrymen, as well. Misguided though they were."

Justin was trying to follow their conversation, but he found himself distracted. He was rubbing his neck, touching his Adam's apple with his fingers. The knife had not done any physical damage, but he kept checking anyway.

Another close shave, so to speak, he thought. *Does everybody in this world come close to death on a daily basis, or is it just me?*

"Your countrymen," said Zechariah, nodding. "As I thought."

"Yes," said Leah. "The soldiers who kidnapped me wore no markings that would identify king or country, but I recognized many of them. I even remembered some of their surnames. They were Nolian soldiers. My own people. They broke into Ahlund's home in the night, claiming they had come to 'save' me. When I questioned this, they took me by force and set fire to Ahlund's home. They would not listen to me, and they refused to give me any answers. Most would hardly look me in the eye."

"Hook and I were part of that company," said Olorus. "We were given the same orders. We chose not to carry them out."

"Um, sorry," said Justin. "I don't know if it's okay for me to ask questions right now, but I'm confused. Why did your own soldiers kidnap you?"

Leah cleared her throat. "When the royal family of Nolia, *my* family, was murdered, I survived thanks to soldiers of the High Guard like Olorus and Hook. The plan was for me to go into hiding until the culprits of the attack could be located, with our prime minister acting as regent until it was safe for me to return. Ahlund took me to Deen to keep me safe, but I've had no contact with Nolia since. In other words, Justin, I don't know."

"Enlighten us, lieutenant of the High Guard," Zechariah said.

Olorus frowned. "The High Guard is disbanded," he said. "By order of Prime Minister Asher."

"Disbanded?" Leah said.

Olorus and Hook exchanged a look.

"My lady," said Olorus. "It's far worse than you think. The government allowed the people to believe you perished. It was meant to give the perpetrators the impression that they had succeeded and, thus, draw them out. But then, a week ago, Asher addressed the public. He claimed he had *uncovered* evidence that you were still alive, and. . . . He told them, my lady, that you had orchestrated the attack on your family."

The blood drained from Leah's face.

"He claims," continued Olorus, "that you hired assassins to murder your family so you could take the throne. He also claims that you fled the country after the incidents, fearing repercussions, and have been hiding ever since."

"He paints me as a killer and a coward?" said Leah. "Of course. He's using my family's murder—and my trust—to his advantage."

Olorus hesitated. "I don't think he took advantage, my lady. I think this was his plan all along."

Leah looked sick.

"Hook and I have been discussing it," said Olorus. "Asher had the most to gain from this plot, and he was . . . *meticulous* in his actions following your departure. By allowing you to live, he set you up to take the fall. Few are privy to the truth of what happened on the night your family was killed. No one would believe that the king and your brothers, all war heroes and great fighters, could be killed in an attack while the young princess escaped unharmed."

"So," whispered Leah, staring at the forest floor. "I didn't escape at all. He let me go."

"That's an old trick," Zechariah spoke up. "Killing the old guard outright turns them into martyrs. But by sowing seeds of distrust, allegiances can be shifted to new leadership at the same time. Framing one of their own by painting him—or her—as a traitor is the most effective method."

"It breaks my heart to tell you this, my lady," said Olorus, "but many of the people believe Asher's lies. He sent those soldiers to Deen to arrest you and put you on trial. The army is loyal to him, now. He has appointed new officials in key seats. Those who know the truth have been spread strategically thin, and they fear for their lives to step forward. Certain legislators have already met with untimely, suspicious ends. He is gaining control, and a guilty verdict against you would secure his hold on the nation. When he ordered your arrest, I knew the end was near."

At this, the dark-haired man called Hook, who had remained quiet thus far, leaned forward and began working his hand in the air, moving his fingers to form shapes.

"He says," said Olorus, "that if loyalty to the royal bloodline makes him a traitor, then so be it. I feel the same way. I never swore allegiance to any prime minister or council. I swore allegiance to the crown, a crown that is rightfully yours, your highness. Hook and I volunteered for the mission, hoping to save you from your own soldiers."

"And you promptly ran away?" said Zechariah. "Fleeing into the mountains? What a credit to your princess you are."

"I didn't flee anywhere," Olorus snarled. "I flee from nothing! But on open ground, no two men would stand a chance against their numbers."

"I see," said Zechariah.

The irony of Olorus's words was not lost on Justin, either.

"Their orders were," said Olorus, "after arresting Leah, to come this way. To travel up the mountain path and return to Nolia across the northern border. Once we learned their intended route, I feigned illness, and Hook volunteered to escort me back to Nolia. We came here instead. We've spent the past two days studying the area, scouting narrow points along the road for raids. In these thick woods, picking off a few at a time at night, we would chip away at their numbers enough for a rescue. And perhaps, if careful, convince some of them to join our cause."

Justin swallowed hard, wondering how close he had been to getting "picked off" today. Or the night before, alone in the dark.

CHAPTER 27

Leah's face had gone from pale to red with rage. Her eyes appeared damp, but she did not cry. She didn't seem to know what to do or say.

"Your story is full of holes," said Zechariah. "Why would these soldiers take the long, hard road to Nolia through these mountains when they could easily return back over the plains?"

"There are those who oppose Asher," said Olorus. "I think the prime minister hoped to sneak the princess into the country discreetly on the lesser-watched northern roads to avoid a possible ambush by loyalists. And as for my *story*, if I'm lying, let me be struck dead! I do not enjoy relating that I was forced to plot against my fellow soldiers. Some of them learned battle under my own tutelage. A nephew of mine was among them. A recruit. Hardly a man."

Olorus paused, visibly upset. Justin recalled the boy lying in the blood-splattered grass, begging for help just before Ahlund finished him, and he felt sick.

Hook signed in the air with his hand, and Olorus translated, "Hook hopes the deeds of our countrymen prior to this disaster will outshine the orders that led them to their ends," said Olorus. "It grieves me to learn that they are dead, but I thank everything holy that it did not have to be by my hand."

"I hold none of them to blame for their actions," said Leah somberly. "I see now why they treated me like a criminal. They could not have known the treachery in which they were taking part." She gestured toward Justin. "Justin saw to it that they received a proper burial. They are at peace."

Olorus nodded to Justin, saying, "Thank you."

"Lieutenant Antony," said Zechariah. "I have one more question. You caught us unaware on the path today. Why not kill us?"

Olorus grinned. "We expected a squad of heavily armed soldiers. Instead, we got a very old man and a boy with the physique of a malnourished stork. We debated killing you in your sleep, but curiosity got the better of us."

Justin shivered. The soldier named Hook smirked.

"If what you say is true," said Zechariah, "then the soldiers we killed will not go unmissed. Surely, other detachments will be waiting to rendezvous with them."

"A company of infantrymen waits along this very road, in fact," said Olorus, "near the snowline, about a two-day march from here. And a cavalry unit waits north of the mountains. They will have standing orders. If the soldiers from Deen fail to arrive after a designated time—seven days, maybe six—they will set out looking for them. There will be scouts at every fork in the road. On every overlook. It's good we intercepted you when we did. It would have been difficult for you to go unnoticed. The best course of action, for all of us, would be to return to the Gravelands."

"That is impossible, now," said Leah. "The gate was closed when we passed through, and its mechanism was destroyed."

"Destroyed?" said Olorus. "By what?"

"We were pursued," Zechariah said.

When it became clear that no one was going to elaborate on the point, Olorus said, "For now, the surrounding area is safe. Monitoring the paths is easy enough. Hundreds of miles of thickly wooded valleys and ridges. An easy place to disappear if need be. Plenty of game and spring water. We have some time before a decision must be made. Even if it means diverting to one of the other mountain gates to reach the Gravelands, we will still be far ahead of them."

The Gravelands, thought Justin.

He shuddered. The last thing he wanted was to willingly chance another encounter with those monsters after so narrowly escaping the first time—and at the cost of Ahlund's life. Leah must have been thinking something similar.

"I would not travel by the Gravelands, if it could be helped," she said.

Olorus hesitated. "There's something you're not telling us. Isn't there, your highness?"

"There appears to be a third party involved," said Leah. "I'm not yet sure what part they play in all this, but I would prefer to avoid them at all costs."

Worry lines crossed the lieutenant's forehead, and Sergeant Hook Bard cracked his knuckles.

"It seems that things are more complicated than I thought," said Olorus. He nodded to Leah. "It is for you alone to decide, my lady. I will follow your command for as long as you have need of me."

Hook nodded as well, putting a hand over his heart.

"Thank you both," said Leah. "Tarrying here, I'm afraid, is no solution; it only delays our problems. But Zechariah has friends in the mountains who may be able to help us."

"Herding people," Zechariah said. "Tribesmen who ask few questions and do not play political games."

"Tribesmen?" said Olorus. He made a noncommittal grunt in his throat. Then he looked skeptically at Zechariah and Justin. "And you two mean to come along?"

"Of course," said Zechariah.

"Well, then," said Olorus. "So long as my lady vouches for you, I'll allow it. And for serving as Princess Anavion's bodyguards in Sir Ahlund's stead, I suppose I owe you my thanks." He smiled at Justin. "And you, I owe a drink."

"I'll take two," said Justin, rubbing his neck.

Olorus's mouth split open with a laugh that echoed through the trees. It had been so long since Justin had heard real laughter that it sounded strange to him. He had to force a smile.

CHAPTER 28

By midday, Justin realized he had been correct about the fog. It wasn't fog. They were walking among the clouds.

He wiped his brow. It was not sweat that beaded on his forehead but misty vapor. The moisture of the cloudy forest clung to his face, hair, and clothes.

The fact that their party had almost doubled in size so quickly—so soon after nearly killing one another—had everyone on edge. The soldiers walked alongside the steeds. They lugged heavy gear and had large metal shields and tall spears strapped to their backs, but they still hustled at an even pace with the steeds and showed little sign of fatigue. Justin knew he wouldn't have lasted long at such a pace and was just grateful to be riding Seabiscuit.

Outstretched hemlock boughs masked the trees' heights as surely as a ceiling. It was a world trapped in perpetual twilight. Even at midday, it was so dark that anything visible through the cloud cover was smeared with the distortion of low light. There were birds everywhere, but he could not see them. The hammering of a woodpecker occasionally erupted above them and was answered half a mile away. At one point, they flushed a deer and two small fawns from a thicket along the roadside. Gracefully, they bounded off between the trees.

Moss of varying shades of green coated almost everything, painting the ancient forest in verdant watercolors. On the ground, the moss was more dominant than grass. It wrapped about the tree trunks and thickly covered every piece of deadwood.

With time, the ground grew steeper. The forest became thinner, and the air colder. Some sections of trail were too steep for the steeds to traverse while bearing the weight of humans, so the riders had to dismount and lead the steeds on foot before mounting back up again. Eventually, this became so frequent that they gave up on riding altogether, and all proceeded on foot, leading their steeds by the reins.

Justin's legs ached. His breath came in cold gasps that made his chest hurt as he panted with the effort of keeping up with his companions. He was not particularly prideful about things like his strength or physical fitness, but he found himself growing self-conscious of the fact that Leah was so better conditioned than he was. Her breathing hardly even seemed labored while Justin struggled just to keep moving. On the basketball team, if the coach called you "princess," it wasn't exactly a term of endearment, so what did it say about Justin if he couldn't keep up with an *actual* princess?

At a blind spot in the path, Justin pulled out his inhaler, took a long hit, and hastily slipped it back into his pocket before anyone could notice.

Soon, the clouds and the moss were gone. The pines were replaced by thick-branched spruces with needles of cyan, and the path was bordered with gnarls of mountain laurel and juniper. Little brown birds flitted within tangles of hawthorn and thistle. The path became littered with loose shale, and the ground frequently slipped underfoot. Several times, Justin fell and had to catch himself, cutting his palms.

They finally stopped to rest in the late afternoon at a rare flat spot amid some spruces. Looking back down the mountain, Justin saw the forest laid out in a belt of deep green below. It looked like a massive expanse from this angle, but the area they had passed through was only a tiny speck of the wilderness that encompassed this mountain range.

Justin remembered that the name, Thucymoroi, meant, "the mountains that shift." The translation had induced in his mind images of seismic activity and apocalyptic crashing of rocky peaks. Now, Justin saw another reason they might have been given such a name. The way the landscape changed between rising and falling ridgelines and valleys, it would be easy to get lost in the treacherous topography. The path they traveled now had been fleshed out over the eons, but without a well-worn road, traversing the mountains would have probably meant never traveling the same route twice, in which case it might seem as if the mountains had physically shifted since one last attempted their summits.

When the reprieve was over, they were off again, climbing upward through bushy, rocky terrain as twilight began to fall. Zechariah had said he hoped to reach the village before nightfall, but that was not going to happen.

The group found a suitable spot and settled down to make camp, and the steeds were let loose to graze among the nearby thistles. Leah built a fire with some brush and a flint while Olorus and Hook chopped wood.

Justin sat down to rest his legs while Zechariah disappeared into the bushes. He returned carrying two hardy sticks as thick as a man's arm.

"That's not much firewood," commented Justin.

Unceremoniously, one of the sticks was pitched into Justin's lap, and he flinched at how close it came to his most tender spot.

"These were the straightest I could find," said Zechariah. "They will do."

The old man swung the stick in his hand and rapped Justin hard on the shoulder. A cloud of dust puffed up from Justin's cloak as the blow knocked him over. He got up rubbing the stinging spot vigorously.

"What was that for?" he demanded.

"Defend yourself," said Zechariah.

The old man lunged forward and poked the stick into Justin's belly. Justin coughed and buckled over. He picked up the second stick as quickly as he could, but he got another whack on the back in the process.

"Ow!"

"Remember what I showed you with the dirk?" Zechariah asked.

"The what?" said Justin, teeth grinding.

"Your knife."

"No!"

"That's good," he said. "Because a sword is altogether different."

"You mean a stick. Is this necessary right now?"

Zechariah came at him again. Justin had the presence of mind to raise his stick in defense, but it was moot. Zechariah hooked his mock sword around Justin's and swung in a wide arc, carrying it away and tossing it across the clearing. He brought the stick around in a graceful extension of the arc and caught Justin in the shin. The area of impact flared with a cool, liquid pain. The next strike—to the back of his head—knocked him down.

"Son of a—!" said Justin.

"You're dead," said Zechariah.

"I'm not that lucky," Justin managed from his knees. "If this is meant to be a lesson, I am learning nothing!"

"Clearly," said Zechariah.

Zechariah stepped forward to kick him, and Justin brought his hands up out of reflex. He caught the old man's boot before it reached his chest, but it still knocked him backward. The stick then rapped him on the neck, sending stars spinning through his vision.

"You trying to kill me?" Justin shouted.

"I did kill you," said Zechariah. "A number of times."

Zechariah smacked Justin's knuckles. In a rage, Justin charged, swinging his fist at the old man. Zechariah caught the attack, spun him around as if he were a dancer, and held him with the mock sword against his neck, clamping his windpipe shut.

"Dead again," said Zechariah, and he dropped Justin to the ground.

At the sound of laughter, Justin glanced over his shoulder. Olorus was watching the battle with one foot propped on his overturned shield, guffawing heavily. Hook was just smiling, and Leah, although pretending not to watch, seemed to be having a hard time keeping it together.

"We'll make no progress tomorrow if the boy can't walk!" called Olorus.

"That's the advantage of having a healer among us," answered Zechariah.

"If I had known he was just a lad in training," said Olorus, "I wouldn't have treated him so roughly on the trail!"

Justin remained on his knees, wheezing. "When do I get to hit *you*?" he demanded.

"After you can avoid being hit," said Zechariah. "And then, after you can catch me."

CHAPTER 29

Justin rubbed tenderly at his knuckles as he sat before the fire. The place where Zechariah had rapped him was red and swollen, with a patch of dried blood where the skin had broken. He had tried his best to avoid being hit, but all he'd gained for his troubles were bruises and a little blood.

He glared at Zechariah, then took a bite of his portion of a roasted rabbit.

Throughout dinner, Olorus talked about Nolia. He spoke of the beauty of the capital city, Cervice, and the labor the history books said went into carving its marble towers. He talked about defending the borders against barbarian hordes, and of the mounting unrest between Nolia and a nation called Darvelle. Hook had yet to say a word. His hearing seemed unimpaired, but his use of signs to communicate led Justin to believe silence was the norm.

As for Leah, she was nearly as silent as Hook. Given all that had come to light, Justin didn't blame her.

After dinner, Zechariah began rambling about the scholarly significance of fairytales, and Justin's head bobbed as he fought sleep. He missed home, where people talked about normal things like TV and football.

The last of the sun's influence faded to darkness, and the sky above the mountain wilderness shone with constellations Justin had never seen before. His old nemeses, those two moons—the little one and its big sister—were visible over a nearby peak.

Justin had closed his eyes and was almost asleep sitting up when Zechariah said, "Leah, I'm afraid Justin will slow us down tomorrow in his current condition. Might you assist him?"

Justin furrowed his brow as Leah approached and kneeled beside him.

"Where does it hurt?" she asked.

It was a ridiculous question. His feet hurt with blisters, his legs hurt from hiking, his arms still hurt from digging graves, and the knocks Zechariah had administered during their exhibition were starting to transform from sharp pains to widespread aches. He wore pain like a bodysuit.

"Everywhere," Justin said.

"Your hand," she said, noticing his knuckles.

"Yeah, but I don't think anything's broken—"

She took his hand in hers, and he promptly forgot the words. But then something happened that made him forget about the softness of her skin. He felt a sensation like lukewarm water creeping inside his hand. Tendrils of it wrapped around his veins. Like soap to dirt, it washed away the pain.

Leah removed her hand from his. The dried blood was still there, but his knuckles were no longer red or swollen. Justin flexed his fingers. They didn't hurt anymore.

"How did you do that?" he said.

"I'm a healer," she said. She pointed to a ring on her finger, as if no further explanation were needed. "Anywhere else?"

Justin rolled up the leg of his trousers. His shin was blackened in a thick line where Zechariah had struck him, and the bruise was so tender that he winced when she touched it. Again, the peculiar feeling spread throughout the area, warming and cooling at the same time, until the pain was gone. When she pulled her hand away, the bruise was gone, too.

"That's amazing," said Justin. "Is it . . . aurym?"

"Of course," she said. "You've never seen aurym-healing before?"

He only shrugged.

She smiled curiously, squinting at him a little. "Some time, when I'm not so tired, I've got some questions for you."

Justin opened his mouth to say something, but nothing came out. She was only a couple of years older than him, but all of a sudden, it was like he was a freshman trying to talk to a pretty senior—struck dumb.

Leah smiled again, this time a bit pityingly. She gestured toward Zechariah and whispered to Justin, "Don't worry. I bet you'll get him next time." Then she raised her hand and pantomimed a closed-fisted jab, pushing her knuckles against Justin's jaw only firmly enough to turn his head a little. It was the kind of thing you'd do to a kid brother who just struck out in Little League, and it made Justin blush.

She stood and began spreading out her sleeping mat a few yards away from the men. Olorus, Zechariah, and Hook stopped what they were doing and likewise began to prepare for the night. Despite her mild manner, she had a way about her that demanded respect; when she was tired, it meant it was time for bed. For everyone.

Justin fished his wallet from his jacket pocket. He wanted to see Kate's face again, as a reminder of life back home. He lay down in his sleeping mat and started to open his wallet to pull out the photo but found himself distracted by the constellations hanging in space high above. The stars burned so much more clearly up here in the thin, mountain air. They tugged at something inside him, making him feel somehow more and less than himself, all at once. He fell asleep with the unopened wallet still in his hand.

CHAPTER 30

Justin woke from dreamless sleep before dawn, chilled to the bone. The sun, when it finally cracked over the tip of the nearby peaks, did little to warm the air, and as the party set out, he pulled his clothing as tight around him as he could to shield himself from the elements.

The path traveled in switchbacks and strange curves, sometimes climbing sharply and other times leveling off into grassy pastures bordered by stands of pines and firs. Wildlife flourished among the flowering mountain brush. Little birds, pheasants, and rabbits fled as the humans crossed their pastures.

Once, topping a rise, they came upon a beast the likes of which Justin had never seen before. It was a huge, elk-like deer, seven feet tall at the shoulders and covered in red fur with white speckles across the back. Atop its head was a set of shovel-shaped antlers like a moose, so large that a full-grown steed could have sat in them. It was a wonder the creature could even stand. It looked at them, then galloped into the trees. The average elephant would have weighed more, but this animal stood just as tall, maybe a little taller.

"What was that thing?" Justin blurted.

"An irelk," said Olorus. "Quite the spread on it, eh?"

"That was, like, probably the biggest animal I've ever seen," Justin said.

"Biggest you've ever seen!" Olorus put his lips together and blew a raspberry. "You must be joking. Why, I've seen cave lions bigger than that!"

Justin blinked. "Lions? Bigger than *that*?"

"Sure!" said Olorus. "But those are tiny compared to a dinoth—giant, tusked beasts with skin like armor. Or an aepy—the people of Endenholm call it the elephant bird. Stands twelve feet tall and will eat a grown man when it can get one."

"Aepies do not eat humans," Zechariah scoffed, "though I did see one pick off a young ox, once. Besides, that's nothing compared to the indrico."

"The what?" Olorus said.

"Indricos make irelk look like house cats," said Zechariah. "Medium-sized ones measure sixteen feet at the shoulders, with long necks and legs like trees. Some people call them land-whales. The cyclopes herd them like cattle."

"Cyclopes!" Olorus said. "You can't be serious, old man. You don't really believe those things exist, do you?"

"I believe what I have seen with my own eyes," said Zechariah.

"Oh, me too," Olorus said. "Say, Hook! Did I tell you about that shug monkey I saw last week? Twenty feet tall and naked as a buck. Feet like wagon wheels—you should've seen the size of his—"

"If you're about finished, I suggest we get moving," said Zechariah.

"And don't even get me started on campes!" Olorus exclaimed as they went. "People say they're just a legend, but who wouldn't believe in a giant scorpion with the head of a woman and the tail of a dragon that lures men underground with their songs to eat them?"

"If anyone's interested," Zechariah mumbled. "There's no such thing as a twenty-foot shug monkey. They don't grow an inch over ten."

CHAPTER 31

The green meadows between ridges ended, and the terrain turned into stony ground and thorny vegetation. Shaggy, gray goats with horns like helmets walked among the shrubbery, munching on bark wherever thorns did not protect. The temperature had dropped so precipitously that it aggravated Justin's lungs, and he was forced to take repeated doses of his inhaler when the others weren't looking. The canister felt light. The aerosol was almost out.

Soon, the temperature was so cold that Justin would not have been surprised to see snow. When he caught a glimpse up the peaks above, however, the snowline was still a long way off. He could only imagine how cold those summits were.

They crested a rise in the path, and suddenly stretching out before them was a mountain valley like a hidden pool among rocks. Lush, green grasses covered a mile or more of rolling plains before abruptly ending at rising, gray rock faces on the other side, where Justin thought he could see the glisten of a flowing stream. Grazing on the plains were herds of animals, and manmade structures were clustered at the valley's center.

"Here we are, at last," said Zechariah, looking down from the top of the ridge.

"Not much of a village," said Olorus.

"It serves the purposes of the *A'cru'u'ol.* Their name means 'trapped people.'"

"You said they welcome travelers," said Olorus. "Let's go, then."

"We wait here until we are invited," Zechariah said.

"Trapped people?" said Justin.

Zechariah cleared his throat. "Their creation lore tells of ancestors who were born below the world and ventured above ground to see the sky. They fell so in love with the sky that when they tried to return home, their eyes could no longer see the way. They became trapped above ground, and their home was lost to them. A'cru'u'ol. The trapped people. An acceptable simplified version of their name is Cru."

"Born below the world," said Leah. "Does that have anything to do with the underground cities? The ones the Ancients built?"

From the side, Justin saw Zechariah's face tighten in a smile.

"Bright girl," the old man said. "The parallel is striking, isn't it? The same thought has occurred to me."

"What thought?" asked Justin.

"That these herding people are direct descendants of the Ancients," Zechariah answered.

"You can't prove that," scoffed Olorus.

"You are probably right," said Zechariah. "But neither can you disprove it. To converse with the Cru people may be to speak with same civilization that built the great walls and dug the mountain citadels. Mortal man will never know."

To anyone other than Justin, the subtle emphasis Zechariah put on the word "mortal" probably went unnoticed.

Twelve centuries old . . . thought Justin.

"Ah," said Zechariah. "We have been noticed."

Below, two steeds with riders had broken away from the village and were approaching the rise.

"The Ancients are to be revered," said Olorus. "How can you compare them to mountain savages?"

"You may want to dispense with that sort of thinking as quickly as possible, outside of your homeland," said Zechariah.

"What sort of thinking?"

"Calling people 'savages.' It's not wise to assume anyone beneath you. Treat everyone you meet as an equal, and you will never be caught off guard."

"Equal?" Olorus chuckled. "Let me tell you what I know of equal. Across the sea, west of Nolia, live barbarian people called the Eeth. Skirmishes between the Eeth and our border guards are as commonplace as the rise of the sun. They cross the sea in their double-sailed dhow boats and attack our ports just for the sport of it. I have personally seen the desecrated corpses of Nolian soldiers, the eyes plucked from their heads to be taken away as trophies. Or ears or noses or scalps. By their very nature, they are a violent and irreverent people."

"No group of people is any different than you by nature," said Zechariah. "Customs may differ, but human beings are the same, able to fear, hate, and love, and instilled with moral law and the capacity to do good and evil. The Eeth's concepts of these things vary from your own, but that is because they are a very old civilization. They have lived on their ancestral lands in Otunmer much longer than your kingdom has existed. They have long memories, and their society has lived through circumstances most Nolians could not imagine. It has shaped them differently."

"I would hardly call them a society," said Olorus. "You mean to tell me you do not believe it indecent, nay, evil, to desecrate the body of a fallen soldier?"

"For a Nolian, perhaps," said Zechariah, "but the Eeth believe that when a person dies, their soul is freed to rejoin a collective consciousness that spans the world. The physical body, in that sense, is only a vessel, and a very unimportant thing. Taking someone's scalp, to them, would be like taking a hat, to you. All I really mean is that the Eeth's intentions may not be as abominable as you presume. To believe that every Eeth is evil would be almost as grave an error as to assume that every Nolian is honorable. The Oikoumene is a big place with many cultures. Living in peace is impossible if ethnocentric thinking skews your view of them."

"Who ever said I wanted to live in peace?" Olorus grumbled.

Justin pondered that strange word again: Oikoumene, pronounced *oik-you-MAY-nay*—the inhabited world. Zechariah's charcoal-drawn map came to mind, with its unfamiliar continents. He'd been trying not to think about it.

CHAPTER 32

The approaching riders ascended the rise and slowed their steeds to a trot. Both were men, and both rode without saddles. Hanging over their bodies were thick, gray-brown furs, and although their faces were woolly with bristly beards, their heads were shaved bare. Their wide eyes seemed to glisten as if always close to tears. Their skin was the rich brown, almost black, of fertile soil. They looked carefully from one traveler to the next with faces that were impassive but not unfriendly. Bows were slung over their backs, and in their hands were long shepherd's crooks.

Zechariah said something in a language Justin had never heard before, rife with glottal stops and heavy nouns. In response, the riders smiled and nodded, returning what Justin guessed was some kind of formal greeting.

"Welcome," the first of the Cru men said in soft tones. "Please pardon my accent. It's been a long time since I conversed in western words. A bit fast sometimes, but a beautiful language nonetheless. You may call me Sif."

"Sif," said Zechariah. "I am called Zechariah. My comrades and I would greatly appreciate food and shelter as we make our way for the northern roads. We have much to trade."

"You do not need trade or tribute to afford food and shelter here," said Sif. "The Cru always welcome travelers. The mountains can be an unforgiving place."

"Very good," said Zechariah. "I wish to speak with your council, if I could."

The countenances of the riders did not change, but their watery eyes seemed to deepen a little.

"You look to be a very wise man," said Sif, "but our council meets with outsiders only under the gravest of circumstances."

Zechariah nodded respectfully. "This, I fear, is such a circumstance."

Sif's shoulders slumped a bit. "Bad news is plentiful of late. I will speak to the council on your behalf."

He turned his steed by use of his legs alone and signaled Zechariah and the others to follow. He and the other Cru set their steeds at a trot and headed down the hill into the valley.

"I thought you said you had friends here, old man," Olorus mumbled. "Your name didn't seem to ring any bells."

"These men are far too young to know me," said Zechariah dismissively.

Justin threw Zechariah a glance, but the old man just kept looking forward as he rode.

"Why did he say you look like a wise man?" Leah whispered.

"You don't think I look wise?" said Zechariah, scrunching up his face as if insulted.

"It just seemed like a strange thing to say," said Leah.

"In Cru culture, wisdom is highly respected," said Zechariah. "A woman's hair is a symbol of her wisdom. The longer, the wiser. The same goes for a man's facial hair." Zechariah playfully tugged at the edges of his long, white beard.

Justin rubbed a hand over his bare chin.

Approaching the village, they passed groups of horned, bison-like creatures with heavy coats the color of black walnuts. A pinprick of cold touched the back of Justin's hand. Then another. Soon, snow was falling all around him in tiny, pellet-like flakes. It melted on the Cru men's bare heads, clung to their dark beards, and blanketed the black fur of the bison.

The Cru village was a circle of domed huts made of bowed logs, sod, and branches. Smoke wafted from chimney holes. There were no windows, and the doors were only flaps of tanned hide. Still, the prospect of a roof over his head—any roof—was a welcomed one.

Men with shaved heads and women with long, braided hair watched them as they passed. Cru people labored at looms, beat at rugs, scraped hides, or collected eggs from the nests of domesticated fowl. Some children dashed by, a shaggy dog barking playfully at their heels. They stopped in their tracks at sight of the travelers and stared with excited eyes. The dog paced a bit, sniffing the air defensively. The smaller boys' hair grew freely but, unlike the girls, was unbraided. The shaving of the head must have been a rite of manhood.

Nearby, a group of women walked with baskets on their hips and babies strapped to their backs. One hunched old woman had a braid so long that she carried it looped around her body in three lasso-like passes from left shoulder to right armpit. Adolescent girls followed behind the older women, some leading little brothers or sisters by the hand. The teenaged girls batted their eyes at Justin as he passed, and he felt himself blush.

The man named Sif took the steeds to be fed, and Justin and his group were led to an empty hut on the edge of town. A fire warmed the interior. Cots lined the circular walls, and Justin couldn't resist. Without a word, he placed his belongings at the end of a bed and flopped down on it.

Zechariah started to say something, but Justin didn't hear the end of the sentence. He sunk into the feather-stuffed mat and was asleep in seconds.

CHAPTER 33

One second, he was sound asleep. The next, he was slammed to the floor on his back with the wind knocked out of him. When Justin gained his wits, he realized he was pinned to the ground. The tip of a sword was pointing at his throat.

"Where is your sword?" Zechariah demanded, letting the blade touch Justin's neck.

"Are you freaking crazy—?" Justin choked out.

"Where is it?"

Justin glanced sidelong at his sheathed weapons at the foot of the bed.

"Well?" Zechariah growled.

"Right there," Justin said, gesturing with this chin.

Zechariah turned in an exaggerated fashion. "All the way over there, eh? Tell me, Justin. What is the purpose of a weapon?"

"To—to kill people?" Justin said.

"The purpose of a weapon is to defend yourself. Understand?"

Justin nodded quickly. It was hard to think with sharpened steel inches from his jugular vein.

"So, if the purpose of a weapon is to defend yourself, why is yours all the way over there?"

"How was I supposed to defend myself? I was asleep! You attacked me out of nowhere!"

"Do you think it will be any different when someone has true intentions of doing you harm? Olorus gave you just as much warning on the trail."

Justin sneered and started to say something, but when the tip of Zechariah's sword pushed his Adam's apple, his resolve broke cleanly, replaced by dumb fear.

"Do you think someone meaning to kill you will give you fair warning before they slice your guts open or separate your head from your neck?" Zechariah demanded. "Take a good look at your sword over there."

Justin did.

"You put it at the foot of your bed. That's too far."

"I was sleeping—"

"An enemy won't care if you're sleeping. The foot of your bed may as well be a mile away. You must be ready to defend yourself at all times." He shook Justin by the collar. "Understand?"

"Yeah."

"Understand?"

"Yes, all right? Yes!"

Zechariah glared at him. "At all times."

Zechariah stood and sheathed his sword. Justin sat up and brushed himself off in a meek attempt at retaining some dignity, but he didn't bother standing. Leah was standing on the other side of the room, trying to hide a smile.

"On your feet," said Zechariah. "You will accompany me to address the Cru elders."

"I will?" Justin said, still without standing.

Of course, the old man did not answer. He exited through the hut's only doorway, leaving Justin alone with Leah. She had changed out of her traveling gear and instead wore a maroon-colored shirt with a dark vest and trousers.

"We traded some supplies for fresh clothes," she said, gesturing to a folded bundle of fabric beside the bed. "There might not be enough time for you to bathe before meeting the elders, but you should at least change." As an afterthought, she added, "Out of respect."

Justin sniffed at his underarm. "I guess you're right."

"Don't feel bad—I wasn't exactly smelling like a daisy either."

Leah took a cross-legged seat on the floor in front of Justin. It seemed like a very un-princess-like thing to do, but Justin was finding that the more un-princess-like she acted, the more he appreciated her.

"It occurred to me this morning," she said, "that I ought to thank you."

"You already thanked me. I remember."

"Well, kind of. But you obviously have no obligation to be here. You act like you don't even know what's going on half the time."

"It's not an act."

She grinned. "Well, you didn't have to come with us. So, thanks."

He shrugged. "I didn't exactly have anything else going on at the time."

"Where are you from, anyway?"

Justin hesitated, wondering how to do this without sounding insane.

"Well, it's a small town," he said. "Bigger than Deen, though. I've lived in the same house my whole life—same bedroom since I was a baby, actually. Our street isn't anything special, but we do have a nice backyard. Dad put up a bunch of birdfeeders because Mom liked to wake up to the sounds of birds."

"Me too," said Leah.

"In the summer," said Justin, "if I leave my window open overnight, it's the first thing I hear when I wake up. It's kind of cool. I learned to identify some of them by their calls. Dad taught me. Nuthatches, chickadees, cardinals, goldfinches. I can always get blue jays, too, but those are easy."

Leah had a strange smile on her face. Justin gave her a questioning look.

"Sorry," she said. "You reminded me of my oldest brother just now." She looked away. Her smile became sad and forced. Without looking at him, she asked, "Do you have brothers or sisters?"

"No," Justin said. "But our street has a lot of families, so there were always kids to run around with, growing up. Plenty of friends at school, too. I barely hang out with anybody anymore, though, ever since Mom died."

"I'm sorry," said Leah.

"It's okay. It's just not the same without her. Nothing is. She always used to say. . . . Whenever something was wrong or I was nervous or scared, she always used to tell me, 'Everything will be all right. I promise.' I always believed her. But she's been gone almost a year, now. It keeps getting harder and harder to believe everything will be all right."

"Time is supposed to heal wounds," said Leah. "But it can be a real bitch about it."

Justin snorted a laugh. He dropped his gaze to the floor. "I don't care what anybody says about *moving on*. Holidays just suck now. Thanksgiving was terrible. Basketball season reminded me of her a lot, too, so that didn't help. At home, it's just me and Dad, and he can't work, so I took a part-time job." Justin used his thumbnail to pick at a loose seam on his boot. "Sometimes, at night, I wake up, and I can hear Dad crying in his room. Or even shouting. Sometimes, he's almost screaming. I wish he would, I don't know, take some medicine or something to help. It's like the grief is haunting him. Mom was his best friend. And now, with me disappearing, it's gonna make things so much worse. He's probably worried sick right now, wondering where I am. . . ."

Justin's words caught in his throat. He looked up, suddenly remembering where he was and who he was talking to. But instead of looking confused, Leah was waiting for him to go on.

"Anyhow," he said, clearing his throat. "Whining about it won't solve anything, will it?"

They sat quietly.

"I—" said Leah.

"I'm gonna change and—sorry—you were going to say something?" said Justin, realizing he had inadvertently cut her off.

"No, no," she said, standing up. "Go ahead. I need to go offer my services to the village, anyway."

Justin pushed himself up off the floor. "Services?" he said.

"I'm a healer," she said. Then, with the up-and-down cadence of recitation, she added dramatically, "*My duty is to the infirm.*" She chuckled a bit at herself, then crossed the hut and ducked under the rawhide flap of the doorway without looking back.

Justin unwrapped the new clothes and changed into a pair of brown trousers, a cotton shirt the color of an autumn leaf, and a thick coat made of gray-brown furs like the Cru wore. He wished a fresh pair of shoes had been part of the new wardrobe. Blisters rubbed painfully against every imperfection of his boots.

Zechariah ducked his head in.

"I know, I'm coming," Justin said, and he followed him out.

CHAPTER 34

"People speak of eyes watching from the rocks. Travelers come wandering into our village, eyes wild and brains wrought with madness. Sometimes, men disappear. Slowly, almost imperceptibly, darkness comes."

They numbered two dozen, sitting cross-legged on the ground before a long, bare table. The man who had met them in the hills—the one called Sif—was there with them. All had shaved heads and thick brambles of facial hair. Some beards were black, some streaked with silver, and some wiry and snow white.

Zechariah and Justin sat on the floor before them, imitating their cross-legged postures. Unlike the circular huts in the rest of the village, the Cru elders held court in a rectangular longhouse. All weapons had been left leaning against the doorway outside, a symbolic gesture of respect for the sanctity of this place. When Justin had tried asking Zechariah again why he needed to be here, Zechariah had told him to think of it as a learning experience.

The head elder had a name longer than a medium-length sentence but had informed his guests that they could refer to him simply as Thid. He may have once been a very tall man, but the years had withered his body, hunching his back and turning him into a shrunken form at the center of the table. Age spots dotted his craggy, bare head. His white beard was so long that it lay in his lap, folded over itself. Yet somehow, the skin of his cheeks and neck did not hang limply off the bone as it already did on many of the younger elders. His face, concentrically creased with lines like plow trenches, was still hard and strong.

"Our prophets say something is coming," Thid continued. "They call it. . . ." He faltered. "I do not know an equivalent word in the western tongue."

A string of syllables followed in what Justin concluded was a Cru word for the thing he was trying to describe. Zechariah seemed to understand him.

"I have sensed something similar," Zechariah said.

"Danger has visited this part of the world before," said Thid. "Wars, plagues, disasters. But always, A'cru'u'ol have survived. We have dwelt in the mountains for millennia, watching kingdoms rise and fall and rise and fall again, all while we endure." His glazed, red-rimmed eyes narrowed on Zechariah. "The prophets say that this time, that will not be the case." He used the strange word again. "It will destroy everything. Nothing will be safe from its touch. Not even the Cru can withstand."

Justin squirmed a little where he sat. He immediately regretted it, for the glaucomatous eyes of Thid, in response to his movement, adjusted to focus their intensity on him. Justin looked away as casually as possible, pretending an empty corner of the longhouse interested him.

"I am afraid I bring bad news regarding the mountain path," said Zechariah. "Evil forces drove us into the mountains. In the chaos, one of our group was killed, and the gate your people depend on for travel was closed. The winch was destroyed. As well as, possibly, the village of Irth."

Some members of the council, Sif included, looked at one another uncomfortably. Thid, in the center seat, remained undisturbed.

"Perhaps your craftsmen could repair the mechanism so the door can be lifted again," said Zechariah. "If not, I'm afraid the only other path I know of to reach the Gravelands is many miles east. It may change your very way of life."

"Seek not the return to old ways," said Thid. "For the coming evil will sever you from your traditions. The strong must forge, instead, a new path. . . . Only one cycle of the moons ago, that prophecy was delivered to our council."

Zechariah seemed stunned. "I was prepared for your wrath, elders, at delivering this news, but it seems you are already quite well informed."

"The other prophecy," said Sif, at the end of the elders' table. "The one with branches."

"Branches?" said Zechariah.

"Yes," said Thid. "Time is not a line. Our present is one branch on a tree of many pasts. The future has not yet grown. It holds many possible branches of its own. Days ago, we received a prophecy of possible futures. On one branch, the Cru people are destroyed. On another, the Cru go to war beneath the banner of a king, something we have never done in our long history. And on another branch, the Cru survive by returning home."

"Home," said Zechariah. It was not a question but more of an appraisal.

"Home," Thid repeated. "And evil will pass over us and destroy all else, leaving only the trapped people to live on, finally returned to our home beneath the world. In all of these possible futures, the Cru must take a new path, because the old one has been shut." Thid let this sink in for a moment. "You bring us news that the first part of the prophecy has been fulfilled. It would be foolhardy to be angry about events that fate foreordained before the beginning of time."

Quite unexpectedly, Thid's eyes turned to Justin again, and this time, their intensity was too much. He wanted to look away but somehow found that he was entranced, or trapped, beneath that gaze.

"What happens when there are branching futures?" said Zechariah. "Is there a way to influence the outcome?"

Thid turned his attention back to Zechariah. "That is the purpose of this council of elders. It is for us to decide what, if any, action should be taken—which branch we should pursue. Or prepare for."

"I understand the gravity of interpreting and acting on prophecy," Zechariah said. "Once, I was a man of wealth and importance. I left that all behind when I devoted my life to the pursuit of a prophecy. I wish you wisdom in the pursuit of your own."

"And we, yours," Thid responded.

Justin stared at Zechariah. Days on the road had taught him next to nothing about this puzzling hermit. And now, here, in the span of a few sentences, the old man had revealed his life's pursuit to a group of strangers.

"My companions and I thank you for your hospitality," said Zechariah. "We will not be long in your village. Dawn will see us on our way. We wish you good fortune in the coming winter."

Thid nodded. Zechariah's old bones creaked as he stood. Justin stood and followed him to the door.

"Young man."

Justin froze mid-step. He turned and was again forced to look into Thid's eyes.

"Me?" said Justin.

"May your travels lead you safely home," Thid said.

Justin swallowed hard. "Home is, uh, a complicated subject for me."

Thid nodded as if he were familiar with it all. "You are your central mountain, and with it, you are always home. But remember, the strong man forges new paths, carrying with him the peace of the knowledge that while he may plan his way, the spirit guides his feet."

The elder raised a hand in farewell, and Zechariah and Justin exited.

Outside, Justin shivered. The sun was going down, and the village was deathly quiet. A thin powder of snow stuck to the tops of the huts. The ground, not yet cold enough for snow to stick, was damp with meltwater.

Zechariah retrieved his sword belt from beside the longhouse door and reattached it.

"What did he mean, *central mountain*?" Justin asked in a whisper. He was fumbling with his belt, trying to reattach his basket-hilted sword.

"Within the Cru community," said Zechariah, "aurym-sensitive individuals are trained to become prophets. They are religious leaders who live apart from the rest of the Cru, on a hidden peak within the Thucymoroi. They call this peak the central mountain, and they consider it the pivot of the world, the axis upon which rotate the sun, the stars, and all of time and space. Somewhere beneath the central mountain is the ancestral home they left long ago and cannot return to, except in death when their souls rejoin god under the mountain. But the concept goes a step further, in that everyone carries their own central mountain with them. Every person is his own center—the axis upon which his worldly experiences rotate. In other words, everyone sees the world from the summit of their own mountaintop."

Justin shook his head. Zechariah seemed to answer questions in two alternating ways: He either gave you no information or more than you could have ever possibly needed. It made Justin seriously reconsider voicing his next question.

"So, what was that word he used?" Justin asked.

"Which one?"

"He said he didn't know the word for it."

"Ah, that one." Zechariah made a peculiar face. "To the best of my knowledge, it means, 'prolonged death on black wings.'" He grumbled something under his breath, then seemed to answer himself. "Indeed."

He turned and started walking away before Justin could get his sword on. Justin gathered his things and jogged after.

CHAPTER 35

Night in the mountains was a different kind of silent—not a sound could be heard except the occasional bark of a dog out in the fields where Cru shepherds guarded their flocks. Their torches hovered over the valley floor like fireflies.

Justin followed Zechariah into the hut. Leah, Olorus, and Hook sat around the fire. Fresh logs had been piled on for the night, resting atop embers that made the little shelter glow with a shadowy, red hue. It was nice and warm, but upon seeing Leah, Justin almost wanted to retreat back out into the cold.

What an idiot she must think I am after all that whining, he thought.

"What's wrong?" Zechariah asked.

At first, Justin thought the question was directed at him, but the old man was looking at Olorus and Hook. Both were frowning deeply.

"We have a problem," said Olorus. "Nolian soldiers."

"We knew they would be posted along the road," said Zechariah.

"But there's something we didn't count on," said Olorus. "Their patrols have this village surrounded."

"Hmm," said Zechariah. "Yes, I believe you're right. That is a problem."

"We were almost spotted just trying to scout ahead," said Olorus.

"Do you think they saw us come into the valley?" Justin said.

"It is almost beyond doubt that they did," said Olorus. "Now, they're waiting for us to attempt to leave."

"Unless they attack the village by night," Zechariah said.

"Nolian soldiers would not attack innocent people," Olorus said.

"Oh, so the Cru are *people* now," said Zechariah.

Olorus scowled. "It's hard to tell their numbers, but they've got the high ground, and they're better equipped. And look at us. Two soldiers, a boy, and an old man. We will be lucky to make it back out of this valley at all. But they won't be expecting an attack! If we split up and rush them, we can create enough of a distraction for the princess to slip back down the path, toward the Gravelands."

"I told you, Olorus," said Leah. "We cannot go back to the Gravelands."

"It is the only option," Olorus said. "With enough supplies and a well-rested steed keeping a swift pace, you can outrun them and reach the eastern borders. All we need to decide is who will escort you, and who will provide the distraction. I have collected straws for drawing—"

"We *cannot*, Olorus," Leah snapped, iron in her voice.

Olorus and Hook looked at her.

"Something chased us into the mountains," she said. "Not a squad of soldiers but something powerful enough to kill Ahlund Sims. You knew Ahlund. Who or what could defeat such a man?" She let the words sink in. "To turn around now would be the death of us."

"Who or *what*?" Olorus said. "If you don't mind me asking, what was this—?"

"We don't know," said Zechariah.

Olorus made a face. Hook frowned.

"Ahlund and I sensed them coming," said Zechariah. "I felt the blackness of their daemyn energies. I think they were demons."

"You mean coblyns?" said Olorus. "Have you any idea how much coblyn blood has greased my blade—?"

"Not coblyns," Zechariah said. "There are other kinds of demons. Higher forms capable of terrible power. But such things have not walked the Oikoumene since before my birth."

Hook's hands worked quickly, making shapes in the air.

"Did you actually see them?" Olorus translated.

"They were—" Zechariah started to say, but Olorus cut him off.

"Not you," he said. "Justin, you tell me. What did you see?"

"Well," Justin said. "It was, uh, kind of, hard to see. We were in the middle of a storm. They were big and dark and riding on these big animals. Like, really big shadows."

"Really big shadows." Olorus turned on Zechariah. "You risk the fate of my nation on fear of shadows?"

"I sensed them," Zechariah said.

"You sensed them! Fortune-telling and nonsense! How dare you implement magic and superstition to decide the fates of others?"

"But don't you see—?"

"You claim to serve the princess, but I see through your deception!" Olorus said, his voice rising with every word. "It is clear to me that you have other ambitions, though you seem hell-bent on keeping them secret. I wonder why! I've a coil of rope for conspirators like you, old man. I will see you hanged before I am manipulated for your hidden agendas!"

"*Enough*, Olorus," Leah said. "This is getting us no closer to a solution."

Olorus spat on the floor near Zechariah's feet. Without a word, Zechariah turned and exited the hut, leaving the rest of them looking at the doorway.

Justin looked back and forth from the door to the others, unsure of what to do. Finally, he ducked under the rawhide flap and hustled out into the night.

"Zechariah!" Justin called. "Wait!"

The snowfall was heavier now, and Justin had to squint to see him marching away from the hut. It was coming down so hard now that there was no time for it to melt, and the mountain valley was turning white.

He caught up to Zechariah a few huts down. The old man turned briskly at Justin's approach. "We cannot risk another encounter with those things!" he said. Snow landed in his bushy eyebrows and stuck in his long, white beard like flies in a web.

"I know, but—" said Justin.

"The High Demon, the 'cythraul,' as the Ancients called it, is a creature no human can contest with. Cythraul wield daemyn power of enormous magnitude. With my own eyes, I have seen a single cythraul kill an entire. . . ."

Zechariah trailed off and turned away. Slowly, it dawned on Justin what the old man had just said.

"An entire what?" demanded Justin.

"House," said Zechariah. "In Irth."

"No," said Justin, shifting around to stand in front of Zechariah, forcing him to look him in the eye. "That's not what you were going to say. You were going to say something else, weren't you?"

Zechariah leered at Justin.

"You *have* seen them before!" said Justin. "What happened to them not walking the Oikoumene since 'before your birth'? You were lying?"

"Never mind that," said Zechariah.

"No, not 'never mind that,'" said Justin. "You said you didn't know what they were. You acted like you had never even seen one before. Why would you lie like that this whole time?"

"It doesn't matter," said Zechariah. "What matters is that they could kill you with a thought. If Leah and her soldiers decide to go south, we will not go with them."

"But isn't there some way to circle wide around them or—wait, *what*? Not go with them? You're not actually thinking of letting them go, are you?"

"You would rather follow them and be killed like a fool?" said Zechariah.

"No, but we can't split up," said Justin. "What if they get into trouble because we let them go? What if Leah gets hurt or killed?"

"Then she should have heeded wiser counsel."

Justin ran a hand through his hair. He could hardly believe what he was hearing. "Aren't we supposed to be protecting her? Isn't that the point of all this? To save her and her country?"

"Nolia," scoffed Zechariah. "If they cannot protect their leaders, then perhaps they do not deserve them. Maybe the insurrectionists have got it right. Anyway, I do not have time to worry about political games."

"Are you kidding me?" Justin said. "Aren't you the same person who told me that if we were able to help someone in need, we 'owed it' to them?"

"It was for your own protection. You needed a sense of purpose to motivate you."

Justin's jaw clenched. He jabbed a finger at Zechariah. "I am sick of being lied to! And I won't let Olorus and Hook take Leah back down the mountain. Those monsters are after her, and if she's caught, who knows what will happen to her?"

"Nothing will happen to her."

"You're lying again!" Justin was almost shouting now.

Zechariah raised his voice in response. "I'm not lying, boy."

"Yes, you are! Why the hell did I follow you out here in the first place? How could I have fallen for all your bull—?"

"That's enough."

"How could you allow her to take that sort of risk?"

"I said, that's enough!"

"How do you know they won't kill her?"

"Because they're not looking for her!"

For a moment, Zechariah and Justin stood silently as snow fell around them. The night was so quiet that Justin could hear individual flakes landing. Finally, Zechariah sucked in a long breath. He let it escape slowly and calmly through his nostrils as he said, more quietly than a whisper, "They are looking for you, Justin."

CHAPTER 36

Justin stared at the old man. He tried to say something. His mouth moved, but no sound came out.

"You, Justin," Zechariah said, deathly quiet. "You want to know what all this is about? Well, no more lies. It's about you."

"No, it's not," said Justin.

"Yes, it is," said Zechariah. He sighed, as if resigning himself to some dirty task ahead. "And Ahlund knew it, too, though he wasn't as keen to believe it, at first. He found you out on the Gravelands, miles from any town or landmark. I don't know what he was doing out there in the first place. I think aurym may have called him to find you."

"What are you talking about?" Justin said.

"There was no sign of where you had come from," Zechariah continued. "No tracks. In Ahlund's own words, it was, 'as if you had dropped out of the sky.' He knew people would be looking for you, so he brought you to me."

"Who would be looking for me?" said Justin.

"After you ran off in the middle of the night," Zechariah said, "I knew I couldn't let you out of my sight, lest it happen again. However, I didn't want you to get the impression that you were being held against your will. Leah's kidnapping seemed as good a distraction as any. An excuse to keep you close. Ahlund didn't like the arrangement, but he tolerated it. It was supposed to be temporary—I had no idea we would end up coming this far."

"Couldn't let me out of your sight?" said Justin, taking a step away. "Why would anyone be looking for me? I don't even know anybody in this world."

Zechariah hesitated. "You're not the first to come here. There have been others. The Ancients called them *ethouli*. There is a term for it in the common tongue. Does the word 'angel' mean anything to you?"

"Yeah."

"An ethoul was a 'fallen angel.' They, like you, are said to have appeared suddenly as if dropped from the sky like angels from heaven. Some people believed they were divine beings sent by a higher power to help mankind. Others believed they were transgressors banished from paradise—fallen from grace, so to speak. I had a modest library in my cellar in Deen. That pack of books I brought along contains all the historical volumes I own that are about ethouli. Or, at least, as many as I could gather on such short notice. Having no need for sleep has its advantages, like plenty of quiet reading time. Thus far, I have been able to—"

"Whoa, whoa, whoa," said Justin. "You think I am one of these fallen angel things?"

Justin's voice had gone up several octaves, and Zechariah waved a hand at him to lower the volume. "Most of what has been written is speculation and mythology," said Zechariah, "but one aspect is consistent. The arrival of an ethoul always brings change. Sometimes, that means chaos, wars—even the rise of empires. Fallen angels were revered and even worshipped as living gods. The accounts say that many ethouli were figureheads used by governments to legitimize a divine right to power. Others became leaders themselves, amassing armies and building their own nations. People tend to fear and hate what they don't understand, and ethouli were no exception. People feared them so much that they eventually worshipped them out of devout terror."

"So you think that's why those cythraul were on the Gravelands? Because they were after me?"

"*Are* after you." Zechariah sighed again. "In a way, it's fortunate that things happened as they did. If not for Leah being captured, we wouldn't have left Deen, and without that head start, we never would have escaped the cythraul."

Justin spread his arms wide, palms open. "Look at me. Is this what a living god looks like? A lanky kid in boots that don't fit?"

"Believe what you want," said Zechariah, "but the demons are hunting you. It was easier to allow Leah—and you, until now—to assume she was their target. Now, you know the truth."

"Zechariah, I didn't fall from anywhere, and I sure as hell wasn't sent. If you had bothered to tell me about any of this, I could have set you straight. I'm just lost. That's all."

"Be that as it may," Zechariah said, "I felt you arrive in this world."

Justin's lips parted with an unspoken question.

"Aurym, Justin," said Zechariah. "It was like a fire in my mind. It was as loud as thunder and as distinct as an eagle's cry. As I was preparing to ride out and search for the source, Ahlund brought you to my home. And therein lies the problem. The aurym power that erupted when you arrived was so great that it could have been felt by aurym-sensitive souls for hundreds, maybe thousands of miles. What I'm trying to tell you is, I'm sure I was not the only one preparing to ride out and investigate. The cythraul must have felt it, too, and they headed for the point of your arrival. When they didn't find you there, I suspect they rode to the nearest town. Deen. By then, of course, we were gone, but they learned which direction we went . . . somehow."

Justin's hands were going numb; the blood in his extremities seemed to have been drawn inward to fuel his racing heart. He remembered the house in Irth, the way the strange energy had blown it apart, and he pictured the same thing happening a hundred times over in Deen.

"If they went to Deen," said Justin, "the people there might need our help."

"With the gate closed, it is at least a two-week journey back to Deen," said Zechariah, "but we would never make it that far."

For almost a full minute, words escaped Justin, but finally, he spoke.

CHAPTER 37

"Me?" he breathed.

Zechariah looked at him. "You believe me?"

"No," said Justin. "But I think *you* believe this crazy story. And if you do, others might, too. If those monsters attacked us just because they thought I was someone I'm not, then. . . . Then Ahlund is dead because of me. And the town at the gate was attacked because of me. And it's my fault Leah's stranded here, instead of on her way home. And if those things hurt anybody in Deen, it's my—"

"Now, hold on," said Zechariah. "You can't claim all the fault. Remember—"

"Why?" said Justin. "Why is this happening? Why am I here?"

"It's like the Cru proverb goes," said Zechariah. "A man can only view the world from the top of his own central mountain. I don't know why you are here, but I can observe the world around me. Fate has charged me with keeping you safe. I am not yet sure what fate has in store for you."

"What if I reject my 'fate'?" Justin said.

"If you can resolve the argument of free will versus fate," said Zechariah, "then you are a greater philosopher than I would have given you credit for. Rejecting your fate—or your responsibilities or even your very life—is your choice. I imagine nothing would stop you if you were determined to do so. But ask yourself this, Justin: Would you have been chosen for such a fate if you were going to reject it?"

Justin closed his eyes, sighing. "I don't know."

"Neither do I," said Zechariah. "But sometimes, wisdom doesn't mean having the answers; it means knowing the questions."

"Get it through your head," Justin said. "I'm not who you think I am."

"You may be right," said Zechariah. "I almost hope you are. But if I am right, people's lives hang in the balance. Do not repeat this information to anyone, Justin. We can trust no one. Especially a princess stripped of her throne who would do anything to get it back. Do you understand? People will use you if they can."

"Leah? She wouldn't do anything—"

"If it meant having a fallen angel to fly her country's banner—to regain the allegiance of her people and restore her family's honor without bloodshed—she might."

Justin frowned. "What about you?"

Zechariah's face hardened. He pinned Justin down with a stony gaze.

"Choose your next words wisely, boy," Zechariah said. "Elaborate."

"You just told me not to trust anybody," said Justin.

"If you are accusing me—"

"Can you blame me? You brought me all this way, you've lied to me at every turn, and you still won't even tell me who you really are. So, if you aren't manipulating me, what *are* you doing? What are you getting out of all this?"

Zechariah chewed the inside of his cheek, and his glare softened. "Nothing." He pulled his cloak a little tighter against the wind. "I'm only doing what I feel is right."

"What you said about Leah," Justin said. "She wouldn't do that."

"Do not be so optimistic. Remember what I told you. The only way to know truth is to entertain doubt. Doubt encourages attention. Attention breeds cunning. Cunning leads to insight, and insight leads to wisdom."

"Leads to paranoia," said Justin.

"Doubt someone, and you will be thrilled when they prove you wrong. Trust someone, and, well, that is a mistake you may not live to tell about."

"Whatever. I won't tell anybody, but I'm still not letting Leah go back down the mountain."

"Not going—?" Zechariah began but finished with only an exasperated sigh.

"Those things killed Ahlund. I don't want the same thing to happen to Leah or Olorus or Hook. And if you're willing to 'let them go,' then you must have some other destination in mind."

The lines of Zechariah's frown deepened, but he said nothing.

Justin shook his head in disgust. "Fine. Keep your secrets."

Justin turned away and started back toward the hut.

"It would be better to let them go," Zechariah called.

Justin turned back and said, "Better for us, maybe, but not for them."

Justin's hands were clenched into fists as he walked. New snow crunched underfoot. Every updraft of wind was a visible entity, with swirling flakes to mark its path. He felt misled, confused, and betrayed. But mostly, he felt bitter. He ground his teeth. He wanted to hit something.

With a frustrated growl, Justin dropped to his knees and pounded his fist against the ground. Then he pulled back and punched it again. It felt good, so he did it again. Snow plastered his fingers. He punched harder. And harder. He stopped, realizing the snow had turned red. Blood was dripping from his hand. He had split the skin of his knuckles against a stone, but he couldn't feel the pain.

For a long time, he sat there, looking up at the sky, ignoring the drops of blood falling from his clenched fist.

CHAPTER 38

He ducked beneath the rawhide door of their hut. Leah, Olorus, and Hook were crouched around the fire in the same positions as before. Everything looked the same. But everything had changed.

"Were you able to talk some sense into the billy goat?" said Olorus.

It was not in Justin's nature to ignore people when spoken to, but he was in no mood to lie. Without a word, he walked past Olorus and sat down on one of the cots, trying to hide the blood on his hand.

Zechariah entered the hut and said, "There are caves."

It caught them all off guard. He had a way of doing that.

"It is a system of tunnels beneath the mountains," he said. "Some are natural. Others were carved by the Ancients. Causeways connecting the underground citadels."

He crossed to the fire and crouched there, bidding Justin to join him. Still spiteful from their conversation, Justin had half a mind to stay right where he was, but he complied.

"The Cru sometimes use them to travel north of the mountains," Zechariah whispered. The fire melted the snow in his beard as he spoke. "It's a maze, and it's dark as night no matter the time of day. Some of the ways have been long caved-in, miles of tunnels leading to dead-ends or chasms."

"Sounds promising," Olorus said. He scratched at his neck where his red facial hair was coming in thick.

"It's better than promising," said Zechariah. "It's perfect. You said it yourself: We're surrounded. Why shed blood when we can pass peacefully beneath them?"

"How close is this entry point?" Leah asked.

"Not far," said Zechariah. "If we act now, while this snowfall keeps up, I wager we can make it there unseen."

"Even if we do, they will come looking for us," said Olorus. "And our trail will be all too easy to follow in the snow."

"I don't doubt they'll pick up our trail, but it won't be easy to follow us once we're underground. Plus, we have a very big advantage."

"What advantage?" said Olorus.

Zechariah's eyes gleamed. "I've been through these caves before."

Leah nodded, but Justin was gaping. "You can't be serious," he said.

All four of them looked at Justin in surprise, Zechariah most of all.

"After what you told us about those caves?" said Justin. "You said monsters live down there. Black aurym creatures and, whatever you called them—coblyns. You want us to go *down there*?"

"There's danger behind, ahead, and beneath," said Zechariah without missing a beat. "The longer we stay here, the more likely that one of them will come to meet us. Better to take an active role and face uncertainty on our own terms. Plus, in this scenario, Leah won't have to fight against her own countrymen. She won't have to go back down the mountain, either."

Justin chewed his lip. True, he did want to prevent Leah from going back down the mountain, but this wasn't exactly what he'd had in mind.

Hook adjusted the strip of cloth over his forehead that kept his long, dark hair in place. His brows were downturned in a frown as he moved his hands, signing a long thought.

"Very foolish," Olorus translated. "The plan relies too much on Zechariah. Only he knows the road. What if he is killed or cannot remember the way? We will be lost in a maze." When Hook was done, Olorus turned to Zechariah and added, "And where does this path lead, anyway?"

"To the base of the northern rim of the mountains," said Zechariah. "Near the city of Lonn. Well removed from any roads the Nolians are likely to be watching. Princess, the decision is yours. I care only for your well-being."

The sincerity with which Zechariah voiced the last statement made Justin cringe and shift his weight uncomfortably. Based on their talk outside, Justin knew for a fact that it was a blatant lie. The old man's skill at manipulating people was frightening.

"Olorus?" Leah said.

Olorus sighed. "I am with Hook. The idea is not without merit, but it puts us at the mercy of one man's memory. And a very old man, at that."

"Humph!" said Zechariah. "I may be old, but I can still—"

"Zechariah," Leah cut in, "I will concede to your plan under one condition. You say the Cru use these tunnels. Will you consult with them to ensure that you remember the path?"

"But we do not have time to—" Zechariah protested.

"Those are my terms," Leah said.

Zechariah made an annoyed sound in his throat. "All right," he said. "Justin, you can help Hook scout ahead. Olorus, you will come with me to consult with the Cru, and let's try to be quick about it."

"I think not," said Olorus. "Hook and I will scout ahead."

Zechariah clenched his teeth. "Fine," he said icily.

Leah stood up to begin packing supplies. Zechariah started to stand, but as soon as Leah turned her back, Olorus grabbed a handful of Zechariah's robes near the neck, holding him down.

"You're going to get her killed," Olorus whispered.

Zechariah looked flatly at Olorus for a moment, then raised his bearded chin as if daring the soldier to take a swing. Olorus seemed to think about it for a moment but ultimately removed his hand and turned away. Zechariah exited without waiting for Justin, and Justin, trying to ignore Hook's dagger-like stare, followed after him.

Outside, the air was so thick with falling snow that Justin could barely see a single hut of the Cru village. He put his head down and hurried after the robed form of Zechariah.

"Do you think we'll find someone to tell us the way?" Justin said. "At this time of night? It must be getting pretty late—"

"We're going to get the steeds," said Zechariah.

"What about talking to the Cru?"

"We're not doing that."

Justin stopped in his tracks. "What?"

Zechariah halted and leaned in close. "The Cru are an upright and honorable people, but they pay allegiance to no king or country. There would be no reason for them, if someone came asking, not to reveal our route. They cannot be allowed to know our intentions."

"Not even if we asked them not to say anything?"

"That would not be the proper conduct of a guest, Justin."

"Oh, right—I keep forgetting."

"I passed through the caves before, as a younger man. I will remember the way. We'll let Leah think I did as she asked, if it makes her feel more comfortable."

"So I guess you never had any intentions of talking to the Cru at all," said Justin. He paused. "Wait . . . didn't you *tell* Olorus to come with you just now?"

"Of course," said Zechariah. "What better way to ensure that he didn't?"

Justin frowned. "Zechariah, this is wrong. She's putting her faith in you—I am not going to lie to her like this!"

Zechariah let out an irritated sigh. "The alternative is that she follows Olorus's plan and goes back down the mountain. Now I seem to remember you saying you weren't going to let that happen. Justin, you are either going to let her go or you are going to lie to her. What will it be?"

"But—but you said it was a maze!"

"I remember the beginning of the maze, and I remember the end. The middle will be the only hard part."

"News flash. The middle of a maze is always the hard part."

"I am confident we will succeed," said Zechariah. "If trouble befalls us, we simply retrace our steps back here, and we're in no worse shape than when we started. Now, keep your head down, unless you want a spear through your guts. If the Nolians in these hills are anything like Olorus, I would not bet my life on their good judgment or their patience."

Justin rubbed his eyes. "I felt a whole lot better when I thought you knew what you were doing."

CHAPTER 39

Justin glanced over his shoulder at Leah, Olorus, and Hook as they walked.

Seabiscuit and the other two steeds, bearing loads of supplies, were being led by a length of rope. Zechariah was in front, leading them along the edge of the Cru village. Hook carried a bow, strung and ready, that he had earlier bartered off the Cru, and Olorus walked with his spear in hand.

Justin shivered against the cold. It might have occurred to him to regret being pulled away from a warm bed—something he'd been so looking forward to—but all he could seem to think about were the increasing number of things that could go wrong at any moment.

He remembered the Gravelands—how one minute they had been riding toward the enemy, and the next, a dozen men were dead. He remembered their scowling faces, their blood, and the smell of burned flesh. If another such encounter occurred tonight, who would he be burying this time? Or who would be burying him?

The ground was sloped beneath their feet. The damp snow clung to the bottoms of their boots with every step upward, leaving a clear, narrow trail out of the valley. Olorus was right: Come first light, their path wouldn't be hard to follow.

Soon, the terrain leveled out, and the ground became rock and dirt. He saw pine trees through the driving snow and realized they were headed into the forest again. They had gone only a short distance through the sparse trees when Zechariah stopped.

"This is the place," he said quietly, facing a wall of thick undergrowth.

"Do you realize the sort of trail we're going to leave by pushing through all that brush?" said Olorus.

"Soon, we will be on the bare rock of a cave floor," whispered Zechariah. "Tracking us then will be no easy trick. Hopefully, we will lose them."

"Hopefully?" Olorus said.

"Hopefully," Zechariah repeated.

Zechariah pushed through the foliage. Branches broke and twigs snapped. The winds had died down, and Justin wondered how far away all this noise could be heard. He could only draw a shaky breath and follow.

Justin had to push limbs aside as he went. A few times, he lost sight of Zechariah in the brush, but he knew he was going the right way by the branches whipping back and slashing his face. He did his best not to let anything swing back and hit Leah, but it could not be helped. He lost his grip on a particularly large branch, and it swung back hard. He looked over his shoulder to make sure it hadn't hit Leah and realized she wasn't there. He stopped, unsure of what to do.

After a moment's hesitation, Justin retraced his steps backward until he found Leah standing still in the brush, alone. She was looking back the way they had come.

"What's wrong?" he said.

His voice made her jump. When she recovered, she whispered, "Hook can't get the steeds to come through! Olorus is trying to help."

Justin turned back around and squinted. It all looked the same in the dark. He looked ahead, then a little to his left, then to his right. His heart fluttered with panic as he realized he had lost track of the place where Zechariah had slipped through the brush.

From behind him, he heard breaking limbs. The steeds were coming, but they were making too much noise. Surely, anyone who hadn't heard the humans would hear this. He saw Olorus and Hook approaching Leah through the brambles. Behind them were the hulking forms of the steeds. The animals seemed to part the whole forest as they pushed through.

"This is no path!" Olorus said, looking around. "Look at the state of this brush. No one has been through here in decades!"

Leah looked at Justin. "Are you sure this is the way the Cru told you to go?"

Olorus looked around. "Where is the old man?"

Justin looked around desperately. "I. . . ."

"*Fool*!" Olorus said. "Don't tell me you—"

Hook made a hissing noise to get their attention. The dark-haired man had his head cocked and his hand raised in the air, calling for silence. No one made a sound.

Suddenly, Hook pressed his palm flat in the air and patted it twice, as if bouncing an invisible ball. This was a sign that needed no translation: *"Get down."*

Leah lowered herself to the forest floor. Olorus crouched with his spear held low. Hook dropped to one knee in front of the steeds, bow in hand.

Justin got down on his hands and knees, trying to ignore the thorns digging into his exposed palms. Almost a minute later, he finally heard what Hook had been hearing from the start. Footsteps. Coming toward them.

Slowly, silently, Hook drew an arrow from the quiver on his back and nocked it to the bowstring.

PART IV

IN THAT QUIET EARTH

CHAPTER 40

Justin could feel his every heartbeat thudding against the forest floor. Someone was coming. He didn't know how many of them there were, but as they closed in, he could hear them talking in hushed tones.

Justin hadn't noticed until now, but the snow had stopped falling. He looked at the steeds. They stood still and quiet, but one sound, one nervous clomp of a hoof, one swish of a tail—

A noise broke the silence: a creaking strain. Turning, Justin saw that it was the sound of Hook drawing back his bowstring. The bow's limbs curved under the pressure, and the arrow's feathered fletching came to rest at the corner of Hook's lips.

Between tree limbs of snow-powdered needles, Justin saw movement. The quick appearance of a hand. A shoulder, visible through an opening for a split second. A helmeted head, followed by another. And another. Less than twenty-five yards away and getting closer. Justin thought he heard the words, "them," "here," and "find."

They heard us pushing through the trees, thought Justin. *They'll see the trail and follow it to us.*

Hook's body swiveled slowly at the hip, keeping aim on the moving figures. His arm shook with the effort of holding back the bow's draw weight for so long.

Then the voices went silent. For a few moments more, Justin could hear their footsteps. Then nothing. They had passed them by.

Hook lowered the bow, easing the string slack.

"Justin," someone said.

Justin turned and saw Zechariah standing in the brush.

"Come on," he whispered. "Leah first."

Olorus got to his feet and led Leah ahead. Justin started after, but a hissing noise stopped him. He turned and saw Hook. The arrow was still nocked on his bowstring. He gestured toward the steeds, and Justin understood.

Justin crept to the three steeds. While Hook watched the forest with his bow at the ready, Justin grabbed the lengths of rope that bound the steeds and tugged gently. The animals began moving, causing a nerve-rattling snapping twigs underfoot. Justin led them in the direction the others had gone. After a moment, Hook followed.

They passed through several dozen yards of brambles and found Zechariah, Olorus, and Leah standing beneath a giant oak tree where a rocky outcropping jutted from the earth at a strange angle. Narrow trees grew upon the top of the rock, twisting around each other like worms. Justin thought Zechariah must be waiting for them, but instead of moving on, the old man just stood there.

"Now where do we go?" Justin asked.

Zechariah only looked at the ground.

"Princess," said Olorus, "I do not trust this old man or his tenderfooted apprentice! This has become far too—!"

Zechariah took a step forward—and down, disappearing into the ground.

Justin moved closer and found Zechariah standing in a deep, hollow opening beneath the rock: a tunnel descending into the earth like a spiral staircase.

"Told you," said Zechariah.

Before anyone could protest, the old man reached up and took the rope from Justin's hands. Then he turned and led the steeds into the cave, down into the earth. Olorus looked on worriedly. When the steeds vanished into the darkness below, Olorus looked around one last time, sighed, and escorted Leah down after them.

Justin turned to Hook. The silent soldier pointed to a large, fallen limb and pantomimed hoisting it up. Justin understood. Together, they bent low, lifted it, and leaned it against the rock formation, partially hiding the cave's entrance. Then Justin swallowed hard, ducked under the branch, and stepped down into the cave.

To his surprise, he was standing on a set of manmade, stone stairs. He saw no one, but he kept moving forward, one stone step at a time, keeping his hands on the walls to feel his way blindly down the spiraling staircase. Within seconds, the bitter cold of the world above was replaced by damp, cool air that smelled like potting soil. It was so dark that he could not tell whether his eyes were open or shut.

He bumped into something in the dark and almost cried out in fright. The feel of coarse fur beneath his fingers invoked images of the cave lions he had heard about, but then he realized it was Leah's Cru coat. He heard Hook coming down the stairs behind him, then felt him bump into his back, too.

"Are we all here?" Zechariah whispered.

Hook tapped Justin's shoulder in response.

"All here," Justin answered. The dryness of his mouth surprised him.

Softly, the world around them became visible with an icy, blue light emanating from Zechariah's palm. The little stone he had called a gauge was glowing in his hand.

They were in a dirt-strewn den, and until now, Justin hadn't realized how close he had been to cracking his head off the rock ceiling. The cave looked more like an animal's hole than a passageway.

"This way," Zechariah whispered.

He led the steeds deeper, and the humans followed.

At the back of the den, the floor became bare rock and proceeded downward at a sloping angle. For a moment, Justin thought the ceiling was getting higher. Then he realized the ceiling was staying where it was; *he* was moving down. Deeper into the earth.

The shadows of stalactites moved like sundial hands as Zechariah's light passed beneath them, and soon, the ceiling was higher than the stone's glow could reach.

They traveled in silence but for the clip-clop of the steeds' hooves and the steady drip of unseen water. The air was thick and stagnant and seemed to push aside like a curtain as they passed. Despite the low temperature, moisture beaded Justin's face.

"Watch your footing here," Zechariah warned. "There's a steep drop. Sergeant, do you think we're far enough from the entrance to light torches?"

Hook signed.

"Far enough," translated Olorus.

Zechariah rifled through a pack on Seabiscuit's back.

"Those people following us," said Leah. "Were they Nolian or Cru?"

"I could not tell," Olorus said.

"I saw helmets," Justin offered.

"Not Cru, then," said Zechariah. "They must have heard us but didn't see our trail in the dark. Lucky."

Hook signed, and Olorus translated, "Luck won't last. If they don't find our trail tonight, they will by morning. We need to be far away by then."

"We will be," said Zechariah.

CHAPTER 41

The drop before them was deeper and steeper than Justin would have imagined. Even after Olorus and Hook lit torches—made of wood and resin-soaked strips of cloth—the world below was still a black void shrouding unknowable depths. How long a fall might last, Justin could not guess.

It was a group effort to lead the steeds down the steep drop. Navigation was up to the humans, as the animals had poorer eyesight and twice as many feet to attend to. It did not help that they didn't like being down here to begin with. Justin didn't blame them. A cave was about as far from home as a steed could get, and Justin knew a thing or two about being far from home.

Justin was guiding Seabiscuit—one hand on his reins and another stroking his neck—when he took a wrong step. His foot flew out from under him. He lost his grip on Seabiscuit, and he tumbled forward over the precipice.

Something latched onto his arm and held him suspended over the black abyss. Several seconds later, the rocks that had torn loose under his foot clacked against the bottom.

He looked up. Zechariah was clutching his forearm with one hand while holding his shining, blue stone with the other.

Justin planted his feet and pulled himself back up.

"Thanks," he said, and the echo of his voice seemed to last for ages.

Zechariah nodded, took the steed's reins, and continued down.

Watching him go, Justin thought back to Zechariah's claims regarding his age. Surely, it was just another lie. But Zechariah had also said he'd traveled through these caves as a younger man. He hadn't specified *how* young—or how long ago that was.

Supposing he really is as old as he said, thought Justin. *What if he didn't pass through twenty or fifty years ago? What if it was more like nine hundred?*

The ground leveled, the ceiling descended, and they plunged into a winding tunnel. They marched in silence. An hour passed, and when Justin could stand it no more, he asked, "Anybody have a watch?"

"Watch what?" said Leah.

"A watch," said Justin. "You know, like a wristwatch."

"Wrist?" Olorus said.

Hook looked at his hand.

"A *clock,*" Justin said. "I was asking the time."

"The time!" Olorus barked. "The boy wants to know what time it is!"

"If Master Holmes can see the sun," Zechariah replied, "I will be more than happy to tell him." Zechariah stopped and took an exaggerated look at the stone ceiling above.

"I was just thinking," Justin said, not bothering to mask his annoyance, "that we're probably far enough away by now. Maybe we could stop and rest?"

"There is a small cavern ahead suitable for making camp," said Zechariah. "Another hour, maybe. But if Master Holmes is so tired that he cannot go on—"

"I'm fine," Justin said.

"Good," said Zechariah, "because I've been looking forward to teaching you a thing or two with that sword."

Justin cursed under his breath. Olorus elbowed Hook and chuckled.

As promised, they reached the cavern within the hour. The walls were spacious to either side and dotted with holes that made the rock look porous. Hook started a fire by striking flint over resin-soaked wood, and Zechariah extinguished his stone when the flames took over. They ate some salted meat given to them by the Cru and shared bread and water with the steeds. Once Seabiscuit knew it was fair game, he would reach out with his trunk and snatch the bread from Justin's hand.

Justin was the first done with his meal and took to exploring the corners of the cavern, touching low-hanging stalactites and peering into the holes in the walls, which were not just holes but deep tunnels about a foot wide. He had never been in a cave before, but he had learned about them. His teacher and next-door neighbor Jeff Emerson had sparked in him an interest in geology. His class was supposed to visit Penn's Cave in the spring. Justin doubted he would be present for that field trip. In fact, he was beginning to wonder if he would see Jeff Emerson or anyone from his school ever again.

Or Dad, he thought.

He leaned against the cave wall and let his body slide down until he sat on the floor.

None of this is right, he thought. *If I've counted correctly, tomorrow will be my sixth day here. Almost a week. . . .*

He picked at his fingernails. In the immediacy of traveling and running and nearly dying, he'd hardly had time to think. Zechariah's hand-drawn map had been a shock, but the old man also had proven to be a talented actor. Who knew how much of what he said was true? Justin was trying to stay alert but didn't feel any closer to learning where he really was or how he had gotten here.

Still looking for the movie monster's zipper, he thought. *But here, the monsters are real.*

"You, Justin," Zechariah had said. *"You want to know what all this is about? Well, no more lies. It's about you."*

No, it's not, thought Justin.

"Ready to try out that sword of yours?" called Zechariah from across the cavern.

Justin looked at him, wondering if "no" was an option.

"Ready as I'll ever be," he said.

He lowered his hand to the floor to push himself up and was surprised to touch a piece of rough fabric. It seemed to be a knapsack of some kind, but the fire provided little light, and it was difficult to see.

"Zechariah!" he said, standing. "Bring your light over here. I think I found something."

As the old man approached, his gauge cast its blue glow into the corner, illuminating a knapsack—and a skeletal hand clutching it.

Justin jumped backward, lost his footing, and hit the ground. Olorus and Hook stood and drew their weapons.

"I don't think he will be giving us any trouble," said the old man, standing over the dull, brown bones.

Justin's eyes locked on a lop-sided skull. It was a whole human skeleton. Tattered clothes hung from the body. Hardened cartilage and withered connecting tissues still held most of the bones together, but half of the fingers holding the pack were lying on the floor. Beside it lay a large, sheathed sword.

"This fellow has been here for some time," Zechariah said.

"Probably the last soul foolish enough to take this path," mumbled Olorus.

"I don't see any injuries," said Zechariah, "but something must have gone wrong. That's what you get for traveling alone."

"What makes you think he was alone?" Justin asked.

"Because no one took his sword or satchel," said Zechariah.

The old man bent down. He picked up the sword and wrenched the pack from the skeleton's hand, shifting the corpse a little in the process. Some of the bones broke and fell to the floor, spilling crumbs of dried marrow.

Zechariah held the pack and the sheathed sword out to Justin.

"They're rightfully yours," he said.

"He can keep them," said Justin with a cringe.

"There might be money or something valuable," Zechariah insisted.

Justin accepted them reluctantly. The sword was huge. It was nearly half again the length of the sword he already had and so heavy he could barely lift it with one hand. The bag jingled with what turned out to be some money: a couple of fat, silver coins that Zechariah called "amples," and some tiny, bar-shaped pieces of bronze he called "kreels." Not a lot of money, Zechariah informed him, but enough maybe for a set of clothes. The only other item was a metal flask of liquid that smelled like some kind of liquor. He slipped the items into his jacket pocket with his wallet and his keys.

"I already have a sword," said Justin, holding out the sheathed weapon. "Does anyone want this one?"

Olorus started to speak up, but Zechariah quickly cut him off.

"Hold on to it," he told Justin. "You never know when it might come in handy. It's a claymore. A two-hander. You're not ready for that yet. Get your other sword and step lively, now. I haven't forgotten about your training. Let's see if we can teach you a thing or two about how not to become a skeleton yourself."

CHAPTER 42

"Defend yourself."

Zechariah drew his sword.

Justin's eyes went wide, and he took a frightened step backward. He had removed his outer layers and wore only his trousers and Earth T-shirt.

"With real swords?" Justin said.

Without a word, Zechariah lunged forward and swung his sword. The blade whizzed by so close to Justin's nose that he felt the musty, cave air move. He stumbled back, tripped over the uneven floor, and hit the stony ground. Zechariah stepped over him.

"You're dead again, Justin."

"You nearly cut my face off!" Justin said, standing. "Why are we doing it here? Why don't we find some even ground?"

"When the need arises to defend yourself, you don't get to choose the circumstances," Zechariah said. "Uneven ground is a condition you'll have to deal with, and if you've trained on nothing but a flat surface, you are as good as dead. Now, draw your sword!"

Justin grabbed the basket-hilted sword and yanked it from the sheath, revealing the scorch marks left by Ahlund's aurym-fire.

Zechariah advanced and hacked like a madman. There was a loud clang of steel, and the weapon was thrown from Justin's grasp. A knee hit him in the stomach, and as he bent over from the blow, an elbow came down on the back of his neck. He hit the ground with a smack.

On his knees, Justin rubbed the back of his neck. "I wasn't ready!"

"Then you weren't defending yourself," said Zechariah.

Justin started to stand.

"Ah, ah, ah, standing won't do you any good," said Zechariah. "Think about your position. Your enemy has knocked you down, and you're unarmed. What do you do?"

Justin paused. He looked around the cavern floor and spotted his sword illuminated by the firelight several yards away.

"That's right," said Zechariah. "Your first thought should be how to regain your weapon—to *strike back*. No thinking about how much it hurt."

Justin's eyes flashed toward Zechariah. He saw him raise his sword for another strike, and he dove. He rolled across the cavern floor, got to his feet, and grabbed his sword.

"Hold it up in front of you!" Zechariah commanded. "You can't block when it's at your side!"

Justin adjusted his grip, but Zechariah swatted the sword out of his hand again. This time, he followed up the move by grabbing Justin and putting him in a chokehold with his sword against his throat—similar to the hold Olorus had used on him.

"How easily you find yourself in these situations, Master Holmes," Zechariah hissed into Justin's ear. "Remember how Leah healed you on the trail?" He pressed the blade harder against Justin's neck. "Care to see how good she is?"

Justin started to struggle but was thrown to the ground and felt the skin on his elbow break open.

"You have to hold the sword *tight* and block *hard*!" Zechariah shouted.

Justin grabbed his sword and stood. He looked at his elbow, saw blood—

Zechariah attacked again. Justin blocked. The weapons connected and slid against one another, squealing and grinding. Zechariah glared at him over their blades.

"No thinking about whether you're injured," he growled. "Injuries only matter if you survive the fight. During the fight, they're nothing but a distraction. Pain is a distraction. Blood is a distraction. Ignore them both. Keep your focus."

Zechariah pushed away, stepped back, and struck again. Justin moved his sword to block, but the old man changed the direction of the swing at the last moment. Zechariah stopped his sword in midair, just before it would have skewered Justin through the chest.

"That is called a feint," said the old man. Then he swung his opposite elbow and cracked Justin in the temple.

Justin hit the ground again, seeing stars.

"You have to pay attention to more than just the sword," Zechariah said. "Don't just sit there!"

A boot connected with the base of Justin's spine. He yelped, rolled over, and stood.

"An enemy won't wait for you to recover," Zechariah said. "If you think a wallop on the head hurts, imagine some iron between your ribs. Injured is better than dead every time. If you get hit, get back up and fight. Remember how he did it and don't let it happen again."

Justin felt blood trickling down his face, but he kept his eye on Zechariah.

"Again," Zechariah said. "Defend!"

CHAPTER 43

"Zechariah is ruthless," Leah said, watching the old man put the young man through his paces.

Across the fire, Olorus laughed. "Not ruthless enough," he said.

Half an hour after it had begun, Justin's training had changed from an attack-and-defend session to an agility exercise.

"Left! Right! Back! Right! Left! Forward!" called Zechariah.

Justin, holding his sword in a defensive position, did his best to obey. He was panting and drenched in sweat. Blood ran from scrapes and minor wounds. Every so often, Zechariah lashed out without warning, prompting Justin to dodge or parry.

"No, not nearly ruthless enough," Olorus reiterated. "The boy is clumsy. He is slow and weak, and he has no stamina. Up to me, I would have him training in the regimen of the Hell Jays. Then he would know the meaning of the word *work*!"

Leah nodded. The Hell Jays, a subdivision of the Nolian army devoted to border defense, were notorious for their grueling training. And rightly so. The Jays lived in open country and were expected to hold their own against the barbarians of the west, coblyn hordes, and anything else that threatened the sanctity of Nolian life. Leah had forgotten that Olorus had been one of them before his advancement to the High Guard. She turned to Hook, who was tending the steeds. She couldn't remember what unit he had come from.

A commotion drew her attention back around. Justin had been knocked off his feet again.

"I don't understand it," she whispered. "The boy seems at least moderately intelligent, yet he can't defend himself, and he seems wholly ignorant. He couldn't even ride a steed when I first met him. Do you think he's a dullard?"

"Touched in the head, certainly," said Olorus. Unlike Leah, he made no effort to keep his voice down. He spat into the fire, and it crackled in the coals. "As for that old man, I tell you, he has other agendas. I can see it!"

"Ahlund trusted him," Leah said with a sigh. "I thought that was enough for me."

The fact that she used the past tense was lost on neither of them.

Leah spun the ring on her finger absentmindedly, feeling the smoothly cut face of the healer's aurstone set in the thick, silver band. To say that Ahlund had *trusted* Zechariah was a bit liberal, of course. In truth, his opinion of the old man had been closer to indifference.

"I just wonder who they really are," said Olorus.

"Upon our first meeting," Leah said, "Zechariah introduced himself as a scholar and scribe. Justin introduced himself as—well, Justin. He told me where he was from, but it was no place I had ever heard of, and I can't remember it now. I thought he was some sort of apprentice to Zechariah. I judged him to be level-headed enough, albeit faint of heart, but now. . . ."

After the way he talked in the Cru village, she thought, *his level-headedness seems up for debate.*

"I know less than I should about politics and diplomacy, Olorus," Leah said, staring into the fire, "but there is something my father told me when I was a little girl that I remember to this day: It is better to make a decision quickly and change one's mind slowly than to make a decision slowly and change one's mind quickly."

"I understand, my lady," Olorus said. "And I meant no disrespect."

"I know." She paused. "Zechariah said this tunnel comes out near Lonn."

"He did," agreed Olorus.

"Lonn's an independent city," she said. "Well fortified, I hear. And protected by a small standing army. Nolia does not hold dominion over them. Neither does Darvelle."

"You wish to go to Lonn?"

"For a time, perhaps. Until we can gather our forces."

Olorus lit up. "Gather our forces! Now you're speaking my language!"

"I do not wish to wage war," she said. "But our options are limited. Prime Minister Asher has regiments searching the countryside to capture me. Nolia is under his thumb. I can't think of a scenario where I gain the throne without an army. That will involve some planning. And some bargaining. My father had allies in the north, some of whom may find it beneficial to see me back on the throne—"

But the rest of her words were cut off by a sudden, screeching roar that echoed through the cavern seemingly from every direction at once.

Before Leah knew it, Olorus and Hook were at her side with shields raised. She looked around but could see no sign of whatever had made the noise. Across the cavern, Zechariah was frowning. Justin, panting from his workout, was pale with fright.

As the wildcat-like wail faded, the call was answered from different directions, at varying distances and volumes. A rush of warm wind issued from the recesses in the cavern walls like an exhaled breath. Leah felt it brush against her skin. The steeds stamped their hooves and circled in fear.

The warm air dissipated, the noises stopped, and the mountain underworld was silent once again.

A bright light brought Leah's attention to the front of the cavern. Zechariah raised his shining stone above his head. The shadows hung strangely, blue in one direction from the stone and orange from the fire in the other. Suddenly, all those many foot-wide holes in the walls seemed less like cavern antechambers and more like. . . .

Burrows, she thought.

"Leave the fire burning," Zechariah said. "Justin, Hook, gather the steeds. Olorus, do not leave her side."

Olorus nodded. Hook and Justin saddled the steeds and loaded their supplies as Zechariah stared into the darkness ahead. Leah felt her chin quivering, and she clamped her teeth together to stop it.

Perhaps, she thought, *this is a decision I should have made a bit more slowly.*

"Follow me," said Zechariah when the steeds were ready. "And keep silent."

They started walking toward the end of the cavern, but they never made it there.

CHAPTER 44

Zechariah stopped. Justin rested his hand on his sword.

It sounded like a cat, he thought. *One of those cave lions Olorus was talking about? Or the things Zechariah calls coblyns? Or worse: the monsters from the Gravelands. But how could they have caught up with us?*

He could hear his own heart beating, could feel his hands shaking as he envisioned shadowy creatures astride giant animals.

He heard a clicking sound from above where the cave ceiling was veiled in darkness. Hook must have heard it too, because he looked up. A slight scraping noise followed, and a bit of dirt dropped on Leah's shoulder.

Olorus's voice was lower than a whisper as he breathed, "The fire."

Justin turned and felt the breath leave his lungs.

Crawling silently over the cave floor were three dark shapes. The smallest was at least three feet in diameter, and most of that was legs—eight of them. Firelight reflected in a dozen tiny eyeballs. The shiny, sectioned plates of its exoskeleton shifted and rubbed against each other as the legs picked their way toward the humans. At first, he thought they were spiders, but in addition to the eight legs were two short, crustacean-like appendages at the front, each wielding eight-inch pincers. The mouths were small, probably built for taking leisurely bites out of immobilized prey. That was surely their preferred method of killing, Justin concluded, because each had a two-foot-long tail curled forward over its back, armed with a giant, scorpion-like stinger.

Further movement drew Justin's attention to the far end of the cavern. Another one was crawling from one of the small holes in the wall. It unfolded itself, blooming like a deadly, arachnoid flower. It opened and closed one of its pincers, and a sharp, little click like snapping shears made Justin's skin crawl.

"Above," whispered Zechariah.

The gauge glowed brighter. The blue light extended upward, illuminating the ceiling, and Justin's blood frosted over. Three more insects were crawling across the cavern ceiling by digging their bony legs into the rock for support. Slime dripped from the needle-like teeth of their tiny mouths. Back at the fire, there were now ten of them. And more were crawling out of the holes in the walls—dozens of them. They did not rush the humans but crept along on their armored legs, making hardly a sound.

They're hunting us, Justin realized.

High above, one let go of the ceiling, but instead of falling, it descended slowly, swinging like a pendulum. It was lowering itself by a strand of web from its abdomen—web as thick as a telephone line.

"On three," Zechariah whispered.

Zechariah's face was ghostly in the pale blue aura. His old eyes watched the creatures intently, and Justin remembered what he'd said minutes ago about never taking your eyes off your opponent. Justin looked back up at the nearest insect. It was so close that he could see wiry follicles of hair sticking out from between its exoskeletal plates.

"One," said Zechariah.

The bug used two of its crab-like legs to pull the thread from its abdomen, guiding itself downward with pincers open. It hung directly over Zechariah. Others began to lower themselves toward the humans.

"Two."

Justin could barely breathe. The creature was two feet above Zechariah's head and closing. The tail uncurled, shifting its half-moon-shaped stinger into attack position. At the head of the stinger, a retractable, biological syringe extended. A tiny drop of venom quivered at the tip.

"*Three!*"

In a swirl of robes, the old man jumped, drew his sword, and sliced the creature in two. Its halves fell to the floor, spraying gooey liquid and spilling soft matter from masses of spasming legs. With a flick of his wrist, Hook launched a knife into the air that buried itself into the face of another bug, which fell with a wildcat-like scream. Leah drew her sword—similar to the basket-hilted model at Justin's side—and Olorus shouted eagerly as he pulled his spear and shield from his back.

With shaking hands, Justin clumsily pulled his blade from its sheath. The initial shock over, the predators shifted tactics, abandoning stealth in favor of all-out assault. They dropped or leaped to the cavern floor and scurried on blade-like legs. One dropped directly for Olorus, pincers and stinger primed to kill, but he drove his tall spear skyward with a roar. The blade pierced its underbelly, and the creature slid down the haft, where he promptly split it in two with the butt of his metal shield like a guillotine. Another pounced and sailed across the cavern, aimed at Leah, but Hook caught it with his shield, threw it to the floor, and drove his machete-like blade through its stomach. The steeds reared and wailed in terror.

The agile spider-scorpions slipped between the humans, separating them from one another. Olorus and Hook used their shields to protect the princess as Zechariah pressed the attack, spinning to slice at the creatures on all sides. One jumped, and he hacked off two legs in midair, sending its maimed body spiraling.

One charged at Justin. Its crabby legs skittered across the floor, and it lunged for him. He stumbled backward. In mid-fall, he gritted his teeth and maneuvered his sword with a quick, upward slice. He hit the floor on his back. To his astonishment, his attacker hit the ground on either side of him, cut cleanly up the middle into two halves sputtering green fluid. He looked at his sword, surprised and a little pleased with himself. With recent lessons still fresh in his mind, he hurried to regain his footing.

Three jumped on Olorus at once, taking him to the ground in a rolling heap. Leah snapped a kick into one insect's face while driving her sword into another. Meanwhile, Zechariah was being driven back by overwhelming numbers. One fell from the ceiling at him, and he sliced backward, cutting it down seemingly without looking.

Olorus gained his feet. His shield and spear were missing, and he was grappling a spider-scorpion with his bare hands. A pincer sliced through the flesh of his forearm as cleanly as a butcher's knife, and he growled in pain. The other pincer reached for his neck. With a roar, Olorus grabbed the tail, pulled hard, twisted, and drove the creature's own stinger deep into its soft belly. It wailed and fell, and Olorus, blood pouring from his arm, drew his sword, hollered with bloodlust, and pressed the attack.

Justin swung with hatchet-like chops at anything that came near him—sometimes dismembering a leg or claw, sometimes striking mortal blows—but every creature that died was replaced by more scuttling from the cavern walls. He caught one through the head with a quick chop, but before he could yank the sword free, a second reached up and grabbed Justin's blade with its pincers. It tugged on his sword, trying to pull him in for a clear shot with the stinger.

Justin held on for dear life. The claw wrenched him back and forth. The tail swung overhead in scorpion fashion and missed his arm by inches. Its second pincer shot forward, catching his left leg. For a confusing moment, he thought he had wet his pants. Then he realized it was blood.

CHAPTER 45

The creature was winning. It was stronger than he was, and it was driving him up against the wall. Its pincers, its teeth, its legs, and its stinger took turns attacking. He couldn't defend against them all. It had more than one weapon.

So do you, he thought. *Pay attention to more than just the sword!*

All at once, he threw his weight forward. The momentum was enough to push the creature off balance, and that was all the time he needed. He let go of his sword, drew his dirk knife from the scabbard on his right leg, and sliced through the insect's arm. It fell back, spraying fluid from the stump where its claw had been. Justin pulled his sword from the severed arm on the ground. The pincers opened and closed without object.

There came a horrible noise from behind him. He turned.

The steeds had retreated to the exit of the cavern, but one broke free of its ties and ran toward the presumed safety of firelight. The spider-scorpions took their chance. They pounced on the animal and drove their stingers into its hide.

"No!" Justin shouted.

He cut through foes, trying to reach the steed, but it was too late. In seconds, spider-scorpions were all over it, stringing web across its back and pulling it farther and farther into the horde. The rest of the bugs retreated from the humans to join in. The steed vanished within a ball of swarming insects, and its muffled whinnies were replaced by snapping pincers, like an army of dressmakers all cutting at once.

One by one, the bugs retreated into their holes, and the horde disappeared into the walls until none were left. The skittering of bony legs reverberated through the cave, taking with it a warm rush of displaced air. All that remained was the sound of the humans' heavy breathing. The only spider-scorpions left were dead, and there was no sign of the unlucky steed. Justin tried not to think about how many pieces it must have been disassembled into, to have been carried away through those small tunnels. His lip curled to realize how few spider-scorpion corpses were left—far fewer than had been killed. The horde must have taken the carcasses with them, perhaps as an appetizer to the main course.

It was Zechariah who finally broke the silence. "Let's move," he said.

Justin grabbed the reins of the remaining steeds, recognized Seabiscuit, and patted the animal's head in relief.

The party started down the exit tunnel, watching the walls and ceilings as they went. The cavern fell away behind them until the firelight was no longer visible, and the only illumination was the blue glow of Zechariah's stone.

Justin limped and trailed blood. The wound had happened so quickly he'd hardly had time to appreciate it. Adrenaline had numbed much of the pain, at first. Now, with every step, throbbing, white-hot pain flared up from the torn flesh. It wasn't like the movies—a nice, clean little nick, right where it would look cool without interfering with function. It was deep, ragged, and dirty. The strike had carried far more blunt force than he would have expected—not like getting sliced with a knife, but more like getting hit with a baseball bat that also happened to be very sharp. He kept his sword drawn, praying the bugs would not return and wondering what else might live in these depths.

CHAPTER 46

"I have a bad feeling about this," Leah said.

"I can't imagine why," said Justin.

"Look," said Olorus. "Holes in the wall here, too."

They had been traveling for at least eight hours straight since the spider-scorpion attack, stopping only once for Leah to heal the wounds on Justin's leg and Olorus's arm.

Justin had been too anxious to be amazed at the way his flesh had fused together like molten metal under her touch. The pain was gone now, leaving only a jagged, whitish-gray scar and a torn, bloody pant-leg.

It felt as if the cave were taking them in circles. The tunnel was less like a meandering river and more like a knotted string. Justin's sense of direction had become so skewed that he could have sworn they were currently traveling beneath or over the same spot they had been in an hour before.

The lost steed was the one Leah had been riding since the Gravelands. They were now without it *and* the cargo it had been carrying: bundles of firewood, waterskins, and precious rations of food.

Justin kept Seabiscuit at arm's length as they passed more holes in the walls. He kept thinking about a passing reference Olorus had made days ago to a folkloric creature: a giant scorpion with the head of a woman and the tail of a dragon that ate men by luring them underground.

Makes you wonder, thought Justin. *How many other myths are based so closely on reality?*

"Those *things* came out of burrows like that," Leah said, pointing at some nearby holes in the wall.

"These are bigger, though," said Justin, "and not as neatly formed. Probably natural."

"Doesn't mean something doesn't live in them," said Leah.

"A bigger hole for a bigger monster," Olorus said.

Justin swallowed hard. "Just trying to look on the bright side, guys; cut me some slack."

"Remember that warm wind before the attack?" said Leah.

"Pressed in, I imagine," Zechariah said. "Air displaced from the tunnels by their movement."

Justin blinked and shook his head. His eyelids were drooping.

What I wouldn't give for a cup of coffee, he thought.

Besides a short nap in the Cru village, he was going on something like thirty-six hours without sleep—and it had not exactly been your typical thirty-six hours, either. He walked on stiff, tired legs, and his wits were getting slow. He had no idea whether it was night or day. All he knew was that he was as tired as he had ever been in his life.

They left the holed walls behind and, a few minutes later, arrived at a fork in the path. Like the branching of a Cru prophecy, their road split in two: one up, one down.

Zechariah started unpacking. "A suitable place for camp," he said. "I don't think I can go another step."

"Maybe we shouldn't make a fire," Leah said. "What if it attracts more spiders?"

"A necessary risk," said Zechariah. "We need light, but I cannot keep the power in this stone as I sleep. A fire will have to do."

While he sleeps? thought Justin with a frown. *Thought he said he doesn't sleep.*

Justin excused himself back the way they had come. Bathroom visits were another reason to hate the caves. No dirt. No leaves. Just bare rock. It felt like a shameful thing, not to be able to cover it up. Even animals did that. Some, anyway; the steeds seemed to let it fall wherever they pleased. In the forest and along the mountain path, it had been easy to leave the road and find a suitable place. But down here, there were only so many places to go, and removing oneself very far from the group just for sake of privacy was ill-advised. It was a strange paradox, but the rarer privacy became, the less important it felt. Life on the road seemed to breed a sort of barbaric intimacy among travelers, and being shocked or offended by the necessities of human existence was a luxury they did not have.

Returning to camp, Justin found a fire already going. Hook divvied out potions from the food stores. Since several canteens had been lost with the demise of Leah's steed, they shared a depressingly small amount of water. Meanwhile, the remaining steeds lazily sucked moisture off the cave walls with their trunks to let it trickle into their mouths.

Zechariah volunteered for first watch. As the others lay in the firelight and drifted off to sleep, Justin, despite his weariness, forced himself to stay awake. He waited and watched.

When the others were asleep, Zechariah stood. He slipped away from the fire, lit his gauge stone, and started up the left-hand tunnel. Justin started to sit up, intending to ask where he was going, but Zechariah turned back, winked at him, and slipped into the darkness.

Suitable place for camp. Yeah right. He's scouting ahead. Probably because he can't remember the way!

Justin made sure his weapons—his dirk, his basket-hilted sword, and his new, heavy two-hander sword—were all within reach as he lay, looking out into the darkness. Being privy to Zechariah's shaky leadership was not all it was cracked up to be.

Try as he might to watch over the camp in Zechariah's absence, Justin couldn't stay awake. He drifted off with visions of giant insects in his head, and morning, if it could be called that, came when Zechariah woke him. He felt as if he'd only just fallen asleep, yet it had clearly been several hours, for their fire had burned quite low.

"I believe it's about time we were moving," said Zechariah.

"You never woke me for my watch," said Olorus, stretching and groaning.

Hook made a sign with his hands indicating the same.

"Justin took second watch," Zechariah explained. "But I had trouble sleeping, so I took over for the rest of the night." He chuckled. "Night. What a concept, in a place where the sun never shines!"

Olorus gave him a look but said nothing.

Zechariah took the path on the right. The one that sloped steeply downward. The others followed, but Justin hesitated. It felt wrong to be going deeper. He knew that the twists and turns of these ancient corridors could change dramatically; the path's initial direction did not necessarily indicate its true course. But some deep-seated animal instinct within him wanted—needed—to go up. Now.

Olorus and Hook carried torches, and Leah walked with one hand on Seabiscuit to keep him close. Justin took a deep breath, gave the left-hand path one last look, and followed them.

CHAPTER 47

He had better know where he's going, thought Leah, watching the self-proclaimed "scholar and scribe" leading the way. They had made four more turns since the first crossroads—three at two-way forks, and one at a five-way intersection.

She stifled a yawn. Traveling was tiring enough, but a healer's spirit energy needed time to recharge after use. She had gotten little rest since healing Olorus's arm and Justin's leg. She felt like a hollow shell of herself. But the exhaustion was a burden she was willing to carry. Olorus's cut had been deep and would have become critical if untreated, and the blood loss from Justin's wound, a long, jagged cut from shin to knee, might have proven problematic.

Healing was Leah's life's work. Or it had been, back before everything became such a mess. She looked back at Justin at the rear of the procession. His pant-leg was dark with dried blood. "I've never been hurt this badly," he had said, almost in wonder, as she healed him.

Strange boy, she thought, not for the first time.

At a sharp corner, Zechariah slowed to a halt.

"Do you see that?" he said.

He reduced the glow of his stone to nothing, yet Leah could see light ahead.

"Daylight!" Justin said.

"No," Zechariah said.

He brought the blue stone to full power and pressed on.

The tunnel became a little brighter with every turn. The source always seemed to be just around the next corner. Soon, it carried a distinctive green hue and was so bright that Zechariah's stone was no longer needed. Finally, they turned a corner, and Leah drew in a sharp breath of dank, cave air.

Shining light emanated from minerals in the walls of a high-ceilinged cavern. Veins of brilliant green, like frozen lightning bolts, ran over every surface. It hung in the ceiling like a floating pool of emeralds. Entire stalactites were made of it.

"Beautiful," she heard herself say.

"What is it?" Justin said.

"It is called *a'thri'ik*," Zechariah said, "which means, 'cat's eye.' Theynrald is its common name. In darkness, it glows, but in the sun's presence, its light dies out. By day, you wouldn't know it from any other rock on the ground, yet by night—or underground—it is better than torchlight. The Ancients used it to light their underground citadels. As you can see, this place was once a mine."

Now that Zechariah mentioned it, Leah did notice pieces of metal tools scattered throughout the cavern. Any wooden components had long rotted away, leaving the rusted buckets of wheelbarrows and the heads of shovels and pickaxes. She looked at Zechariah. He was smiling at her.

"As good a place as any to take lunch," he said.

"I should like to have a piece of this!" said Olorus. He rushed to a stalagmite jutting out of the ground and broke off its tip. "Aha!" he cried. He dropped his torch, stamped it out, and held up the cone of green light. "A man need not be a sorcerer to use lightstones! Now Olorus Antony can see in the dark as well!"

As they ate, Leah found herself filled with a depression that was difficult to reconcile. She had always thought she was born for adventures, but now, with Nolia in true jeopardy, she found herself wishing only to go home. Maybe adventures weren't as fun as stories made them out to be. Or maybe she just wasn't as equipped for them as she had hoped. She didn't know which answer was worse.

The cavern was so beautiful that she wanted to take some of it with her, like Olorus, but breaking off pieces of it just didn't seem right. She wanted it to remain as it was.

Maybe I'll have adventures again someday, she thought. *Good ones. And maybe, when the world is not so cruel and life is not so hard, I can return to this place and see it again.*

CHAPTER 48

Zechariah took point with his glowing, blue gauge, Olorus held his plundered a'thri'ik shard, Hook followed with a torch, and Leah walked alongside him. Justin, at the rear of the procession with the steeds, followed in their shadows. He tripped over a lip in the rocky floor and grumbled under his breath.

"I was expecting a maze down here," said Leah, "but we've encountered few intersections."

"Our chosen path," said Zechariah, "travels through probably half a percent of the caves beneath the mountains. Elsewhere, navigation is not so favorable. Fortunately, I'm an experienced navigator. And it is equally fortunate that the Cru were willing to remind me of the way."

Hook moved his hands, and Olorus translated. "Hook says you did a good job convincing us that the dangers were fewer beneath the ground than above. He is sure he would have preferred Nolian soldiers to venomous beasts."

"Count yourself lucky we haven't encountered any coblyns," said Zechariah. "And thank you, Sergeant Bard, for voicing your opinion." He did not put any noticeable emphasis on the word "voicing," but his point was clear, nonetheless.

As inconsequential as the exchange may have seemed, it put Justin on edge. Olorus and Hook had made it no secret that they distrusted Zechariah. Justin wondered what they would do if they knew what he knew: that Zechariah had never consulted with the Cru regarding the way, and the only reason he knew which path to take was because he had scouted ahead while he was supposed to be guarding the camp.

I wonder how far he went searching for the right path, thought Justin. *Maybe all the way to the green cavern. Maybe that's how he knew it was the right way.*

Or maybe—and Justin hardly dared consider this possibility—Zechariah was making a series of major guesses. It made Justin wonder how many guesses a dishonest, prideful man would be willing to take before admitting he didn't know the way. Would he gamble with their lives just to save face?

To distract himself, Justin untied his new sword from Seabiscuit's saddlebags. In all the excitement, he had not gotten a proper look at it yet. The sheath was made of beautifully carved, red wood. The pommel was inlaid with runic symbols, and the crossguard's arms sloped forward, toward the blade, giving it a *V* shape rather than the traditional *T* shape of most swords. The handle was easily ten inches long, meant to be held hand-above-hand, and the blade was four feet long and astoundingly heavy. He pulled it from the sheath to inspect the steel—

Justin was so startled that he nearly dropped the sword. A bit of the double-edged, dark steel blade was exposed, showing lines in the metal like veins. The veins glowed green.

He didn't realize he had stopped walking until Olorus, a dozen yards ahead, called back, "Everything all right?"

The rest of the party turned to look at him. Justin stood silent and stupefied.

"Justin?" Zechariah said.

Justin replied by drawing the sword fully from its wooden sheath. The blade erupted with bright light. He held it aloft with both hands, bathing everything around him in an emerald glow. Leah gasped. The others looked on in stunned silence—Justin included. Running along the dark steel were veins of the same green light as in the cavern, winding about the steel like tiny, glittering threads, pulsing like starlight.

"Amazing," said Leah.

Zechariah walked to Justin's side and touched the sword with his fingertips. "An a'thri'ik blade!" he said. "Forged in the style of the Ancients. Imagine that."

"Huh?" said Justin.

"Cat's eye stone," said Zechariah, "incorporated into the blade during the forging process. That sort of metallurgy is a lost art."

"And to think you were going to leave it behind!" chuckled Olorus. "Hold on to that, my boy. It may fetch a fine price if ever you find a buyer who knows its worth."

Justin smiled. He playfully moved the sword, watching its green light shift against the cave walls. They continued walking—now with Justin and his glowing sword leading the way.

CHAPTER 49

"Nolian folk are typically a darker-haired and darker-skinned race," said Olorus. "The princess here is a prime example of that. Two hundred and fifty years of the noble blood of western conquerors! My father was a picture of the Nolian race. He fell in love with the daughter of an indentured servant from Endenholm, and that is where I get my red hair and fair skin. But I could not be prouder. The folk of Endenholm are known for their quiet strength."

Justin muttered, "Quiet. Right."

Leah smiled over her shoulder at him. Ahead of her, Olorus went on talking, none the wiser.

"There are many races in the Oikoumene," he continued. "The Cru are nearly as dark-skinned as the natives of Raeqlund. And some would say that the Thubestines are closely related, though their skin has a more reddish hue, if you ask me, almost like an Ecbatan. The Castydocians are a curious lot. Their hair turns silver with age, but from birth it is snow white. Almost as white as the skin of a Rorrdvuuk barbarian—big, barrel-chested men, those savages are."

"What did I tell you about calling people savages?" Zechariah said wearily.

"Old man, even you must admit that some races carry more esteem than others," said Olorus. "Why, even within Nolia's capital city of Cervice, they say west-enders are duller in the head than most. . . ."

Olorus kept talking, but Justin was hardly listening. He was too busy with his own thoughts. At lunch, Leah had revealed her destination: a town called Lonn. The prospect of leaving the caves behind should have been a relief to Justin. Instead, he found that the thought of open country put him on edge. Those shadow-monsters were looking for them out there—or, if Zechariah was to be believed, looking for *him.*

You, Justin. You want to know what all of this is about? Well, no more lies. It's about you.

Justin breathed out, slowly and shakily. His insides—from his esophagus all the way to his stomach—had a nasty habit of seizing up coldly whenever he thought of those words.

"There!" Zechariah's voice startled Justin back to the present. "Do you hear that?"

"Hear what?" said Olorus. "I can't hear anything."

"No one can hear anything over your mouth," said Zechariah.

Justin strained his ears, but all he could hear was the same crypt-like silence and the occasional drip of water from the ceiling. Hook must have heard it, though, because he made a quick sign with his hand.

"Running water?" Olorus translated.

"The Greenspring River has its origins in these caves," said Zechariah. "Our path follows it down into the foothills."

They picked up the pace, reinvigorated by the prospect of escape. Soon, Justin could hear the water, too. It started as distant white noise and intensified into a loud rushing sound. An hour later, their tunnel turned a sharp corner and opened at the threshold of a cavern that reverberated with the sound. Here, visible by the light of their green and blue lanterns, was a spring that gushed right up from the depths of the rock, feeding an underground lake.

A loud splash alerted Justin. He turned his heavy sword in the direction of the noise, and the green glow illuminated ripples near the shoreline. He wondered what terrible beast had berthed to cause the disturbance—sea serpent, aquatic dinosaur, or some other, unimaginable horror. But then he noticed a frog about the size of a man's fist sitting on the rocky banks. The green of Justin's sword reflected in its black, globular eyes. It hopped into the lake, creating a second splash and ripple—incommensurate with its diminutive size—and Justin sighed in relief.

The steeds tugged at their reins, eager to get to the water.

"Is it safe to drink?" Olorus asked.

Zechariah knelt at the shore. Using his hands as a cup, he slurped some and swished it in his mouth before spitting it back out.

"For four-legged creatures, I would say so," he said, wiping water from his beard. "But not for us. The next few days would be unpleasant. Just make sure they don't wade in."

Justin wondered uneasily what knowledge or experience warranted this warning.

The steeds couldn't drink quickly enough. For days, they had survived only on moisture from rocky walls. Now, they gratefully snorted up trunk-fulls of the lake water and poured it into their mouths. Soon, Zechariah located a narrow ditch where lake water spilled down a tunnel, and they left the cavern.

The ditch grew in size as they followed its path. Adjoining tributaries joined it until it became a stream, and suddenly, the cave did not seem so dark. Zechariah extinguished his blue stone, and Justin sheathed his sword. A dull sheen still glistened on the water.

"Daylight," said Leah.

Around the next corner, a patch of mushrooms grew on the cavern wall. Justin picked one to look at it, and Seabiscuit reached over with his trunk and thoughtlessly stole it as he passed, popping it into his mouth.

They picked up their pace as the light became brighter. They spooked a swarm of tiny bats from the cave ceiling that flew off, squeaking in annoyance.

Turning one final corner, they emerged into daylight so bright that it was nearly blinding. Justin stepped out into soft blades of knee-high grass. The sun hurt his eyes wonderfully. A crisp wind caressed his face.

"Justin!" hissed Zechariah. "Get *down*!"

CHAPTER 50

Though Justin could hardly see in the light of day, he squinted in Zechariah's direction. The old man was crouched low in the grass. Behind him, Olorus, Hook, and Leah were doing the same.

"Back in the cave!" Zechariah whispered. "Quickly!"

"What's going on?" Justin said, looking around in bewilderment.

Zechariah grabbed him by the arm and pulled him to the ground. Hook ushered the steeds back into the cave, and the humans followed. Zechariah dragged Justin along, tossed him in, and pushed him flat against the rock wall. Justin started to protest this treatment but silenced himself at the look on Zechariah's face.

"Something's coming," said Zechariah. "Not a sound, now."

All Justin could see of the world outside was a thin sliver between the rocks.

Is it . . . them? he wondered.

The light shining through the crack was overwhelmingly bright, but Justin could make out some of the countryside. Visibility was clear for almost a mile. This place was neither a rocky pass nor a sprawling grassland. The river burst forth from the mountain and spilled down grassy uplands. Ahead, downhill, the river entered a forest of dogwood trees, wide-leafed maples, and birches.

While examining this scenery, Justin finally spotted what the old man had apparently already seen—or maybe sensed through the tenuous vibrations of "aurym."

At the point where the Greenspring River entered the trees, about a quarter-mile away, a line of dark shrubbery appeared to be moving. Justin squinted and realized it was not shrubbery. It was a group of something. And they were on the move.

People marching? Justin wondered. *A herd of animals?*

Zechariah stepped forward and raised a spyglass to his eye. It was the same one Ahlund had used what seemed like a lifetime ago to search for Leah's kidnappers on the Gravelands.

"What is it?" Justin whispered when he could take it no longer.

Instead of answering, Zechariah lowered the spyglass and handed it to Justin. Justin leaned against the cave wall to steady himself and looked through the eyepiece.

"What the. . . ?" Justin said.

There must have been a hundred of them, walking in a strange, unmeasured gate that was part bipedal locomotion and part ape-like knuckle-walking. They were long-limbed creatures the size of children, hairless like humans, but with black, leathery skin, and bodies lean and corded with muscle. Their hunched, deformed frames slunk along the ground. Short tails dragged behind.

The faces were like exhumed corpses: black, mummified flesh stretched over misshapen skulls. Broken and jagged incisors hung from their upper lips. If they had any eyes to speak of, Justin couldn't see them from here.

"Coblyns," said Zechariah.

Olorus snatched the spyglass from Justin.

"So many of them," Olorus whispered. "I've never seen a pack larger than ten or fifteen at a time."

"Usually, they hunt only in small groups," said Zechariah. He paused and raised his hand, letting the sunlight play over his knuckles. "They also don't come out in the daylight."

"Are you sure they're coblyns?" Leah spoke up.

"Certain," said Zechariah.

Olorus nodded his agreement.

Coblyns. Justin remembered that word. Zechariah had described them as soulless creatures that fed on the living innards of prey to consume their spirit energy. Justin had hoped they were only myths, like goblins or trolls in his world. No such luck, apparently.

"What in blazes are they doing?" Olorus said. "They're not fighting each other. They don't appear to be searching or tasting the air. Doesn't look like they're hunting at all. Just walking. Just—"

"Marching," said Zechariah. "They are marching."

"Impossible," Olorus said. "Coblyns do not march."

"It appears these do," Zechariah said.

"Impossible," Olorus said again, this time half-heartedly. "Where did they come from?"

"I think a better question is," said Zechariah, "where are they going?"

CHAPTER 51

After the coblyns disappeared into the forest, the humans emerged from the cave again, albeit less eagerly. It was midday, and the sky was clear. The caves had brought them far below the mountains' snowy altitudes and forested ridgelines. Here, it felt like summer again.

Without looking back, Zechariah grabbed the steeds and began leading them down the foothills. Justin was about to follow when he saw Olorus take something out of his pocket. He might never have known what it was, had he not recognized its shape: a cone with a jagged base. The cat's eye shard, or a'thri'ik. It no longer showed even the faintest hint of green. It was just a dull, dirty, gray stone. Justin stole a peek at his new sword's blade and realized that, in the light of day, it looked like any other sword. He shrugged. The intricate handle and carved sheath were still pretty, at least.

At first, the Greenspring was narrow enough to hop across. But as they followed the river down the wooded hills, many adjoining side channels came in to meet it, and the river grew deep and wide.

Soon, they reached the place where the coblyns had crossed. The vegetation was trampled. The banks were beaten to a muddy slop where the small army had forded the shallows of the river. From there, their trail continued through the trees.

"They're going east," Olorus said.

"Southeast," said Zechariah. "But for what reason?"

"Reason?" Olorus said. "Coblyns do not act on reason. They do not think or plan; they only crave. Self-preservation and hunger are all a coblyn's brain can comprehend."

"Today's events seem compelling evidence to the contrary," Zechariah said.

Hook signed. Olorus translated, "Could they be migrating?"

Zechariah stroked his beard. "Perhaps. But I have never heard of such a thing."

Justin stared at the tracks in the mud. There were footprints, hand-prints, knuckle-prints, and the snake-like trails of tails. He crouched to examine one of the clearer prints and stretched out his hand for comparison. The track was two-thirds the size of his hand, with five digits he presumed were toes. The big toe was stubby and shifted back along the side of the foot, looking a bit like a malformed human thumb. At the end of each toe were sharp, triangular imprints. Claws.

Justin stood and looked cautiously into the forest, thinking about the shadow-giants. What if they had circled the mountains? Maybe they were already out here waiting for them. He watched Olorus, Hook, and Leah examining the coblyn tracks, and he envied their ignorance.

Travel along the Greenspring's winding path was more difficult than Justin would have anticipated. There was no road, and navigating through trees and thick shrubbery made the going slow. Eventually, a benched floodplain developed alongside the river, and the vegetation was limited to only the largest and hardiest of trees bordered by secondary growth.

By midafternoon, the woods thinned and ended abruptly. Large, fungi-ridden stumps marked the places were trees had once stood. Their flat tops were a sure sign of human tools. He saw an unhitched wagon loaded with logs, and a rutted, dirt road led from the timbered land across a valley dotted with farmhouses and fields.

Emerging from a copse of trees, Justin spotted a fortified city ahead, atop a hill. Its beige, stone walls gave it a solid, geometric appearance. The city proper was atop the hill, and the rest draped over the hillside, where the walls extended all the way to the bottom, ending at parapets around a wide elbow in the river.

"That'll be Lonn," said Olorus. He turned to Leah. "Last chance to change your mind, my lady."

Leah said nothing.

The forest, a mix of oaks, maples, and pines, had been clear-cut for nearly a mile around Lonn in every direction. Fields of wheat and corn grew on the fertile floodplain along the road, but there were no storage barns or farmhouses. On the Greenspring River, Justin saw dozens of sails. Boats were being piloted up and down the river with fishermen tossing nets into the water.

"Is this part of Nolia?" Justin asked.

"Hardly," Olorus said. "These are uncontested, free lands, all the way to the sea—but you must know that, Justin! You're from Deen, aren't you?"

"Yeah," Justin said quickly. "Never been this far away from home, though."

The second part was true, at least.

"Lonn is an independent trade center," said Leah. "One of several in this region."

"How they manage to keep the peace in these places, I will never understand," said Olorus. "Three types of people live in these towns: native-born yokels, money-hungry traders, and outsiders hiding from the rest of the world."

"Like us," said Zechariah.

"Not like us," said Olorus. "I mean people hiding from past lives, from debts unpaid or crimes unpunished. Or, just hiding from themselves."

CHAPTER 52

The sun was disappearing over the mountains as the group approached the doors of Lonn. Guards were posted atop the fifteen-foot walls. They wore chain mail armor and helmets with long nose guards that divided their faces in two. Quivers of arrows were strapped to their backs. They picked up longbows as Justin and the others approached, but Justin could see, even from here, that the bows were not strung.

"Coming from the mountains, I presume?" one of the guards called down. His words were choppy and heavily accented to Justin's ears. "Only trouble comes from those mountains."

"Or that which has prevailed through trouble," Zechariah replied loudly.

"Just as dangerous," the guard said, bored. "State your business."

"I am a cooper from Darvelle," Zechariah said. He indicated Justin, then Leah, then the soldiers, saying in turn, "This is my apprentice, his betrothed, and my bodyguards. Our business was in the Gravelands, but we are in need of supplies and rest before we can return home to Isabelle."

"How many nights?"

"One."

"You've no wares with you."

"Which is why my business venture is complete."

"You should have plenty of coin, then. A little gold might loosen these gate hinges."

"Any gold I carry will be spent *inside* your gates."

"You're heavily armed," said the guard. "With only a couple of steeds for the five of you. You probably killed somebody for them."

"If you must know, these steeds are purely for cargo. As for our swords and shields, the mountains are, as you know, a dangerous place for tradesmen with coin."

"And you've brought along your apprentice's betrothed for what reason?"

"Do you accept travelers after nightfall?" Zechariah shouted. "Because it may be morning by the time all of your idle curiosities have been satisfied!"

The guard smirked. "Five coming through!" he shouted down behind the wall. "Three men, one woman, a couple steeds, and one ornery mountain goat."

Zechariah played the character well, cursing at the guard and threatening to take his money elsewhere as the doors swung open. The guards laughed at him as he led the party in. Leah had drawn the hood of her riding cloak over her head, covering her black ponytail and hiding her face. She adjusted the hood even tighter as they entered.

"Mountain goat," Zechariah said quietly. "That reminds me, Olorus. I seem to remember some unkind names being thrown around upon our first meeting. Billy goat, I think it was?"

Zechariah clicked his tongue in his mouth thoughtfully. Olorus seemed to blush a little.

Though few people could be seen, the sounds of the city seemed to echo from all directions. The gates closed behind them as they entered, and a young boy approached and took the steeds by the reins, informing Zechariah that they would be stabled on the north side of town.

"If you need a place to stay," the boy added, "try Gunnar's Brig. Downhill, port side. Gunnar pays me five elths a week to say that to travelers. Hurry and you'll see them bring in the catch!"

Zechariah placed a piece of copper in the boy's hand as Olorus and Hook removed the saddlebags.

Justin was interrupted from admiring the city when Zechariah put a hand on his shoulder, cleared his throat, and gestured to the sack of books on Seabiscuit's back. Justin frowned. He removed the bag and tossed it over his shoulder, only to have Olorus hand him his new two-hander sword as well. Beneath the combined weight, he felt as if he were about to collapse. The stable boy led the steeds up an adjoining side-street, and Zechariah led the humans deeper into town.

The sounds of the city grew louder near the river. Stone and wood buildings stood shoulder-to-shoulder, and the narrow streets were arranged in patterns even more random than the snaking turns of the Greenspring. Emerging from a cluster of houses, they found Lonn's port. Beneath his cargo, Justin felt like a burdened steed. He looked up and started to complain, but what he said instead was, "Wow."

The wide street was choked with a bustling crowd of humanity. Sails were everywhere on the river's bay. Flags flew from the masts of ships and poles along the dock. At the front of the crowd was a moored boat, and standing on its deck were scruffy-looking men holding large buckets. Dozens of other boats were cruising in from the river. The fishermen stood proudly on their decks, and the crowd in the street whistled and cheered as if greeting conquering heroes. On nearby balconies, people hung over the railings trying to get a look.

The boats ranged in size from canoes to skiffs to seaworthy vessels as big as houses. As the boats docked, the fishermen onboard would hold up their fish, prompting cheers from the crowd, and then throw them to partners onshore. One of the men—a big, fat fellow with a beard and trousers with suspenders—reached into his bucket and pulled out the biggest crab Justin had ever seen. The crowd roared. He flung it sailing, and a man on the dock scrambled to catch it, which delighted the crowd.

Justin dropped the bag of books and massaged his aching shoulder. "What's going on?"

"The fishermen who help keep Lonn self-sufficient are local heroes," Zechariah said. "Bringing in the catch is a daily event."

A man in a canoe presented a fish with a long, pointed nose. He nearly fell trying to pick it up. A second man joined him, and together, they tossed it ashore to the waiting recipient, who was promptly knocked over flat on his back. The people laughed and applauded.

Meanwhile, a tall ship, much larger than the others, was coming in. The town grew audibly excited at its arrival. Great, white sails were lowered. Its shining hull was made of a dark, red wood, and several men stood upon its double-leveled deck. Flying atop the mast was a white flag bearing a sword with thorny ivy wrapped around the blade.

The door of its cabin opened, and a figure emerged: a tall man dressed all in dark leather with a sword at his belt. Hanging from his face was a long, black, braided mustache that only half-covered his toothy smile. Perched atop his head was a huge hat with a feather stuck through it. A scar ran down the left side of his face, and over his left eye was an eyepatch.

"Gunnar! Gunnar!" called the crowd.

He walked to the ship's prow with a spring in his step and placed one foot upon the railing. A member of the ship's crew approached the eyepatched man, lugging a wooden bucket. The eyepatched man reached into the bucket, and, with a flourish, pulled out a slimy, purple octopus with eight dangling legs. The crowd roared as he tossed it ashore. The individual doing the catching was so surprised that he barely managed to hold on to it.

In response to the cheers, the eyepatched, mustached man removed his hat. Long, curly locks of black hair tumbled out from under it. Beneath the hat, a small trout was sitting on his head. He reached up and removed it from his head, bowed grandly to the fish as if granting it a royal pardon, and dropped it over the side of the ship into the water. The crowd laughed.

The eyepatched man signaled to his crew, and they began turning cranks on the ship, hauling up nets that were filled to bursting with fish, crabs, and other aquatic animals.

By now, Justin was grinning at the display, but when he turned to look at the others, his smile vanished. Olorus had inched close to Leah and was wearing a look that spelled danger.

"What's wrong?" asked Justin.

"We have a tail," Olorus said under his breath. "At least one man, maybe more."

"Just one," Zechariah answered without looking. "He is alone. I think he's been following us since the gates."

"Somebody who recognized Leah?" Olorus whispered.

"Possibly," Zechariah said.

"We could split up, see who he follows, and have the others swoop around behind," said Olorus.

"We can't afford the attention," said Zechariah.

The eyepatched man was leaping off his ship to help haul in the catch, and the crowd was dispersing, leaving Justin and his friends exposed in the street.

Olorus growled impatiently. "We'd better get inside, then. Draw them into close quarters."

"I say again, he is alone," said Zechariah. "And we can't afford the attention. Let us wait until the situation presents itself."

Olorus hazarded a glance over his shoulder, and his eyes widened. His voice was no longer a whisper as he said, "I think the situation is about to present itself right now."

Justin turned and gasped. Something in a dark, hooded cloak, taller than the rest of the crowd, was coming straight toward them.

They're here, thought Justin. *They found us!*

Olorus and Hook dropped the saddlebags and turned to face the advancing figure. Justin laid his two-hander sword on the ground with the sack of books and grabbed the handle of his basket-hilted sword.

After all this running in the darkness, it happens now, thought Justin. *In broad daylight, in front of all these people.*

The figure was only a few steps away when it raised its hands—human hands with empty palms—toward Olorus and Hook. A sign of surrender. Sensing an ambush, Hook spun around, searching for other attackers. Olorus's knuckles were white on the haft of his spear.

The figure turned to look at Justin. Beneath its dark hood, Justin saw a high-bridged nose, a sharp jaw, and a scarred face as hard as a statue. Gray eyes, piercing as daggers, stared back at him.

Justin's breath caught in his throat. "Ahlund?"

PART V

APERÇU

CHAPTER 53

Leah couldn't take her eyes off Ahlund as he led them through the tavern called Gunnar's Brig.

With dusk approaching, the enthusiastic crowd had moved inside for drinking and music. Smoke hung in the air. The walls were decorated with giant seashells, patched sails, nets, and old harpoons. On a makeshift stage, a trio of musicians played a quick-stepping jig. The entertainers consisted of a barmaid on a miniature harp, a round, gruff-looking flutist, and the same eyepatched man for whom the dock had erupted with applause just minutes before. He sat on a stool, madly plucking the strings of a dulcimer in his lap.

Leah blinked, forcing herself to stop staring at Ahlund. Finding her lost bodyguard alive was like seeing a ghost.

But is it him? she wondered.

His clothes were new, and his beard had been trimmed. In the street, he had uttered only a quick, "Follow me," before leading them into the Brig. Judging by the silence of her companions, they must have been just as thunderstruck as she was.

As they passed a table of rough-looking men sharing a liquor bottle, she tugged her hood tighter over her face. Most Nolians wouldn't have recognized their own king, let alone his daughter. It was unlikely that anyone here, so far from home, would know who she was. Still, there was no way of telling how far Asher's rumors had spread or how many prying eyes might be on the lookout for a fugitive princess.

Half-drunken cheers filled the hall at the sweeping conclusion of the musicians' song while Ahlund led Leah and the others to a room on the tavern's second floor. Zechariah sat on the only bed and offered the other side to Leah. She gladly accepted and, for the first time in a long time, enjoyed the feel of a soft mattress beneath her.

Ahlund shut the door. He, Justin, Hook, and Olorus remained standing.

Justin was the first to break the silence. His boldness continued to surprise her—even if it was born of ignorance.

"Is it really you?" Justin said.

"Yes," Ahlund said with a voice like the crunch of gravel.

Leah smiled and thought, *Would the real Ahlund say anything more?*

"Sir Ahlund," said Olorus. "It rejoices me to see you alive."

"Likewise, Lieutenant Antony," said Ahlund. "And Sergeant Bard. I assume the two of you are deserters."

"Loyalists," Olorus corrected, thrusting out his chin.

Ahlund turned to Zechariah. "When the gate dropped, I thought you were all dead. The great walls were built with the magic of the Ancients as mortar. Nothing can penetrate them."

"Not even aurym," Zechariah said, smiling. "Ah, that explains it! I could no longer feel your presence, either, so I was convinced that you had been killed. I should have guessed that the walls were cutting off my perception. If I had known you survived, we would not have left you behind."

"But how *did* you survive?" Again, it was Justin who posed the question.

"After the gate shut," Ahlund said, "I turned on the demons, ready to fight to my death. Instead, they turned their sights on the village of Irth. They killed without discrimination. Everything standing was destroyed."

Leah's cheek quivered with the effort of keeping a stern face. She knew why Nolian soldiers were hunting her. She could understand what independent agents might have to gain from her capture. She did not, however, understand why these *things* wanted her. The people of Irth, it seemed, had been killed just for being in the wrong place at the wrong time: between her and those monsters.

She bit her lip. Across towns, countrysides, and several major cities, three-quarters of a million Nolian lives were currently under the rule of a tyrant. It was up to her to avenge her father—her whole family—and take her rightful place on the throne. But innocent bystanders were now dying, all because of her cause. At what point did the loss of life outweigh the returns? How many of those three-quarters of a million Nolians would perish in her fight for the throne? At what point was it better to forgo the suffering? At what point would it be better if she, a single person, died rather than all those innocent people? Was her cause really worth the price?

She turned away from Ahlund and found herself looking at Justin. To her surprise, his face was pale, and his eyes were damp. She frowned. None of this was any fault of his. Was he really so affected by this story—disturbed to the point of tears?

"I tried to stop them," Ahlund continued. "The last thing I remember is the ground beneath me erupting in a blast of daemyn energy. My steed was torn asunder, my body hurled against the walls. When I woke, the storm had passed, and the sun had risen on a new day. I was half-buried beneath wreckage, and it took all my strength to crawl free. Irth was a smoking ruin, desolated by the touch of daemyn. The demons were gone, but I could still sense them, far to the east, working their way around the mountains."

"But that makes it true, then," Olorus said, looking at Zechariah. "What you told us about monsters on the Gravelands."

"It was always true," Leah snapped. "I'll thank you not to doubt my word in the future."

Olorus's eyes met the floor as he bowed to her. Hook, too, looked sheepish. For their lack of trust in her, they probably deserved a harsher reprimand, but these men were soldiers. But when it came to marching orders, they were accustomed to submitting to authority earned by experience and expertise, not inherited. She couldn't blame them for being skeptical.

"You . . . you say they traveled east?" said Olorus.

Ahlund nodded. "Yes. And fast. I do not know what physical limitations, if any, that these cythraul have. They may not require rest or sustenance in the same way humans do. Difficult to say how long it would take them to circle the mountains."

"But what about you?" Justin asked. "How did you manage to get here before any of us?"

It was a good question and one Leah had been meaning to ask next.

"I was not the only survivor of Irth," answered Ahlund. "I helped a family escape the wreckage of their home. They sought to travel north, to seek refuge with relatives along the coast. When I asked how they planned to attempt such a journey, the old matriarch of the family informed me of a route. A tunnel that led beneath the walls, beneath the very mountains, and emerged in the north."

"Seems there are many hidden passages in those mountains," Olorus said. "It is lucky those *demon* things did not know of any."

"Humans, it appears, are the superior species in at least one regard," Ahlund said. "We have the strength to fight but also the humility to plan our escape. Apparently, this tunnel has been a well-kept secret for generations. I offered to travel with the family, to protect them during their passage, if they would show me the way. We rode an ancient ferry along an underground creek that emerged from the earth and connected to the Greenspring River. We came here, to Lonn. The family arranged travel and departed for the coast. That was two days ago. I stayed here. This city is the only safe place for many miles. It was your only logical destination."

Zechariah cleared his throat. "Ahlund, before we discuss things further, you and I should speak privately."

"Agreed," said Ahlund.

"What do you mean, privately?" Leah objected.

"My sincerest apologies, my lady," said Zechariah, as sweet as could be, "but Ahlund and I must take temporary leave. Won't be but a minute."

"And Justin," said Ahlund.

"Me?" Justin said.

"Yes, you," said Ahlund.

Ahlund left the room without so much as a look back. Zechariah followed, and Justin, after shrugging apologetically to Leah, rushed after them.

"We could always just cover our ears!" Olorus called. There was no response. Beneath the strip of cloth tied over his forehead, Hook was glaring at the doorway.

After all this time apart, Leah had expected more out of Ahlund than a few mildly expository answers. Instead, he was gone again. Apparently, whatever he and Zechariah had to discuss was too sensitive for her to hear, yet it was appropriate for Justin's ears.

"That old man," grumbled Olorus, taking a seat in the corner. "He's got a lot of nerve, treating royalty in such a manner. Blatant disrespect."

Leah was enticed to agree, but she left the sentiment unspoken.

Father taught me that a strong ruler saves rebuke for the face of its object. A wise woman talks behind no one's back. It breeds distrust, and besides that, there is never a moment when every back is turned. Better to encourage unity than provoke discord.

"He is as eccentric as his beard is long," said Leah. "But he has been a valuable ally so far. We should save hostility for the enemy."

Olorus thoughtfully ran his hand over the knife at his belt. "I wonder if shortening that beard might shorten the attitude."

Leah smirked. "If it comes to that, you can hold him down and I'll do the shearing. All I want right now is to go to sleep."

Hook dimmed the oil lantern. The soldiers took up positions on the floor in their bedrolls, and Leah took the bed. As she lay on the mattress, she tried not to think, not to worry about tomorrow, but she couldn't help staring at the sliver of light streaming in from the bottom of the door, and wondering what was going on out there.

She hazarded a look across the room. Olorus and Hook were breathing deeply in sleep. She held her breath as she slipped out of bed, picked up her boots, and tiptoed out the door.

CHAPTER 54

An almost nude woman with the head of a catfish looked down at Justin.

The night was dark and overcast. The Greenspring lapped against the pier supports, and lantern light from the city windows reflected in a glossy sheen on the water. Twelve-foot-tall, anthropomorphic effigies of gods and goddesses stood guard along the docks. They were half-woman and half-fish, or half-man and half-turtle, or half-child and half-crab. Around their feet—or fins—were little stacks of bronze and silver pieces, bundles of flowers, and other offerings for the deities.

Ahlund stood there, tall and silent. He looked only slightly more human than the ligneous totems of the dock. Zechariah had his hands folded in the sleeves of his robes. Justin stood between them.

Finally, Ahlund said, "He knows something."

"He knows something," agreed Zechariah.

"Zechariah told me those monsters weren't after Leah," said Justin. "That they're after me."

Ahlund nodded.

"Jeez, not you, too," Justin sighed. "Has everyone gone crazy?"

"What do you remember about your arrival here?" Ahlund asked.

Justin shrugged. "It's hard to tell. It was Christmas Day—but you probably don't know what that is. There was something about a model ship. The last thing I remember is shoveling snow off the driveway. Then I woke up at Zechariah's house."

"In your world, were you capable of using aurym powers?" asked Ahlund.

"Aurym doesn't exist in my world," said Justin. He looked back and forth between the two men. "Is something wrong?"

"Things have recently come to light that require our attention," said Ahlund. "In another lifetime, I belonged to a band of knights called the Ru'Onorath: the Order of the Guardians. Warriors devoted to upholding righteousness and destroying evil. Defenders of the Oikoumene. Years ago, I was . . . excommunicated from their brotherhood. Upon my arrival in Lonn three days ago, I encountered a figure from my past, a Ru'Onora named Kallorn. Before he left to return to the home of the Guardians, he told me that there are reports of armies in the far east. Hordes of refugees are fleeing west. And legions of coblyns are migrating."

"Migrating," Justin said. "That must be what we saw."

Ahlund looked at Zechariah.

"He speaks truly," said the old man. "Just south of here, we saw several hundred in broad daylight, moving as a unit. Heading southeast."

"Kallorn described similar phenomena," said Ahlund. "He claimed to have seen armies of coblyns marching in ranks. He tracked one such group for days, to a small village west of here. By the time he got there, the coblyns had attacked it and had moved on. He estimated one hundred people dead. Fed upon."

Justin remembered Zechariah's description of a coblyn attack. Hollowed-out corpses. People being eaten while they were still alive. He closed his eyes and shivered.

"Coblyns working together, as a unit," said Zechariah. "Very strange."

"It's the sort of thing the Ru'Onorath are meant to handle," said Ahlund, "but Kallorn informed me that the Guardians are dwindling. Strong warriors disappear without a trace, never to be seen or heard from again. For a long time, a distant darkness has been slowly looming in my soul, but now, it's closing in very quickly. In Kallorn's words, 'the light of righteousness is being doused by the rising tide, and soon, it may drown us all.' And there are other signs. Ask any Lonnman and he'll tell you the rumors of the black fleet: a thousand ships massing in the Raedittean Sea north of Athacea. No one knows who they are or where they came from. And shadowy forces are roaming the countryside. Searching."

Ahlund let this last word hang in the air deliberately. Justin had been staring at the ground but now looked up sharply.

"You're not suggesting. . . ?" said Justin. "You think they're looking for me?"

Neither Ahlund nor Zechariah said a word.

"You think all these the demon creatures and armies and fleets are looking for me? I've only been here a week, you know."

"But I have been here for fifty years," said Zechariah.

"So?" said Justin.

Zechariah cleared his throat. "Justin, you have learned much about me during our travels together—"

"That's a bit generous," retorted Justin.

Zechariah cleared his throat again, this time in annoyance. "But you should know me well enough by now to know that I'm not the sort who belongs in a broken-down, old shack on the Gravelands. An immortal man with so much knowledge and experience could do better, don't you think?"

"Immortal," said Justin. "You're still sticking with that story?"

Zechariah ignored the comment. "Until rather recently, I was a person of some importance in the southern world," he said. "I served as advisor to the boy-king of Raeqlund, training him in the ways of leadership, practically ruling the nation myself until he was old enough to take the throne. I had all the riches I could have desired, yet something prompted me to leave it all behind in favor of seclusion on the plains. That something was a prophecy. It foretold the arrival of an ethoul, a fallen angel, in Athacea. So taken was I with this prophecy that I retired from my position, left my riches behind—besides what I could carry on my back—and traveled hundreds of miles to the Gravelands. That was fifty years ago. The boy-king of Raeqlund is dead. His son rules now, from what I hear, with a just hand."

"Are you trying to tell me," said Justin, "that you think I'm the person you were waiting for?"

"No," said Zechariah. "What I'm trying to tell you is that I was not the only one waiting."

CHAPTER 55

"The demons we encountered on the plains were waiting for you, too," said Zechariah. "They had been probably been there for years, like me, shrouding their presence from mortals. And I feel very strongly that there will be others searching for you."

"Well," said Justin, balling his hands into fists, "I feel very strongly that you two are nuts. All this traveling has scrambled your brains or something."

"I've been researching the ethouli for years," Zechariah said. "Your kind is—"

"I am a *person*, damn it!" Justin shouted.

The outburst startled Zechariah badly enough that his shoulders twitched. Ahlund only stared at Justin.

"I'm a person, and I am lost—that's all," Justin said. "I'm not an angel or anything else. I wasn't sent here, and I didn't fall. Get it through your heads. I. Am. Lost. And nobody seems to care about helping me find my way home."

"There's no going home," said Ahlund. "If you're not ready to hear that yet, I'm sorry."

"You two are delusional," Justin said. "I don't even know why I'm here! If you think I'm just going to believe your lies—"

"This is not an argument," Ahlund said. "If you would stop sniveling like a child, you would realize the truth."

Justin sneered. “What truth?”

“That it does not matter what you believe,” said Ahlund. “It doesn’t even matter if you really are a fallen angel. What matters is what *other* people believe.”

“I told you, Justin,” said Zechariah. “People have rallied around the ethouli in the past. They were used as figureheads to legitimize divine right to power. The fallen angel is a symbol that inspires hope, worship . . . and domination. You have seen only a very small portion of Athacea, which is only one small continent of the Oikoumene, which is only a small part of the world. Athacea is mostly small kingdoms like Nolia and independent towns like Deen and Lonn. But in other parts of the world, there are vast nations ruled by powerful centralized governments. Some rule justly. Others do not. Life in Athacea is generally peaceful and prosperous, in its own way. Elsewhere, life is not so kind. There are heavily populated urban centers full of downtrodden, impoverished people desperate for something to believe in. Entire races of people are enslaved and awaiting hope. If word spread that a fallen angel had appeared, people would rally. Hope would become faith, and the meek would rise up. Regardless of the truth, if the common masses could be brought to believe, the fallen angel would *become* true. The symbol would become the divine.”

Justin squinted at him. “I knew it,” he said. “You are trying to use me.”

Zechariah rolled his eyes.

“No!” Justin said. “Admit it. You just said, if people ‘could be brought to believe.’ That sounds like a goal, Zechariah. That’s been your plan all along, hasn’t it?” Justin took a step away from them. “This entire time, you’ve been trying to gain my trust so you could use me. That’s why you keep lying to me and hiding the truth.” He took another step away. “Well, I won’t let you. The two of you can’t make me—!”

In an instant, Justin was flat on his back with the wind knocked out of him. It took a second for his brain to catch up with what had happened to his body. Ahlund had grabbed him by the neck of his shirt, tripped him with a quick instep of his foot, and slammed him down on the dock on his back. Now, the mercenary had Justin pinned to the ground with his fist.

“You would shut your mouth if you knew the foolishness of your words,” Ahlund said. “If you had any idea—”

Zechariah touched Ahlund’s shoulder, interrupting him. “We have a visitor,” he said.

Justin managed to shift his gaze and spotted a cloaked figure on the dock not far away, half-hidden in the shadows. It stepped forward, raised its hands, and drew back the hood. Leah’s black hair fell free. She wore an expression like she’d just been slapped.

Ahlund pulled Justin to his feet but did not let go of his shirt.

“Do not make enemies out of your allies, Justin Holmes,” Ahlund snarled. He shoved Justin hard enough to knock him over, but Zechariah caught him by the shoulders. “You have enough enemies already,” Ahlund added. Then he pulled his hood over his head, turned, and walked past Leah without a glance.

Leah stepped forward.

"I owe you an apology, my dear," said Zechariah. "I should not have kept you in the dark. As for Ahlund, his tenure as your bodyguard, I think, is over. In his heart, Ahlund is still a Ru'Onora. A Guardian of the Oikoumene. His duty is to this world as a whole. He will honor that duty the way he feels is best."

"What do you think that will be?" she asked.

"To keep moving. We must protect Justin from the enemies we encountered on the Gravelands. We'll travel north, across the Raedittean Sea."

"Into Mythaean territory?" said Leah.

"Briefly, yes. Our journeys lie on different paths now, princess. But you still have two capable bodyguards to see you home."

Justin bit his lower lip angrily. He wasn't thinking about future plans. All he could think about was how unfair everyone was being to him, and how disgusting it was, the way they talked about him as if he wasn't standing right there in front of them. He wanted to yell at them, but he couldn't think of anything good to say. The unarticulated frustrations stewed in his gut. Leah was giving him a stupid look, almost like she was disappointed in him for something. Finally, he could take it no longer.

"If you're going to say something, spit it out," Justin snapped at her.

Leah blinked in surprise.

"No?" said Justin. "Then quit staring at me."

She averted her eyes.

Beneath the scrutiny of the wooden idols, Justin followed Zechariah and Leah back to the Brig and up to their room. He lay on the floor, staring at the ceiling, too tired to think, too angry to sleep. After a few minutes, anger gave way to a sinking, debilitating sorrow.

"Everything will be all right," he whispered in the darkness. His mom had always told him that. "Everything will be all. . . ."

Silent tears slid down his cheeks as he prayed, *God, please help me. God. Please.*

They seemed to be the only words he could think of.

CHAPTER 56

"Five hundred," said Gunnar. "That'll get you as far as Matellus."

"Five hundred kreels?" Ahlund replied. "Look at me. Where do you think I would carry that kind of gold?"

"You don't want me to answer that, friend," said Gunnar.

The two men faced each other across a desk in the back room of Gunnar's Brig. The room seemed to be a sort of office, but so much junk lay scattered across the tabletop and floor that Ahlund found it hard to believe that work could be conducted here. The large, feathered hat usually worn on Gunnar Erix Nimbus's head was currently on the desk, sitting on top of some of that junk. His hair, locks of flowing, black curls, rested on his shoulders. A long, curved-stemmed pipe hung from the side of his mouth, unlit, and bobbed up and down when he spoke. His chin was clean-shaven, but his braided mustache nearly reached his chest. He watched Ahlund with a single eye. Where the other eye should have been, there was an eyepatch over a long, jagged scar.

Ahlund had met the man several days ago upon first arriving in Lonn. He was the captain of a fishing vessel and the owner and operator of the Brig. Ahlund had come to know him by reputation as a sort of local celebrity. Discerning folk spoke of him as a liar and a thief. But there was no one in Lonn more experienced at navigating the Greenspring River—and certainly no one with a better boat than the *Gryphon*.

Ahlund remained silent. He knew he didn't need to say anything to progress the conversation. For a man like Gunnar, a man who enjoyed talking, silence would get under his skin more effectively than anything Ahlund could have said—and getting under someone's skin was always good leverage.

Gunnar leaned back in his chair and brought his boots up onto the table, crushing beneath his heels an object that looked like it might have been a music box. He was undeterred by its destruction, however, and said, "Look, I'm simply naming my price. I mean, we're not talking about a hop, skip, and a jump to Castydocia. A trip through the Drekwood ain't my idea of a holiday. I've got other investments. Other fish to fry, literally. Our kitchen is dismally understaffed."

"I'm not paying five hundred," said Ahlund.

"Oh—that's right," said Gunnar, snapping his fingers. "I forgot. There'll be an additional ten-kreel convenience charge for your steeds. And I'll mention this now because I don't want you to be surprised later: I ask for at least three elths a day for their hay and water, plus a small security deposit that will be returned providing their stalls have been thoroughly cleaned at the end of the—"

"No steeds," said Ahlund.

"That's a shame," said Gunnar. "Loyal companions, they are."

"We do not have five hundred kreels," Ahlund said.

Gunnar shrugged. "Well, the weekly game is tonight. Table buy-in is twenty amples, if you care to give luck a shot."

"I don't have time for this," said Ahlund, standing up. "I'm sure I will have no trouble finding someone in the port quarter willing to sail for less than two hundred."

The muscles in Gunnar's jaw tightened a bit, causing the unlit pipe in his teeth to shift. "All right, all right," he said. "Sit back down."

Ahlund remained standing.

"There's something you should know, friend," said Gunnar. "People around here are afraid of the Drekwood. Some go so far as to say it's haunted by souls of the condemned. I don't subscribe to ghost stories, but I do know from experience that you're proposing to go through a dangerous bit of real estate. And you're right—somebody else'll likely brave your nautical misadventure for some quick gold, but have you ever heard the phrase, 'a scholar and a fisherman'? Me neither. My point is, you'll probably find someone to sail for two hundred all right, but your volunteers are apt to be the stupidest sons of mothers in the western world—and me. The difference is, I can get everyone through it alive. And, seeing as you intrigue me, just this once I may be willing to accept twenty percent down now and the remainder on credit."

Ahlund said nothing.

Gunnar stood. The thing under his heels fell to the floor with a dull ringing of broken gears. He smiled widely, revealing several gold teeth amid the genuine ones, and extended his hand.

"To Matellus, then?" he said.

Ahlund, in no mood to argue to the point further, grasped Gunnar's dirty hand. Gunnar pumped his hand enthusiastically.

"Confidentially," said Gunnar. "I'm actually glad you came callin'. Been far too long since I sailed up the East Branch. Far too long since I been away from this town, in fact." He picked up a burning candle from the desk and used it to light his pipe, drawing quick puffs and expelling curls of rich, white smoke until the bowl glowed red. "Fools hootin' and hollarin' over seafood every blessed day. Sometimes this place makes me wanna stick my head in a sack of suckerfish." He took a very long draw on the pipe, savored the smoke, and then let it out in twin trails from his nostrils. "Well, my esteemed financier, when do we shove off?"

"Can you sail by dark?"

"*Tonight*?" Gunnar removed the pipe from his mouth and scratched his forehead with the stem. "Three-quarter moons. Water's high. I suppose providing no clouds roll in, shouldn't be a problem."

"Then we leave at sundown."

"You don't fool around, friend. I like that. I'll prepare my crew and load the ship, and you can go get that down payment in order. Pleasure doing business."

Without another word, Ahlund exited the back room and headed toward the main hall where the others were waiting.

Ahlund knew something wasn't quite right about the bargain he had just struck. Greed alone could not explain why this innkeeper and boat captain—who had taken until midday just to roll out of bed and see to negotiations—would be so willing, almost eager, to accept the credit of a badly dressed, ill-groomed stranger. But no matter. If Gunnar's game was robbing and murdering the passengers, he was in for a surprise.

Ahlund could not stop thinking about his conversation with Kallorn days before. Maybe it had been the long years or the severity of those years, but Kallorn had looked a century old. He had once been a picture of the noble strength of the Ru'Onorath: the Order of the Guardians. Now, his yellow hair was thinning, and his beard, once gold like wheat in autumn, was dull like seared sandstone and streaked with gray. Most telling of all was his posture, hunched as if perpetually at the mercy of some great burden.

I have probably aged far less gracefully, Ahlund thought. Entering the main hall of Gunnar's Brig, he spotted Zechariah. *A pity we cannot all have the powers of the undying. Though the old man may come to regret living long enough to see these times.*

Ahlund knew of the darkness in the east, but he had not expected Kallorn's reports of armies, black fleets, and coblyns on the move. Kallorn had been just as surprised to hear Ahlund's news of daemyn-wielding monsters on the Gravelands.

And all of it, thought Ahlund, *coincides with the arrival of Justin Holmes.*

Ahlund was torn from his thoughts as Zechariah turned toward him. Anxiety was visible on his face. Leah and her soldiers were at a nearby table, drinking tea and looking none the wiser to whatever had the old man so concerned. Their sixth companion was nowhere to be seen.

"Where is Justin?" Ahlund asked.

"That's just it," said Zechariah. "I don't know."

CHAPTER 57

The road north of Lonn left the valley and plunged into a forest of maples and paper birches. It had not taken long for Justin to lose sight of the Greenspring River upon this winding road. A mile or two later, the city of Lonn was shrouded by the forest behind him, and he was officially on his own, with no idea where he was going.

But there's a road, thought Justin. *All roads lead somewhere.*

Fortunately, he was not entirely alone. He had Seabiscuit. He had told the stable boy that a business deal required that he leave ahead of his master, and that Zechariah, still in town, would take care of the stable fee.

Justin heard the quick trampling of hooves racing up the road behind him, and he knew what was coming. He made no effort to flee. He turned Seabiscuit around and waited. The sun reflected brightly off the surrounding birches' white trunks.

A cloud of dust followed Ahlund's black steed. It came to a skidding halt before Justin and Seabiscuit, and for a few long moments, Justin could hardly see Ahlund or his panting steed through the cloud of kicked-up dust. When the dust did settle, Ahlund was staring at him. For a few moments, no one said a word.

"You expect me to do the talking?" Justin finally said.

"You're the one who left," said Ahlund. "I expect an explanation. A defense. Anything but silence."

Justin frowned. "Well, seeing as I've been causing so many inconveniences for you and Zechariah, I figured it might be in everyone's best interest if I just—"

"Shut up," Ahlund said.

"First you tell me to talk, then—"

"Do you have a father?" demanded Ahlund.

Justin's frown softened. "Yeah."

"What do you think he'd say if he saw you now? Running away from your problems. Acting more like a child than a man. Would he be proud of your petulance? Your lack of heart? Would he be proud to call you his son?"

Justin's first instinct was to lash out, but his gaze shortly fell to looking at the dirt. Ahlund had called him a child, and he felt like one. A little kid caught disobeying.

I know things have not been easy, rang his father's words in his head. *But you can't keep doing this. You're not a child, so I can't keep you here, but that doesn't mean you get to storm out of the house every time you get a little upset. Running away like that doesn't work the way you think it does. Your actions have consequences.*

Justin winced. It was the last conversation he'd had with his father—maybe the last he would ever have with him.

"I'm sorry," he said, and he meant it.

"My people, the Ru'Onorath, have a saying," said Ahlund. "'Fear is a wolf, and the coward and the fool are its prey.' What did you hope to accomplish out here?"

Justin shook his head. "I don't know. It just felt good to be acting on my own decision for once instead of being told what to do, I guess. Ever since I got here, I've just felt . . . helpless."

Ahlund made a face.

"I know, I know," said Justin. "It was a stupid thing to do. Can we just forget this ever happened?"

Ahlund said nothing for a moment. Then he said, "There is a second half to the saying. 'The righteous man is a lion. Wolves cannot harm him.' Do not ask for forgiveness for your actions. Change them. Decide who you are. Then act like it."

Justin nodded. "Okay."

"Zechariah said you tried to use a gauge," said Ahlund.

"Um, yeah," said Justin. "But it didn't do anything."

Ahlund fished through his pockets. "He asked me to bring it. So you could try again. If I found you."

Ahlund took out the tiny stone, and it transformed into a swirling torrent of color. It was not blue, as it had been when Zechariah had used it to light their way through the caves. Instead, it was an orange jewel burning with a light so intense that Justin turned away and could still feel its heat from several yards away. But it wasn't physical heat; it soaked through him, warming him to his bones.

Aurym, he thought.

Ahlund let the stone fade back to its natural form, and the warm feeling in Justin subsided.

"New initiates to the Ru'Onorath are accepted during childhood, sometimes at birth," said Ahlund. "They're brought up in the ways of the Guardians to become spirit warriors. We use gauges to determine who possesses the gift."

He handed the stone to Justin.

"I already tried," said Justin. "I can't."

"Try again."

"Aren't you going to tell me how?"

"It doesn't work that way."

"So how does it work?"

"That's what you have to learn."

"Zechariah said something about a spark that I had to—"

"But that didn't work, did it? So try something else."

Justin studied the rock's features, rolled it around in his hand, and shut his eyes. He gripped the stone, thinking about the aurym-heat he had felt, imagining the stone springing to life. He opened his eyes. It was still just a rock.

"Keep it," said Ahlund. "Keep trying. Supposedly, ethouli were strong in aurym power."

"I'm not one of you, though," said Justin. "People in my world can't shoot fire."

Ahlund shrugged. "Will you come back with me?"

"Yeah," said Justin.

Ahlund nodded. "We're sailing north along the Greenspring. If anyone asks, we're on our way to the coastal city of Matellus, but our true destination is an island northwest of Darsida. We're going to Esthean, home of the Guardians. You will be safe there."

"Safe," said Justin. "Right. Look, no matter what happens, no more running away. I promise."

"Good," said Ahlund. "Let's go. We depart tonight."

Ahlund turned his steed and sent it racing back along the road. Justin prodded Seabiscuit's ribs with his heels to follow. The paper birches whizzed past. Justin thought about his father. What was he doing right now? It had been one week since Justin had woken up here. Were the police searching for him? Were they dragging the Allegheny River for his body? What scenarios must be running through his father's mind? And could Ben Holmes survive the heartache of losing his son, so soon after losing his wife?

There's got to be a way home, thought Justin. *There has to be.*

CHAPTER 58

"There you are, boy!" Olorus said. "I owe you a debt, and it was getting warm."

"Huh?" said Justin.

Ahlund watched from the doorway as Justin took a seat across from Olorus. The lieutenant slid a large mug across the table. Justin looked unsure but brought the mug to his lips and tipped it back for a swig. When he lowered it, he wore a face so painfully sour that the dishes rattled with Olorus's laughter.

"That didn't take long," Zechariah said in the old language as he joined Ahlund in the doorway.

"He's weak," Ahlund replied. "Lets his emotions get the better of him."

"Doesn't every boy, at that age?" said Zechariah.

"We'll have to break him of it. It is too dangerous to be tolerated."

"Remember, Ahlund: You Guardians may discourage passion, but it is not inherently a fault. It can lead people to do brave things. Great things above and beyond oneself. . . . Did you tell him?"

Ahlund hesitated. "I mentioned it."

"And?"

"We must get him to Esthean. The Ru'Onorath elders will know what to do."

They have to know what to do, he thought.

"I take it the soldiers do not yet know we are leaving," Ahlund said. "Olorus is far too merry."

"Actually, they do," said Zechariah.

Ahlund frowned.

"You're not going to like it," said Zechariah.

Ahlund waited.

"Leah has *decided*," said Zechariah, "that she is coming with us."

"Where is she?" Ahlund demanded.

"Don't bother," Zechariah said. "I already tried. She's using our voyage across the Raedittean as pretense to join us. She hypothesizes—correctly, I think—that returning to Nolia without an army would be the death of her. She says her father had good relations with some Mythaean nobles. She plans to offer future economic and political assurances in exchange for military aid in reclaiming her throne."

"And you plan to allow this?"

"I was a royal advisor for years," said Zechariah. "Her tactics are sound, and the Mythaeans have the largest standing armies in all of Athacea."

"Because they are constantly at war with themselves."

"True. I doubt that our young princess fully understands the subsequent entanglements she might be getting herself into, but it may be her best chance. And the Mythaeans are greedy. A military investment for future returns would appeal to their avarice." Zechariah paused and stroked his beard. "The leadership of Nolia is far from my utmost concern, but if we can help Leah without going too far out of our way, then what is the harm? I daresay she deserves it."

Ahlund was tempted to agree. Leah had always struck him as too frail for leadership. Too quiet, too humble, and too kind to be put at the helm of a nation. But he had occasionally glimpsed another side of Leah Anavion. Behind the quiet was calculation. Behind the humility was wisdom. And her kindness was not timid; it was merciful and virtuous. She was untested in government, but her birthright demanded her a chance, and Zechariah was right. She did deserve it.

"Besides," added Zechariah. "I cannot think of any way her presence would cause great harm. I warned Justin that deposed royalty would be dangerous, but I do not think that Leah would covet power to the extent that I previously feared."

Ahlund turned and walked away.

"Just where are you off to now?" Zechariah called after him.

Ahlund did not turn back as he said, "To renegotiate our contract. Our number of passengers just doubled."

CHAPTER 59

Justin had not realized how strong his bond with Seabiscuit had become. Until he had to sell him. After the terms of sale had been concluded, he lingered at the stable, stroking Seabiscuit's snout. Steeds would be an unnecessary expense on a boat, Ahlund had said. Since the group already owed Captain Gunnar several hundred *somethings*—it was a form of money Justin had never heard of—the steeds were sold to the Lonn stables.

Coins were counted out by the stable master and given to Zechariah, and Seabiscuit's reins exchanged hands.

"See you, buddy," Justin whispered. "You've been a good steed, all the way back to the Gravelands when I gave you such a hard time not knowing how to ride. You're the only one who hasn't given me grief about anything."

"Come along, Justin," Zechariah said.

Justin scratched Seabiscuit behind the ears one last time. "I hope somebody really nice buys you," he said.

Halfway down the street, he paused to look back. Seabiscuit was watching him go.

The sun was setting on a clear day over Lonn. The two moons were in the three-quarter phase, the bigger one shining bronze and the smaller one almost blue. The distance between them seemed greater than before, and Justin wondered if it changed depending on the cycle of their orbits around the planet—whatever planet this was.

Approaching the docks, Justin spotted Captain Gunnar climbing up the mast of his ship, the *Gryphon*, yelling orders at a crew of four men. The *Gryphon* was a beast of a ship, with a mast so tall and thick that it reminded Justin of the pines in the uncut forests of the Shifting Mountains. Flocks of white gulls and black crows circled, cawing at the sailors. Nearby, Ahlund, Leah, Olorus, and Hook stood around their supplies.

Leah broke off from the group and met Justin and Zechariah.

"May I speak to Justin privately?" she asked Zechariah.

The old man nodded and continued down to the riverfront.

"I hear you're coming with us," said Justin. He paused. "Why?"

"With every transfer of power, there is bloodshed," she said. "I need an army. If that means making a deal with a foreign nation, so be it."

"Do you need to come with us to do that?" said Justin.

"It's mutually beneficial," said Leah. "Our combined efforts—"

"You coming along isn't beneficial to anyone," Justin said.

He said it louder than he meant to, and she winced in surprised.

"Don't you remember those demon things on the Gravelands?" Justin said. "Remember what they did? You heard what Ahlund said. That town at the gate was completely destroyed. And it was all my fault. Everywhere I go, people end up dying. I wish this would all just end so nobody else would have to suffer anymore."

An emotion flashed across Leah's face that Justin couldn't identify. She started to say something, but he cut her off.

"Honestly, what would be beneficial," said Justin, "would be for you to get as far away from me as you can. The more people around me at risk, the greater the burden."

Leah pursed her lips. "Are you finished?" Before Justin could answer, she said, "You think you're the only one who wants it all to end—the only one who thinks things would be better if she'd just never been born?"

Too late, Justin realized his mistake. Leah kept going.

"I remember the Gravelands too, Justin," she said. "I remember them as the place where I watched my own countrymen cut down, run through, beheaded, and burned alive. Men I knew. Men who had wives, sons, daughters, and parents waiting for them to return home. All dead. Because of me. And now, I'm looking for an army to help me invade my own nation, to fight *against* Nolia's native sons. I think I'm doing the right thing. But sometimes, I'm not sure. Olorus and Hook say I am. They would follow me to the ends of the world, and that scares me. It puts a fear in me I can't describe. The only thing that gives me strength is knowing that Asher, the man who killed my family, commandeered my country, and sent so many people to their graves, must be stopped, and only I can do it. The youngest of my brothers was crippled. Did you know that? Did you know that the prime minister of my country had a crippled boy murdered in his sleep? That tyrant rules over my people. I can either leave them at his mercy, or I can attack my own home." She cleared her throat. "I realize you're upset, Justin, but you'll pardon me if I don't pity you for your *burden*. I came over here to tell you that your secret's safe with me. And to apologize for being rude last night."

Justin started to say something but found himself looking at Leah's back as she briskly walked away.

"Well, Justin," Justin whispered to himself, "at least one thing transcends worlds. Even across the unknowable boundaries of space and time, you're still terrible with girls."

Justin made his way abashedly toward the ship. He could see several men out on the river in a small skiff, waiting to extend the boom—a giant, steel chain that was extended and locked across Lonn's harbor every night to prevent ships from entering or leaving. Apparently, Gunnar had used his influence to delay the boom's extension tonight, but the men in the skiff looked impatient. Zechariah, Ahlund, and Leah had boarded the *Gryphon*, but Olorus and Hook were still standing onshore.

"I don't know, but what the princess says *goes*," Olorus was saying as Justin approached.

Hook made some quick signs with his hands, including pressing one hand flat and moving it up and down in flowing, hilly patterns.

"That's the point of the boat," Olorus said. "As long as you're in it, you don't have to know how to swim."

Hook signed quickly and vividly.

"Filthy!" said Olorus. "Do you hug your mother with those hands?"

Justin stepped up the gangplank and tried not to panic at the way it bowed beneath his weight. This would be his first time on a boat, ever. Just one of many recent firsts.

"I want this ship moving!" Gunnar was yelling. He'd climbed back down from the mast and was stomping across the deck. "If we ain't out of this harbor before that boom goes across, someone's arse will get a taste of cold steel!" He paused a moment, scratched his chin, then added loudly, "To clarify, it will not be mine."

The four crewmen hustled with their duties. One of them Justin recognized as the short, round flutist who'd been playing onstage the night before. The other three were dirty, bearded men in ragged clothing, so unsavory that they made Gunnar look like a saint in white robes. Justin tried not to make eye contact with them as he joined Ahlund, Zechariah, and Leah at the bow of the ship. He tried not to look at her, either.

"How long will we be sailing?" Justin asked.

"A few days," answered Zechariah.

Olorus and Hook, having finally made it onboard, approached the company at the bow. Olorus joined them, but Hook kept going and leaned over the side of the ship, his shoulders tense.

"Is he all right?" Leah asked.

"I think so," Olorus whispered. "But he doesn't much care for the captain. He won't say why. I know he hates boats. Might just be nerves." He lowered his voice to an even quieter whisper. "These sailors are in a foul mood. I don't blame them, either. Bad luck to set sail at night."

"Everything else is against us," Zechariah said. "Why not add luck to the list, just for good measure?"

"Your observation is noted, Olorus," said Ahlund. "We'll tread softly with the crew to avoid complications."

"Should we tire of treading softly," said Olorus, "we outnumber them, *and* we are better armed."

"Last resort," said Ahlund.

The one-eyed man named Gunnar sashayed over to them. "A more mismatched troop of brigands, I have never seen," he said, shaking Ahlund's hand. "I ought to have told you to shove off when I still had the chance."

"You'll wish you had, I'm sure," Zechariah said.

Ahlund introduced the passengers, and Gunnar shook hands with each of them—all except Hook, who remained off by himself. Ahlund used everyone's true names except for Leah, whom he introduced as Lee Tensong. Justin didn't know if the false name had been decided upon beforehand or not. Either way, Leah took it in stride.

"Delighted, Miss Tensong," Gunnar said, kissing Leah's hand. "You may well be the first human female to board this ship."

"Human?" Olorus said.

"There have been fish, of course," said Gunnar, "but telling the boys from the girls is no easy trick, so admittedly, that's only a guess." He then marched off, shouting, "All's aboard! Let's shove off!"

Mooring lines were loosed. Long poles were used to push off from the dock, and Justin watched the moonlit waters slide by. The current caught them, and he almost lost his balance as the ship swung in the direction of the Greenspring's flow.

Gunnar hopped across the deck and took a wild leap. For a moment, Justin thought he was going to go flying overboard, but his body stopped in midair when he snatched a hanging line. He hung suspended by one hand, dangling haphazardly over the side of the boat like a monkey on a vine. He removed his great, feathered hat and made a gracious bow toward the men on the skiff with the boom.

"Sorry for the delay, my good fellows!" he yelled. "Your patience is rewarded. Free drinks at the Brig! Tell 'em Gunnar said so!"

"Hear, hear!" one of the men shouted, and the others joined in.

As the ship passed the walls and cleared the end of the harbor, a warm wind hit Justin's face. He closed his eyes, smelling the summer air.

The river narrowed. The *Gryphon*'s speed increased. In the clear sky above, the bronze and blue beacons of the double moons lit the way, and ahead, along the shores of the Greenspring, yellow-green bulbs of fireflies danced between the white birch forest.

CHAPTER 60

His father was driving. His mother was in the front passenger seat. Justin was in the back.

Through streaming trails of rain, a green light shone above them. The wipers swiped the windshield with a dull *thunk-thunk*.

There was no warning except for Justin's mother, Claire Holmes, reaching up to grip the dashboard and saying, "Ben, watch—!"

A loud bang. Gravity changing direction.

The car was rolling. The vehicle's interior seemed to shrink, folded in on itself like a metal accordion. On the second roll, there was a pop, and pieces of broken glass exploded from the window beside Justin. His body became a rag doll carried along by the momentum, and one of his flailing arms slammed against the frame of the broken window beside him. Glass punctured the skin and ground against bone.

Midway through the third roll, while the car was upside down, Ben Holmes's body went through the windshield and disappeared.

Then final roll completed with a violent slam forward. Justin's mother made a surprised, exhaling sort of sound.

CHAPTER 61

Justin sat up in bed, gasping for breath. His room was dark, lit only by slivers of sunlight penetrating the boards in the ceiling. People were talking. Their shadows walked above him. Someone—Gunnar, probably—shouted something and laughed.

Justin ran a hand through his hair. It was the dream again. But this time, for once, he remembered it.

The door to the tiny room swung open without a knock. Light spilled in around the silhouette of an old man in gray robes.

In the blink of an eye, Zechariah leaped across the room, whipped his sword from its sheath, and brought it to Justin's throat.

"I thought I told you to keep your weapon on you at all times," said Zechariah. He gestured to the sword Justin had left propped in the corner. "Across the room isn't close enough."

"It's pretty effective where it is," Justin said. "As a diversion."

Zechariah looked confused. Justin raised the weapon in his hand, the long, single-edged knife called a dirk, and pressed it gently against Zechariah's stomach, just below the ribcage. The old man blinked in surprise. Then he smiled. He removed the sword from Justin's throat and stepped back.

"It seems this time I made the critical error of underestimating my enemy," Zechariah said, sheathing his sword. "We're going ashore for lunch, if you care to join us."

"I'll be there in a minute," said Justin.

Zechariah nodded, smiled again at the dirk, and left the room.

Justin sat quietly, thinking back to the dream—not a dream at all but a memory.

It hadn't been his father's fault. He'd had a green light and was midway through an intersection when the SUV plowed into them, striking the passenger side at full speed. It had been dark and raining, but the SUV had been driving with its headlights off. It would be discovered later that the driver's blood alcohol content was .27.

Justin didn't remember the end of the roll but must have woken up a few times before the paramedics arrived because he did remember the cold, hard rain pelting his face. The next clear memory was being in a hospital bed. They gave him the news about his mother shortly after.

Ben Holmes was a different person after that night—physically, of course, but mentally, too. Before losing his wife, Ben had been ambitious, loud, and kind. His kindness seemed to have intensified after the crash, but the other qualities had all but died out. Before losing the use of his legs, he had exercised every day. He had been a three-sport athlete all through high school and had wrestled the one-sixty-five weight class in college. After dropping out during his sophomore year, he worked at a sawmill in southern Pennsylvania for a few years. He reconnected with his college girlfriend, Claire, now a real estate broker working in her hometown in mid-western Pennsylvania, and they eventually married and had a son. Shortly after moving north to start his new life, Ben took the real estate license exam and became an agent at Claire's firm.

Ben may have never finished college, but in every other way, he was a scholar. He was a voracious reader and a lover of the sciences and philosophy. He loved sports and had been Justin's coach for wrestling, Little League, football, and basketball. As for Claire, she never missed a game. Literally. When Justin thought about it, he could not remember a single match or game when his mother hadn't been there. Always in the stands. Always cheering him on. Before every game, she would tell him, "Winning isn't everything. Remember to have fun. But win if you can, because it's more fun."

As Justin got older—and taller—basketball became his chief athletic endeavor and eventually the focus of his entire life. Basketball was everything. The painted square on the backboard above the garage became worn and faded from ten thousand practice layups and probably twice as many downtown buzzer-beaters to score the winning three points in OT in his imagination. All those were to say nothing of the innumerable games of H.O.R.S.E. Between Justin and Ben over the years—or P.I.G., when pressed for time.

Justin had made the varsity team in ninth grade and was a starter the following year. His junior year, he was the team's leading scorer. College scholarships were a possibility.

Ben was incredibly proud of his son's achievements, but he frequently reminded Justin that athletics and academics were not mutually exclusive. "Use your muscles on the court, but keep your head in your studies," he would say from the front door, calling Justin in from the driveway to do his homework. "Knowledge stays with you. Your body doesn't."

Looking back on it now, those words seemed brutally ironic.

Everything changed after the accident. Justin's father was in a wheelchair. And his mother wouldn't watch from any stands ever again.

By the beginning of his senior season, Justin felt like he had become a completely different person. All passion for athletics was gone. Competition seemed pointless. Winning seemed pointless—*everything* seemed pointless. Friends and adults thought they were motivating him when they said things like, "Your mother loved to watch you play. She would want you to do your best." Or, "Think of your dad! He wants to see you shine now more than ever." Or, "You've gotta give it your all, because she's watching from a different set of bleachers, now." His least favorite was being told that this was "all part of God's plan." Everyone always seemed to think that one was particularly comforting for some reason. But to Justin, it was like he was drowning, and instead of these people jumping in to help him, their solution was to tell him not to worry—it was part of the plan, after all.

A few practices into the season, he had quit the basketball team. Who cared about scholarships? He didn't want to go to college, anyway. What was he supposed to do? Pack up and leave his father all alone? Sure, the Emersons were next door and Uncle Paul and Grandpa came around when they could, but it wouldn't be the same. Justin would be gone, and his dad would be all alone in an empty house with no one to take care of him.

"Don't worry about me," Ben had said once. "I'm tougher than I look, you know. All I want is what's best for you."

Looking around the dark cabin room in the bowels of the *Gryphon*, Justin sighed. For years, he'd worried about doing well enough in basketball and getting good enough grades to get into a good college. His mom had him looking at Ivy League schools. But all the practice, all the stress, all the work—it had all added up to nothing in the end. And despite Justin's best efforts, his father was alone anyway.

He rolled out of bed and gathered up his things, throwing on his shirt and jacket. He attached the basket-hilted sword to his belt. The dirk was sheathed at his calf, and the newest addition to his armory was strapped to his back: the cat's eye sword.

All this just for lunch, he thought. *And somehow, knowing this place, it doesn't seem excessive.*

He stepped into the narrow hallway that ran below the ship's decks. A circular, metal shield hung on the wall, and Justin stopped short at the sight of his reflection in its surface. It had been a long time since he'd seen himself. The boy looking back didn't look much like a boy at all. His face was leaner than it had ever been. His hair was getting long, and a bit of thin facial hair had sprouted around his mouth and chin.

He pulled up his shirt sleeve. A pink, hairless scar ran from his forearm to his bicep—the place where his arm had come down on the line of broken glass framing the car window. He didn't remember how many stitches it had required, but it had been a lot.

The midday sun momentarily blinded him as he emerged on deck. The *Gryphon* was anchored along a sandy shoreline below a hillside covered in birch trees and cedars. The opposite side of the river was made up of wetlands, where the skeletal fingers of drowned, dead pines stood limbless and pallid. Zechariah, Ahlund, and Leah stood conversing on the beach. Olorus and Hook were near the forest line, keeping to themselves. Farther down the beach, tossing gathered wood into a smoking fire, were the *Gryphon*'s crewmen.

"Ahoy, lad!" Gunnar said, hip-deep in the river with a fishing pole in his hand. His single eye looked up at Justin. "Get down here and catch your lunch!"

Justin descended the gangplank to shore. He paused along the riverbank, reached into his jacket, and took out his wallet. His keys, he had recently noticed, were missing, and he suspected they had fallen from his pocket at some point—possibly during a wrestling match with a humongous insect. He wondered if someday someone traveling beneath the Thucymoroi mountains would find them and wonder what magical, ancient mechanism they had powered. His dad's pickup was pretty ancient. But magical? Not so much.

Flipping open his wallet, Justin breathed a laugh at the goofy sixteen-year-old with the crooked smile in the photo on his driver's license. He started to search for Kate's photo but realized he didn't really care. He found himself wishing he carried pictures of his parents instead.

He closed the leather wallet, put it back in his pocket, and took out the only other artifact that remained of his old life. He looked at his asthma inhaler and gave it an experimental shake. It probably had one, maybe two good hits left in it. With a shrug, he swung his arm over his head in a hook-shot, giving the inhaler a toss.

As the little piece of plastic sailed in a high rainbow arc above the river, Justin imagined it as an orange basketball. In his mind's eye, the scoreboard clock flashed to zero. The buzzer went off. The ball passed through the hoop just about as perfectly as any ball ever had.

Teammates jumped in the air. The stands roared. Dad sprinted out onto the court and grabbed him, hugging him, picking him up and hoisting him high above the others. In the stands, Mom had her hands folded over her mouth, barely able to contain her pride.

The inhaler landed in the water with a plop, floated for a second, and sank.

CHAPTER 62

"That boy just don't learn!" called one of Gunnar's crew.

"Gettin' a smart lickin'!" another taunted. "Hey boy, yer bleedin'!"

Justin got back up, ignoring the comments and the blood running over his eyebrows. Zechariah rushed him, attacking high. Justin blocked. The sound of scraping metal lit up the air, and they broke apart.

For a while, Justin had fished with Gunnar and his crew in the river's shallows. He had always liked fishing when he was a child, and today, he managed to stay on pace with Gunnar and the sailors, landing four small, blue-gray trout. His friends had only watched from a distance.

Justin found that he enjoyed the sailors' company. They passed the time by telling stories that seemed to consist entirely of two subjects: fish, and water creatures that were not fish. Among other things, he had learned that an *eachy* was a giant, slimy sea serpent that lived not in the sea but in the Greenspring River. At least, that was what the sailors seemed to think.

He'd eaten lunch with the sailors instead of with his friends. They ate separately, though they did not seem to mind accepting the freshly caught fish that Gunnar offered them. As soon as Justin finished his meal, however, Zechariah approached and told him it was time for more practice with his sword.

Justin feinted left, then hacked to the right. Zechariah blocked easily with one hand and hit him over the head with a closed fist. Gunnar and his crew laughed loudly.

Justin was gaining confidence with a sword, but the better he got, the harder Zechariah was on him. Every error was penalized with a lump—much to the sailors' delight. He certainly hadn't expected to be the after-dinner entertainment, but, knowing the old man, the humiliation was probably an auxiliary lesson.

Justin pretended to be injured from the blow, purposefully leaving himself defenseless; there was nothing Zechariah enjoyed more than punishing a mistake. When Zechariah came at him, Justin sprang and stabbed with his blade. The surprise showed on Zechariah's face as he blocked the attack. He still managed to shoot his leg out, tripping Justin by the ankle and sending him rolling across the sand.

Justin stood and adjusted his grip beneath the basket-hilt, preparing to charge.

"That will do, for now," Zechariah said.

Justin knew better than to let his guard down. He didn't relax his stance until Zechariah turned away. Only then did he sheathe his sword and wipe the blood from his eyes.

"Not bad," said Olorus as he and Hook stepped up beside him. The lieutenant looked appraisingly at the split skin near the crown of Justin's head. "At the very least, you're learning how to take a beating."

Justin cracked a smile. Olorus grinned and slapped him on the back. Hook offered him a canteen, and Justin took it and made the sign with his hands that he had learned meant "Thank you." Hook's eyes lit up. He responded with the sign that meant "You're welcome."

Justin was in the middle of taking a drink when Leah approached. Without a word, she stood on her tip-toes to examine the wound on his head.

"You don't have to," said Justin awkwardly, bending down so that she could reach his head.

She paid him no mind. She parted his hair with her fingers and touched the injury. He felt the odd tugging sensation of his skin crawling. Soon, the pain of the cut subsided, and she walked away. He reached up to his head, touching the spot. Some of the blood was still wet, but the skin was closed, fully healed.

"Thanks," he called after her, but she did not even turn around. She had not spoken a word to him since their confrontation at the docks. He didn't blame her.

Justin handed the canteen back to Hook and said, "I'm going to wash up."

At the river's sandy bank, he knelt and splashed his face and forehead. An unexpected smile tugged at his lips as the water turned red with his blood.

"Boy."

Justin turned to find Ahlund standing behind him. His approach had been silent.

"Have you tried the stone again?" Ahlund asked.

"The stone?" said Justin. "Oh, the gauge. Not since you gave it to me."

"Try it again," Ahlund said. "You need to practice every day."

"Okay," said Justin, "but, like I said, where I come from, the average person can't shoot fire."

"Where I come from, the average person can't do such things, either," said Ahlund. "I am not average. And neither are you."

Ahlund handed Justin his cat's eye claymore. Justin had given it to him for safekeeping while he sparred.

"One other thing," said Ahlund. "We are approaching a forest. The Lonn people call it the Drekwood. It is a place of daemyn energy."

"Daemyn?" said Justin as he strapped the claymore to his back. "I remember Zechariah using that word. He said it was an evil version of aurym."

"Something like that. Fire has water. Birth has death. Good has evil. Aurym has daemyn."

"So, can people use daemyn, too?"

Ahlund gave him a look. "No, Justin. People cannot *use* evil. It is evil that uses people. Daemyn has a will of its own. It has wants. It seeks to manipulate. Even if a person's intentions are good, anyone who seeks to use daemyn becomes a slave to evil. The Drekwood's life force is a twisted, deformed shadow. Daemyn energies feed the very roots of the trees. Such places are breeding grounds for coblyns."

An involuntary shiver tingled Justin's spine as he thought of the creatures he had seen crossing the river south of Lonn. Child-sized demon monsters with mummified, blackened flesh, who fed on the living innards of their prey to absorb their life energies.

"There is a duality within the human soul," said Ahlund. "Increased familiarity and sensitivity to aurym will amplify a person's sensitivity to both sides of the energy."

Justin cocked an eyebrow. "What does that mean?"

"When a person first begins to understand aurym and realize his own potential, his heart will desire to do good. But the more a person becomes one with aurym, the more daemyn will seek to corrupt him. The closer you get to the light, the more the darkness wants you. Temptations become stronger. Evil draws nearer. An invisible war is waged within the soul. As the Ru'Onorath proverb goes, 'Bright light casts deep shadows.' It is not enough to simply train your body. Being quick on your feet and sure with a blade will not save you from every foe. It is not even enough to train your mind. You must also train your spirit."

With two fingers, Ahlund touched his head, then his shoulder, and then the center of his chest, saying, "Mind, body, spirit. A true warrior holds them in balance."

Justin was about to say something but was distracted by raised voices. He and Ahlund turned toward the source.

Having missed the setup to the situation, Justin wondered how Hook had found himself sitting alone in the center of the four sailors. They stood over him, speaking to one another in jeering, bullying tones.

"Don't got the look of a western man, do he?" said one.

"Eyes set all apart like a bloody islander," said another.

"You an islander, boy?" asked the short, fat man.

Hook, of course, said nothing. He was peeling an apple with his knife, giving the process his utmost attention.

"Can't ye talk, lad?" someone said.

Anger began to boil up within Justin. He looked toward Olorus some distance away and wondered why the lieutenant didn't intervene or say something on his friend's behalf. He was just standing there, watching . . . and smiling.

"Crab's got his tongue, I guess," said a sailor. "Thinks he's some kinda pirate with that bandana."

The short, fat sailor leaned forward, reaching for the strip of cloth Hook always wore tied around his forehead. "Why don't ye let a real sailor wear that, boy? You can have it back if—"

One instant, Hook was sitting on the ground with the fat sailor leaning over him. The next, the sailor was on his knees, and Hook stood behind him, his left arm wrapped around the sailor's neck in a chokehold. In one hand, Hook held his knife, the tip of the blade pressed against the sailor's chubby cheek just below his eyeball. In the other, he held the apple.

"What the—?" the sailor said. He tried to pull free, but Hook stepped into the back of his knee, pinning him to the ground and making him holler.

Justin grabbed his sword, counting the number of steps it would take to put himself between the sailors and Leah. Ahlund's hand was on his sword's hilt, and smoke rose threateningly from the sheath. Zechariah's sword was already drawn and at the ready. Gunnar stood on the balls of his feet, trying to look everywhere at once.

Suddenly, Olorus started laughing. It started low and grew to a belly laugh. Then he bent over, slapping his knee.

"Just what is so funny?" Gunnar demanded.

"Your first mate's not the first person to learn the hard way," Olorus said, "that you ought never try to touch that piece of cloth on Hook's head. If you're lucky, he'll just kill you." Olorus laughed even harder. "But if he's feeling inventive, he'll make a right fool out of you first!"

"I—I meant no. . . ." stammered the fat sailor. "I didn't mean to—*ack*!"

His voice was abruptly cut off with a sickening, wet crunch.

The sailors gasped. Justin drew his sword, readying himself for all-out war.

Hook released his captive, and to Justin's surprise, the fat sailor stumbled forward and got unsurely to his feet, looking dumbfounded to be alive. Hook's half-peeled apple had been jammed into his open mouth, and there it was stuck, giving him the appearance of a wide-eyed, roasted pig in a shirt and pants.

The display was too much for Olorus. He fell backward and landed on his rear, laughing harder than ever. Hook stood with a smile, twirling the knife between his fingers.

Gunnar puffed out a sigh that flapped his braided mustache. "Somebody get me something to calm me bleedin' nerves. Where's the wineskin? A flask? Anything."

The fat sailor indignantly spat the apple into the sand. He looked down at it, reconsidered, then picked it back up and took a bite.

CHAPTER 63

"I'm afraid you've lost me again."

Justin sighed. "The object is to get the most points, and every time the ball goes in the basket, it's two points."

Olorus scratched his head. "And it takes ten people to do this?"

The *Gryphon* floated down the Greenspring. The sailors had brought out a table and a deck of cards, and Hook had accepted a challenge from one of the sailors—a stringy fellow named Vick. Justin, Olorus, and two of the other sailors stood together, watching the game. Justin had commented that he was better at athletic games than card games, and Olorus had said he was the same way. As a result, their conversation had regrettably devolved into a crash course on the rudiments of Justin's favorite sport.

"There's a basket on each end of the court," Justin said. "One team of five is trying to score in one basket, and another team of five is trying to score in the other."

"It seems like it would go faster if they both used both baskets," said Olorus.

"No, no," said Justin. "Because while one team tries to put the ball in the basket, the other team has to try to stop them. And if they steal the ball, they can put it in their basket to get two points."

"Where is this peculiar contest waged?" Olorus asked. "And for what purpose must the contenders be continuously slobbering?"

"*Dribbling* just means that if you have possession of the ball, you can only take a step if you keep bouncing it at all times."

"And you say grown men play this game?" said Olorus.

Justin decided to drop the subject.

The Greenspring wound its way through woods teeming with wildlife. Many of the animals, Justin recognized: woodpeckers, deer, squirrels. But for every one he knew, there were three he had never seen or heard of before. Upon mentioning this to Zechariah, the old man gladly took to describing them in greater detail than was really necessary. There were furry animals swimming in the water called lavellans, aquatic rodents with a poisonous bite. Along the shoreline, feasting on an unlucky crayfish, was a mammal that seemed to be half raccoon and half dog, which Zechariah called a magnut. But perhaps strangest of all had been when Justin had spotted movement amid the marshes on the eastern shore. To his astonishment, he realized it was a furry, hippo-like head sticking out of the water to nibble on reeds. It was, Zechariah had informed him, a bowtooth: a giant, hairy, four-legged water-dwelling mammal. Justin hadn't seen any large predators yet. He was hoping not to.

"That smarts!"

The exclamation came from one of the spectators of the card game in response to a move Hook had made, apparently sealing his victory. It was hard for Justin to tell, though; he couldn't read the numbers on the cards.

"What's happened, Vick, you roll over?" asked one onlooker. His name was Borris, and his scraggly beard only partially hid a facial scar that had healed badly, fusing his lips together on one side and forcing him to talk out of the side of his mouth.

Vick, the skinny sailor at the table, threw his cards down. "Just as well. If I don't lose now and again, I start to suspect me-self of cheatin'."

"Hey, boy!"

Justin turned his attention to the short, fat member of the crew named Pool, the one Hook had thoroughly embarrassed hours before.

"How you feel?" said Pool. "I bet yer one big bruise!"

"Huh?" said Justin.

"He don't even remember!" Pool said, laughing.

"Understand, gentlemen," Olorus said, taking Vick's place at the table to play against Hook. "Once you take so many beatings, they start to blend together."

"Oh, that," said Justin.

"Old man whooped you somethin' fierce," Vick said.

"Why didn't you lie down?" asked Borris.

Justin shrugged. "I've tried playing dead, but he just hits harder."

The crew laughed, and Justin was glad to see that there was no lingering enmity among them. Hook and Pool's confrontation seemed to have been forgotten—Pool perhaps being sufficiently put in his place, and Hook not one to hold a grudge. Such was the way among soldiers and sailors, Justin supposed, that squabbles and aggressions were as common as they were quickly forgotten. It had been a fight, nothing more. Justin remembered a time when he would have cowered from such violence, but having seen the gore and terror of real battle, a good, clean fight seemed not such a bad thing anymore.

Justin's gaze wandered upward, to where Gunnar hung on the mast. The captain had a habit of swinging around the top of the ship, barking occasional orders to the helmsman: a little gent with white, wispy hair named Samuel. "Steady as she goes!" Gunnar would say. Or, "Take her wide!" Or, "Mind those rocks!"

Justin watched Gunnar hanging from a rope by one hand and twirling his braided mustache as he surveyed the river ahead. Zechariah had told Justin never to trust a person implicitly, but to first entertain doubt so as to gain insight. At the time, it had sounded borderline sociopathic, but the old man had a point. And after Justin's discussion with Ahlund on the road north of Lonn, he had quietly resolved to think a little harder before he acted—and to learn as much about this place as possible.

"Can I ask you guys something?" Justin said, gesturing to Gunnar. "Who is he?"

"The cap'n?" said Borris. "He's Gunnar Erix Nimbus!"

"I know. But who is he really? He's not from Lonn, is he?"

"No, no, no," Pool said. "Came from the far east. Magician, don't you know."

"You're mistaken," Vick said. "From his own mouth, he told me he was once a knight in the Zorothin cavalry. Stole a bundle of gold from the king himself and fled west to become a riverboat captain."

"Wasn't no knight!" said Borris in his half-mumbling lisp. "Got royal blood, he does! Men fought *for* 'im. He wasn't a king, but near it, I believe."

"Wait a minute!" Olorus said. "You mean to tell me not one of you knows who he is?"

"Course we know who he is!" Borris objected, looking a little hurt. He straightened up haughtily and said, "He's the captain."

The others agreed.

"Magician," Olorus scoffed, slapping a card down on the table.

"I tell you, he knows magic!" said Pool. "Has himself a little garden—"

"If you *must* know," came Gunnar's voice from above.

All turned their attention to where the captain hung from the mast, his black locks unfurled in the wind.

"I was born at sea!" he said. "When I's no more than a week old, the ship wrecked, and an otter carried me up the Greenspring. Dropped me as a baby in the middle of the Drekwood where a pack of wolves took me in as their own. I suckled wild wolf-mother's milk—only till me teeth came in, of course—then ate nothin' but raw ursushound livers till I grew to manhood. Built this ship with me bare hands out of Drekwood trees and spit-shined her buxom hull every blessed morning. Been sailin' the world ever since." He twirled one end of his mustache. "'Tis a rags-to-riches sort of story, you might say."

For a few odd seconds, the only sound was the river water lapping against the ship's hull. Then Pool clutched his round belly and roared back in heavy guffaws. Vick and Borris joined in, and at the helm, wispy-haired Samuel shook with silent laughter.

"Raised by wolves, he says!" Borris squeaked between chuckles.

From the mast, a toothy grin spread across Gunnar's face. He removed his hat, threw his head to the sky, and howled high and long like a wolf. "Ah-*ooooo*!"

It was too much for Pool, who turned red, tears spilling down his chubby cheeks. Borris slapped Justin on the back and leaned on him for support.

"Put the kettle on, momma!" Gunnar screamed into the air. "Your baby boy's comin' home! Ah-*ooooo*!"

The display was so distracting that Justin hardly noticed as the *Gryphon* took a fork in the river, toward a place where the trees grew thick, dark, and shadowed. At the bow of the ship, Ahlund and Zechariah were not laughing.

Part VI

PEEL THE PAINT

CHAPTER 64

Ahlund Sims's lip curled at the sight of the Drekwood.

Twin moons glowed overhead, and tiny licks of moonlight reflected off the lapping waters of the Greenspring. Grass along the banks swayed in the night breeze. But ahead, the river disappeared into a tangled mass of darkness. The passage into the Drekwood was so choked with trees that the Greenspring seemed to enter the forest by way of a narrow, dark tunnel.

The low groans of the *Gryphon*'s wooden joints echoed over the river and bounced back from ancient, black trees. Black vines hung like disemboweled entrails, some so long that they floated on the water's surface.

The gate of the underworld itself must be more inviting than this infernal portal, thought Ahlund.

Common folk were right to fear this place. Ahlund could feel its presence crawling within him, sending shoots of darkness slithering into his soul. It put an ache in his head and a nausea in his stomach. But to bypass these woods would have added several days to their journey. Too much time. Every moment wasted was an advantage to the enemy. Ahlund and Zechariah had agreed that they would rather brave the Drekwood than risk the evils pursuing them.

"A terrible thing," Zechariah whispered beside Ahlund. "It is like an infectious boil. A blight upon nature."

"Daemyn craves that which it cannot have," Ahlund said. "It hungers for the purest aurym most of all. That makes you and me the most susceptible. Leah's aurym has practical applications but is not overly powerful. Daemyn will ignore her, I think. Everyone else should be fine. But that won't save us from anything that chooses to make this place its home."

"Our captain seems oblivious to the danger."

"He is also a wielder of aurym."

"Him?" said Zechariah. "That fisherman?"

Zechariah threw a glance over his shoulder at Gunnar on the wheel, steering the *Gryphon* toward the Drekwood, swaying with the movements of the ship. The others—the sailors, Justin, Leah, Olorus, and Hook—were sleeping below deck.

Zechariah shook his head. "I don't sense anything in him."

"I did not either, at first," said Ahlund. "He hides it well."

"Why would he hide it?" asked Zechariah.

"A very good question," said Ahlund.

"Fair weather for a funeral!" Gunnar suddenly called down from the helm. "May as well have a batch of them, don't you think?"

The offhanded comment rubbed Zechariah the wrong way. He turned to face the captain, snapping, "Do you have any idea what this place is? Have you really traveled through it before?"

"It's a den of daemyn, my elderly friend," said Gunnar. "Nesting place for coblyns, revenants, lost souls, and any other hocus pocus the locals can dream up. And, hell yes, I've traveled through here. It's a nice little pick-me-up anytime the fish ain't biting. . . . Here we go."

The river narrowed. Its pace quickened. And the *Gryphon* slipped into the gaping maw of the Drekwood. The air thickened around Ahlund like congealing blood. Hanging vines dragged over the ship, leaving slimy trails across the decks. One brushed against Zechariah's robes and seemed to curl lovingly at the touch.

Warped, tangled trees walled the river's banks. Arthritic fingers of branches intertwined with one another, forming a thick, unbroken ceiling over the *Gryphon*. If the river had been any higher, the main mast might have scraped the canopy.

A baritone, predatory howl echoed through the darkness.

"Hark! A homecoming!" Gunnar said, cupping his ear. "For little old me? Such dears!"

"You're mad," said Zechariah.

A small oil lamp hung at the helm, and Gunnar turned it to full brightness, illuminating the wild look in his lone eye. "Gunnar Erix Nimbus, they call me," he said. "Though 'Mad' was me mum's maiden name, rest her soul."

Ahlund watched the banks. Worse things than wolves lived in these woods. Ursushounds. Hyaenodons. Coblyns.

Ahlund's attention was torn away from the banks at the patter of footfalls below deck. Up the stairs they came, and Leah burst from the doorway and ran to Zechariah.

"Something's wrong with Justin!" she breathed.

Zechariah looked sharply at Ahlund.

"Check him," Ahlund said. "I'll keep watch."

Leah and Zechariah hurried through the doorway and below deck.

"I've heard it said that those endowed with the magics can be sensitive to this place," Gunnar said, leaning casually on the wheel and cleaning his fingernails.

Ahlund looked at him.

Gunnar shrugged. "Heard it said, is all. What would a fisherman know of such things?"

"Just steer the damn ship," said Ahlund.

Gunnar appeared unsurprised when Ahlund drew his sword, called on aurym, and set its blade glowing red hot. Ahlund used the burning blade to start lighting the lamps hanging on the *Gryphon*'s railings.

CHAPTER 65

Leah held her palm against Justin's forehead. He lay in his cot. His pale, cold skin was slick with sweat, and he breathed in shuddering, arrhythmic gasps. His eyelids quivered with rapid movement. She touched his chest. His heart was pounding.

Olorus and Hook stood grim-faced at the boy's bedside. In the doorway, Samuel, Borris, Vick, and Pool were huddled together, growing uneasier by the second. Justin's yelling had woken them all. He had been tossing and shouting as if caught in a nightmare, but try as they might, no one could seem to wake him.

Leah gritted her teeth and extended her reach, feeding yet more aurym through the aurstone in the ring on her finger. With the power of the spirit, she reached inward, sifting through Justin's physiology.

"He isn't injured," she said. "And I can't find any sickness or poison in him."

Zechariah used a finger to pull open one of Justin's eyelids. As Zechariah leaned in to listen to his breath, a sick, wet moan escaped Justin's lips followed by a string of gibberish muttered in a voice that did not sound like his own.

Hook placed a comforting hand on Leah's shoulder, but it only startled her.

Justin turned toward Zechariah. His lips peeled back, and more nonsense syllables rose in his throat. Leah saw a flash of emotion cross Zechariah's face: recognition.

Not nonsense, Leah realized. *Another language.*

"Is he . . . talking?" she said.

"Leah," Zechariah said. "Please tell Ahlund to come down here."

"What can we do?" said Olorus.

"Take the crew and guard the decks," said Zechariah.

"Guard them from what?" asked Olorus.

Zechariah didn't even look at him. "Now, please."

Olorus and Hook exited the room, and the sailors were more than happy to follow. Leah followed as well but paused to look back. The old man was mumbling something back to Justin—speaking in the same language that had come from the boy's mouth.

Olorus was waiting for her in the hallway with his spear and shield in hand. They walked wordlessly down the hall and up to the top of the stairs. The *Gryphon*'s sailors stood frozen in fear at sight of the Drekwood, blocking the way to the deck. Olorus pushed them aside to clear a path.

Ahlund stood near the prow, looking out over the river with his sword alight.

"Ahlund!" Leah said, jogging to him. "Zechariah needs you."

Ahlund sheathed his sword. Smoke rising from the sheath stung Leah's nostrils. "Stay here with the soldiers," he said. Without waiting for a response, he crossed the ship in a few long-legged strides and ducked through the doorway below deck.

An animal's call echoed in the distance, and an answering shriek resounded from the underbrush just a stone's throw from the *Gryphon*.

"We—we're in the Drekwood, ain't we?" the sailor named Vick said. He had a long knife in his hand, but his feet were rooted to the deck.

"More foul'n I ever imagined," Borris said from the side of his mouth.

Without warning, Olorus beat his spear against his shield with a clang, jolting them all to attention.

"Spread out!" he barked even louder than the clang of the shield. "A lot of good you'll do huddled together like kittens. You, get on the stern! You, patrol aft! You, hold that weapon like you mean it!"

The sailors, visibly shaking, rushed to comply. Their weapons were the ramshackle tools of highwaymen. Vick gripped his knife's handle with two hands. Samuel had a hatchet. Pool had a blunt mace. Borris had two-thirds of a broken, rusty old sword.

"Steady, lads," Gunnar said from the helm. "It's a two-day trip to the other side. No use jumping at shadows and bird calls. Keep this up, and the stress is gonna kill ya 'fore anything with teeth gets the chance."

Leah swallowed hard. The captain's words did little to calm her nerves.

CHAPTER 66

"I've never seen this before," Ahlund said.

Justin arched his back, tossed his head, and gargled. Ahlund quickly turned him sideways, allowing vomit to spill from his mouth to the cabin floor. Zechariah wiped his lips with a rag.

"I don't understand," said Zechariah. "What's happening to him?"

"Daemyn," said Ahlund. "Something's gotten hold of his spirit. During Ru'Onorath training, some of our tests involve deliberate exposure to daemyn, to teach the trainee to defend against it. Students who fail the test sometimes lapse into a state of delirium a bit like this. But I've never seen it so severe."

"Delirium?" said Zechariah. "Look at the boy. He is dying."

"He *will* die if we don't break its hold on him," said Ahlund. "There was an herb that the elders sometimes administered in these cases. Grilcin. It's medicinal. Maybe Leah carries some. Otherwise, we'll have to turn around and row back upstream; the closer it is in proximity, the more easily he will be to control."

Justin moaned long and low. Zechariah squeezed the boy's hand. "Go," he said. "I'll watch him."

Ahlund exited the cabin, and his swift emergence back on deck startled Borris so badly that he dropped his two-thirds of a sword. It clattered to the floor, prompting a vulgar comment from Olorus about slippery hands.

"Leah," Ahlund said. "We need grilcin."

Leah removed the leather pack from her belt and began rooting through it. It was filled with glass vials containing seeds, dried leaves, nuts, berries, nectars, and powders.

"Grilcin's a hallucinogen," she said. "It's not really the sort of thing you carry in a field kit. I may have something here that could mimic its properties, but I've only ever heard of grilcin being used in surgeries—"

"You're forgetting its recreational potential!" Gunnar spoke up from nearby. "I don't reckon you'll find any growing along the riverbanks, but if you do, save me a pinch, won't you—?"

"We've got a sick man below deck," Ahlund said, raising his voice over Gunnar's. "Your crew had better know how to row because we're turning back. Now."

"There'll be a surcharge for that," said Gunnar.

Leah, who had emptied her entire bag on the deck to search through it, shrugged and said, "I'm sorry."

"It was worth a try," said Ahlund. "If we turn back now, Justin may survive."

"May survive?" said Leah. "By the spirit. . . ."

"Grilcin, you said?" Gunnar called over. "Might be that I've got some."

Ahlund turned. Again, Gunnar was casually cleaning his fingernails. For someone so generally foul, he did that an awful lot.

"You do?" Leah said.

"I don't say I do," said Gunnar. "But I might, for the right price."

Leah sneered. "Do you realize Justin could die, you son of a—?"

"What price?" said Ahlund.

Gunnar seemed to think hard about it. He was steering the ship with his pinky finger. "Well, I couldn't help but notice the boy's sword."

"A sword?" said Leah. "For a plant?"

"Aye, but what a dear plant it is at a time like this!" said Gunnar. "Need determines value, Miss Tensong. Supply and demand. Basic economics."

"We have swords," said Ahlund. "We'll find you one."

Gunnar grinned, flashing his gold tooth. "But you know the one I mean."

Ahlund's jaw clenched. Justin's cat's eye sword—forged with a'thri'ik shards in the blade. That treasure was not one to be bartered away on a whim. At what point Gunnar had noticed it or how he'd realized its value, Ahlund didn't know.

"Or if that's not an option," said Gunnar, "I'd be willing to consider *your* sword, Sims."

This time, Gunnar's smile stretched so far that it tugged at his eyepatch.

"You'll have my sword," Ahlund said, "when I sheath it in your pelvis."

Gunnar laughed. "I'm sure that would make you feel better, but it won't help the boy much. If we can't agree on a deal, I'll simply turn us around, and we'll start doing a little hard rowing and a lot of hard praying."

Ahlund stared Gunnar down. The man didn't budge.

"The boy's sword is yours," said Ahlund.

"Deal," said Gunnar. "Vick, take the wheel, will you?"

With Vick at the helm, Gunnar sidled to Ahlund and extended his hand. When Ahlund refused to shake it, Gunnar said, "O—kay. A verbal contract, then. Follow me to my garden."

Gunnar turned and walked the opposite direction.

Leah looked at Ahlund incredulously. "Garden?" she said.

On the lower deck, Gunnar stopped before a giant crate, unlocked it with a key hanging from his neck, and threw back the lid with a thud, revealing a folding, multi-layered case. The interior was sectioned off into hundreds of compartments, each with a tiny label to identify its contents. Every last one of the compartments contained plant specimens in vials, like those in Leah's field kit.

"This is no garden," said Leah. "You're a healer, aren't you?"

"Sometimes, I guess," Gunnar said. He ran his finger across the rows, muttering, "Grilcin, grilcin, grilcin. Ah! Here we are!"

He pulled out a vial and gave it a shake. It must have contained over a hundred seeds. He undid the cork, carefully withdrew one seed, as tiny as the head of a pin, and presented it to Ahlund.

"There," Gunnar said. "Grilcin."

"The seed is worthless," said Ahlund with a sneer. "We need the plant. Its leaves."

Ahlund started to turn away, but Gunnar grabbed him by the shoulder. Ahlund's arm twitched, but he forced himself to resist the reflex to snap the captain's wrist.

"Patience is a virtue," said Gunnar, holding the seed in his calloused, scarred palm. "Any good gardener knows that."

He brought his opposite hand down over his palm.

"All good things come with time," he said, "and just a little tender care."

He removed his hand, and Leah gasped. The seed had split open. A stalk had grown up his finger. It circled his knuckle and ended at a blue flower wreathed in a tuft of leaves. There was no soil; fine strands of roots spider-webbed across his hand as if trying to anchor into his skin.

CHAPTER 67

I want to go home, thought Justin as vomit bubbled at the top of his throat. High on the wall, a clock with symbols he did not recognize ticked out its heartbeats. He looked around the kitchen at the woodwork, the mounted antlers, the diamond-shaped window pane in the front door. He felt sick, and he was having a hard time remembering how he'd gotten here, wherever here was. *I shouldn't be here. But where should I be?*

A boat. For some reason.

He was thinking of a boat.

A model ship. A door opened, and out stepped an old man with a white beard, dressed in gray robes. "Justin Holmes?" he asked.

On the first attempt, Justin's mouth was too dry to speak. He licked his lips, tried again, and managed to say, "Yes."

The old man smiled. "I've been expecting you. I imagine you are confused and maybe even a bit scared right now. Don't worry. I can help."

Justin faltered. He couldn't remember why he was here. He didn't even know this person.

The old man seemed to sense his apprehension. "You've been listening to deceivers, Justin Holmes," he said. "They were trying to take you away. To a place where you would never see home again. But you can go home now."

It was hard to remember, but Justin felt certain it had been a very long time since he had been home. "But where—?" he said.

"There is a door," said the old man. "I will take you to it, but it will require hard work, determination, and trust."

Justin craned his neck, trying to look into the adjoining room where the old man had come from, but the door slammed violently shut, making him jump. He flinched in surprise. Had the old man even touched it? "Come with me," the old man said, "and all will be explained." The old man extended his hand. Justin stared at it. He couldn't remember the old man's name but was too embarrassed to ask at this point. He took his hand, and they walked to the front door. They left the house, and the air was bitterly cold. They were in a mountain village. Bald-headed men in furs roamed the town with bows and quivers on their shoulders. Women with babies strapped to their backs sat scraping animal hides. A thin layer of snow like butter scraped over bread covered everything, even the men's bald heads, and little flakes fell from the gray sky. All around loomed mountain peaks. Justin felt sure he had seen this place before, maybe in a dream. The trouble was, he couldn't remember if it was a good dream or a bad one. They shared a hut with a dark-haired woman and two soldiers. Justin sparred with the old man using sticks as swords so he could learn how to fight. When he got hurt, the woman healed his wounds. They left in the night and found a burrow that led deep underground. Cave beasts tried to hurt them, but the soldiers were fierce and kept them safe. Time slithered tangentially. The world swirled with mist, and everything seemed shrouded by a dark pall, persistently limiting visibility. Justin inquired about this, and the old man answered, "Can you not tell that you are in a dream? This is only a dream world in which you have become trapped. The creations of this place want to keep you here, to use you for their own gain, to keep you from waking. This world is an illusion. That is why I will help you escape. But first, we must find the man with the crown." Justin went on to ask about this as well, but the old man would reveal nothing further on the subject. All he said was, "I told you this process would require trust."

Trusting him was not easy.

There was . . . something . . . foul about the old man.

Something Justin only noticed if he paid very close attention.

Sometimes.

His eyes weren't the right color.

Or the edges of his cloak faded to black when they should have been gray.

As soon as Justin noticed these things, they always changed back.

On the third day in the caves, they reached a crossroads.

Justin found himself leading the procession—he knew the way because he had been here and done this before—and he took the path that led right.

"Stop," said the old man. "You are going the wrong way."

"No, I'm not," Justin said. "This is the way."

The old man looked confused in the blue light of his glowing stone. "You continually doubt me, even after I have seen you through all sorts of dangers and hardships. Don't you understand that this world is trying to trick you? Down that path is a cage you will be locked in forever. Come this way."

Justin would not move. The path to the right did seem darker and more menacing, but he knew it was the correct way.

"Justin is right!" yelled the soldier with the red beard. "Why do you try to mislead us, old man?"

The dark-haired woman drew her sword and said, "Justin, you will take the path to the right!"

The second soldier, the man with the strip of cloth tied over his forehead, threw his spear at the old man. It hit the old man in the leg, and he fell with red blood squirting from the wound.

"*Stop!*" Justin yelled.

The soldier with the strip of cloth jumped on the old man, but the old man threw him off and managed to stand. The bearded soldier and the dark-haired woman had murder in their eyes. They were coming for Justin.

"I don't want to fight you!" Justin pleaded as he drew his sword. "Please, don't!"

The dark-haired woman raised her sword to strike. Justin dropped his sword and put his hands up. He would rather die than fight a friend. He braced himself for the impact.

The old man raised his hand. A bolt of purple electricity shot from his palm. It sizzled through the cave air, hit the woman in the hand, and sent her sword cartwheeling through the air. She clutched her hair and wailed in fury. The bearded soldier advanced on Justin, and the old man shot another bolt that picked the soldier up off the ground and slammed his back against the cave ceiling.

"Run, Justin!" yelled the old man, pointing down the left branch of the cave.

The woman and the silent soldier pounced on the old man. With inhuman strength, they drove him to the ground, plunged their hands into his body, and tore through his flesh with their teeth. Through the screams, Justin thought he could hear the old man saying, "Run! Hurry!"

Justin could hardly move, but he forced himself to do as the old man said. He sprinted up the left branch of the cave.

CHAPTER 68

The stone floor turned into a staircase, and he raced up the steps without looking back. He could still hear the old man screaming when he reached the top of the stairs and arrived at a heavy door trimmed with gold. Justin threw the door open and shut it behind him.

"Not everything is as it seems, is it?"

Justin wheeled toward the voice. A man stood before him. He was dressed in ceremonial steel armor colored scarlet and white, trimmed with glistening silver. The armor's shoulder-plates were sharply upturned, and the armguards as sharp as blades.

The man's skin was fair. His light brown hair was short and perfectly in place. Atop his head was a crown—not a big, pointed one but a rather unassuming gold band that wreathed his brow like a thin halo. At the front, a trio of diamonds was set in the crown the shape of a triangle.

The man stood before a large globe on a stand. The room around him was brightly illuminated by windows looking out onto a blue sky, but Justin could not see any land. They must have been high above the ground. In a tower, perhaps.

The man with the crown spun the globe ever so slightly. Even from across the room, Justin could tell that the spherical map was not a representation of Earth. Its landmasses were all wrong.

"So," the man said. He tapped his finger against a spot on the globe. "Here is where you are." He was rather soft-spoken, and his voice was lightly accented.

"Where—?" said Justin but quickly changed his question to, "Who are you?"

"My name is Avagad," said the man in the crown. "I'm glad I was able to locate you before any harm could befall you, Justin. This world is a dangerous place."

It was then that Justin noticed an altar at the far end of the room. Floating above the altar was a long rectangle about the size of a full-length mirror, hanging in the air like a suspended pane of glass. Its surface swirled and bloomed like colorless sunspots, bubbling and overlapping in marbled shades of black.

"What is that?" Justin said.

"That," said the man with the crown, pointing at the floating pane, "is what you seek."

"The way . . . home?" Justin said.

Avagad nodded. Sunlight from the windows caught the diamonds on his crown. "They misled you," he said. "They told you that people would try to deceive you to gain your friendship, and time and again inexplicable danger presents itself. Danger they continually save you from. It is an act played out to gain your trust. What sort of friends would whisk you off into the wilderness instead of helping you? You wanted to go home, and instead, they took you farther from it." He placed one hand behind his back. With the other, he gestured toward Justin with an open palm. "They would try to use you for their own purposes, but I won't let that happen. They think you are an ethoul. The word means 'fallen angel' or 'angel cast out.' But you and I know the truth."

He crossed the room and stood beside Justin, barely a foot away from him.

"You did not fall from anywhere, did you?" Avagad said. "Nor were you cast out. You simply found yourself in this place, and now, you would like to simply find yourself home, wouldn't you?"

With one hand, he pointed at the energy pane. The other, he placed on Justin's shoulder.

"Through there lies your salvation," he said. "There are many doors like this one, leading to many faraway places. You stepped through one accidentally, it would seem! Fortunately, it is easily remedied."

Justin eased away from Avagad's hand. "Why would you help me?" he asked. "You don't even know me."

"I am a king, Justin," said Avagad. "Upholding peace and order, helping the downtrodden. Those are the duties I accepted when this crown was placed on my head. I ask nothing of you in return but the names of the people who deceived you."

"Their names?" Justin said.

"So that I may prosecute them for their crimes," he said. "Do not worry. I won't harm them. I believe in mercy for offenses born of ignorance. They are badly misguided, it's true. But we can help them, I hope."

Justin hesitated—not on purpose but because he was having the hardest time thinking.

"I. . . ." he said. "I can't remember. My head's all foggy."

"Ah, well," Avagad said with a shrug. "More important is your safety, I suppose. You are free to go. My greetings to your world."

Avagad strode back to the globe and stood there, studying one of its landforms. Justin watched him a moment, then turned toward the altar. The energy pane was a two-dimensional vortex of swirling blackness—not pitch black, not midnight black, but a muddled, imperfect black, as if a child had mixed too many paints. The pane was as thin as a sheet of paper, yet through it, things appeared three-dimensional: like a window opening to the heart of raging storm clouds.

"Step through it," said Avagad, "and you will arrive in the very place. That you. Exited your. World."

Justin turned. Avagad's voice had become halting and strange.

"Go," Avagad said. "They are. Trying to. Infiltrate. This . . . place."

Over the course of speaking the sentence, Avagad's voice dropped like a soundtrack slowed to half-speed. Looking around, Justin realized *everything* was slowing. The vortex in the energy pane was decelerating, and outside, the clouds in the sky were frozen. He tried to move and found that he, too, was in slow motion. The only thing operating at normal speed was his mind.

"Quickly . . . before . . ." said Avagad's deep voice, "they . . . sever . . . the . . . conn—ec—tion. . . ."

A corner of the room broke from its foundations and started to float away in zero gravity. Other parts of the room shattered. The windows twisted, and their glass broke under the strain. Blocks of stone cracked through their centers with puffs of dust and floated away from themselves in opposite directions. The globe lifted off the floor, stretched like a wad of chewing gum, and snapped.

Justin tried to run for the energy pane, but his body was moving more slowly than ever. It was like the air had turned to sand. Everything was fading and blurring. The doorway home cracked through the center and shredded into pieces. Then everything was gone.

CHAPTER 69

Leah watched Ahlund strip the leaves from the grilcin plant and grind them between his calloused hands with quick, abrasive motions. Its acrid aroma gave her pinpricks in her sinuses.

Leah glanced at the captain patrolling the deck with his crew.

"How did he do that?" she said under her breath. "It wasn't sleight of hand, was it? He *grew* that plant."

"How do you think he did it?" said Ahlund.

"Aurym?"

"I knew he possessed some kind of power," said Ahlund, "but it was impossible to anticipate the form or its degree."

"He doesn't have the feel or look of an aurym-user."

"He is not who he would have others believe he is."

"He is a fool and a lowlife."

"A lowlife, certainly," said Ahlund. "But what does it say about us, to be outsmarted by a fool? This mixture. Justin must swallow it."

"I have something for that," she said.

Leah searched through her field kit and found what she was looking for: a spool of cloth-like material. She was careful to dry her hands before touching it, as the delicate material, used to create medicinal capsules, would begin to disintegrate the moment it was exposed to moisture. Ideally, it was to be handled only with kidskin gloves, as even the natural oils on human skin were enough to begin the process. But these were far from ideal circumstances. A healer's work rarely was.

She tore a piece and presented it to Ahlund, who poured the grilcin powder onto the material. With practiced hands, Leah rolled and folded it into a compact capsule.

Then she heard screaming below deck.

Ahlund sprinted to the stairs and down below deck. Leah did her best to keep up. She rushed down the stairs, into Justin's room, and all intelligent thought escaped her.

Justin lay in bed with a foaming sneer across his whitened face. The words of another language were booming from his lips. Beside the bed, on his knees, was Zechariah, screaming in pain. He had been holding Justin's hand for comfort when she had left. Now, Justin held Zechariah. The old man's hand was crushed within Justin's grip. Blood poured down Zechariah's arm. His fingers pointed in all the wrong directions, and shards of off-white bone could be seen in the sticky gobs of blood that fell to the cabin floor.

Ahlund grabbed Justin's arm, trying to pry open his grip, but the boy's fingers were like stone. Justin thrashed in the bed. His chest pointed skyward as if something inside were trying to burst forth. His eyes were lifeless, white orbs.

"The capsule!" Ahlund shouted.

Leah rushed to the bedside. Ahlund snatched the grilcin capsule from her hand. He grabbed Justin's jaw and held it open in mid-wail, and he tossed the capsule into his mouth. With both hands, Ahlund clamped the boy's jaw shut.

Suddenly, Justin let go of Zechariah and reached for Ahlund's throat instead. Ahlund ignored it, keeping a tight hold on the boy's mouth. Zechariah tucked his bleeding hand under his opposite armpit. With his good hand, he grabbed Justin by the neck and worked his fingers against his esophagus, trying to force the capsule down his throat.

Within seconds, Justin's thrashing lessened. The low, guttural voice died off in his throat. His eyes were still open, but the whiteness was clearing. Still, Ahlund did not remove his grip until Justin's head lolled back onto the pillow and he lay dormant. His eyelids drooped, then closed, and the color returned to his face. Aside from some lingering spittle at the corners of his mouth, he appeared to be sleeping normally.

Ahlund leaned in to listen for breath. "He's out," he said. "He can't be controlled while so deeply unconscious."

Zechariah let go and plopped to the floor on his rear. Leah was at his side. She wrapped her arm around his shoulder for support as she examined him. Tears clung in his beard. He pulled his injured hand from his armpit, and the sight made Leah's stomach turn. His hand looked like it had been crushed beneath a millstone. Blood leaked from puncture wounds where bones had broken through the skin. She placed her hand above his, called on aurym, and quickened his blood's clotting to staunch its flow.

"How long will the drug last?" Zechariah asked through gritted teeth.

"It varies," said Ahlund. "Several hours, at least. If we can barter for more grilcin, he might survive long enough to reach the other side of the forest."

"We can't keep him drugged for that long," Leah said.

"It's not healthy, I agree," Ahlund said. "But it's less dangerous than leaving him at the mercy of the Drekwood's power."

"No!" Zechariah said. "No, it isn't the Drekwood doing this!"

"No?" Leah said. "Then what—?"

"It used Justin as a medium," said Zechariah. He pulled away from Leah and got to his feet. "It spoke to me!"

"What is it?" demanded Ahlund. "What spoke to you?"

"A demon," said Zechariah. "A cythraul."

Leah's lips felt thin and bloodless. "You mean . . . it knows where we are?"

Zechariah turned and faced the cabin wall. He stared ahead, eyes unfocused, as if he were seeing straight through the ship. "It doesn't just know where we are," he said. "It is here."

Zechariah wheeled around to face Leah.

"Leah," he said. "Can you fix it?"

She stared at him stupidly before realizing what he was talking about. She looked at his hand. "Given enough time, it might be possible to—"

"No time," he said. "For now, I shall fight left-handed."

Zechariah's short sword flashed from its sheath. He held it in his off hand, upside-down, the tip pointed toward the floor. He strode past Leah to the door. Ahlund drew his sword, too. He looked at Leah.

"Lock the door," he said. "No matter what happens, do not leave this room."

Leah could only nod.

The door closed, and Leah found herself alone with Justin, staring at Zechariah's blood drying in the cracks between the floorboards.

CHAPTER 70

The flames in the oil lamps flickered as if fighting a breeze. But there was no wind. The air was thick and still.

Ahlund followed Zechariah out onto the deck. The only sounds were the groans of the *Gryphon* and the gurgle of the Greenspring. Even the predators of the Drekwood had gone quiet.

"What happened?" Olorus said, staring at Zechariah's mutilated right hand.

"I'm fine," Zechariah said.

That, of course, wasn't true. The old man's hand hung bloody and useless at his side. It looked like a broken tree limb coated in raspberry jam.

Hook signed something, and Olorus translated, "What about Justin?"

"He is safe," Ahlund said, "for now."

"It's not one of those . . . demons?" said Olorus. "Is it?"

"It tried to take the boy through possession," said Zechariah.

"Tried to *take* the boy?" Olorus said.

"We stopped it," said Ahlund. "But now, it's coming for us. Physically."

Olorus sneered. "Let it try."

All at once, a bitter cold pressed in from every side. The lamps dimmed even further, fighting against being snuffed out by an unseen force. Gunnar's crew backed away from the sides of the ship. Their breath issued as puffs of steam—proof that the chill in the air was no illusion.

From all around them came a dull, scratching noise, like many spoons scraping many empty bowls.

Claws, Ahlund realized. *On the ship's hull.*

Something moved in the branches over the river, sending black leaves drifting down to the deck. Undergrowth along the banks rustled and shook. Hisses and growls started low and grew louder by the second.

"Coblyns," Gunnar whispered, sliding his cutlass from its sheath.

A blood-curdling howl cut through the darkness.

In unison, dozens of creatures suddenly dropped from the trees. They leaped from the banks and scrambled over the sides of the ship—long-limbed demons the size of children, with leathery, mummified skin and hairless bodies lean and corded with muscle. Their hunched, bowed, deformed shapes hopped on swift, clawed feet. Dripping fangs bared, tails dragging behind them or extended for balance.

Ahlund called on aurym and set his sword alight. It thrummed with living power, turning the cold air to steam. The orange, glowing blade looked fresh from the smith's furnace—so hot that it hurt Ahlund's hands and face just to be near it.

"*For Nolia*!" Olorus roared.

The coblyns threw themselves at the men, screaming with bloodlust, gnashing their teeth. Ahlund cut high, rending asunder a coblyn in midair. Zechariah slashed upward with his downward-pointed sword and followed with a quick, raking stab, leaving two coblyns spewing black blood.

Gunnar kicked one in the head, knocking it overboard, then ran another through with his cutlass. Hook drove his spear through two coblyns at once while Olorus struck one with his shield, snapping its spine and sending its beady eyes rolling back in its head. Pool, Samuel, and Borris swung their clumsy weapons at anything that came near them. Vick, at the helm, held a white-knuckled grip on the wheel.

What the creatures lacked in intelligence they made up for in numbers and animalistic abandon. They threw themselves on sword and spear. Their claws flashed even in their death throes. One jumped at Vick on the helm, and Ahlund sent a jet of flame from his sword, frying it in mid-leap. Then he drew his long knife, plunged it into an attacking coblyn's eye, and tore the face from the skull.

A coblyn charged through Hook's defenses. It slashed him across the face with its claws, but the silent soldier grabbed it and twisted its head full around to the tune of a crunching snap. Nearby, Zechariah swung his sword and sent a head rolling. But even as bodies piled up, more coblyns fell from the trees and jumped from the shores. Ahlund, cutting, hacking, and shooting flames, found himself surrounded. Despite a fine effort, the humans' perimeter was breaking, forcing them apart, making them vulnerable.

We should be winning this, Ahlund thought as his burning sword did its deadly work. *But they're hitting us in all the right places, separating us. Behaving more like an infantry unit than a herd of beasts.*

All at once, a mass of coblyns broke from the rest and charged for the door at the rear of the ship—the stairs that led below deck. Ahlund ran for the door but was overtaken. Coblyns drove him back, using their numbers to ultimate effectiveness. He could only watch as they scratched, tore, and beat at the door that led to Justin and Leah.

"The stairs!" Ahlund shouted.

The rest of the men tried to respond. Zechariah started for the stairs but was quickly pinned down. Olorus shouted in rage as he attempted to break through, but he could do nothing. Hook threw his spear. It needled through several coblyns at the stairs, but it wasn't enough. The door was ripped from its hinges, and the coblyns spilled in.

Gunnar and his crew had dropped back to defend the helm where Vick was trying to navigate amid the chaos. But all at once, Gunnar abandoned his defenses and sprinted into the heart of combat. He hurdled an attacker, planted a foot on another, and leaped for the doorway.

CHAPTER 71

Gunnar came down in the middle of the coblyns at the stairs, catching them by surprise. With cutlass flashing, he hacked down beast after beast with quick strokes.

A black, leathery body crashed into him, and he lost his footing and fell backward. He tumbled down the stairs. His sword was thrown from his grasp as he hit the bottom. The coblyns bounded down at him, eager for his living entrails.

Gunnar pulled a small pouch from his belt, opened the drawstrings, and threw it at the stairs. Tiny seeds spilled everywhere. With a grunt of effort, he raised his hands. Veins bulged in his forearms as he called on his power. Seeds grew to full-grown plants in a split second's time. Roots grew into spears, jousting through coblyns' lower jaws and bursting from their heads in full bloom. Vines strangled lanky bodies as flowers blossomed on the branches.

Gunnar fed life into the plants, weaving them together, constructing a barricade to substitute for the broken door, but one coblyn managed to get through the attacking plants. Before Gunnar knew it, he was flat on his back with the lone coblyn pinning him down. He caught a lucky grip on its neck, and that was all that held back the jaws snapping inches from his face. Hot breath doused him with the stench of decay. He gritted his teeth against the pain as claws ripped through his clothing and raked his skin.

Gunnar lurched against the creature, grabbed another pouch from his belt, and tossed it into the little devil's mouth. With a burst of power, he willed the seeds into bloom. The skull expanded, then burst like popping corn.

Black blood and gray cranial matter painted the walls. The coblyn fell limp on top of Gunnar with arms and legs spasming, its head replaced by a bouquet whose loveliness would have rivaled any florist in Castydociana.

Gunnar pushed the dead body off of him and stood. His shirt was in tatters and dotted with red from multiple cuts across his stomach. He touched the wounds and whistled through his teeth at his good luck. About an inch deeper, and that'd have been all she wrote.

"Are you all right?"

Gunnar turned. Standing in the hallway, sword in hand, was the girl who'd been introduced to him as Lee Tensong. Naturally, he'd known better.

Lee, thought Gunnar thought. *No one strained any muscles coming up with that one.*

"I recommend you go back inside, princess," Gunnar said.

"You're injured," she said. "Do you need. . . ?" Her expression changed. "What did you call me?"

"And bolt the door," he added.

Without waiting to see if she listened, he turned and waved at the plant life. A vine slithered across the stairs, fetched his sword by the hilt, and brought it to his awaiting hand. At his command, the bramble barricade parted like a curtain, and he stepped through.

He climbed the stairs to the deck, expecting an all-out assault waiting for him at the top, but there were only corpses. With a flick of his wrist, the plants closed behind him. The only coblyns left on deck were dead, hewn bodies. The passengers—who were proving every bit as formidable as Gunnar had anticipated—stood with weapons ready but no enemy left to fight. The crew of the *Gryphon* was accounted for. Pool, in fact, was patrolling the ship and taking pleasure in using his mace to smash the skulls of any coblyns still clinging to life. Not a big-time thinker, that one, but refreshingly versatile.

"Did we finish them off?" Gunnar said.

"They stopped," said the one with the red hair and the overactive mouth—Olorus. "They . . . retreated?" He looked at Ahlund and added, "Coblyns do not retreat."

"They do not attack in ranks, either," said Ahlund.

"It was not a retreat of their choosing," said the elderly chap, Zechariah. "They were called back."

"Called back?" Gunnar said. "By what—?"

"Cap*taaaaain*!" Vick screamed.

A sudden shift in weight threw the *Gryphon* off-kilter so violently that Borris and Samuel fell sprawling to the deck. Several oil lanterns on the bow went out, plunging the front half of the ship into darkness.

From the darkness came a loud smashing sound. Broken, splintered pieces of the ship's railings came flying and spinning out of the shadows. Something had hit the deck—something heavy enough to shatter the railings to toothpicks and throw the seaworthy *Gryphon* off balance. Gunnar wondered if a tree had fallen on the front of the ship.

Repetitive, booming vibrations shook the deck beneath Gunnar's feet. Rhythmic tremors that felt like—

Footsteps.

Then into the light stepped a black boot the size of a tabletop. Deck boards bowed beneath its weight.

With another step, a giant emerged from the shadows. It had two arms and two legs and walked fully erect like a human, but its size and dimensions were so disproportionate that there could be no mistaking this thing for human. Its shoulders were five feet wide, and it stood at least twice as high. Other than some crude rags draped over its midsection, it wore no clothing. Instead, its body seemed to be constructed of jagged, black bone armor. Muscles flexed and shifted beneath exoskeletal plates. The head was fleshless—a deformed, human-like skull made of jagged, black bone. Sharp, interlocking teeth lined the end of a wide, heavy jaw. Sprouting from its forehead were two black horns like iron spikes. The eye sockets were empty pits radiating a red glow from within, as if a fire burned somewhere inside, just out of sight.

It took another step into the light, revealing a sword held in one of its skeletal hands. The notched blade was half a foot wide and the length of a full-grown man. The lantern light around the monster—not the flames of the lamps, but the illumination they produced—rippled and warped, as if not even light could escape the pull of its presence.

"A High Demon," said Zechariah.

"A cythraul," said Ahlund.

The silent soldier, Hook, was nearest the monster. He bravely stood his ground at the giant's approach, but it lunged forward faster than its towering frame should have allowed. Hook had no time to react as the massive arm swung forward and swatted him like he was a pup. The blow lifted Hook off his feet. Judging by the way his arms flopped, he was either unconscious or dead before he ever left the ground. His limp body hit the deck and rolled unnaturally. Olorus rushed to his aid.

Borris and Pool dropped their weapons and retreated to the far side of the ship, whimpering and cowering. Tears covered Samuel's rosy face, but he could not move. Vick tripped over a coblyn corpse as he retreated from the helm. Without anyone to tend to the wheel, the ship drifted aimlessly down the river.

Gunnar stepped forward. "All right, you big son of a whore," he said. "Ain't no such thing as a free ride. You board my ferry, best be ready to pay the toll."

Olorus growled a series of rage-fueled nonsense syllables, clanging his spear against his shield as he stepped up to stand beside Gunnar. Hook's motionless body still lay at the rear of the ship. Ahlund and Zechariah took up places alongside Gunnar and Olorus. Coblyn blood dripped from their weapons, mingling with their own.

The cythraul breathed out, as if savoring the moment, venting yellowish fumes from between teeth the shape—and size—of daggers. Inside the empty eye sockets, the unseen fire seemed to burn a little more brightly.

CHAPTER 72

The sounds of battle overhead had been replaced by a deathly hush. Whether the silence meant the battle had been won or lost, Leah did not know.

She watched Justin closely. Under the drugging effects of the grilcin plant, he slept calmly, but his breathing was rapid. Her healer's instincts, along with countless hours spent at the bedsides of the sick, told her to hold his hand for comfort, but each time she reached for it out of habit, she remembered Zechariah's hand and decided that a gentle grip on the upper arm was the wiser choice.

It was a summer evening, but she was freezing right down to her bones. It left her weak and lightheaded. Only once had she felt this way before. The Gravelands. When those monsters had pursued them.

"Are they here, now?" she wondered aloud. Her teeth chattered as she spoke. "Could they have—?"

The ship rocked, nearly knocking her over. She heard the sound of breaking boards. In the aftermath, she looked at the cabin door and realized the knob was turning.

Leah's throat went dry. The knob spun full around, then caught against the lock she had secured at Gunnar's request. The doorknob wiggled. Someone or something was trying to come in.

Quietly, Leah let go of Justin's unconscious arm, drew her sword, and put herself between the door and the bed. The door jumped on its hinges.

A thud. A crash. The latch broke free with a dry crack, and the door flew open.

CHAPTER 73

So, we meet again, thought Ahlund, looking up at the black skull of the cythraul.

"Wish I could say it's been nice knowing you boys," said Gunnar, "but I'll be honest, this is turning out to be one of the worst excursions I've ever been associated with."

Olorus started to say something in response, but the cythraul opened its blade-toothed mouth and bellowed a roar—the same voice that had come from Justin's throat, now amplified a thousand times. The monster lifted its giant sword high. The four humans roared battle cries of their own, and they bolted forward to meet it.

Zechariah slashed upward. The cythraul swung its giant weapon, blocking, and the force of the impact sent the old man stumbling backward. Gunnar drove his sword at an opening, but the monster backhanded him with its off hand. Like Hook, he was lifted and thrown like a plaything. He would have soared overboard had one desperately flailing hand not caught a line that hitched up the ship's sails. His arm wrenched nastily against the momentum, but his grip held firm, and he hung suspended from the mast.

Olorus charged, driving his spear at the cythraul, but the monster brought its gargantuan blade down like an axe to the chopping block. Olorus was forced to roll sidelong to avoid the cythraul's sword as it broke through the deck boards and stuck there. Seeing his opening, Ahlund swung his sword in midair. The blade turned white-hot and issued a jet of angry flame at the skull-like head.

The cythraul lifted its free hand and seemed to catch the blast. Ahlund's fire warped and swirled as if caught in a whirlpool. The fire shrank, dimmed, and then disappeared entirely, absorbed into a singularity.

The cythraul opened its heavy jaw and bellowed a laugh, flexing its unscathed, skeletal fingers into a fist. It wrenched its sword free of the deck, pulling several boards up with it. Then the cythraul's blade whistled through the air in a horizontal swipe at Zechariah. The old man ducked it, then narrowly avoided a huge foot as it stomped and burst a hole through the deck.

Olorus took advantage and circled around from behind. He drove his spear into the back of its leg. The cythraul roared in pain and swung its weapon. Olorus raised his shield in time to block with a deafening clang, but the blunt force sent him rolling.

Gunnar dropped from the mast and landed spryly beside Ahlund. The two were about to advance together when the ship rocked violently again.

Another one? thought Ahlund, but he saw nothing.

"We're scraping the rocks!" Gunnar shouted as another violent shake knocked him over.

Ahlund heard cracking, splintering boards at the bow of the ship. With no one on the helm, the *Gryphon* had drifted into the shallows and was bouncing against an embankment. In the resulting turbulence, the cythraul had just as much trouble staying on its feet as the men, but it went after Zechariah nonetheless, swinging its sword in wide arcs, seemingly intent on him and him alone.

Suddenly, Vick—who had previously fled the helm—broke from the rest of the crew and bound across the deck, shouting, "I'm on it, cap'n!" He grabbed the wheel and wrenched it sideways to pull the *Gryphon* back on course, but the strange angle at which the vessel now drifted bore testament to some unseen damage.

Ahlund charged and swung his flaming sword. The cythraul snuffed out his attack again. It wheeled back to Zechariah, feigned an attack with its fist, then swung its sword in an upward slice.

The old man had no time to dodge. He brought his sword up to block. Their blades connected with a crash, and Zechariah's sword snapped. Ahlund could only watch as Zechariah was lifted off his feet, surrounded by glittering, steel pieces of his shattered blade. His robed body flipped backward, crashed through a wooden railing, and plummeted overboard. The monster roared in triumph.

Ahlund unleashed his aurym fire in a wide curtain. Beneath the shroud of flames, the humans charged. Gunnar stabbed the underside of the cythraul's arm. Olorus drove his spear between the bone plates of its lower back. Ahlund slid across the deck and slashed his white-hot blade into the back of the cythraul's knee, chopping through flesh, muscle, and tendon. Black ichor squirted from severed arteries and splashed his face as he jumped back to avoid a stomp.

The cythraul raised its hand and pointed at him. Indigo electricity danced across its fingers. A ball of concentrated darkness grew within its palm.

Remembering the monsters' daemyn attacks on the Gravelands, Ahlund planted his feet and readied himself like a coiled spring.

With a sharp pulse, the ball of energy shot from the monster's hand like a loosed projectile. Ahlund dove sidelong. He felt the chilling blackness of daemyn as the orb zoomed dangerously close to him as he dove. The projectile continued on past him and hit the helm, where Vick still held the wheel.

The ball of daemyn hit the ship's deck and exploded with a sound like underwater thunder. Items at the periphery of the blast were either set aflame with black fire or shredded by the shock wave. Ropes, boards, and shards of metal whizzed through the air, propelled outward by the concussion. Sections of the deck lifted and fractured. Anything within the blast zone disintegrated like sugar in water. At its epicenter, Vick's body was visible as a shadow for half a second. Then the shadow drifted apart from itself, dispersed into a haze, and vaporized.

"*No*!" Gunnar screamed.

Heedless of the debris raining around him, the captain charged the cythraul. He reached into the pouch at his belt and tossed a handful of seeds. They scattered, harmless as sand, until he called on aurym. Vines and shoots exploded outward in a torrent of greenery, wrapping around the monster's legs and climbing up its body. With hands outstretched, Gunnar orchestrated their rapid germination. The cythraul sliced at the plants with its sword and tore at them with its massive arms. Gunnar drove harpoon-like branches between exoskeletal plates. He knotted tree limbs and wove webs of vines, and soon, the cythraul's sword arm was pinned to its side. Olorus and Ahlund took the opportunity to stab and hack repeatedly, spilling black blood, but it only seemed to anger the thing.

Olorus backed away and unsheathed the spear from his back. With a war cry, he crow-hopped for momentum and hurled it at the cythraul's head.

His aim was true. The spear broke on impact, but not before entering the empty, red eye socket. The blade cracked a hole in the back of the skull, leaving the long, wooden haft protruding all the way through the head.

The uninjured eye blazed redder still.

The monster thrashed against its floral bonds with renewed rage. Ahlund doused the cythraul's body in liquid, blue flames that ignited Gunnar's plants into a brushfire. Anchored in place, burning alive, a spear stuck through its skull, and losing black blood by the bucketful from a score of wounds, the cythraul fought on.

CHAPTER 74

Where are you, old man? thought Ahlund.

An impact shook the *Gryphon*. The ship was slamming into the banks again, but with its helm destroyed by the daemyn blast, all means of steering—and any chance of correcting their course—were lost.

Snapping timber echoed through the night. The ship bounced off the rocks and careened back out into open water, rotating like a wheel.

Gunnar was on his knees, shouting with the effort of maintaining his aurym attack. His hat was gone, and his long, black locks hung sweat-soaked and disheveled. Thus far, his plants were slowing the cythraul down enough to prevent it from finishing them off, but he was tiring.

Finally, Gunnar's shoulders slumped. His arms dropped to his sides. He had nothing left to give.

The cythraul's maw opened in an eager roar. Bathed in flames, it broke free of the brush, raised its massive sword overhead, and took aim on Gunnar. Gunnar lowered his head, resigned to his fate.

Suddenly, the flash of a distinct aurym presence from above.

There you are.

Ahlund hauled back and tossed his sword spinning through the air. It sailed high over the cythraul's head.

Zechariah dropped from the mast's rigging like a diving hawk. He landed on the cythraul's shoulders. With his only good hand, the old man caught Ahlund's sword by the hilt. The blade was still hot with Ahlund's power as Zechariah drove it into the cythraul's neck.

The blade caught on bone. The cythraul bayed a strange roar and reached up, groping for the old man, but Zechariah pulled the sword free, hauled back, and chopped twice more, severing the spinal cord and the connecting tissues.

Zechariah dismounted and landed roughly. Olorus's burning spear was still protruding from the cythraul's head as the disembodied, fleshless skull fell and bounced across the deck.

The monster took one more step, then froze. Its headless neck became a geyser of viscous, oily fluid. It dropped its sword, raised its arms in shock, and fell to its knees.

Purple energy rose from the neck, then expanded, sizzling over its body. The daemyn energies that had fueled it were turning on their host—imploding. Pieces were torn inward, ripped off the bone like succulent meat. The body collapsed inward one piece at a time, shrinking into a broken fossil of its former self.

Finally, with a bright flash, the residual daemyn energy exploded.

The blast knocked Ahlund off his feet. Chunks of the deck were torn from their supports, flaming and electrified with otherworldly energies.

Ahlund looked up just in time to see the main mast, broken in twain, plummeting down on him like a felled oak. He scrambled, dove, and felt the rush of displaced air as the top half slammed into the deck behind him.

The spinning, damaged ship rocked upon its axis. Debris rained into the Greenspring with muffled plops.

The ship's rocking lessened, and Ahlund got up. The air was not so cold. The oil lanterns shone brightly again—those that remained, anyway. Olorus, Gunnar, and Zechariah all watched the place where the cythraul had been. Nothing remained but its head.

At the ship's aft, Hook was slowly regaining consciousness. The frantic sailors were leaning over the ship's railings, calling for Vick, apparently in the misplaced hope that his death had been an illusion. All the while, the *Gryphon* floated downriver in lazy circles like a maimed water bird, no longer even capable of moving in a straight line.

Gunnar winced, coughed, and hacked, spitting up thick blood onto the deck. When the fit passed, he wiped his mouth and said, "Would someone mind fetching the healer? Think I got something pretty well busted up in here."

Olorus started for the stairs but stopped in mid-step and turned to face Gunnar. "How did you know she's a healer?" he demanded.

"I know exactly who she is," Gunnar said in an impatient sort of way. "Tell the princess if she fixes me up she can have all the grilcin she wants."

Olorus's brow furrowed. With a wave of Gunnar's hand, the plant barricade at the top of the stairs parted, allowing Olorus to pass through freely.

Ahlund approached the head of the cythraul on the deck. It lay propped upside-down on its twin horns. He kneeled and pulled Olorus's smoking spear free from the head, and the skull, twice the size of a man's, broke apart as if it were made of charcoal and disintegrated into a pile of black ash. The monster's sword must have gotten caught in the implosion. No matter. Not a man alive could have lifted such a weapon.

"You mind telling me what that thing was doing on my ship?" said Gunnar. It appeared his jovial irreverence was spent.

Ahlund only stared at the pile of ash. Zechariah nudged him, then wordlessly handed him back his sword.

Finally, Gunnar yelled, "I'm talking to you two, ya bloody—!"

"Turn the ship about!" Olorus shouted as he scrambled back up the stairs. "Turn about now!"

Gunnar appeared to be armed with a sardonic reply, but Ahlund cut him off.

"Why?" Ahlund said.

"Justin and Leah," Olorus said. "They're gone."

CHAPTER 75

"If they fell overboard, maybe they've made it to shore!" shouted Olorus.

"What do you mean they're gone?" Ahlund demanded.

"Vick! Vick!" shouted the sailors into the murky, churning waters.

The smoking *Gryphon* raced uncontrollably downriver, turning this way and that as everyone onboard tried to be heard at once—all except Hook, the ever-silent soldier, and Zechariah, who just sat down cross-legged.

"Turn about!" Olorus repeated. "This instant!"

"Are you certain they're gone?" Ahlund said.

"You think me a liar, mercenary? Move aside!" Olorus tried to elbow past Ahlund, but instead, he bounced him ineffectually. He appeared surprised. Opting for the high road, he swung wide to march across the deck to Gunnar. "I say again, turn this ship around!" he shouted at the captain.

"I'm waiting," Gunnar said, watching Ahlund, ignoring Olorus. "What was that thing doing on my ship?"

"You heard the lieutenant," Ahlund said. "Do as you're told."

Gunnar's single eye glared at Ahlund. Any of his good nature that had remained was now, without question, gone. "Who the hell are you people?" he said.

Ahlund focused his aurym, trying to find Leah or Justin's presence, but he got nothing. Olorus was right. They were gone—not dead, necessarily, but certainly not here. Snatched right out from under him during the cythraul's attack.

"Answer me!" yelled Gunnar.

"I thought you feared nothing in the Drekwood, captain," Ahlund said, turning toward the forest, trying to extend his senses through the darkness and into the trees. "So much for getting everyone through it alive."

Ahlund heard Gunnar's sword being drawn from its sheath and realized, almost too late, that turning his back on the man had been a mistake.

Ahlund wheeled back around just in time to lean away from Gunnar's cutlass as it sliced in a horizontal arc at his head. Judging by the breeze against Ahlund's nose as the blade passed by his face, it had missed by about an inch. There could be no mistake. That was meant to be a killing blow.

Across the ship, shouts were raised. Weapons were drawn. In a fury, Gunnar slashed at Ahlund a second time—another earnest attempt at a lethal blow—but he had squandered the element of surprise. Ahlund didn't bother drawing his sword. No need. He ducked the attack. With one hand, he seized the captain's weapon-wielding wrist. He clamped his other hand on Gunnar's throat.

Ahlund felt Gunnar's pulse pounding under his grip. His own blood was pumping hard, too. So hard he could hear it in his ears. The battle, the panic of finding Justin and Leah missing, and now the added adrenaline of defending himself from a would-be death strike, had Ahlund on the brink of a point of no return. The textbook coup de grâce of this counterattack maneuver was an abrupt up-thrust of momentum to Gunnar's sword arm with a simultaneous downward pull with the hand clutching his throat. The opposing forces would tear the tendons of Gunnar's shoulder, rendering his weapon arm physically incapable of resistance. Then all that was left was to turn the opponent's weapon on himself with a quick, upward stab into the belly and up under the ribcage, shredding stomach, liver, and lungs all in one go. If done perfectly, one could even puncture the heart on the first try. Ahlund had only done it perfectly a few times. He wondered if he could do it again.

Gunnar inched his free hand toward a knife at his belt, but Ahlund squeezed his neck as a warning, and the captain withdrew. Ahlund held Gunnar inert, staring into the captain's single eye as he debated what to do with him. The rest of the men watched. No one dared say a word.

Ahlund considered for a moment. A slow death would be preferable to a quick one, in this case. To make an example out of this man.

"You. . . !" Gunnar gagged beneath the force of Ahlund's grip. "You mongrel cur! It killed him. Vick's *dead*."

"Yes," agreed Ahlund. "Vick is dead, and it is my fault. You thought killing me was the solution? Best-case scenario is I'm dead and you're no better off than you were a moment before. Worst-case scenario is this." Ahlund squeezed again. Gunnar's cheek twitched. His face was turning blue.

Ahlund hesitated, then released his grip.

Gunnar pulled away, his sword raised threateningly as he doubled over, gasping for air.

"You want to know why a cythraul was on your ship," stated Ahlund. "Has it yet occurred to you that *a* cythraul may be the least of your worries? That there may be more of them?"

"So it was a cythraul," Gunnar said hoarsely, rubbing his neck.

"It was," Zechariah said. He alone, Ahlund noticed, had not armed himself during the altercation. He remained seated cross-legged, staring into his lap, cradling his maimed hand. "Our combined efforts were barely enough to defeat it," he added. "And if you two kill each other, our chances against the next one are diminished."

"Is this why you wanted to sail through the Drekwood?" said Gunnar. "Because these things are looking for you people?"

"Heavens, no," said Zechariah. "They're only looking for one of us."

The others waited for the old man to elaborate. He held the undivided attention of everyone onboard the *Gryphon*, including his companions, and he chose it to mumble, dryly, "Drat. A fine thing to happen to my favorite hand."

"Start talking, old man," Olorus said. "What do you mean 'one of us'?"

"This ship had a lifeboat, did it not?" Zechariah said.

"It does," said Gunnar.

"It did," corrected Zechariah.

Gunnar and the crew looked starboard.

"It's gone, cap'n," said Pool.

"Must'a broke free in the tussle," Borris offered.

"You'll find the mooring lines have been cut," said Zechariah, "yet no one abandoned ship."

"Maybe the boy and the princess did," Gunnar said.

"Possible," said Zechariah, "even likely—had I not spotted a squad of soldiers rowing them both to shore a few minutes ago."

Ahlund's panic flared. His pulse raced yet again.

"You mean to tell me that you saw soldiers kidnapping the princess and the boy?" Olorus shouted. "And you let them *go*?"

"I saw it while clinging to the side of the ship!" Zechariah shouted back. The volume of his voice was so unexpectedly loud that Olorus recoiled in surprise. "With one hand, I might add!" he roared. "Did you expect me to fly over to them, you fool? It's a miracle I managed to hold on at all!"

A miracle? thought Ahlund. *If that is a miracle, what do you call climbing back onboard, scaling the mast one-handed, then dropping down to attack the cythraul from above? I should be grateful this old man is my ally. He would make a fearsome enemy.*

"Judging by the torch fires I could see on the shoreline," said Zechariah, "there were many of them."

"We're probably miles away by now," said Ahlund, "but with a little luck, we may still be able to track them down—"

"Maybe you did not understand me, Ahlund," said Zechariah. "There were many of them. Too many. And who knows how many more were beyond my sight?"

Ahlund frowned. He did not like the tone of Zechariah's voice.

"Too many or not," Olorus chimed in, "if we can kill a demon from the bowels of hell, I pity any denizens of this world caught before us!"

"Do not be blind," said Zechariah. "We paid a high price to kill that beast. We are weary. We are injured. We have no time to recover. Outnumbered against an unknown enemy, it would be suicide."

"Better is suicide by bravery than to live another moment as a coward!" Olorus said.

"Spoken like a true jackass," said Gunnar.

As Olorus targeted Gunnar with a profane threat, Ahlund considered Zechariah's words. Normally, the old man was not one to back down from a fight for anything. How could he even consider not pursuing them?

We are their only hope, thought Ahlund. *We are the only ones who can save them. We are. . . .*

"We are the only ones," Ahlund mumbled, finally understanding.

"What say you, Sir Ahlund?" Olorus encouraged. "Help me talk some sense into this gray-headed fool!"

Ahlund locked eyes with Zechariah. He hesitated, then said, "It is sometimes a virtue to charge forward no the matter the odds. But not today, Olorus."

"What?" barked Olorus. "You're not suggesting—!"

"We have no allies," said Ahlund. "No reinforcements. I do not fear death, but if we are killed, there is no one left, and Justin and Leah will be lost. Only we can save them, which leaves us with the responsibility of choosing our next steps wisely. Impulsivity, however lionhearted, is not an option."

Hook stepped forward. He was still bleary-eyed from getting knocked out by the cythraul but worked his hands fervently in the air, nevertheless. Olorus translated his signs: "You sound like the old man. More bureaucrat than soldier."

"We failed to protect the princess from the enemy," said Ahlund. "To rush to our doom, however valiantly, would be a greater failure still."

"Did you say 'princess'?" said the lisping, scar-faced sailor named Borris.

Ahlund hesitated, but he saw no point in concealing it any longer. "Yes. Princess Anavion of Nolia."

"There is something else you should know," said Zechariah. "It's about my apprentice. Justin is an ethoul."

CHAPTER 76

"An ethoul?" said Gunnar. "A fallen angel?"

"Ever'body knows fallen angels ain't real," said Pool. "Just fairytales and—"

"I *knew* it!" Olorus suddenly bellowed, drowning out everyone else.

The lieutenant took several aggressive steps toward the still-sitting Zechariah, jabbing a finger at him.

"Ever since I laid eyes on you, I knew you couldn't be trusted!" Olorus snarled. "To think how many times we have deferred to your demented judgment—I should have split you from gut to ear the first moment we met!"

Olorus raised his sword. Zechariah's head perked up in alarm, but he did not have time to move.

Ahlund stepped in front of him. "Stay your hand, Olorus!" he said.

Slowly, Olorus lowered his sword. His eyes shifted to stare at Ahlund, murder in his gaze. Ahlund could see it on the man's face: Intervening in this matter was as good as betrayal in Olorus's eyes, and he would not forget it.

"Gunnar," Ahlund said. "Can this ship be repaired?"

Gunnar's jaw muscles tightened. There was an expression on the young captain's face that Ahlund could not place. He ran a hand over his braided mustache and said, "I wouldn't even know where to begin."

"We can't keep floating aimlessly," said Ahlund. "Can you at least bring us to a stop?"

Gunnar considered, then said, "Man the oars, boys."

"What?" said Pool.

"But, cap'n—" said Samuel.

"Get your sorry arses moving!" yelled Gunnar. "Get on those oars and wait for my command!"

The crew jogged below deck.

"Rowing won't do much good in this current," said Zechariah.

"No," said Gunnar, "but it may get us to shore if you lads are willing to lend a . . . never mind." He marched to the aft of the *Gryphon*.

Olorus threw Ahlund a deadly look, then followed. Ahlund looked around, realizing to his surprise that he had misplaced someone. Hook had been standing several yards across the ship a moment before. But he wasn't there now, and Ahlund hadn't heard or seen where he'd gone.

Instinctively, Ahlund looked over his shoulder. The silent soldier stood less than a foot behind him. A long knife was in his hand. The point was touching the fabric of Ahlund's shirt just below his ribs—one effortless thrust from Ahlund's kidneys, one quick sideways rake from his bowels.

Hook allowed the moment to sink in. Then, without a sound, he sheathed his knife, stepped back, and followed Olorus. Ahlund breathed out, long and low.

A few moments later, Gunnar, Olorus, and Hook returned hauling a long coil of rope. Gunnar cut it into sections and gave each man a good-sized length. Zechariah extended his good hand, and Ahlund helped him to his feet. The old man took a portion along with the rest.

"On my order," said Gunnar, "I'll have the boys veer to port. That'll drive us ashore, but it won't keep us there. We need to tie up real quick, or the current will just pull us back out."

"That will work?" asked Olorus.

"Either that," said Gunnar, "or the force will rip the ship to pieces. Doesn't much matter now, though. Maybe you've noticed you're standing at an angle. That's because we're sinking. Tether these lines to anything sturdy onboard. When we hit shore, find a good, strong tree to dog the opposite end."

The men hurried to find anchor points. Zechariah worked one-handedly to throw his rope over itself. He used his hip to hold it in place while he pulled the knot tight. Ahlund, watching his back all the time, had just finished tying his rope to the stump of the felled mast when a rustling sound overhead caused him to grip his sword. A few seconds later—it took that long for rain to permeate the nearly impregnable canopy—

water came pouring through. Somewhere high above, in the outside world, it was raining.

"On my mark," Gunnar shouted down a trapdoor that led below decks, "we go hard to port! Ready, steady . . . *mark*!"

The oars were lowered, followed by a change of direction so swift it nearly threw Ahlund off his feet.

"Hold, boys!" Gunnar shouted down the trapdoor.

The front of the ship took a hard turn to port as the back drifted lazily around to starboard. But rather than veering toward shore as intended, the *Gryphon* just rotated on its axis. The ship seemed doomed to execute a complete spin and continue on its present course.

Halfway through the turn, Gunnar sprinted across the deck and propelled himself overboard. Ahlund rushed to the side to see Gunnar land on the dark shoreline. With his rope trailing behind, the captain dashed through the rain toward the woods. Following the captain's lead, Ahlund held his rope tightly, backed up a few steps, and leaped.

Ahlund's landing was not as graceful as Gunnar's. He crashed hard in the rocky shallows, then scrambled up the bank. Ahead, Gunnar was tying his line doubly tight around the base of a tree trunk, but the rope was uncoiling in his hands almost faster than he could tie it.

Ahlund tossed his rope around a lip of granite. He stepped on the rope to hold it in place, threw his knot together, and finished it just as the line drew taught with an audible twang and a creak of tension. It slid dangerously against the sharp edge of the rock, but it held.

With the two lines dragging against its weight, the *Gryphon* swung toward shore, hit an unseen obstacle downriver, and crashed to a halt. Olorus's shouting was audible over the rain as he, Hook, and Zechariah jumped ashore to find anchor points. The crew emerged from below deck and rushed to assist.

At a sudden crashing amid the undergrowth, Ahlund wheeled around with sword drawn. Gunnar came pushing through the bushes. He stopped before Ahlund, unbothered by the red-hot blade pointing at his face.

"I think it actually worked," Gunnar said. "Tell me the truth. That boy. You don't really believe he's—"

He was interrupted by a snapping noise downstream. Ahlund turned in time to see the *Gryphon*'s hull crack. The rope he had tied to the nearby rock fell slack. Boards splintered and fractured as the ship broke apart. One by one, the oil lanterns were doused as the remnants of the *Gryphon* either floated away or were sucked below the water's surface.

In the dim glow of the last lantern, Ahlund saw Gunnar bow his head Then the final lantern succumbed to the river, and all light went out.

PART VII

STONES OF YEARS

CHAPTER 77

Justin woke beneath deep, dark water.

Panicking, he flailed and kicked, swimming hard toward the surface. His lungs burned. His heart pounded. An interlude from one of the songs in his father's strange record collection was inexplicably spinning in his head: a driving bass guitar, a screeching organ, and snare-heavy drums in a 10/8 time signature.

There was something at the bottom of the water. A nightmare that was real. Sinister things that had snared him, trapping him in the murky depths for what seemed like ages, showing him things, whispering, burrowing dark shoots into his consciousness. But all the things he'd been told and shown faded until he could no longer remember them, leaving only sickly cobwebs in his mind. His soul quivered with reverberations of faceless fears. He tried to keep swimming up toward the surface of the pool, but there was no life left in him. Pinpoints of light flared in his vision like camera flashes. Was this what it was like to die? He could hold his breath no longer. He sucked in, knowing that his mouth, throat, and lungs would fill with the murky waters, and all would be over soon.

Instead, oxygen filled his lungs. The flashes of light before his eyes became spots. Then the spots expanded and opened up, consuming his vision, changing the dark pool into a bright blur. He thought he could still hear the snare drum and the screeching organ as the bright blur gained focus, until it became a campfire. A perfectly normal campfire, and a relatively small one, at that. The music faded to silence.

Not dying, he thought. *Living.* And for the first time, he wondered what that really meant.

He lay on his side, on the ground. His body ached. He was hungry and thirsty, and his mouth tasted like bile. Was he in the old man's hut? On the grasslands beneath starry skies? On the floor of a cave? Before he could decide, he heard a woman shout.

"Leah?" he muttered, but the name left his dry throat as an indiscernible groan.

He tried to move and realized his arms were bound by the wrists behind his back. He arched his back and repositioned his legs, trying to gain a vertical base, but weariness and vertigo made it a futile gesture. Just beyond his field of vision, he heard the woman's voice again, followed by the sounds of a struggle.

"Let *go* of me!" said the woman.

A man was laughing—no, giggling.

What is happening? screamed Justin's fevered mind as he struggled against his bonds. *Come on, Justin, get up, get up!*

Suddenly, Justin heard a strange sound: blunt impact, like a mallet hitting a slab of uncooked meat. Drops of liquid pitter-pattered on the ground around Justin. The man's giggling was replaced by a startled cry. Tiny spit-crackles emanated from the fire's embers as sputtered fluid sizzled in the flames.

Something hit the ground within Justin's field of vision. He thought at first that it was some yet-to-be-prepared dinner item, like a leg of lamb. But then he noticed that it was wrapped in a shirtsleeve, and still-moving fingers on the end were scratching in the dirt.

The man's startled cry rose in volume and timbre.

"Quiet," said a deep voice.

The screaming man obeyed. His cries died down to pitiful, jaw-clenched moans.

"She is not to be touched," said the deep voice somewhere behind Justin and high above him. "Anyone who lays a hand on her will lose it."

Justin stared at the arm on the ground, severed above the elbow and leaking in the dirt. It groped once more, as if trying to grasp hands with an invisible ally, then stopped moving altogether.

"Pick it up," said the deep voice.

"W—what?" said the moaning man.

"Pick it up. You will carry it."

A one-armed man, half his body painted red with trailing gore, mournfully approached the limb. His remaining hand trembled as he reached down and picked up his own arm.

"Time to go," said the deep voice from above.

Justin was unceremoniously hauled to his feet. His legs were like jelly, but he managed to lock his knees in place and stay standing. Walls of ancient, forbidding forest encircled a camp of fifty or more people he did not recognize. He tried to scan the crowd for Leah, but soldiers were kicking the logs of the fire, spreading the embers and snuffing them with dirt. The fire died, and all was darkness but for a few torches whose dim spheres showed grim, unfamiliar faces and shadowed silhouettes.

Soon, the torches were moving into the trees. When the men in front of Justin started moving, he was shoved roughly from behind. With his hands bound behind his back and no arms free to catch himself, Justin stumbled forward and bumped into the man in front of him. The man turned and backhanded Justin across the mouth so hard that he immediately tasted blood. The aggressor from behind pushed him again, forcing him to move dazedly onward.

Justin spit the blood out of his mouth.

P—pain, he thought. *Pain is a . . . a distraction. Blood. Blood is a distraction. Ignore them. Think. How did you get here? What's the last thing you remember? You were in a tall tower, weren't you? Yes. And there was a man. A man with a crown.*

No. No, that wasn't right.

A boat, he thought. *You were on a boat—*

Brilliant pain erupted at the back of his skull as a fist connected with his head. He stumbled forward again, buckled over from the blow.

"Keep moving!" someone shouted.

Justin put his head down and followed the man in front of him. He thought more blood was running down his face, but then he realized it was lukewarm rainwater.

Focus on what you know, he thought as he tried to block out the throbbing pain in his head. *Trees and darkness. The Drekwood.*

His hands were bound, and his weapons were gone. The girl he had heard—was it really Leah, or had it been his mind playing tricks on him? And what about the others? If the woman he'd heard was Leah, these people must have captured her. But none of them were allowed to touch her.

Of course, thought Justin. *She's wanted for murder. The people searching for her finally caught up with us. But if it's the princess they're after, why keep me alive?*

It was difficult to imagine a scenario in which he and Leah were captured while Ahlund, Zechariah, Olorus, or Hook still lived. Each of them, for their respective reasons, would have fought to the death to keep this from happening.

Dead, thought Justin. *That's the only way this could have happened. They're dead.*

Justin closed his eyes. He had problems with all of them, and most of them had problems with him. They had deceived him and one another, but they had also taken care of him, taught him how to survive, protected him. He didn't know if he could trust anyone in this world, but surely they were the only ones who came close. They were. . . .

My friends, he realized.

His sorrow broke open, and inside was rotten guilt.

I accused Ahlund and Zechariah of double-crossing me, he thought. *I even tried to run away. And now, they're gone.*

The rain was falling harder now. It soaked his hair, trickled through the patchy stubble on his cheeks, and turned the forest floor to slick mud. In the bobbing torchlight, all he could see were passing tree branches and the shadows of his captors.

CHAPTER 78

"Over here!" shouted Olorus.

Ahlund set his blade even brighter, doing his best to pick a path toward the crash site of the *Gryphon*. The Greenspring's banks were marshy wetlands, and try as he might to stay on solid ground, his boots sunk up to the ankles with every other step. His sleeve caught on a sharp patch of branches. He pulled free, ripping a hole in the fabric.

"Can't you do something about these trees?" he growled over the rain.

Behind him, Gunnar called back, "What do you expect me to do about it?"

"Make them grow out of the way."

"These plants are too old," Gunnar said in an almost contemptuous tone of voice. "Their spirits are too mature—too wise to be controlled."

Ahlund swung his sword and chopped through a tangle of branches. They burst into flaming embers at the blade's touch, then shriveled to ashes.

At the crash site, someone had managed to light a makeshift torch. Pool, Borris, and Samuel could be seen wading through the water, trying to salvage what they could from the *Gryphon*'s wreckage. Olorus and Hook had piled up some scrap wood. They were shielding it from the rain with their bodies, trying to start a fire with the torch, but the wet timber would not take a flame.

Ahlund cut through the brush, strode into the clearing, and shot a fireball into the center of the pile of scrap wood. Olorus tripped over his own feet as he jumped back from an instantly blazing bonfire.

"All right, boys!" Gunnar yelled as he stepped into the firelight, flagging down his crew. "You did what you could. Time to let her go."

The panting sailors gave up on their salvage. As the captain and his crew watched the remains of their ship slip beneath the water's surface, Ahlund took inventory of his human assets. Olorus and Hook now looked more defeated than angry. Pool, Borris, and Samuel looked at their captain, awaiting orders that, by the look on Gunnar's face, he was not ready to give. Zechariah stood at the water's edge, staring off into the trees, absently rubbing the piece of cloth he had used to bind his crushed hand. The fabric was soaked dark red. The only sound was the rain.

"Several years ago," said Ahlund without preamble, "I began to feel a dark presence."

He waited a moment, and when no one offered protest or quip, he continued.

"Like one may feel rain in the air before it falls," he said, "I could sense daemyn spirits stirring, oceans and continents away, in the far east of the Oikoumene. I didn't know what to make of this, but as time passed and it continued to grow, it became clear that something in our world was changing. In recent months, this sensation became drastically more vile. I became concerned that the Ru'Onorath, the Guardians of the Oikoumene, had not purged whatever it was. The Ru'Onorath are aurym warriors devoted to fighting daemyn. They would not let such a force go unchecked—unless it was beyond their power to stop it. In another lifetime, I was one of them. But that was long ago. I'm just a soldier now.

"I was living in a small town called Deen, working as a sword for hire to protect the princess of Nolia, when I first met Zechariah. Lieutenant Antony, your distaste for Zechariah is no secret. You know him only as a meddlesome codger. Perhaps your opinion would change if you knew his true identity. Imagine my own surprise when, a few weeks after we first met, I learned that this seemingly plain old man was not only the legendary advisor to the boy-king of Raeqlund but a surviving member of the Brethren."

Olorus's lips parted slightly. Even Hook could not hide his surprise.

"The Brethren?" Gunnar said. "The order of immortal warrior-monks?"

"If the Brethren ever existed at all," said Olorus, "they were supposed to have died out five—nay, six hundred years ago."

"Killed off by a betrayer," said Zechariah, nodding. "Most of us, anyway. Five hundred and eighty-nine years ago, this winter."

"But, then, your age!" said Olorus. "That would make you—"

"Twice as old as the kingdom of Nolia," Zechariah said. "Or older. But let's not dig up ancient history."

"Zechariah told me that he could feel the same darkness in the far east," Ahlund said. "We discussed the matter many times. One night, I awoke for no apparent reason and felt a strong urge to ride out into the Gravelands. I obeyed the instinct, and just before dawn, something happened. An explosion of aurym power."

"It was indescribable," said Zechariah.

There was a strange look on Gunnar's face.

"Have you something to say, Gunnar?" asked Ahlund.

"Well, I . . ." said Gunnar. "A week, maybe a week and a half ago, I went to bed drunk but something woke me up that struck me sober as a nun. I thought it was a dream, but I could still feel echoes of it for a long time after that."

"One week ago," said Ahlund. "The timeline fits."

"If you, Gunnar, could feel it many miles away," said Zechariah, "imagine what Ahlund and I felt, being so close. Imagine how many others must have felt it as well."

Gunnar shook his head. "So what was it?"

"The epicenter was near my location," said Ahlund before Zechariah could say any more. "I rode toward it. The sun was coming up, and I saw buzzards circling in the sky. Beneath them lay a human body. I was almost too late. I had to kill one of the carrion birds before it could begin feasting. I found a young man, unconscious but alive. There were no tracks, no sign of how he had gotten there. It was as if he had fallen from the sky."

Ahlund let the words sink in.

Hook signed something.

"Justin?" Olorus translated.

Ahlund nodded.

"What we felt was the aurym energy expended to bridge a gap between worlds," said Zechariah. "It was an ethoul's arrival. Justin's arrival."

CHAPTER 79

Olorus spoke up. "My patience grows thin sitting here listening to tall tales!"

"I have yet to witness this mythological entity you call your patience, Olorus Antony," Zechariah said. "If you put half as much effort into thinking as you put into speaking—"

"I'm sharing this story with you now," said Ahlund, "so that we may choose our next course of action with every pertinent fact in mind. Listen a little more, and you will all be free to act as you see fit.

"I have told you about the daemyn in the east. Now, you have seen a cythraul with your own eyes. These are not the only strange goings-on. Refugees flood westward, fleeing war in Erum. Coblyns migrate in hordes. And less than one hundred miles north of us, an armada patrols the Raedittean Sea. A fleet of warships of unknown origins."

"I can vouch for that," Gunnar said. The rain had let up, and he pulled his pipe from his pocket, packed it, and lit it with a flaming piece of debris pulled from the fire. "Travelers staying at the Brig have been talking about it for weeks. Hundreds, some say thousands of black sails. No one knows where they came from or what they're doing."

"I have a guess at their intentions," said Ahlund. "They're here for Justin."

"You really believe Justin is an *angel*?" said Olorus.

"What I believe," said Zechariah, "is that thousands of years ago, there were individuals like Justin who came to this world from other places. Individuals the Ancients called 'fallen angels.' Whatever they were, I believe Justin is one of them."

"You're speaking as if all that stuff really happened," Gunnar said. "How's the story go? Demons enslaved mankind, so angels came down to save humanity? That's just the folklore of the western world. In other regions, folklore is different. What makes this drivel any truer than any other?"

"Until an hour ago, Vick probably thought that cythraul were only folklore and drivel," said Ahlund. "Belief notwithstanding, you saw what happened to him."

Gunnar glared over his pipe at Ahlund. The sailors hung their heads.

"This drivel is as real as you or me," said Ahlund. "You don't need to believe in it for it to kill you."

"It is only rational thinking that restrains my hand, Sims," said Olorus growled. "It is one thing for *you* to believe such nonsense, but you've dragged a lady of royal blood along on this witch-hunt! And now, she's gone because of you two. And for what?" Olorus kicked viciously at their campfire, sending flaming embers flying. "As all that is holy as my witness, if any harm comes to her, I will cut out both your hearts."

"Your feelings are noted, Olorus," Zechariah said wearily. "But Ahlund is correct. Your belief in the matter is not a requisite for reality. Fifty years ago, a prophecy foretold that an ethoul would appear in the Gravelands and that this event would mark the beginning of a time of unrest. I went to the Gravelands in pursuit of that prophecy, and there I waited for a fallen angel. Supposedly, ethouli were powerful warriors. Can you imagine what I thought when Ahlund brought Justin to me? A weakling of a boy, pitiful, delusional, infuriatingly helpless. I expected a fighter. But Justin did not know where he was, how he had gotten here, or why. As you mentioned, Gunnar, it's said they helped liberate humans from slavery beneath the demon overlords. Later, fallen angels were like living idols, worshipped as gods, inspiring populations to rise up and unite."

"If properly trained, Justin could still help us fight this enemy," said Ahlund.

"But," said Zechariah, "if he fell into the enemy's hands, he could destroy us. And that is what I fear may have happened tonight."

The circle was silent. Hook raised his hands and signed.

"You are lying by omission," translated Olorus. "Living idol? That, I understand. But how can he destroy us?"

Ahlund hesitated. "According to the legends, ethouli were capable of immense aurym power. Some say that one ethoul possessed the power of one hundred ordinary humans. Others say one thousand."

"They could build monuments by raising a hand," said Zechariah. "They could kill with a thought. Their whim was reality. Some ethouli *were* just living idols and figureheads. But others seized their authority by force. The same individuals who defeated the demons turned against humanity. Few historical accounts remain from those dark periods of history, when superpowered tyrants held the Oikoumene at their mercy."

"We're still talking about Justin, aren't we?" Olorus mocked.

"I admit, I don't sense any power in him," said Ahlund. "Perhaps that part of the legend has been exaggerated."

"Or perhaps," Zechariah said, raising a finger, "Justin simply has not yet discovered his potential. With some training and practice with his gauge stone—"

"Wait a second," Gunnar interrupted. "Justin doesn't know any of this. Does he?"

"Justin knows some of it," said Zechariah, "but not much. The boy is lost and confused. And he can be . . . temperamental. My repeated attempts to tell him the truth have been met with rather emotional reactions."

"I mentioned to him, in passing, that ethouli were supposedly powerful," said Ahlund. "I should have told him everything I knew. I fear he is woefully ill-prepared for what may await him."

Olorus translated for Hook: "You do not even know if any of this is true."

"It hardly matters whether or not it's true," said Zechariah. "If people believe it, it becomes true. If word were to spread that a divine being had been sent from heaven, true or not, people would take up arms to join the cause. Some nations would renounce his divinity; others would pledge themselves to it. This would lead to public outcry and perhaps even rebellion. If things progressed far enough, battle lines would soon be drawn. New alliances would form, and old ones would be broken. World power could shift. Belief would lead to radicalism. Radicalism would lead to conflict, would lead to martyrdom, would lead to war—not a war of nobles squabbling for territory. A holy war fueled by faith. People will kill for their leaders, but they will die for their faith. So the truth is quite elementary."

"You fools may have devoted yourselves to this cause," said Olorus, "but I have not. And neither has the princess. It sickens me to think of the way you've used her like a pawn!"

"Do not presume to speak on her behalf," Ahlund cut in. "She knew almost as much as Justin did. She insisted on coming with us."

"She . . . knew?" said Olorus. He opened his mouth to say something else, but no words came out. He seemed hurt.

"So you think the people you saw kidnapping Justin and Leah are working *with* the cythraul?" said Gunnar.

"I can't say for certain," said Zechariah.

"But if Justin's the one they're after," said Olorus, "why take the princess, too?"

"I don't know," said Zechariah. "There may be more pieces on this game board than we currently realize."

Hook worked his hands in the air.

"Hook says," said Olorus, "that he knows of at least one additional piece on the board. A valuable asset on *our* side, which could be put to use." Hook made another series of signs. "With Gunnar's help," translated Olorus said, "we could have a fleet of ships at our disposal."

Ahlund looked at Gunnar. His pipe had gone out, but he didn't seem to notice. When Gunnar said nothing, Hook signed some more.

"I know Gunnar is capable of this," Olorus translated, "because I know who this man is."

"Don't know what you're talking about," said Gunnar.

Gunnar opened his mouth to say more but trailed off because, at that moment, Hook was doing something that, judging by the look on Olorus's face, not even he had ever seen Hook do before. He was untying the strip of cloth around his forehead.

Hook let the cloth fall free. Previously hidden beneath it was a long, ugly scar running horizontally across his forehead. It was about an inch thick, and it wreathed his forehead just above the brow, running from the top of one ear to the other. Ahlund could not tell if the scar had been made by a cut or a burn, but it was an almost perfectly straight line—clearly done intentionally and with a steady hand.

"Where did you get such a scar, Sergeant?" asked Zechariah.

"That's no scar," Gunnar said. All eyes turned to him. "It's a brand. The brand of a galley slave."

Hook signed, and Olorus translated: "I was a youth when I was sentenced to life at the oars. My tongue was cut out, I was given this brand, and for years, I sat in the guts of a ship and rowed. I came to know well the name of Gunnar Erix Nimbus, along with the rest of my slave masters."

CHAPTER 80

"Slave masters!" said Olorus.

Long seconds passed, and Gunnar said nothing. Finally, Hook signed, *"The man's silence says it all. He is no fisherman. He is nobility. A royal admiral and a descendant of the Mythaean Sovereign King."*

Gunnar's crew murmured among themselves.

"And how does Mythaean royalty find himself fishing the inland rivers?" asked Zechariah.

"That's a long story," Gunnar said.

The way he dismissed the question instead of responding with a smart remark was enough to convince Ahlund that it was true. The Mythaean Thalassocracy was an ocean empire that ruled the Raedittean Sea. To Ahlund's knowledge, it was less a cohesive nation than it was a group of colonies sharing a similar culture and ancestry. Their nobles were the progeny of a warlord who had once conquered and united the entire Raedittean Archipelago. No small task. He left the empire to be ruled by his two sons, naming one a count and the other an admiral—one to rule the lands, one to protect the seas.

Such sovereign rule was a thing of the past. The Raedittean had fractured into many feuding city-states, yet to this day Mythaean colonies were governed based on the same system. One count and one admiral: two military leaders with theoretically equal power. If Gunnar was a royal admiral, it made him the equivalent of a prince among his people.

"So, you are a slaver in hiding," said Olorus.

Gunnar's lone eye burned fiercely. He ripped the unlit pipe from his mouth and pointed the stem Olorus. "I never owned slaves," he snapped. "I never took them or used them—not once. Not all of us are like that."

"Most are," Hook signed. "Bef*ore fate freed me of my bonds, I spent years at the oars. Time enough to learn much about my masters. There is a Mythaean colony just west of where the Greenspring meets the sea. Hartla. They will give Gunnar warships and soldiers. With a sufficient military force, we can proceed inland from Hartla and track down whoever took Leah and Justin."*

"But we don't know where they're headed," said Olorus.

Hook replied, and Olorus translated, "If Ahlund and Zechariah are right, they will be taking them east. They will not know we are looking for them, so there will be no reason for them to hide. Warships will allow us to patrol the coast and intercept any ships attempting to set sail from Athacea and cross the sea—"

Hook's thought was cut off by a deep cutting through the night. Ahlund grabbed his sword. Borris, Samuel, and Pool huddled closer to the fire.

"I think we have done enough talking," Zechariah said.

"Agreed," said Gunnar, surveying the trees. "Coblyns wouldn't even make a fitting appetizer for some of the things in these woods. The sooner we get out of here, the better." He turned to his sailors. "Boys, grab anything useful you can find. If we can't carry it on our backs, we leave it behind."

"But where we going, cap'n?" asked Pool.

"Hartla," said Gunnar.

"So you mean to go through with Hook's plan?" asked Zechariah.

"Hook's plan is not my concern," said Gunnar. "I have no ship thanks you to people, and if there are more of those demon things following you, I certainly don't intend to walk *back* toward Lonn. Hartla is a fortified city. I have some old friends there who might invite me in. Or they used to be friends, anyway. . . . Zechariah, feel free to tag along if you want. It might be your best chance to keep that hand. If anybody else wants to follow, that's his decision, but quit asking me favors."

While Gunnar and his crew packed up and prepared to move downstream, Ahlund turned his gaze upstream in the direction of an unknown enemy that had captured Justin and Leah. If mere human beings had committed this kidnapping, Ahlund would not have hesitated. It did not matter that they were already many miles away or that Ahlund was weary from the previous battle. He would have traveled to find their trail, hunted them down, and destroyed them all.

But there were, in a literal sense, bigger things to worry about than human beings. Sacrificing himself in a hopeless pursuit would help no one. But if Gunnar could be convinced, maybe Hook's plan would work. Maybe they could gain reinforcements at Hartla and intercept this enemy instead of hunting them down.

Ahlund was aware of Zechariah, Olorus, and Hook watching him, waiting for him to make a decision.

Gunnar and his sailors started downstream. Ahlund followed them, and the others followed Ahlund.

CHAPTER 81

This is torture, thought Justin's fevered brain as it happened. *Literal torture.*

He never saw their faces. They were always hooded. He had determined that he wouldn't tell them anything, no matter what they did to him, and that would have been a noble gesture if they had asked any questions. They barely said anything. They just hurt him. Over and over.

It was difficult to discern night from day in the Drekwood, but not impossible. Four days had passed since Justin had woken up as a prisoner, and on each day, the hooded men had come for him. They punched him, kicked him, beat him. Presently, they had left him lying in the mud, half-conscious.

There were too many injuries on his face to tell them apart anymore. He coughed and tasted blood. It was a struggle to draw breath. For the first time in a while, he wished he had his inhaler, but who was he kidding? This was the end. He would stop breathing entirely, soon enough.

Someone approached. Without looking, he knew they were bringing her to him. He could hardly see her through his swollen eyes, but he felt her kneel beside him.

"Oh, Justin. . . ." Leah said.

"Think my," Justin said. "Rib, broken. Hard to, breathe."

Leah placed her hands on his midsection. He felt her aurym wrap around the broken piece inside him. He braced himself. The fixing was often even more painful than the breaking.

He cried out at the tight wrench within his body as the rib was pulled and positioned back into place. Warm, healing hands willed the pieces of bone to grow and knit together, to build into each other until they were one again. The pain lessened as the surrounding inflammation reduced, and breathing became easier.

"Thank you," he said.

"I should just refuse to do this," she said. "If I didn't heal you, they wouldn't be able to—"

"I thought of that," Justin breathed. "You can't."

"Why not?"

"You can heal yourself, can't you?" he said.

"Within reason."

"How long until they figure that out?" Justin said. "If you don't do as they say, they might hurt you, too. I think that's why you're here. To fix what they break." Despite the pain, he forced a smile. "Just like Zechariah's training sessions."

Leah smiled too, and Justin thought he could see tears in her eyes.

She healed his broken nose—one of the most painful and most consistent of injuries—and forced down the swelling in his eyes by healing the traumatic tissue and draining the blood that had pooled beneath the skin. One by one, she reset his broken fingers.

Justin forced himself to sit up. He was bare-chested, and his skin was covered with bruises, dried blood, and cuts where the skin had been broken. Leah closed the open wounds, and Justin watched in dull fascination as the skin melted together like hot butter. The resulting scars were noticeable but not disfiguring. In spite of the circumstances, he enjoyed watching Leah work. The only time they were allowed near one another was when she healed him. The rest of the time, they were kept far apart.

"You're pretty good at that," said Justin.

"It used to be my job," Leah said.

"They haven't done anything to you, have they?"

"No. They leave me alone except when they need me to heal you."

Justin lowered his voice to a whisper. He knew there were guards somewhere nearby. "Have you learned anything?"

"They say we'll be out of the Drekwood soon," she said softly. "After that, I think they're taking us northeast."

"What's northeast?"

"The sea."

Justin tried not to react visibly to this news, but inside, he felt sick.

"Some of them have accents I've never heard before," Leah said. "I still don't know why they're doing any of this."

"If only I had been awake when they came for us," said Justin.

He had learned that during the raid on the *Gryphon*, he had not only been unconscious but drugged against the symptoms of a strange sickness. Leah said there had been a coblyn attack on the *Gryphon*, and she'd felt something big climb aboard the ship. Then strange men had broken into the cabin, grabbed both of them, and dragged them out through a cargo door. Leah and Justin had been tossed into the *Gryphon*'s lifeboat and taken away. The last thing Leah had seen was Zechariah's limp body thrown overboard into the darkness.

It must have been one of those cythraul things, thought Justin.

He tried not to think about the implications—that Zechariah was probably dead. The others, too.

"Have you overheard anything?" Leah asked.

"Not much worth repeating," said Justin. "From what I can tell, they were waiting for us in the Drekwood. I don't know how they knew we were coming. It sounds like they snuck in while Ahlund and the others were fighting that demon, but I don't understand how they timed their attack so perfectly. This Lisaac they talk about—I think he's in charge."

"I haven't seen him yet," said Leah, "but the men say he's a giant. They say he's part cyclops."

"Cyclops?"

"Human-like creatures that grow twenty-five feet tall. They are said to live on the ice fields of Otunmer in the far south. Probably only fairytales."

"I know what they are," said Justin. "Or at least, my world has stories about them."

"Supposedly, cyclopes carry a type of weapon called a voulge. It's a polearm, kind of like a spear but with a wide cutting blade. It's like a meat-cleaver on a long pole. Maybe Lisaac buys into the myth too, because I've heard them say he carries one."

Justin shuddered, thinking back to that first night when Lisaac had cut off a man's arm just for trying to touch Leah, then forced him to carry it. The wounded man had done all right for a mile or so, but gradually, he had fallen behind, growing weaker with each passing minute. Leah had tried to help him, but they would not allow her. When the one-armed man could walk no more, he had been left behind. Justin hoped he had bled to death before coblyns or anything else could get to him.

"I'm sorry, Leah," said Justin. "This is my fault. You should have left in Lonn when you had the chance. You could be on your way home right now with Olorus and Hook. Now you're here, and they're probably—"

"Stop apologizing," said Leah. "I made my choice. I bet you would rather be home, too. But what good is going home if you have to leave your friends behind to get there?"

The sound of approaching footsteps signaled that their time was up.

"Leah—" Justin said.

"Try not to tense up next time," she said.

Men came out of the trees and hauled Justin roughly to his feet.

"If you can relax your muscles," Leah called as he was dragged away, "the hits won't be as bad."

Justin kept his eyes on Leah for as long as he could.

See you next time, he thought as she disappeared in the darkness.

CHAPTER 82

Justin was tossed to the ground before a campfire. As usual, a bowl of foul-tasting, watery gruel was waiting for him. He picked it up and started to eagerly slurp down the contents, but a boot connected with his hand. The bowl hit his face, and the contents spilled down his front.

He didn't know how many soldiers were around him. Ten or fifteen, maybe, judging by the volume of their laughter. Some pointed fingers. Some made vulgar threats. In that moment, Justin wanted to kill them.

The rage made him dizzy. He wanted to put each of these men through the same physical torture he had endured at their hands, and *then* he wanted them to die.

If you get hit, get up and fight, Zechariah had once told him. *Remember how he did it and don't let it happen again.*

Justin picked his bowl up off the ground and brought it back toward his mouth, leaving himself open. His aggressor did not disappoint, but this time, Justin saw the boot coming.

Justin dropped the bowl, repositioned his body to lean into the oncoming kick, and caught it in the shoulder rather than the face. There was a vocalized sound of confusion from the attacker as Justin wrapped one arm around the man's leg and grabbed him by the shirt with the other. With all his might, Justin threw his weight forward. The man's feet were lifted from the ground, and Justin heaved him into the campfire.

The soldier tried to catch himself, and his outstretched hands sunk up to the wrists in burning coals. If he'd had the presence of mind to focus on gaining his feet, he might have removed himself from the situation promptly. Instead, he panicked. Every time a body part touched the flames or the coals, he recoiled, causing him to fall back into the same trap again and again. Coals and sparks flew as he thrashed. He screamed.

Several soldiers grabbed Justin. Others rushed to the aid of the man in trouble. After a few aborted attempts, someone finally grabbed him by the arm and pulled him free.

The injured man rolled around on the ground. "Put me out!" he yelled. "Put me out!"

"Settle down," someone said. "You ain't on fire."

It was true. Smoke trailed from his singed clothes in lazy spirals. In a few places—his hands, a corner of his chin, his legs—his skin was blistered and charred, but otherwise, he was fine. When he finally understood that he was not on fire and was not going to die, the soldier stopped rolling and lay there, looking at his burns and moaning.

"Ya swine!" snarled a soldier beside Justin.

A bony fist jabbed Justin in the stomach. He coughed and gasped for breath.

A deep, booming voice said, "What happened here?"

The men visibly tensed. Everyone went silent. Still wheezing from the punch, Justin looked up and saw, for the first time, the man they called Lisaac.

At first, Justin assumed he was hallucinating. No human being, he thought, could possibly be this big. He blinked, but Lisaac stayed the same.

He must have been eight and a half feet tall. His torso was rounded and unnaturally bulky. His shoulders were slouched, with arms that seemed much too long. If he had been able to stand fully erect, there was no doubt in Justin's mind that he would have surpassed nine feet, but his back was badly hunched, as if the weight of his own body were too much to carry.

Odder still was his face. His forehead was prominent. His jaw was thick and elongated. The cheekbones were wide. His eyes appeared tiny by comparison, sunken beneath a bulging brow ridge. This was not just a taller-than-average man, Justin realized. He seemed to be suffering from near-debilitating physical deformities, possibly the side effects of some disease. His voice was deep—unnaturally, gut-shakingly deep—as he repeated, "What happened here?"

"The—the kid," stammered one brave soul. "Threw him in the fire."

Sunken eyes like marbles came to rest on Justin, then shifted to look at the injured soldier on the ground.

Lisaac approached Justin. Instinctively and shamelessly, Justin tried to back away from the giant, but the soldiers held him in place.

"This is true?" Lisaac said, looking down at him.

A second after Lisaac spoke these words, Justin was hit in the face by his warm, stinking breath, expelled from between gapped teeth that seemed much too small for the man's mouth.

"Well?" said Lisaac.

Justin nodded.

"Your name is Justin," Lisaac rumbled.

Justin hesitated, unsure if it was a question. "Yes," he said.

Lisaac turned away. He walked past the fire and toward the burned man. How much did a body that size weigh? Six—seven hundred pounds? Yet his stride was surefooted; his size did not appear to hinder his movement.

"You are fine?" Lisaac said, looming over the burned man on the ground.

The burned man had to clear his throat twice before stammering, "F—fine, sir."

Lisaac's gaze turned back to Justin. "This man," he said. "You intended to kill him?"

Justin looked away.

"Have you ever killed a person before?" said Lisaac.

The question caught Justin by surprise, but he could think of nothing to gain by bluffing, so he said, "No."

"He is your first, then," said Lisaac.

At first, Justin thought Lisaac meant the first person he had ever *tried* to kill. But then Lisaac reached over his shoulder and freed his weapon: the voulge. It was nearly as long as he was tall, with a bladed, metal head that looked like an oversized meat cleaver.

Lisaac swung the massive weapon over his head and brought it down as if he were splitting wood.

"No!" Justin yelled.

The burned man's desperate shout was cut off as the cleaver blade fell through his neck and buried itself in the damp forest soil beneath.

Justin shut his eyes tightly and turned away. Nearby, someone gagged.

Justin heard Lisaac pull the voulge out of the ground.

"It took longer than I expected," boomed Lisaac's voice, "but finally, you show some spirit, Justin. We can work with that."

Despite Justin's best efforts, tears broke from between his eyelids and trickled down his face as the soldiers hauled him away. His heels dragged in the mud in defeat. He tried not to open his eyes, but he couldn't help it. At the campfire, two men were picking up the burned man's body by his legs and armpits. A third carried his head by a handful of hair.

Justin was thrown to the cold ground. He lay there, shirtless and plastered with mud. He knew he would be allowed to rest only a little while before once again being forced to march for hours on end. Then there would be another beating.

Everything will be all right, he thought. He had never in his life believed it less than he did right now.

I'm going to die here, he suddenly realized. *No one is coming to save me.*

I'm never going home.

He slipped his hand into his pocket and discretely withdrew the gauge stone. It was the only thing he had left—too small for them to find and only a pebble to untrained eyes, anyway. With the gauge in his palm, he concentrated, trying to will his inner strength through it, trying to block out his surroundings, trying to make the stone glow.

CHAPTER 83

A fist connected with his face, and he felt his nose break. Again.

He hit the forest floor with blood flowing from both nostrils. He blinked away tears, trying to see where the next attack would come from.

A boot heel stomped down on his hand, and the bones of two fingers broke at the knuckles. He could not clench his teeth quite hard enough to hold back the cry of pain, and it came out as a squealing hiss. He remembered the first time his fingers had been broken, just a few days ago. The backward, wrongly bent thumb and forefinger, seemingly knuckled in all the wrong places, had filled him with disgust. The pain was unpleasant, but nothing was worse than the horror of seeing a part of himself so quickly and callously ruined—to have seemingly permanent damage done to the only body he would ever have.

Those things no longer bothered him, nor even merited much attention. Leah's aurym abilities would heal the wounds. His body was not being destroyed. Just tortured. That freed him to focus on the pain.

Pain was a funny thing. It was not like warmth or cold or other sensations that the body adapted to after prolonged exposure; you never got used to pain, it seemed. Because no matter how many times they hit him, it always hurt exactly as much as it had the first time. The only real way to cope with it was through distraction, so Justin busied his mind by studying their attack patterns, learning what to expect next. Even now, he was automatically bracing himself for—

A booted foot kicked him in the kidneys. Nerves in his lower back fired with sharp pain. He never stopped feeling the pain, but he no longer felt the fear. He had become desensitized to it. It was the same beating every time. Pain was just pain. What was the point of being afraid? It would only further empower these men. They were just muscle. Faceless thugs. They were not worthy of his fear.

Justin started to look up, but someone punched him in the jaw. When he looked again, the man who had hit him was shaking his hand and rubbing the knuckles.

"Aw . . . you hurt yourself?" said Justin. He spit blood onto the ground. "Poor thing."

It was a stupid thing to do, but it distracted him from the pain. Even made him smile a little.

Someone grabbed him by the hair, and another man grabbed his arms and pinned them behind his back. Ahead, he spotted the dull reflection of a dagger in the torchlight.

This is new, he thought.

Hands gripped his face to hold it in place. A hooded surgeon kneeled before him and brought the dagger to his eye.

"Boys," said a deep voice.

The dagger's tip was resting against the ridge of Justin's broken nose—so close to his eye that he couldn't see it.

"The general approaches," Lisaac's voice rumbled. "He would like to . . . *talk* . . . with the prisoner."

The men dropped Justin into the mud. The dagger was gone. The hooded men were walking away. No. Hurrying away.

Justin felt a pang of sickness in his gut, emanating from deep below a newly broken rib. As the feeling intensified, expanding and contracting, becoming a cold, sucking darkness within him, he recognized it for what it was. Fear returned to him.

No, he thought. *Bring back the dagger.*

Justin scrambled in the mud, trying to look everywhere at once in the darkness. Turning, he spotted the eight-and-a-half-foot-tall silhouette of Lisaac in the lingering light of a dropped torch. Justin blinked. And suddenly, standing beside Lisaac's silhouette—no, *over* it—was the massive, shadowed frame of a ten-foot-tall monster.

No. . . !

A thousand-pound body constructed of armor and bone. Shoulders six feet wide, curled upward with bony crests. A fleshless, black skull for a head. Two horns protruding from above the brow. Crude, tattered clothing hung from its midsection, and slung over its shoulder was the jagged, crescent-moon blade of a notched scythe.

The cythraul pushed past Lisaac as if the giant man were a child. The ground shook as it stepped toward Justin. Justin turned and pumped his legs to break for the trees, but before he could take two steps, a giant hand grabbed him by the arm and plucked him bodily from the ground.

Higher and higher he was lifted. His forearm, caught within the grasp of a monstrous fist, burned with a pain the likes of which he had never felt before. It was like a chemical burn. Sizzling, melting, disintegrating his flesh. All the pain he'd ever felt, combined, was nothing compared to this. It seeped into his bones, boiling his marrow.

His body finally stopped rising and was held suspended before the great skull of the cythraul. He stared into its pitted, eyeless sockets. He heard someone screaming in agony. As the cythraul's mouth opened to reveal serrated teeth running in double rows like those of a shark, Justin realized the scream he was hearing was his own.

The mouth was big enough to bite off Justin's head at the shoulders. He kicked and thrashed, but it made no difference. His arm felt as if it were submerged in acid, and with each passing second, the pain somehow grew worse. Dark spots formed in his vision as his own screams faded to dull, faraway echoes. The last thing he heard before the world fell away was a voice—a voice like cinder blocks dragging over pavement—as the cythraul said, "JUSTIN."

CHAPTER 84

A cythraul, thought Ahlund. *Close. And getting closer.*

Ahlund wondered if anyone else among their little group had noticed the way the temperature had dropped so suddenly and so unnaturally or the way the shadows around them seemed darker, as if they had thickened into physical manifestations.

For a while, Ahlund thought he could sense a cythraul following them. Then the feeling had disappeared suddenly and reappeared miles ahead. Now, it felt like one was right on top of them.

Ahlund walked at the rear of the procession. The group had followed the Greenspring for a whole day after the *Gryphon*'s crash. Then, on Gunnar's assurance that he knew the way, they had left the river and blazed a trail straight into the untamed Drekwood. A windstorm besieged them on the third day. Limbs had crashed down from high above, but the deep-rooted, demonic trees of the Drekwood did not sway or shift. Every night, predators circled, and on the third night, Ahlund had been forced to slay an ursushound—a carnivore with the size and strength of a bear and the swiftness and cunning of a dog. They were viciously territorial, and this beast had proven too insistent for its own good. They had cooked its meat over a fire, but it tasted of blood and rot. Today had been uneventful thus far, save the sensation of the cythraul close by.

A crash in the underbrush ahead brought Ahlund to full alert, but it was only Borris tripping on a root.

"The gods curse this place!" Borris hissed out of the side of his scarred mouth as he stood and brushed the leaves from his shirt. "Been told all me life it were haunted. Shoulda listened to me mum and been a farmer."

"Your mother was a whore," spat Pool.

"Aye, she was," Borris agreed, "and thank the stars. 'Twas the dirty coin of lonely farmers that put pants on me arse."

"Quiet," Olorus commanded. "I think I saw something."

Ahlund reached for his sword and squeezed a white-knuckled grip on the hilt. Smoke rose from the sheath.

Olorus craned his neck to get a better look through the trees.

"What is it?" said Zechariah.

"A bit of light, I think," said Olorus. "A reflection of some kind?"

Gunnar stepped up beside Olorus and squinted with his single eye. "Dawn hitting the cliffs, I believe," he said. "Means we're nearly out of these woods."

Ahlund was no native of the western world, but he knew that the northern edges of Athacea were wooded coastal plains that bordered wild scrublands. One of the most well-known characteristics of the region was a series of sandstone ridges that ran perpendicular to the coastline. They zigzagged along the continent like a thunderbolt, creating sheer cliffs and canyons. Their destination, Hartla, was situated where those cliffs met the sea.

Gunnar looked smugly at Olorus. "See, Red? Told you we weren't lost."

Olorus scratched self-consciously at his ginger stubble. "It is not your sense of direction that worries me," he said. "It is the fact that I still think I should have gone to search for Leah! Were it not for Hook's plan, I never would have agreed to—"

"Hook's plan *this*, Hook's plan *that*," mumbled Gunnar as he pushed his way through the trees. "I don't know if you've noticed, but Hook's plan is contingent on the selfless cooperation of one person in this group whose goodwill has surpassed its breaking point. You bastards owe me a hell of a lot of gold, plus a new ship and/or financial compensation in equal value of the vessel in question, plus the supplies lost in the wreck, hazard pay for continuing on foot through hostile territory, surcharges for general pain and suffering—don't think I'm not keeping track. Hell of a time to call in favors."

Gunnar continued protesting, but Ahlund was not listening.

Zechariah tripped on a rut in the path and steadied himself on Pool for support. He patted the stout little sailor on the shoulder as a thank you, then kept walking. Ahlund frowned.

"Old man," Ahlund said.

Zechariah halted. Slowly he turned to face him. "I wish you would stop calling me that."

"Your hand," said Ahlund.

Zechariah sighed and rolled up the right-hand sleeve of his robes. He had bled through his wraps again. Ahlund had managed to stop the bleeding a few times, but the wounds kept reopening. They had no medical supplies, and fresh water was difficult to come by in a poisonous place like the Drekwood; they hardly had enough for drinking, let alone for cleaning wounds. They were running short on fabric for clean wraps, too. Beyond some basic first aid, Zechariah's wound had essentially gone untreated for four days.

"Quite the time to lose our healer," said Zechariah.

"Pray that Hartla is close," said Ahlund. "It will be difficult to stave off—"

"Infection has already begun in earnest," said Zechariah. His head wobbled a bit as he spoke, as if fighting dizziness. "This hand is beyond saving. It's the rest of me I am wondering about."

Ahlund leveled his gaze at him.

"I know the Brethren were famously *immortal*," said Zechariah, "but immunity to the adverse effects of time and decay is not strictly immortality. We are no better protected from physical damage or violent deaths than anyone else. Our immortality only applies until it is acted upon by an outside force, like the sickness brought on by a badly infected wound."

Ahlund remained silent. Death by infection was a unique brand of unpleasantness. If the hand was as bad as Zechariah said, their only recourse would be amputation. The question was, would it happen in Hartla under a surgeon's saw, or in the field beneath Ahlund's sword?

CHAPTER 85

The foliage thinned near the sandstone cliff faces. No longer was the path choked with rock-hard branches and brush. The blackened, daemyn-fed trees were replaced by less sinister sycamores, cypresses, and oaks. Soon, Ahlund felt a nearly forgotten sensation: the warmth of the sun on his shoulders.

It was mid-morning when they reached a jagged rock wall. Trees and flowering brush clinging to its façade hung over a creek that hugged the base of the cliffs. They rested and gathered water. Zechariah removed himself from the group to wash and bandage his wound in private. He refused to let anyone look at it.

An hour later, as they followed the creek along the base of the cliff, Ahlund heard a sound that stopped him in his tracks. A distant roar echoed through the forest. The call of a cythraul.

The rest of his party walked on, undisturbed. Even Zechariah seemed not to have heard it. Ahlund gripped the hilt of his sword and resumed marching.

"I hope this city truly holds allies of yours, Gunnar Erix Nimbus," Zechariah said, quite loudly.

"Even if it does," Gunnar said from the front of the procession, "intercepting the people who took Leah and Justin might not be as easy as you think."

"You are certain these people will remember who you are?" Zechariah asked, again very loudly.

Gunnar looked over his shoulder, making a face at Zechariah's uncharacteristically noisy voice. "I don't think it'll be a problem."

"I hope you are right," Zechariah replied. "Because several of them seem to have arrows aimed at your head."

As Zechariah finished his sentence, Hook and Olorus threw themselves to the ground. Gunnar got down on his haunches, unsheathed his cutlass, and scanned the surrounding forest. A few seconds later, the sailors managed to get their weapons free and duck down as well.

"No need for all that," Zechariah said. He gestured toward the cliffs. "They've got us penned in. If they want to kill us, there'll be little stopping them."

Ahlund squinted into the forest. Now that the old man mentioned it, he noticed the places where the canopy was unnaturally unimpeded by branch-cover, clearly manipulated by human hands. Once these areas were evident, it was not hard to trace them to the geometric shapes of camouflaged guard posts in the trees. Archers were stationed within them.

You're slipping, Ahlund thought. *So focused on distant dangers that you're walking into avoidable ones. As the Ru'Onorath proverb says, it is the man watching for bears who steps in a bear trap.*

Suddenly, Zechariah wobbled and fell to his knees. Ahlund hurried to him and placed a hand on his shoulder. Even through the robes, Ahlund felt heat emanating from Zechariah's body. And despite burning with fever, he was not sweating.

Ahlund turned toward the sentry posts and waved a hand, shouting, "Come quickly! The old man is hurt! He needs water!"

"Old man," Zechariah grumbled. "No bloody respect."

The voice of someone unseen reverberated off the cliff. "Lower your weapons! All of you!"

Ahlund unbuckled his sword belt and let it fall. Olorus and Hook exchanged unsure glances before dropping their weapons, too. Gunnar did the same, and the sailors followed his lead. Zechariah tried to remove his sword from his sheath, but he couldn't. Ahlund drew it for him and laid it in the grass.

"You there," shouted the same voice. "Did he speak truly? Are you Gunnar Erix Nimbus?"

"Aye," Gunnar called. "And through wind and tide and squall and foe, I shall ever journey on."

Some sort of formal greeting, Ahlund thought.

"Archers," said the voice in the trees. "Keep your bows up. The rest of you, approach with caution. Bind their hands."

Branches moved as sentries climbed down from the posts.

"Bind their hands?" Olorus whispered. "I should like to see them try."

"Does it come naturally?" Gunnar asked. "Or do you have to work at being such a halfwitted goon?"

"You are the one who is halfwitted, fisherman," Olorus said, "if you think I will not remember and repay each of your comments in due time."

"That'll be the first payment I receive on this venture," said Gunnar. "I suppose you aren't too worried, if the bowstrings start twanging, anyway. Your skull is probably dense enough to stop an arrow."

"Arrow through the skull," said Olorus without looking at him. "Is that what happened to you?"

Gunnar glared at him with his lone eye but said nothing.

"First tenet of the High Nolian Guard," whispered Olorus, eying the sentries as they approached. "Never surrender."

"Yet you just laid your weapons down," said Gunnar.

"I can have my weapons back in my hands and thick with the blood of these fools in an instant!" hissed Olorus. "A High Guard swears a life-oath to protect the royal house by any means necessary, including death. We will die before we are taken as prisoners. And we certainly do not allow our hands to be bound."

Ahlund was about to reprimand Olorus, but Zechariah spoke up.

"Which is more sacred?" asked Zechariah, breathing shallowly as he sat on the ground. "Your oath to the royal house, or the tenets of the High Guard? The order to never surrender was probably meant as inspiration for courage—not as an excuse not to *think*. But if you are so blindly devoted to the tenets of the High Guard, a mostly extinct order that as good as betrayed its own benefactors, then your life-oath ends today, I think. I would only ask that you first please distance yourself from the rest of us so that none of the arrows loosed at you accidentally hit me."

Olorus growled but said nothing.

Two squads of sentries clad in orange-trimmed leather armor approached. There were short swords at their belts, but they did not draw them. Ahlund offered his hands and did not make eye contact with the young man—almost a full twelve inches shorter than him—who tied his wrists with sturdy leather cords. When the same soldier bent over to bind Zechariah, he saw the bloody wraps and instead helped the old man to his feet, unbound. Nearby, Olorus and Hook both allowed their hands to be tied. No one approached Gunnar.

Gunnar raised his hands to the closest sentry. "You forgot one, sonny."

"Our commanding officer ordered that you not be bound, sir," said the sentry.

Gunnar's face changed, taking on a look of such disapproval that the sentry shrank beneath it.

"You see these men you have bound?" said Gunnar in a voice that was deadly quiet. "I am one of them. Either we are all prisoners, or none of us are. Now bind my hands. That is an order."

The sentries fidgeted. After some hesitation, the young man stepped forward and bound Gunnar's hands.

With guards at their flanks, the group was led into the woods. As a pair of soldiers gathered the discarded weapons, Ahlund looked over his shoulder. He could have sworn he had just heard another roar.

CHAPTER 86

A small military outpost of log-built shacks sat along the edge of the cypress and oak forest. By the look of it, no more than thirty soldiers were stationed here, and half were evidently out on patrol. While Gunnar met privately with the outpost's commanding officer, the rest of the prisoners waited.

Ahlund and the others still did not have their weapons, but they had been freed from their bonds and provided with fresh water, and several soldiers were currently fetching bandages for Zechariah. After facing so much darkness, it was refreshing to be reminded that while not all the world was honorable, good people did still exist. Virtue and decency still had a place. And that was worth fighting for.

Ahlund kneeled beside Zechariah. Gunnar was speaking to the outpost commander. Their words were inaudible from this distance, but body language spoke volumes. Gunnar, cool as ever, paced before the officer and did most of the talking. The officer was not only listening but standing at attention. It looked more like he was being addressed by a superior than a prisoner.

"Aurym," said Zechariah.

Ahlund looked at him.

Zechariah smiled. "We hire a ship captain to ferry us down the Greenspring, and he just happens to be Mythaean nobility . . . with, perhaps, precisely the connections we need to keep hope alive."

"We hired him because he had the best boat," Ahlund said. "In hindsight, he had the best boat because of who he is."

"Logical," Zechariah agreed. "But logic cannot explain us finding you in Lonn after we were separated. Nor can logic explain why you were drawn out into the Gravelands that night to find Justin. Or how the destruction of your home, which led us north, saved us from a pack of cythraul we did not know existed. Aurym is at work."

"Selective memory," Ahlund said. "You forget most of the story, and you credit aurym with the rest."

"Oh?"

"Was it aurym that took Justin and Leah from us?" demanded Ahlund. "Was it aurym that allowed the town of Irth to be destroyed and its people slaughtered? Was it aurym that separated us from our healer just when we need her the most? You are a great man, Zechariah, but sometimes, you are blind."

Zechariah looked away, and Ahlund sighed. He almost pitied the old man. He remembered a time when he, too, suffered from the same blindness and naiveté. As a young initiate in the Ru'Onorath, there had been a fire in him: faith in the will of aurym. Belief that the power of the spirit was not just an energy source, but that its perfect will had a hand in the world.

But that was a long time ago, before Ahlund had been forever exiled from the Ru'Onorath.

There had been no conspiracy against him. No mistake, no plot, no injustice. Ahlund had simply exercised his free will. The fire of faith within him had gone out, so he had turned his back on the order. He had walked away from it all.

He had secretly prayed for something to stop him—for aurym's will to intervene. An unexpected event to prevent his leaving. A twist of fate to lend him divine inspiration. A voice speaking his name from the clouds and chastising him for his faithlessness. He had prayed for something—*anything*—to happen. Something to save him from himself and prove that his faith was not unfounded and that aurym really did have a hand in the world.

Instead, he had walked away, and nothing had stopped him.

Few transgressions among the Ru'Onorath were graver than direct, unapologetic renouncement of the order. His exile was self-imposed, but it was final. He was forbidden to return.

Ahlund knew now that aurym was an energy source and a powerful weapon, but there was nothing spiritual about it. It was not an intelligent entity. It did not have a will of its own, and it was not the sacred, metaphysical ally that Zechariah and the Ru'Onorath thought it was. Some cultures made gods out of the sun or the moons. Zechariah and the Ru'Onorath were no different, worshipping something they did not understand, seeing signs and portents where there were none.

Ahlund could produce fire through his sword. Much like normal fire, it could be harnessed and controlled if used properly. Or it could burn you. It was a tool. Nothing more. And since leaving the Ru'Onorath, he had used it whenever and however he pleased. For money. For gain. For killing.

"Putting trust in the will of aurym might be comforting," said Ahlund. "But wishful thinking is no substitute for reality. And 'faith' is not an acceptable scapegoat for failure."

Zechariah turned and squinted at Ahlund as if suddenly realizing something. "You blame yourself for this," he said.

The old man's insight was infuriating at times.

"What's done is done, Ahlund," said Zechariah. "Regret solves nothing. We must focus on the path ahead."

"The path ahead?" Ahlund said. "On the Greenspring, I was so focused on the path ahead, on fighting the enemy in front of me, that I did not see the one that snuck up from behind and took Justin from us. Deciding to come here, following Gunnar, putting our hope in a farfetched plan. I wasn't thinking clearly. I should have hunted down those kidnappers when I had the chance. Now we don't know where Justin is or if he's even alive."

"That's logic talking," said Zechariah disdainfully.

"You have a problem with logic?" said Ahlund.

"Logic itself is infallible," said Zechariah. "It's like a knife's edge. Even a skilled wielder can cut himself from time to time."

Ahlund looked sharply at him.

"You speak of logic as if it is infallible," Zechariah continued. "But logic is only as infallible as its user. I can use critical thinking and my own informed reasoning to determine truth based on facts, inference, and observable proof. However, as a fallible human, I also know that I am capable of making mistakes—and how *many* mistakes I have made in my long life, Ahlund! I would have to be quite naïve to trust in the reasoning powers of someone who is as great a fool as me."

"You call yourself a fool?"

Zechariah made a noise in his throat. "Faith in logic would only be an acceptable doctrine if I had never made a mistake before, which is why I find the notion to be quite overrated. It would be very—what was the word you used? *Comforting* to believe I had all the answers. It is much more difficult to be a realist and own up to how little I know.

Besides, Ahlund, you are the one who charged into a burning building not so long ago. Maybe your behavior is not as logical as you think."

"Maybe you don't know me as well as you think," said Ahlund.

"You rode out in the middle of the night on nothing more than a feeling," said Zechariah. "That's how you found Justin. Everything you have ever done and everything that has ever happened to you brought you to that moment. As a mercenary, the path you chose was self-serving, but aurym has had a hand in all of it—even when you were at your worst. Perhaps, in the interest of profit, you even considered delivering the princess *to* her enemies instead of protecting her from them. . . ?"

Zechariah waited for a response. Ahlund said nothing.

Zechariah ran his good hand over his beard. "Regardless of how you got here, Ahlund," he continued, "you are here. Olorus and Hook are here out of a sense of duty. Gunnar happened to be where we needed him, when we needed him. It all converged to bring us here. Imagine if a single piece of the puzzle were lost. Imagine if Gunnar were still an admiral instead of an outcast. Imagine if I had not been on the Gravelands. Imagine if you were still a Ru'Onora. You would be halfway across the world. Instead, you were exactly where you needed to be, exactly when you needed to be there."

"Are you trying to say—?"

"And," Zechariah cut in, lifting a finger. "Princess Anavion not only willingly joined us but is an aurym-gifted healer. You are right to say that she was taken from us when I needed her the most. But she is, presumably, with Justin instead, perhaps when *he* needs her the most."

Up ahead, Gunnar was concluding his conversation with the outpost officer. The officer saluted him smartly. Gunnar nodded in a bored sort of way, then came walking toward Ahlund and Zechariah.

"Justin was cast out of his world and fell into this one," Zechariah said. "Are we any different? Torn from the worlds we knew and borne off like pollen on the wind? Was it all by chance and coincidence? You may feel that you have failed Justin, but no one is a failure so long as he soldiers on. Gunnar, Olorus, Hook, and the others look to you for courage. When you give up, that is when you fail."

Zechariah grabbed Ahlund's shoulder with his good hand and squeezed with bony, pale fingers. The strength of his grip was remarkable.

"Don't give up, Ahlund," he said.

Gunnar arrived and knelt down beside them. "They're giving us passage to Hartla," he said. "Shouldn't be more than a few hours' journey by wagon, but I really can't promise what'll happen when we get there. I'm taking an awful risk here."

"It does not go unappreciated," said Ahlund.

Gunnar made a face. "Don't thank me just yet. Wulder Von Morix was a friend, once upon a time, but people drift apart. Allegiances change. As far as I know, we're just as likely to be welcomed with open arms as we are to be slapped in irons. Keep that under your hats, though, will ya?" He gestured toward Olorus and whispered, "Wouldn't want that one doing anything characteristically stupid."

"Not to question your integrity, captain," said Zechariah, "but I'm beginning to think the story of your upbringing among the Drekwood wolves is full of holes."

Gunnar smirked.

"What news, fisherman?" asked Olorus as he and Hook joined them.

"All's well so far," Gunnar said. He nodded to Hook. "There's a chance your plan may work."

Olorus perked up. "You'll do it?"

"Look, don't get too excited," said Gunnar. "Hartla's shipbuilders are the best for hundreds of miles. At some point, I'll have to stop there anyway to get a new ship, given that the *Gryphon* fell victim to your manipulations. The way I figure, the only thing better than one ship is a fleet of ships. With a few words in the right places, I might be able to convince a disenfranchised captain or two to abandon their posts and follow me out to sea—could be the start of a lucrative privateering venture."

"Do you think the Hartlans will give you ships?"

"That's the real trick, ain't it?" said Gunnar. "They're leaders. Politicians. We might be able to convince them to see the political benefit of saving a lost princess, though I can't vouch for what they'll want to do with her."

Olorus squirmed but said nothing.

"Hook," said Ahlund. "Do you anticipate any trouble?"

Hook looked at him but did not sign.

"What do you mean, 'trouble'?" asked Olorus.

"Were you freed?" Ahlund asked.

Hook signed, *"No."*

"Escaped?" said Ahlund.

Hook signed, *"Yes."*

"And the Mythaeans," said Ahlund. "What is their policy regarding runaway slaves?"

Hook's next sign required no translation: an index finger pulled across the throat.

"What?" Olorus gasped. "Then you need something to cover that slave brand better than a blasted piece of cloth!"

Ahlund had learned enough of Hook's signs to fill in the blanks as the silent soldier replied, *"I knew the risk in this plan. I accept it. I knew if I ever came north again, I would have to face my past."*

"But what if they find out?" Olorus whispered.

"They will," signed Hook.

"We'll fight it," said Olorus.

"We cannot," signed Hook. *"It would jeopardize any hope of gaining their help. We have to honor their laws."*

"It will be a cold day in hell before I honor the laws of slavers," Olorus said. "How could you place yourself in this danger?"

"I may not have been born a man of Nolia," signed Hook, *"but Nolia took me in. They made me one of their own. They saw value in me. Within a mute, beaten galley slave, they saw my character. When I became a High Guard, I swore to protect the royal blood. I will give my life for my princess. Or perhaps I should say, my queen. Queen Leah Anavion. And for Nolia. My true homeland."*

CHAPTER 87

"Get up," someone said.

Leah opened her eyes to a sight she hadn't seen in days. A blue sky.

"Come on, healer," said the voice.

She pushed herself up from the dirty, ragged bedroll. The sun was up and shining through the trees. The forest was still thick, but it somehow felt less sinister. The canopy was less solid, and the sun shined through naturally. It seemed they had finally left the Drekwood.

"Better hurry," the voice said. "He's pretty bad."

Leah quickly forgot the joy of the blue sky. They always called on her to heal Justin after they hurt him, but no one had ever told her to hurry before.

She followed the soldier past smoking fire pits and men sleeping on the ground. Soldiers stood guard around the perimeter with bows, swords, and spears. Justin had estimated their numbers at fifty, but she was beginning to think it was closer to one hundred.

Something caught her eye, and she stopped. Imprinted in the moist, muddy earth before her was an impossible sight. It was a footprint—no, a *boot* print—the size of a wine barrel.

"Come on," the soldier said and reached to grab her.

"Your friend may need your help," boomed a thunderous voice.

The soldier drew back his hand from Leah as if scalded. Leah turned to see Lisaac standing at the edge of a clearing. No matter how many times she saw him, his size was no less shocking.

But not even he is big enough to leave a track like that, thought Leah, looking back at the giant boot print. *Only one thing is.*

She tried not to falter beneath Lisaac's gaze as she approached. The beady eyes sunken in his malformed head always watched her in a suggestive manner. She stopped before him, entirely shadowed by his giant form.

"Do you see that footprint over there?" she said.

"Yes," said Lisaac.

"I think it was made by a cythraul," said Leah. "A High Demon. They are extremely dangerous. If one is close, we need to get out of here before. . . ."

She trailed off at the look on Lisaac's elongated face. His lips curled into a smile, baring tiny, gapped teeth like rounded pebbles lodged in his gums.

"The cythraul are indeed dangerous," he said. "Your friend can attest to that."

Lisaac gestured toward the center of the clearing. Leah's eyes went wide. Only now did she notice Justin's body lying in an immobile heap in the mud behind Lisaac. She sprinted to him. Sliding across the ground on her knees, she summoned her aurym for the healing process.

"By the spirit. . . ." she said.

Justin looked like a corpse. He lay crumpled and lopsided, like a doll tossed aside by a fickle child. He had all the usual injuries, but one thing stood out above the rest: his left arm.

"What happened?" she shouted, her voice cracking.

"He was touched," said Lisaac. "By a cythraul."

Carefully, Leah repositioned Justin's arm to get a better look at the wound, and what she saw made her stomach convulse. His hand seemed fine. His shoulder, likewise, was normal. Yet everything in between, from his bicep to his wrist, looked as if it had been eaten away, burned bone-deep. The skin, the muscles—everything was gone. Stripped to the bone. Dissected like a cadaver in the healers' academy operating theater. What remained looked like the blackened, desiccated flesh of a carcass after several weeks of decay.

Leah's hands were shaking. Panic threatened to drown her in its icy depths. She felt like an initiate at the Academy again, seeing her first potentially lethal injury and frantic beyond words at the thought of a life resting in her unsteady hands.

Remember your training, she thought. *Detach yourself. See the person as they should be, not as they are. See the injury, see the problem, and see the solution.*

She shut her eyes, trying to convince herself that this was not Justin; this was not a friend. It was a stranger. A wounded soldier brought in from the front lines. And she was his only chance.

So do your job!

She opened her eyes. She could use her aurym to start blindly rebuilding tissue and staving off infection, but to heal effectively, she needed to know the nature of the wound. It looked like the arm of a burned corpse, but she could see no peripheral burns. No signs of charring to the surrounding skin or clothing. She squinted, letting a lack of focus lend a new angle of perception, and a subtle pattern emerged. Just as the boot print in the muddy ground was impossible yet unmistakable, so too was the way this wound seemed to wrap intentionally around the arm—not in the amorphous blob pattern typical of a violent burn.

It's a handprint, she thought. *A giant handprint.*

It appeared that, somehow, the physical contact of the cythraul's touch had caused this damage—

"Heal him," boomed Lisaac from behind.

"I'm examining him," Leah said. "I've never seen this kind of wound before."

"Heal him."

She shook her head. It was no use talking to this man. Not at a time like this, and maybe not ever. She held her open palm over the blackened remains of Justin's arm and willed her aurym to flow through the aurstone in the ring on her finger.

She drew her hand back, blinking in shock at what she felt. Reaching her healer's aurym into another person was a bit like touching them physically. It was usually warm, but touching Justin's arm felt cold as ice.

She shook off the surprise and forced herself to stay linked with the patient. She pushed her aurym's healing hands into the frigid darkness and loosed the power that influenced the production of blood and the growing of tissue.

Nothing happened.

Leah pushed harder, willing her aurym stronger, but the subject remained unresponsive.

There had been times in her career when patients had been beyond saving, but this was different. Even when someone was rapidly approaching death, parts of their body would still heal and rebuild under the correct influence. The only time a body was completely unresponsive was when it was. . . .

Dead.

Frantically, Leah kneeled down and pressed her ear against the skin of Justin's bare sternum. A heartbeat. He was still alive.

"What are you doing?" Lisaac demanded. "Heal him."

Leah held her hand over Justin's face where his lip had been split. She willed her aurym to work, and the skin quickly fused, leaving barely a mark. She tried the arm again, but nothing happened. There was still only coldness. It was unprecedented. Why would a specific wound reject a healer's aurym while the rest of the body accepted it?

Worry about that later, she told herself. *For now, just do what you can.*

She focused on Justin's shoulder. The barrier between the living and seemingly dead flesh was as distinctive as fire and ice. She poured her power in, repairing the flesh and encouraging the body to produce great excesses of blood. When she had shored up every piece of the shoulder, she moved down to the wrist and repeated the process. She placed a palm on Justin's forehead and used her aurym to test his condition. Lisaac stepped up beside her.

"He's stable," she said. "Hopefully it won't take him long to regain consciousness."

"His arm is still damaged," Lisaac said.

"I can't repair it," she said.

"You will."

"I can't!" Leah said, wheeling on Lisaac. "The most skilled healer in the world couldn't fix this."

Towering over her, Lisaac frowned. "Why?"

"I don't know," said Leah.

Lisaac seemed to consider this. "He will survive?" he asked.

"I think so," said Leah.

Lisaac squinted at her suspiciously. "I will be displeased if he is permanently damaged."

"Your displeasure is the least of my worries," Leah said. She turned to look at the arm again. The arm was dead. That much was clear. The question was whether it would need to be amputated.

"How did it get in here, anyway?" asked Leah.

Lisaac looked confused.

"The cythraul," she said. "Did it break through your defenses? Is it gone?"

"You misunderstand," said Lisaac. "It came and went, and it will be back."

Leah started to say something else, but Lisaac cut her off.

"Take her away," he ordered.

Two soldiers came forward. She swung her elbow and caught one in the mouth, but the other grabbed her by the arms.

"Get off me!" she said. "He's still hurt!"

Lisaac bent over, down and down, until he was face-to-face with her. His head was almost twice the size of hers. His gaze slowly traced her up and down.

"All I require is that he lives," said Lisaac. His stinking breath seemed to stick to her cheeks. "You said he will survive. For your sake, my dear, you had better be right."

The soldiers dragged her away.

Part VIII

EVERMORE

CHAPTER 88

Justin's eyelids fluttered open, and he had to squint against the brightness. Looking around, he realized he was in an ornately furnished room, surrounded by things made of bronze and gold. He was sitting in a soft upholstered chair. Lining the walls were large windows looking out on clear blue skies and white clouds.

He sat up straight in the chair. As his eyes adjusted, he spotted a globe in the center of the room, a raised dais at the far end, and a two-dimensional doorway of swirling, twisting light.

"I'm back in the tower," Justin said.

"Good," said a voice. "You remember."

Then Justin saw him. He stood beside the globe, clad in the same ceremonial scarlet, white, and silver-trimmed armor as before. The golden, diamond-studded diadem sat upon his brow.

"I was worried you might have forgotten," said the man with the crown—Avagad, he had called himself before. "Never fear. The doorway home still awaits you."

Justin looked past Avagad at the strange doorway-like object hovering above the dais, remembering how the two-dimensional vortex had shattered before he could reach it.

"What happened last time?" said Justin.

"Someone managed to sever our connection," said Avagad.

"Connection?" said Justin.

Avagad's armor glistened. His body seemed to emanate an almost holy light. The diamonds shined brightly in his crown.

"Things in this world," said Avagad, "are not always as physically sound as one might assume. For instance, you currently find yourself in a chair, in my tower. But can you remember how you got here?"

"I remember something," said Justin. "I was in mountains, then caves. . . ." He trailed off. He shut his eyes, trying to remember.

"You were taken from your home against your will," Avagad said, putting his arms behind his back. "To a place that did not seem real. Correct?"

"I think so," said Justin.

"Your first instincts were astute," Avagad said. "You knew this world wasn't real, and you knew there must be a way home. But time and again, people who claim to be your friends have found ways to prevent you from discovering the truth. I've been watching you, Justin. I watched as they pulled you farther and farther from home. Deeper and deeper into their world, a place held together by paper-thin walls and delicate threads. It might look real. It might even feel real. Don't be fooled."

Justin stood from the chair, looking around the room. "What about this place?"

"Does it seem real?"

Justin ran a hand over the arm of the upholstered chair, feeling the texture beneath his fingertips, letting his nails drag across the individual threads.

"You're currently trapped in a dream-world called the Oikoumene," said Avagad. "When you are there, the things around you seem genuine, much like a dream. It's only after you leave that you realize it isn't real. You may appear to move from place to place or experience the passage of long periods of time. You may even feel pleasure or pain. For instance, wasn't your arm hurting just now?"

Justin's brow furrowed. Now that Avagad mentioned it, he thought his left arm had been hurting. He held it up to look at it, but there was nothing wrong with it. Not a scratch.

"The pain felt real, didn't it?" said Avagad. "But you sustained no injury. The woes of the dream-world are all inventions. They may trick your mind, but, as you can see, your body is untouched. Now, finally, you can leave that world behind." Avagad swept his upturned palm toward the vortex of light hovering over the dais: a frameless, gravity-defying window pane. "You need only step through the door."

Justin stared at the pane, trying to make his mind work. There was a world beyond this room. He had seen so much and met so many people, but he was having a hard time remembering any of it.

He raised his arm—the arm that had been hurting—and stared at it. Nothing was wrong with it. There wasn't a single mark.

But that's not right, Justin thought. *There should be a mark. From an accident.*

An image flashed across his mind: a heap of twisted metal and shattered glass. His left arm sliced nearly to the bone. That had happened. He *knew* that had been real. So why didn't he have the scar?

Justin put his head in his hands. Why was it so hard to think?

"You may want to hurry," Avagad advised. "Remember what happened last time? The connection was broken, and your time since then has been filled with pain, fear, and torture."

Justin closed his eyes. Avagad was right about that. He had been hurt. He had been beaten and injured enough times to kill a man.

"I was tortured," Justin said, eyes still closed.

"Yes."

"They nearly killed me, but they didn't."

"They failed."

"No," said Justin, riding a brief flash of insight. "They didn't fail. I was healed."

"Ghastly!" said Avagad. "They healed you so that you could be tortured anew? Is there no end to this cyclical misery?"

Justin opened his eyes. "They didn't heal me. Leah did."

"Who?" said Avagad.

"Leah," said Justin. "The princess. She healed me. Of course! She's my friend."

Avagad looked at him pityingly. "Their deceptions run deeper than I feared. Remember the caves? That girl is no friend. She tried to kill you."

Justin shut his eyes again. Avagad was right. In the caves, she and the two soldiers had turned on him. They had gone wild. They had savagely murdered the old man, and Justin had fled.

But they also had *not* turned on him. He remembered fighting together with them against monsters. They had made it through the caves, found daylight, followed and a river to a town, and. . . .

I have two memories, Justin suddenly realized. *Two memories of the same event, with different outcomes. But that's impossible. Only one can be real. But where did the other one come from?*

"They continually deceive you," said Avagad. "They've used your fear of the unknown to gain your trust. They want to use you."

Justin's eyes shot open. Avagad was watching him.

"I thought you said Leah tried to kill me," said Justin.

Avagad nodded. "And she will try again. It's only a matter of—"

"But you just said they were trying to gain my trust and use me," said Justin. "If that's true, why would she try to kill me?"

"Yet another clever misdirection," said Avagad. "More manipulation to increase your reliance on them—to prevent you from ever returning home. But that is all in the past. Your long nightmare is finally over."

Justin frowned. He started across the room, walking toward the strange doorway. He passed the windows and approached the dais where it hung suspended above the ground. A doorway home: exactly what he desired. And it was right in front of him. All he had to do was walk through it. After everything he had been through, could it really be so simple?

He stopped before the dais and turned to look at Avagad. The man with the crown stood stock-still, watching Justin, barely breathing—as if a single wrong move might dissuade the boy from his current course.

It's like he's watching an animal, thought Justin, *approaching a trap.*

"The only way to know truth," a wise old man had once told him, "is to entertain doubt."

Suddenly, Justin knew what he had to do.

CHAPTER 89

Justin said, "You describe the Oikoumene as a place where the walls are paper thin and suspended by threads."

He paused, watching Avagad for a reaction, but the man showed none.

"My head's a little fuzzy," Justin said, "but as far as I can remember, in all the time I spent in the Oikoumene, it remained solid." He looked around the room—at the globe, the windows, the dais, the portal—remembering how they had twisted, torn, and broken.

"Come to think of it," Justin continued, "this is the only place I've seen fall apart before my eyes."

Justin took a step away from the portal and did not miss the look of concern that flashed across Avagad's face.

"You've placed the burden of proof on them," said Justin. "You have a lot to say about everyone else. Not so much about yourself."

Avagad grinned diplomatically. "I have nothing to hide, if that's what you mean. You have your free will to do as you like, of course. If you choose not to trust me, all that is hurt are my feelings. You, however, stand to lose an awful lot more on the deal."

Justin looked around the tower room. "This place is very nice."

"It suits my needs," said Avagad.

Justin took another step back. "I think the deceivers went about it all wrong. The Oikoumene is dark. Unpleasant. Pretty dangerous at times. If anyone were trying to trick me into trusting them, *this* would be a much more effective way to—"

"I see," Avagad cut in, his serenity faltering for the first time. "I offer you free passage home, and instead of gratitude, you accuse me of treachery."

"That doorway doesn't lead home, does it," said Justin. It was not a question.

His mouth was bone dry, but somehow, he managed to force out the rest.

"It's not true. It's a trick. I don't think anything you've told me is true."

Avagad's lips narrowed into a thin, tightly pursed line. He exhaled sharply through his nostrils. "I did this for you," he said. "I tried to save you. But if you prefer an existence of pain and fear and suffering, I suspect that is exactly what you will find."

"I don't care," said Justin. "I'm not walking through that door."

Avagad sneered slightly. "I would have preferred to be your ally, Justin," said Avagad.

"What does that mean?" said Justin.

Avagad started walking slowly toward Justin, his hands folded behind his back. "You know," he mused, "you fell far short of my expectations at first. But now, to my pleasant surprise, you are exceeding them. I will admit, I did not anticipate that. Especially from a child who until now has exhibited such habitual cowardice. Perhaps like steel you have been tempered in the fires of conflict. Further physical and mental hardships will only make you stronger. We'll be doing you a favor."

Justin's hands balled into fists. "You're the one behind all this."

"I'm the one trying to help you," said Avagad. "I am the one with the answers."

Justin took a step back. "I don't believe you."

"That's because you haven't seen what I have," said Avagad. "If you knew what I knew, you wouldn't walk through that door—you would *run* through it. If you understood a small fraction of what is at stake, the magnitude of what's coming, you would race to stand alongside me instead of fleeing."

"First the door takes me home, then it makes me stand alongside you?" said Justin. He shook his head. "First rule of telling a lie is to stick to your story."

Avagad's nostrils flared. He walked forward, closing the distance between him and Justin. He somehow seemed taller than he had been a moment before. The sharply upturned shoulder-plates of his armor were broader, and the sunlight catching the diamonds in his crown became shadowed.

"If you don't want to stand beside me, so be it," said Avagad in a voice that echoed through the tower room. "Instead of standing, you may kneel."

Justin took a step backward. "I'm not walking through that door," he said, but he struggled to sound defiant. Even to him, his voice sounded weak and hollow.

"I don't care," said Avagad. "I wanted an ally, but a servant will do. As for those friends of yours, don't worry. I won't kill them. Not anymore. You will kill them. This girl, Leah. A princess, you said? Thank you for that information, Justin. It will prove most useful."

Justin suddenly realized he had involuntarily backpedaled all the way to the edge of the dais, and Avagad was still coming, walking more quickly now, getting closer by the second. Justin reached for his sword, but it was not there.

"The princess will be first," Avagad said, marching toward him more quickly now. "I will make you look her in the eye as she begs you for mercy while you pull out her heart and feast on royal flesh."

In a panic, Justin ran. The large globe was only a few feet away from him, so he stepped sideways to put it between him and Avagad. Avagad kept coming, his broad shoulders now heaving with rage. Justin pushed the globe off its supports, hoping to send it rolling toward Avagad to slow him down. Instead, the wooden frame snapped. The globe fell to the floor—and straight through it, as if the solid stone floor were made of paper.

The tower floor ripped wide open, and a rushing wind sucked and tore at the atmosphere of the room. Avagad stepped back, shielding his face. Trinkets, books, and other items within the tower flew from their shelves and shot across the room in a whirlwind, sucked through the hole like water down a bathtub drain.

The torrent was too much. Justin's body was lifted up and wrenched downward through the chasm. The roar of the swirling wind assaulted his ears. He saw a blinding flash.

CHAPTER 90

"No weapons," said Olorus. "That's a start."

Ahlund was tempted to agree. It was encouraging to see that unarmed representatives were being sent to meet them rather than a squad of guards to escort them straight to prison. Ahlund and the others had been transported via a caravan of oxen-drawn wagons across miles of rolling countrysides. The Raedittean Sea had appeared first as a strip of dark blue visible between hills, then grew closer and closer until the white knuckles of its breakers could be seen punching the rocky shores. Their wagons had passed trader camps, agricultural fields, farmhouses, and groves of walnut and olive trees, their leafy heads tousled by the ocean breeze.

With so many signs of civilization, it seemed as if Hartla proper should have been very close, yet Ahlund still saw no city. Instead, what he saw were the sandstone ridges—sheer cliffs rising high from the plains, extending out toward the sea.

Their dirt road had turned to laid stone, and now the group stood at the edge of canyon cutting a narrow path straight into the cliff formations. The road led down the center of the canyon. Carved into the sandstone on either side were the larger-than-life figures of two kings. One held a scepter, the other a sword. This, Ahlund assumed, was the gateway to Hartla, urban center must have been hidden somewhere beyond or within the cliffs.

The unarmed representatives currently emerging from the mouth of the canyon wore formal togas adorned with badges and emblems of rank and prestige.

Statesmen, thought Ahlund. *Better than headsmen. Though not by much.*

Ahlund had paid attention to which wagon carried their confiscated weapons, and he took a casual step toward it, mentally calculating how long it would take to break the nearest guard's neck, reach the wagon, locate his sword, put it to its deadly work.

The first representative approached Gunnar.

"Nimbus, Admiral of Eppex," the representative said in a loud voice. Smiling, he gave Gunnar a graceful, exaggerated bow, holding one edge of his toga with an upturned hand. "What an unexpected delight! Allow me to be the first to welcome you to fair Hartla. Through wind and tide and squall and foe, may you ever—"

"Can't you see we've got a sick man here?" Gunnar snapped.

The representative wilted. "My—my apologies, admiral. I was only trying to. . . . What I mean to say is, yes, sir. Right away. You there, guards! Run ahead and alert the healers!"

As some soldiers rushed to obey, the representative bowed to Gunnar several times in quick succession.

"Nine hundred apologies, my lord, for my foolish inattention to—"

"And nine thousand blessings to yer mum's arse," Gunnar said. "May she warm the nethers of every lusty sailor she waddles past."

The representative's face turned red. A few of the guards bit their lips to hold back smiles. Pool, Borris, and Samuel, on the other hand, made not even the slightest effort to mute their heavy, boisterous laughter.

"My lord," said the representative. "Count Wulder has been informed of your arrival, and he will be ready to receive you shortly. In the meantime, please allow us to extend any and every courtesy to you and your crew."

"Hot food," Gunnar said. "And for gods' sake, strong drink. Buckets of it. And our weapons and supplies. Now."

"Of course, of course," said the representative. "Guards, return them their effects."

One by one, the prisoners were handed their weapons. Olorus let out a happy growl. Taking his sword, Ahlund squeezed the hilt, savoring the way his fingers fit so perfectly into the contours of the grip—worn down by his own hand from long years of use. He felt whole again.

"Right this way, gentlemen," said the representative, and he turned smartly on his heels and started down the road into the canyon. Gunnar, Ahlund, Zechariah, and the rest followed, with the guards bringing up the rear.

The canyon road cut deep into the cliffs, and a hundred yards from the entrance, it took a sharp turn. Here, Ahlund paused to appreciate the twenty-five archers looking down from the tops of the ridges on either side of the canyon, all with bows in hand.

They rounded a second corner, and their path intersected with an adjoining canyon, through which flowed a narrow river spanned by a fortified bridge. Beyond, tucked deep within the rock walls, was Hartla. The city was surrounded on two sides by sandstone ridges and on the other two sides by water.

At first, Ahlund thought the river fed a reservoir for the city, but then he realized what he was really seeing: It was an inlet of the Raedittean Sea. This inland cove was encircled by cliff walls as tall and sharp as mountain peaks. Upon the inlet's waters, hundreds of ships bobbed in the surf: Hartla's fleet.

People crowded the streets, their bodies deeply tanned by the cloudless skies of the coastal weather. The architecture consisted of stone-cut buildings three and four stories high, and in the distance, built into the side of the cliff, was a castle with flags flying atop its palisades.

"The canyon and the inlet are the city's only entry points," Gunnar whispered. "The cliffs mean the city can be defended from above and below, and invaders are forced into choke points along the canyon, making overall numbers useless."

"Incredible," said Olorus. "A defensive masterpiece."

"And a well-kept secret," said Gunnar. "With enough supplies, it is said that a few hundred can defend this city against an army of ten thousand."

With a good strategist at the helm, thought Ahlund, *that might not be far off the mark.*

They reached the city-side of the bridge, and an empty cart was wheeled to them, pushed by several young men and women. They offered the cart to Zechariah for transportation to the healers' hall, but he waved it away and proceeded on foot. Ahlund pulled Gunnar aside.

"I'll go with Zechariah," said Ahlund. "When the count calls on you, send for us."

"Aye aye," said Gunnar.

As Gunnar, Olorus, Hook, and the sailors were led off toward food and drink, the lisping Borris could be heard whispering to his fellows, "*Told* you he was noble blood!"

Ahlund walked alongside Zechariah and the team of healers. One of them, a young man, held a hand over Zechariah's injury as they walked, using aurym to alleviate the pain. Guards followed behind.

"At the very least, Hook may get a good last meal," Zechariah mumbled, speaking in the old tongue so that no one else might understand.

"With any luck," said Ahlund as they approached the healers' hall, "Gunnar's word may be enough to pardon his crimes."

"With any luck," replied Zechariah, "our captain does not face an equivalent sentence."

Ahlund had been wondering the same thing. Warfare between the noble houses that ruled the city-states of the Mythaean Thalassocracy was a longstanding tradition. What would be considered civil war in other parts of the world, the Mythaeans called politics. It was entirely possible that by following Gunnar to Hartla, they would be considered accessories to his actions.

"And with a little more luck," said Zechariah, "he won't decide to betray us outright."

Ahlund said nothing.

CHAPTER 91

The palace of Hartla, cut into the side of the cliff, was encircled by a deep, rocky chasm acting as a dry moat. The only access to the palace was a bridge across that moat, which Ahlund and the others were currently being led across.

Halfway across the bridge, they passed into shadow. Looking up, Ahlund saw that they were beneath the cliffs; the castle and its fortress had been built into the walls of the canyon, and rock formations hung suspended over portions of the city.

Ahlund kept a close eye on his old friend beside him. Zechariah really should have still been with the healers, but this was where he was needed most. His diplomatic expertise would be their only hope if Gunnar turned out to be unwelcome here. Even after the healers' best efforts, Zechariah's right hand was still was a bloody mess of gnarled bone and illogical flesh. It was currently covered in medicinal salves and tightly wrapped. Just as Ahlund had feared, there was no hope of healing the hand. The only recourse would be to remove it.

Ahlund looked at Zechariah. The old man was stone-faced.

They crossed the bridge and entered the castle through high gates. The antechamber was a cavernous, high-ceilinged hall. Ahlund could not tell if this place had been carved into the cliff-side or if it had been adapted from naturally formed caves, but there were no windows. The room was illuminated by two great, burning hearths at either end of the hall and a chandelier suspended from the rocky ceiling, its candlelight reflecting brightly in its silver and bronze mountings.

The men escorting Ahlund and the others brought them to a halt in the center of the room.

"Blimey!" blurted Pool. His voice echoed through the hall, and he hastily clamped his hands over his mouth.

On a raised platform at the far end of the hall were two thrones: the seats of the count and the admiral. One was currently occupied by a portly, broad-shouldered man clothed in orange and white. His gray-streaked beard was tied in a long braid. He wore not a crown but a great helmet adorned with the thick, ivory tusks of some sea creature. The tusks curved downward from the helmet, so that the tips pointed forward above his shoulders. At the base of the thrones stood several diplomats and advisors in togas.

"Your Highness Morix, Count of Hartla," announced one of the escorts, "may I present His Highness Nimbus, Admiral of Eppex."

The man on the throne nodded impatiently.

Gunnar stepped forward with his hands resting on his belt. "Wulder!" he said. "Been too long. I trust you've been well?"

The count responded only with a cold, calculating scowl.

"Okay, then," Gunnar said. "Now that we've got the pleasantries out of the way, let's get down to business. I require a flagship and several escort vessels—as many as you can spare. Each with a crew of Hartla's best sailors. And weapons. Lots of them. Food and drink, by the plenty—I like my men and women to feel like they're taken care of. As far as entertainment—"

"You are as insolent as ever!" the count bellowed.

"And you're fat as ever," said Gunnar.

The count's scowl deepened.

"Maybe you've forgotten that by definition, there cannot be insolence among equals," said Gunnar.

Ahlund did not think Gunnar had intended the statement to be a joke, but given the difference in appearance between these two men—a count on his throne, crown and all, and a stinking, travel-beaten man wearing the flag of his sunken ship as a bandana—the idea that they were equals was comical.

The count sighed and rubbed his temples. "Do I even dare ask who the rest of this rabble is?"

"This is my crew," said Gunnar.

"Even that runaway slave?" said the count.

Ahlund looked at Hook. His expression was blank. Olorus, however, clenched his hands into fists. His stubbled cheek twitched.

"Runaway slave?" said Gunnar, looking around. His eyes found Hook. "You mean *this* worthless dog? He's a slave, all right—serves onboard my ship—but he's never run away. Nor will he if he values his life."

"I can see this is going nowhere," the count interrupted. "Guards!"

CHAPTER 92

Ahlund looked from side to side, trying to estimate how long it would take the palace guards to reach him—calculating whether he could put Wulder to the sword before they massacred his friends.

"Leave us," Wulder finished.

For a moment, even Gunnar's bravado faltered. He let out an audible sigh of relief as the palace guards began dispersing in ranks.

Wulder waved a hand at the scribe and advisors, saying, "You, too. Get out." They hurried to leave.

Gunnar breathed a humorless laugh. "Very funny, Wulder. You had me going for a second—"

"Gunnar, dismiss your crew so that we can speak in private," said Wulder.

"Very well," said Gunnar. "But the captains of my fleet convene with me in all matters. Captain Sims, Captain Zechariah will stay with me."

Wulder Von Morix made a sound of exasperation but conceded with a nod.

Gunnar turned to the others in the group. "The rest of you, go find something to do," Gunnar said loudly. Then he leaned in and whispered, "Olorus and Hook, take Pool, Borris, and Samuel outside. *Tread lightly.* Wulder hasn't decided to kill me yet, but there's still plenty of time for him to change his mind. If anyone tries to speak to you, tell them you're part of a military convoy from the fleet of Admiral Gunnar Erix Nimbus of Eppex, and you're not at liberty to discuss anything at present." Gunnar looked at Hook. "My apologies for insulting you, sergeant. Purely deception, that you might avoid the gallows. Your liberty is unquestioned."

A smile tugged at Hook's lips. Then Olorus, Hook, and the crew of the *Gryphon* exited the main hall.

"Captain Zechariah?" whispered Zechariah. "I rather like the sound of that."

No sooner had the palace's outer door shut than Wulder shot to his feet and bellowed, "Damn it, Gunnar!"

In a decidedly un-noble move, Wulder bypassed the stairs and hopped down heavily from the thrones' raised platform, his boots thudding against the floor.

"It's been years since anyone has even seen you alive!" he said. "Now you barge in here demanding soldiers and ships? What in blazes do you expect me to do?"

"Soldiers and ships would be a good start," said Gunnar.

Wulder was grinding his teeth. "Do you realize how much influence Yordar now has within the Thalassocracy?" he yelled. "He has consolidated four more city-states under his singular rule. No one has done that since the days of our ancestor the Sovereign King! Some say he intends to return our people to a totalitarian empire—blood will color the sea!"

Gunnar was quiet for a moment, allowing Wulder's words to echo through the cavernous hall.

"You need not lecture me on Yordar's ambitions," said Gunnar. "Don't forget, Eppex was the first to fall."

Wulder walked up to stand before Gunnar. He was the same height as Gunnar but at least a hundred pounds heavier. He stared him down, stroking his gray, braided beard as if trying to make up his mind about something. Finally, he reared back and wrapped his arms around Gunnar in a bear hug, easily lifting the lighter man off the floor.

"You damn fool!" Gunnar laughed, trying to pull away.

"By the seas, it has been too long!" Wulder said.

"This why you kicked out your court, isn't it?" said Gunnar. "So they wouldn't see what an emotional ass you are."

Wulder dropped Gunnar. "Right," he said. "Let us discuss these uncouth demands of yours. But first, I'll hear where you have been hiding all these years—you and your *captains*."

Wulder chuckled as he led Gunnar toward one of the hall's large hearths. Ahlund and Zechariah exchanged a look of relief, then followed.

CHAPTER 93

Justin was falling, falling. Through darkness and light and darkness again. Spun and flipped and buffeted by tornado winds. He tried to swing his arms against the ripping, tearing forces, but someone was restraining him.

"Justin!" someone said.

The winds stopped. He opened his eyes and saw Leah kneeling over him, holding his hands to prevent him from thrashing.

"Justin!" Leah said. "Look at me. It was a dream. You are okay. Understand? You were dreaming. Everything is all—"

"Avagad," Justin blurted.

The details of the dream—or vision or out-of-body experience or whatever it had been—were already slipping from his memory. He tried to get them out while he could still remember.

"It wasn't a dream—I was *there*," he said. "There was a man with a crown. A doorway. He wanted me to walk through it. But he's a liar. I talked to him—I think I've talked to him before, but it's hard to remember. He wants to use me. To. . . . He said he would. . . ."

Suddenly, Justin noticed that his left arm was wrapped in bandages from his shoulder to his wrist, and he lost his train of thought. He turned his arm, trying to get a better look. Leah gasped in amazement.

"By the spirit! You can move it!" she said. She grabbed the hand of his bandaged arm. "Careful. Don't overdo it. I can't believe it! How bad does it hurt?"

"It doesn't hurt at all," said Justin. "Feels a little funny, though."

"Do you remember how it happened?"

Justin shuddered as the memory came back. The massive, dark form of the cythraul pushing past Lisaac. Plodding forward. Grabbing him by the arm.

Justin scanned their surroundings. It was midday. Smoke from cook-fires hung in the air. Dozens of armed men encircled the encampment, and others could be seen moving between the trees. They were no longer in the Drekwood, and high above, the bright blue sky hurt his eyes wonderfully.

This is all Avagad's doing, he thought. *These men working for him. Including Lisaac. . . . Including the cythraul.*

"Yeah, I remember," said Justin. "A cythraul did it. Lisaac called it their general. It picked me up by the arm, and after that, I don't know what happened." He gestured toward his bandaged arm. "Thanks, as always."

"I didn't heal you, Justin," she said.

"Huh?" he said.

"I tried, but I couldn't. I promise, I'll do everything I can to get it back to normal, but I've never seen anything quite like this."

Leah's words, or maybe it was the defeated way she said them, made Justin feel sick. He raised his left arm and flexed his fingers. Everything seemed in working order, but beneath the bandages, he felt a strange sensation: a *tugging* of the flesh. Scar tissue? He started to peel back the wrappings for a look and realized the bandages were much thicker than he had expected.

Justin looked up and saw fearful apprehension on Leah's face. He removed his hand from the bandages.

"I can move it," he said. "That's all that matters. And it doesn't hurt a bit, so you must have done something right." He looked around at the guards, squeezing his hands into fists. "I've had enough of this, Leah. I don't know if all this torture is supposed to break me or what, but all it's doing is making me angry."

"Maybe that's what they're trying to do," said Leah.

Justin took a deep breath. For a moment, he sat quietly, looking up at the sky, trying to think. Leah remained crouched beside him.

"You said you've had that dream before?" Leah said.

"Yeah," said Justin. "When they took us from the ship, I think. It was the night Lisaac cut off that man's arm."

"It's the cythraul," Leah said. "That's what's doing it."

"The cythraul?"

"Back on the river," said Leah, "Ahlund and Zechariah thought your sickness was the cythraul trying to take control of you. This time, a cythraul touched your arm, and the same thing happened."

Suddenly, something from his conversation with Avagad came to his mind: "I wanted an ally. But a servant will do. As for those friends of yours, don't worry. I won't kill them. Not anymore. You will kill them."

Justin smiled.

"What?" asked Leah.

"Avagad," said Justin. "He threatened to hurt my friends if I didn't join him. He said he would make me kill them."

"That's awful," said Leah.

"It's great!" Justin said. "He's been watching us—all of us. For a long time, I think."

"So?"

"So he couldn't make me kill them if they weren't still alive, right?"

Leah's face broke into a reluctant grin.

"That means at least some of them must have survived," said Justin. "They're out there, probably looking for us right now. I bet Ahlund, Zechariah, Olorus, and Hook been following us this whole time!" He leaned a bit closer to Leah, lowering his voice to a whisper. "One way or another, we're getting out of here. We'll either do it ourselves, or we'll be ready to act when the others do find us."

"You are full of surprises, Justin," said Leah.

Justin shrugged. "I thrive on low expectations."

Leah took Justin by the hand and kissed his cheek, causing the breath to leave his lungs. He felt himself blushing and had to clear his throat before he was able to speak.

"You, uh, are full of surprises, too," he said.

Leah snorted a nasally, pitying sort of laugh, and ruffled his hair.

CHAPTER 94

The four men took seats on the benches in front of the hearth. The cavern that housed the royal palace was cool, being sheltered from the sun, and the fire provided both heat and light in this otherwise shadowed place.

"Your second throne is empty," observed Gunnar.

"And half my harbor, as well," said Wulder. He had removed his crown-like horned helm, revealing a mostly hairless head. "You remember my younger brother Drexel? He took his place as admiral, and he's got half our ships out patrolling the northern coast."

"Looking for that black fleet?" Gunnar asked.

Wulder shot him a look. "You've heard about that, I see. Yes. A thousand or more unidentified warships with black sails are performing unsanctioned maneuvers in our waters. They've been at it for weeks. We have tried engaging them peaceably to learn their intentions, but anytime we draw near, our ships are attacked. We have yet to learn the nationality of the sailors and soldiers manning the ships. It appears to be a mixed bag. Could be Yordar's doing. Drexel thinks it's an invasion fleet aimed for Hartla."

"Who is this Yordar?" Zechariah spoke up.

"A warlord," said Gunnar. "His . . . *actions* . . . are what drove me from the Thalassocracy."

"Yordar rules from Pel," said Wulder. "In addition to Eppex, he has conquered four other city-states. He accepts nothing but unconditional victory. His invaders pillage and burn and murder. He executes ruling nobles and installs puppet leaders in their place whom he calls governors. And he has taken the title of 'Lord-Count of the Raedittean.' To me, the title confirms his ambitions to rule the entire archipelago. All this, he does under the pretense of restoring us to our 'former imperial glory.' The Sovereign King who unified the archipelago and formed the Thalassocracy did it to defend against barbarian invaders from the west. He did not build his empire through betrayal and murder!"

"Speaking of which," said Gunnar, "does Yordar know I'm alive?"

Wulder sighed. "I never told a soul about your visit here before you journeyed inland, but palace walls have ears. Rumors always get out, one way or another. Word must have reached Yordar, because he came here personally to question me about your whereabouts. I told him I hadn't seen you. Whether or not he believed me, I do not know. He has had a sharp eye on Hartla ever since. You can understand our unease, therefore, regarding this black armada sailing in our waters."

Wulder paused to growl in anger and slam his fist against his leg. "Why, Gunnar? Why now? Don't you see what this will do? Yordar already desires Hartla—the gateway to Athacean trade routes—and now, you show up, announcing your name in front of soldiers, statesmen, and anyone who will listen. We won't be able to quell the rumors this time. Yordar will find us guilty of harboring a fugitive, and he will bring all his military might down on us!"

Gunnar said nothing. For the first time, Ahlund understood the true risk Gunnar had taken by returning to the Thalassocracy, not only to himself but to others.

"Gunnar," said Zechariah, "what grudge does Yordar hold against you that is great enough to move armies?"

Before Gunnar could say anything, Wulder spoke up. "You mean to tell me, Gunnar, that you haven't told them?"

"It's ancient history," said Gunnar. "I am not normally keen to dwell on it."

"Not enough among your *captains*?" asked Wulder disdainfully.

"You clearly see through our ruse, Count," said Zechariah, "but once you have heard our story, I am certain you will realize why Gunnar risked returning to Mythaean territory. Our errand, you see, is of the utmost importance."

Wulder laughed and rubbed a golden-ringed hand over his eyes as if fighting a headache. "Just what I need," he sighed. "High ideals from low places." He leaned forward and locked eyes with Zechariah. "The word of a Mythaean admiral is sacred. Therefore, I accept Gunnar's claim that you two are captains and that the rest of those lowlifes are your crew, but I cannot imagine who you think you are to speak to me. You two—a crippled, dusty old man and an ugly, long-legged hedge knight. You are nothing." He adjusted his significant girth on the bench. "And nothing will speak when nothing is spoken to, not before."

Zechariah chewed on his tongue in annoyance, but Ahlund almost smiled. The count could hardly be faulted for his ignorance. In a way, such a blunt display of authority was to be admired.

"They might speak out of turn," said Gunnar, "but they speak truly, Wulder. Recent events found me ferrying some passengers—these men and their companions—toward the coast. Along the way, we were attacked by an unknown enemy force."

Ahlund did not miss the change in Wulder's face. It was no mistake that Gunnar referred to their attackers as an "unknown enemy." It played to the count's existing fears.

"One of my men was murdered," said Gunnar. He paused. "And my ship was destroyed."

"Not the *Gryphon*!" said Wulder.

Gunnar gave a stiff-lipped nod.

"My condolences," said Wulder. "A fine ship, she was."

"Two others of our party were kidnapped," said Gunnar. "One was the princess of Nolia."

Wulder looked at him suspiciously. "They say the Nolian royals are all dead."

"I had heard the same," said Gunnar. "But—"

A loud banging interrupted their conversation, and Ahlund turned to see the palace's outer door thrown open.

CHAPTER 95

A man marched into the throne room. He was dressed like a common Hartlan soldier but wore a large hat, similar in style and size to the one Gunnar had lost. Though not as heavily built, he was the spitting image of Wulder, right down to the braided beard, which was shorter and showed no gray. He couldn't have been much older than Justin.

"I nearly called the heralds liars!" the man said as he strode toward them. "Gunnar Erix Nimbus, back from the dead! Through wind and tide and squall and foe, may you ever journey on!"

"Morix, Admiral of Hartla," said Gunnar, standing and gripping hands with the newcomer. "Drexel, you must have been a much younger man when last I was in Hartla. I'm sure I would have remembered such an off-putting face. Meet my captains, Ahlund and Zechariah."

Drexel sat down without looking at either of them.

"What news from the north?" said Wulder. When Drexel hesitated, Wulder added, "No need for discretion. Gunnar is harmless."

"Our scouts have been patrolling all corners of the surrounding waters," said Drexel. His voice was raspier than Wulder's—deceptive for his younger face. "This morning, several of our ships did not check in. They are still missing. And the black fleet moved again in the night. The whereabouts of the majority of the fleet are unknown, but a small fraction of it seems to have blockaded the old port town of Gaius."

"Isn't that just north of here?" said Gunnar.

"Aye," said Wulder. "A wildfire burned down the town a few decades ago, and it was abandoned and never rebuilt. Now, it's a hideout for bandits and such."

"There is only one reason for the fleet to occupy those ruins," said Drexel. "To use it as a staging ground for the invasion of Hartla."

"Yordar has you jumping at shadows, Drexel," said Wulder. "Our southern borders are far more vulnerable. Why would anyone mount an invasion from the north? The cliffs prevent passage by land."

"We can't rule anything out," Drexel said. "We still don't know who these invaders are. They wear no uniforms and fly no colors except black."

We theorized that the enemy who took Justin and Leah would take them across the ocean, thought Ahlund, *and now a fleet appears. Is it possible that this isn't an invading force but an escort?*

"There's more to this story," said Zechariah, who must have been thinking along the same lines as Ahlund. "We have information that might explain some of what's happening. If you'll bring our associates back in here, we can explain everything."

The old man's words caused a flash of anger from Wulder. The count stood, stepped toward Zechariah, and raised a finger at him, shouting, "I thought I told you to keep your *stinking mouth*—!"

Ahlund stood, drew his sword, and swung it in a rainbow arc over his head. In mid-swing, he set it ablaze.

The Von Morixes barely had time to jump back before Ahlund hacked his sword through the bench, mere feet from where Wulder had been sitting a moment before. The bench split cleanly into two flaming pieces. Wulder tripped and hit the ground on his ample rear. Drexel leaped to his feet with his hand on the sword's hilt, but he dared not draw it.

"This is no frail old man you speak to!" Ahlund roared, his voice rattling the chandelier overhead. "This is the Brethren Zechariah! Last of the Immortals of the South! And I am no hedge knight. I am Ahlund Sims of the Ru'Onorath, a Guardian of the Oikoumene and wielder of the Sacred Stone!"

Slowly, Ahlund pointed the tip of his sword at Wulder's face. The fire intensified. The flames dancing furiously across the blinding blade could be seen reflected in the count's eyes.

"We will endure no further disrespect from the likes of you," Ahlund said.

Ahlund allowed Wulder and Drexel to watch the blade a moment longer. Then, with a flourish, he extinguished its flames and drove it into the sheath at his side.

"With credentials like that," said Gunnar, "I pretty much had to make them captains."

CHAPTER 96

Olorus and Hook were called in to join the gathering, and a condensed version of the company's tale was related to the Von Morixes. Soon, Wulder and Drexel—who had at first required the threat of Ahlund's flaming sword to remain attentive—were listening closely.

"So you mean to say," said Wulder, "that you believe the black fleet at Gaius is the same enemy that waylaid you in the Drekwood and captured Princess Anavion and the boy?"

"That is our theory," said Zechariah. "After everything that happened in the Drekwood, we would have been slaughtered if we had attempted to follow them. Sergeant Bard suggested we come to Hartla and that Gunnar request to borrow a force of ships and soldiers to intercept this enemy and attempt a rescue."

Wulder threw a sidelong glance at his younger brother—a silent question.

"Our scout ships report that the ships at Gaius fly no colors," said Drexel. "The ruffians manning the vessels look more like mercenaries or highwaymen than Mythaean soldiers. I had already begun to suspect that this was none of Yordar's doing. Unless they are hired swords—"

"No matter who it is," Gunnar cut in, "no unsanctioned warships should be allowed to maneuver unchecked through Mythaean waters. The longer you allow this to go on, the more emboldened they will become and the weaker Hartla will appear. You've got to pull this thing up by the roots."

"Weak!" bellowed Drexel, leaning forward heatedly. "I protect our waters every day! Hartla faces more threats than you know, and we do not have the luxury of pursuing every dog that barks in our direction!"

"What stake do you have in all this anyway, Gunnar?" said Wulder. "After all these years, why do you risk your life and return to the Thalassocracy on nothing but the word of a few ferry passengers?"

"These passengers hired me on credit," said Gunnar. "They got one of my men killed, they got my ship destroyed—they owe me a hell of a lot of gold. I only have one good eye, and it is fixed firmly on them until I get what's owed me. The only way I seem likely to get my money is to take up this debt with their friend, the princess of Nolia. She is indisposed at the moment, so you can see my predicament. It is financially prudent that I help them find her."

Olorus shifted his weight uncomfortably but remained silent. Hook's eyes were glaring at Gunnar, yet his mouth seemed upturned, almost in a smile.

Wulder turned to Drexel, "I believe Gunnar is right in one regard, at least. There was a time when an unidentified warship in Mythaean waters would not have been tolerated. When did that change?"

Drexel's face twisted. He looked ready to voice another protest when Zechariah intervened.

"Send couriers to every city-state that calls itself an ally of Hartla," said Zechariah. "This Yordar's actions have disrupted your very way of life. You cannot be the only colony unable to function effectively. Call on your allies to act alongside you."

A few moments passed. Wulder looked at Drexel. Drexel was glaring at the floor.

"For once, I agree with the old man," Gunnar finally said. "Yordar's operation thus far has been focused on ruffling as few feathers as possible. His power will continue to grow. By the time someone takes it upon themselves to check his ambitions, it may be too late . . . but the three of us could be the start of a new military alliance. A challenge to his authority."

"You mean that, Gunnar?" said Wulder. "You would return to the Thalassocracy? Truly?"

Gunnar grinned. "Why not?"

Wulder smiled broadly.

"You will need a show of solidarity—and force," said Zechariah. "A demonstration, as a call to arms for your allies and a clear message to your enemies."

"The black fleet at Gaius," said Wulder.

"That is what I have been saying!" said Drexel. "Let us act. Let us bloody our swords against this enemy!"

Ahlund shot Zechariah a look. Not for the first time, he noted that the old man's skill at manipulation was impressive—and frightening.

CHAPTER 97

Hours had passed since the conversation with Leah, and dusk had fallen. Justin, yet again sitting alone in the firelight in a corner of camp, on yet another dark evening, reached for the bandages on his left arm.

He touched the edge of the bandage, but he hesitated.

Do I even want to look? he thought.

The thought gave him the strangest feeling of déjà vu. He remembered what it had felt like to wake up in a hospital bed on Earth, staring at bandages encasing the same arm like a cocoon and wondering, *Why am I here?* He remembered thinking his arm felt very, very dirty, and he had been wondering if he could take a shower when the doctor had arrived with the news.

"There's some pretty bad damage to the muscles in your arm," the doctor had said. "But, with recovery time and rehab, most people can usually prevent or minimize any long-term problems." He paused to look at a mobile device in his hand. "I am also supposed to tell you that your dad is in critical condition—I can't say much more than that, at this point, but he's really very fortunate. He was thrown from the vehicle and over a steep embankment. Apparently, first responders initially assumed it had just been you and your mother in the car. It is amazing he fared as well as he did, given that he was admitted several hours after you and your mother. . . . Unfortunately, I have to tell you that your mother did not make it."

Justin only remembered bits and pieces of what the doctor said after that. Phrases like, "In situations like this," and, "Her injuries were, quite frankly. . . ." and, "We will bring somebody in for you to talk to."

The conversation ended when the doctor asked, "Justin, do you understand what I'm telling you?" and Justin answered, "My mom died."

After that, Justin still kept wondering, *Why am I here?* But now the "why" didn't bother him so much; it was the "I." Why am *I* here? Why *my* family? Why *my* mom? Why me?

Sitting before a campfire in the wooded wilderness, Justin closed his eyes, grabbed the edge of the bandage, and pulled.

It gave a bit. He felt no pain, so he pulled some more. He heard the bandage tearing, but, strangely, he felt nothing. He pulled and pulled until all the bandages had been removed. Eyes still closed, he inched his fingers toward his arm. They brushed against something that did not feel like human flesh: a cold, hard surface that reminded him of blacktop. His arm registered no sensation. Convinced that it must yet be wrapped in some other substance—rawhide or leather or something—he opened his eyes.

Justin gasped so hard that his lungs filled nearly to bursting. His hand was the same as he remembered it, but his flesh ended at his wrist. From his wrist to his shoulder, he seemed to no longer have skin.

Instead, the surface of his arm was a dull, chitinous material the color of ebony. He moved his arm experimentally, and the material shifted, sliding against itself with grinding, cracking sounds. At the elbow, it seemed to be divided into sections like scales or plates. He might have been able to convince himself that it was some sort of covering growing over his skin, but that was very clearly not the case. On the contrary, his arm was quite a bit narrower than it should have been. It was as if the skin, muscles, and all other living tissues had been removed—peeled off to reveal *this* underneath, where ordinary bone should have been. His arm was the same diameter as his wrist all the way up to the shoulder. His bicep was missing. Just gone.

Justin should have been horrified, but it was too strange—like he was watching the whole thing happen to someone else. He lifted his arm and examined it, wondering in dull fascination how he could even move a body part that had no muscles in it. The blackish material looked like the exoskeleton of an insect. The arm didn't even seem alive, yet it obeyed his command.

Experimentally, Justin picked a little at the boundary where the black substance ended and his real flesh began. Digging his fingernail under the skin drew blood, and it hurt badly—as it was supposed to. He rapped his knuckles against the narrow, blackened forearm and regretted it. His knuckles flared with pain. It was like hitting solid rock. His arm, however, felt nothing. There was no sensation of touch. It just felt cold. And dead.

Justin crawled toward the fire and pulled a burning piece of kindling from the flames. Holding it in his right hand, he pressed the hot end against his blackened left arm. He twisted, grinding the glowing embers back and forth against the hard surface of his left arm. He felt nothing. Pulling it away, he could see no trace of a burn.

Justin braced his arm against a stone on the ground, drew back, and, with all his might, smashed the burning wood against his forearm. The kindling snapped in half in a shower of sparks. The force of the strike would have probably been enough to break his arm under normal circumstances. Yet he still felt nothing. The arm was completely unharmed. Not a mark. It was like his arm was made of—

Armor, thought Justin. *Bone armor.*

"Like a cythraul," he realized aloud.

"I wanted an ally," rang Avagad's words in his head. "But a servant will do."

"He wasn't bluffing," Justin said, staring at his new arm.

The cythraul could do worse than kill Justin. They could . . . *turn* him.

Movement nearby caused Justin to look up. The soldiers were moving. The campfires were being spread and snuffed out, and items were being gathered up, prepared for a march.

Since when do we travel by night? he thought.

Soldiers with torches approached. Justin didn't wait for their command. He stood and fell in line. His handlers were, surprisingly, empty of their usual threats or taunts as they marched. In fact, *all* the soldiers were being abnormally quiet.

Almost an hour in the march, Justin heard shrieks and cries in the darkness surrounding them. The soldiers drew into tighter ranks, throwing nervous glances into the shadows. There were hisses, howls, and giggles. Soon, Justin saw shadows skirting the edges of the torchlight, flashing between trees, skittering over dead leaves. Black, lanky bodies the size of children, knuckle-walking like apes.

Coblyns, thought Justin. *But they're not attacking.*

The soldiers around him shuddered. But strangely, Justin felt no fear. Only heightened senses and cold calculation.

A particularly close hiss in the darkness made the soldier in front of Justin miss a step and freeze in place, trembling. Justin pushed the man aside in annoyance and marched on. For a split second, he saw torchlight reflected in a pair of red, pea-sized eyes watching from between the trees.

CHAPTER 98

The palace of Hartla was filled to capacity. Five hundred or more people had been called for an emergency council. There were ship captains, infantry officers, lesser nobles, city officials—anyone important enough to weigh in on matters of war.

Upon the thrones sat the Van Morixes. Gunnar sat in a chair beside them, still wearing his dirty clothes and the *Gryphon*'s sword and ivy flag as a bandana. Below their raised platform stood court advisors and scribes. Zechariah and Ahlund, Olorus and Hook, and the sailors lingered nearby.

The up-and-down white noise of the crowd echoed through the hall until Wulder hushed the room by raising a jeweled hand.

"No use sugarcoating it," Wulder bellowed. "Even as I speak, a fleet is massing at the ruins of the old port town of Gaius in an apparent bid to invade our lands."

The room broke into mayhem. Advisors shouted to be heard. Military officers waved their hands as they demanded answers.

"Quiet, quiet!" Wulder shouted.

The cacophony was gradually dying down until one brave soul stepped up onto a chair, pointed at Gunnar, and shouted, "This is his fault!"

Dozens of "Ayes" and "Hear, hears" were thrown up in support of the protestor.

A female politician much closer stepped forward and leveled a finger at Gunnar, declaring loudly, "Let us not pretend we don't know who this man is! If a fleet gathers, it is Yordar searching for *him*! And now he has been granted asylum within our city. We as good as asked for war when we let him in here!"

The crowd cheered in agreement.

Drexel stood and raised his fist as he shouted, "I have seen this enemy with my own eyes, and this is none of Yordar's doing!"

"No matter who it is," Gunnar cried out, "it ends now!"

"Empty words!" replied a scar-faced military man at center stage. "We all know the stories of your defeat, Gunnar. How you failed Yordar and he drove you from the Thalassocracy in disgrace. Now you are here, telling lies and spurring our country to war! An admiral without a colony, out for revenge and nothing else—"

"Silence!" Wulder bellowed.

The entire court was brought to order.

"You speak to a noble admiral of the Thalassocracy," said Wulder in a low, deadly tone of voice. "The blood of the Mythaean Sovereign King flows through the veins of Gunnar Erix of House Nimbus! Speak your peace, countrymen, but know that an offense against any noble blood is an offense against all."

"Your concerns are all heard," said Drexel in his raspy voice. "It is no secret that Hartla is within Yordar's sights. We must be economical with our fleet. But Gunnar is right. There was a time when news of an unknown fleet, miles from our city, would have spurred shouts of action from this court. Are you so fearful of what Yordar *might* do that you would compromise your principles? Your honor? It is clear that the plots of this insurrectionist threaten the very effectiveness of the Mythaean Thalassocracy."

"Which is why today," boomed Wulder, "we publicly label Yordar Erix Nimbus a sworn enemy of Hartla."

Ahlund turned to look at Gunnar.

Yordar . . . Erix Nimbus? Well, well.

Wulder went on: "This house declares war against Yordar Erix Nimbus, his forces, and any who bow to his counterfeit title of lord-count of the Raedittean!"

To Ahlund's surprise, a few tentative cheers went up among the crowd.

"Let us be the first colony stouthearted enough to stand against Yordar's tyranny!" roared Drexel.

The tentative cheers spread. Ahlund could see a few statesmen and city officials attempting to quell the wave of approval, but it was no use. The fervor only spread.

"Let others fall in behind us!" Wulder shouted. "Let couriers be sent to every ally of Hartla, calling on them to join us in a new military alliance devoted to toppling the barbarous despot, Yordar Erix Nimbus."

The zeal increased. Soon, the people's fists were rising and falling as if striking the drums of war. Olorus and Hook were smiling. Borris, Pool, and Samuel, caught up in the excitement, stood and shouted with the rest. To Ahlund, such a reaction was a strong testimony to the tensions that already existed within their hearts. These were people who had been pushed for too long and were ready to do some pushing of their own.

"Our first action," said Drexel, "will be a show of unrelenting force! We will run this unknown enemy—this black fleet that has parked itself so close to our lands—out of our territory! We will prove our military superiority to our brother and sister colonies and show that we cannot be governed through fear of a false lord-count, a foreign fleet, or anyone else! We will show that the strength of this race lies not in tribute paid to a tyrant but in our allegiance to one another! And we will show the world what it means to be a true-blooded Mythaean! We will make our enemies tremble!"

Gunnar and the Von Morixes bowed to the thundering court and descended from their platforms. They gestured for Ahlund, Zechariah, Olorus, and Hook to join them, and the makeshift war council gathered together. The plan had already been decided upon; tonight, Gunnar, Zechariah, Ahlund, Olorus, and Hook would lead an infantry force north along the coast and make camp south of Gaius. Meanwhile, Drexel and Hartla's fleet would sail north to meet them. At sunrise, the two branches would hit the enemy simultaneously by land and sea. A ground war and a naval assault all at once.

"Tomorrow, we must not forget about the deadliest player on the board," said Drexel. "The force at Gaius is only a fraction of the whole black fleet. The rest is still somewhere in nearby waters, and there is hardly a force in all the Oikoumene that could contend with it at full strength. I fear we may be kicking a hornet's nest."

"No battle was ever fought without great risk," Ahlund said.

Wulder nodded solemnly. His gaze wandered to the crowd of cheering Hartlans. "I only wish," he said, "that I felt the same confidence in us that these people do."

"Half would be good," Gunnar said.

"So goes the plight of the leader," said Zechariah. "All the more so on the eve of war."

"May our shields hold strong!" Olorus proclaimed. "And our spears strike true!"

"Through mind, body, and spirit," Ahlund said, "may aurym will that we should meet again." He touched his head, shoulder, and heart in succession, drawing a smile from Zechariah.

The three Mythaean nobles, Gunnar, Wulder, and Drexel, lowered their heads and recited as one, "Through wind and tide and squall and foe, may we ever journey on."

CHAPTER 99

They had marched through the entire night. The sky was lightening with the approaching sunrise, and there was still no sense of touch in Justin's left arm. No one had backhanded him or kicked his knees out from under him in what seemed like a long time—the soldiers seemed too focused on the coblyns darting between the trees.

Justin wasn't sure what to make of it all. The coblyns didn't act like mindless beasts driven by insatiable hunger as he had heard them described. The soldiers were terrified, yet they did not flee; the coblyns hunted them, yet they did not attack.

Justin ran a hand over his blackened arm. It had hardened overnight like a monstrous chrysalis, but he could still move it normally despite having no apparent muscles. Judging by the healthy appearance of his unaffected human hand, it must have been capable of circulating blood, though he could not imagine how.

"The hell's wrong with yer arm, anyway?" one of the soldiers demanded.

Justin kept silent as he marched.

"I asked you a question, maggot."

"Hurts," Justin mumbled, which was untrue.

"What?"

"Hurts," Justin repeated at the same volume.

"Think it hurts now," said the soldier. "You don't pick up the pace, I'll show ya hurt."

Justin wondered if this soldier had ever had *his* nose broken, and decided, *He's about to.*

"I said pick it up!"

A boot kicked Justin in the base of the spine, and he went down. He braced himself, getting ready to ram the elbow of his rock-hard arm into the man's face, but the soldier didn't come after him. The commotion of Justin hitting the ground riled the coblyns, and they shot between hiding spaces with renewed fervor, snarling and screaming. The soldiers froze in place with their hands on their weapons. The coblyns still did not attack.

"Get up, you cur," commanded the thug who'd kicked him. He said it halfheartedly, not quite brave enough to take another shot. "Yer lucky I don't make you crawl the rest of the way."

"I think we're already here," someone else said.

The front of the line was coming to a stop. It was difficult to see much in the darkness, but the forest was thinning. The coblyns remained back in the thicker trees, but he could still hear rustling leaves and the occasional snarl or giggle.

"Bring me the boy!" bellowed Lisaac from somewhere up ahead.

Justin might have cooperated if given the chance, but his keepers grabbed him roughly and half-dragged, half-carried him forward through rows of waist-high standing stones covered in moss and lichens.

Headstones, Justin realized.

It was an entire field full of ancient grave markers so eroded that they bore little resemblance to the cutters' intended shapes. But this was no ordinary cemetery. Ahead was a large stone structure with walls at least twenty feet tall. It looked like a coliseum, elliptical in shape, with broken archways lining its heights. The headstones were arranged in concentric rows, all radiating outward from this central complex.

The soldiers quietly watched Justin being led forward. There were about fifty of them in all: bedraggled men with crude weapons hanging from their belts and heavy bags slung over their shoulders. He had come to think of them as monsters for the way they had treated him. But out here in the open, in the half-light of the coming dawn, they didn't look like monsters. They looked shockingly ordinary. Instead of the evil or hateful expressions he might have expected, they just looked tired. And scared. Some, as they watched Justin being led forward, almost looked like they pitied him.

Justin spotted Leah amid the crowd. She tried to come to him, but a few soldiers stepped in front of her to block her way. Justin tried to flash her a reassuring smile, but it felt cold and phony on his lips.

If they turn me fully, thought Justin. *If they do to my whole body what they did to my arm, will I be* me *anymore? Will I know who Leah is . . . or who I am?*

CHAPTER 100

Hidden away beneath the palace of Hartla was a system of tunnels—secret passageways that had been designed for tactical personnel movements. Tonight, beneath the sandstone ridges, the footfalls of five hundred Hartlan soldiers thundered down the corridors.

They wore orange-trimmed leather armor and gauntlets. Torchlight reflected off circular, steel-plated shields. Most were equipped with cutlasses. Others had flanged maces or longbows with side-swords and quivers full of arrows.

Ahlund and his group, at the front of the procession, had donned the same orange-trimmed armor. Pool, Borris, and Samuel had been supplied with proper weaponry to replace their rusty, old equipment and having bathed and shaved, were hardly recognizable. Gunnar had been offered a ceremonial commander's helm but had opted to keep the *Gryphon*'s flag as his only headdress. Olorus carried a new spear, his Nolian kite-shield, and a short sword. Hook was equipped with a spear, a shield, and a long knife. Ahlund felt reasonably at home in the new armor. As long as he had his sword, it didn't much matter what he was wearing.

Zechariah was the only one not wearing Hartlan armor. Instead, he wore the same gray robes he always did, looking much the same as he always had, except for one change. His right hand was gone.

Ahlund kept an eye on the old man. He had remained silent on the subject of his hand, and if he spoke at all, it was about the upcoming battle. A wooden buckler-shield, about one foot in diameter, was strapped to his back. Come tomorrow, he would wear the forearm-mounted shield on his hand-less right arm. For now, the bandaged stump hung uselessly at his side.

Presently, they came to a wide, stone staircase that extended upward for two hundred yards or more. Upon reaching the top of it, Gunnar ordered a halt. The face of every one of the five hundred soldiers looked up the staircase.

Only five hundred, thought Ahlund. He had hoped for more, but the Hartlans were no fools. Despite public support for their plan, the Von Morixes and their city's officials were not about to empty the barracks in such uncertain times. Thus, the quota that had been allotted for the operation at Gaius was frustratingly conservative.

As for Ahlund's group, this plan relied heavily on the theory that the fleet at Gaius and the enemy who had captured Justin and Leah were one and the same. It was a theory that Ahlund feared was closer to a guess. He just hoped that going to war for Hartla was not the latest entry on his growing list of mistakes.

"I must admit," Zechariah muttered to Ahlund, "when I left my little hut to join you, this is not where I expected to end up."

"I told you not to follow me," said Ahlund.

"I have been through wars as a soldier, as an officer, as a general on the battlefield, and as an advisor in the war room," said Zechariah. "But not for many years. The Oikoumene has been peaceful of late. . . . I fear that era may be coming to a close."

Olorus and Hook stepped up to join them. "How you managed to drag me into this," said Olorus, "I will never know."

"How do you think I feel?" whispered Gunnar from the steps above them. "I knew I should have charged you bastards full price."

"You'll have to square that debt with the true guilty party," Ahlund said. "Justin."

"Still harping on about that, eh?" said Olorus. "A common squire could best the boy in single combat, yet you think armies and navies traverse the world to find him! If you are right—which I doubt—and Justin really is to blame for it all, I will make sure he never hears the end of the trouble he has caused."

Ahlund decided not to press the issue. It seemed unwise to test everyone's shaky tolerance of one another—on top of their sudden and rather tenuous commissions as officers in a foreign army.

Gunnar cleared his throat and climbed a few more steps to look down on the soldiers assembled on the stairs.

"Listen up, boys," he said in a voice that echoed through the tunnel. "We're at the threshold, here. In a few minutes, I'll send scouts ahead to recon the countryside. Then we march north out of the cover of these tunnels, toward enemy-controlled territory."

Gunnar paused. He took a deep breath before proceeding.

"But before we go any further, it's time I cleared the air. Your count could have and probably should have chosen any number of other more experienced and more qualified commanders to lead you. Instead, because of my noble blood, he chose me. And now, out of loyalty to your count, you are expected to follow me. It has been years since I led soldiers into battle—years spent mostly fishing for trout."

A few of the troops laughed, apparently thinking this was a joke.

"I think, at least for today," said Gunnar, "we need to stop pretending that 'noble blood' means anything. My father's father's father was a somebody, they tell me. That's all. That don't mean a thing today. My blood ain't any nobler than yours. I'm just some guy, like the rest of you. No, actually, not like the rest of you. If anything, you're better than me. I had duty thrust on me at birth. My performance of my duties was lackluster at best, and even that was taken from me by the actions of my brother. But the rest of you have chosen to be here. From the day you enlisted to defend your homeland, your lives took on greater meaning. Entrusted to you soldiers, in addition to your own mortal souls, are the souls of the citizens of the land you swore to protect. Every one of you holds in his or her hands the lives of your mothers and fathers, your lovers, your children, your friends. Your failure could mean their deaths. And your triumph, or your sacrifice, can mean their continued existence. Today, *your* lives are entrusted to me. So I want you to know that I feel the full weight of those many lives in our hands, and I will not order you into battle lightly. Whatever happens next, I don't ask that you obey me, and I don't ask you to follow me because of who my father's father's father was. What I ask is that you to trust me. . . . Trust me out of loyalty to all those mothers and fathers, lovers, children, and friends whose souls rest in our hands—whose futures depend on us. I have not earned the right to be your admiral, but, if you can find it within yourselves, I would be honored to be your brother."

Others in Gunnar's position might have taken the moment to try to rouse the group into a frenzy of support, or request a show of solidarity from them. Gunnar simply stepped down from the stairs without another word.

Olorus turned to Ahlund and raised both red eyebrows as if to say, "Not bad."

The tunnel remained quiet, but the five hundred Hartlans seemed to Ahlund to stand a bit taller.

CHAPTER 101

They camped in the forest and made no fires. Somewhere in the distance, unseen, waves crashed against the rocky Athacean coastline.

Ahlund looked up at the moons. There were nine miles of wooded hills between here and Gaius, but their plan of attack relied too heavily on the element of surprise to risk moving any closer tonight. While Ahlund, Zechariah, Gunnar, Olorus, and Hook scouted ahead, the rest would remain here.

Ahlund found Gunnar with Pool, Samuel, and Borris, speaking to a Hartlan soldier.

"I'm surprised Wulder never established a presence at Gaius himself," said Gunnar.

"It's a decent inlet," replied the soldier. "Couple years ago, the count sent a platoon to clear out some bandits, but a permanent settlement would be more trouble than it's worth."

"Cap'n," said Pool. "Er—I mean, admiral. What ought we be doin'?"

"You ought be rowin' home, you rotten bilge lavellans," Gunnar said, reverting to Lonn-speak.

"Nothin' doin'," said Borris, from the good side of his mouth. "We're with ya till the end, admiral!"

"Me—a Mythaean soldier!" Samuel said. "If me da could only see me now!"

Gunnar smiled. "Well, if I can't run ya out, then I'll need me crew by me side. Tomorrow, you three are the admiral's personal bodyguards. Any harm wants to befall me, it's gotta get by you lot first. It's hard enough to woo a girl with only one eye to wink with, so see to it I don't get any uglier, ya hear?"

"Aye aye, admiral!" the three chorused, saluting.

Upon spotting Ahlund, Gunnar's demeanor noticeably darkened. "Would you boys excuse us?" he said. "I need a private word with Captain Sims."

The soldiers and sailors-turned-bodyguards took their leave. Gunnar and Ahlund stood alone, but it was still a long while before the admiral spoke.

"Listen," he said. "Don't think for a bloody second that I believe in any angels. But after what happened in the Drekwood, I would have to be an even more obstinate ass than Olorus to deny that something strange is going on." He paused. "Maybe you and the old man aren't as chock-full of excrement as I originally thought. So if anything weird rears its head again, I'm deferring to your judgment."

My judgment, thought Ahlund. *The judgment of a thug who turned his back on everything he believed in, to bloody his sword for anyone who would pay. . . . Would Gunnar defer to my judgment if he knew how many souls have died beneath my sword for the sake of a little gold? Would Zechariah trust in me if he knew how long it has been since I believed in the faith he holds so dear? And what would Olorus and Hook do if they knew that after the Nolian government hired me to protect Leah, I accepted a higher rate of pay from the prime minister personally to betray her into his hands. . . ?*

"Gunnar," said Ahlund. "I am not the man for this job. I am unworthy."

"Hell, aren't we all?" said Gunnar.

Ahlund said nothing for a moment, then looked at Gunnar. "This Yordar they speak of. He is your brother?"

"Yeah," was all Gunnar said.

"You know what the old man will say," said Ahlund.

Gunnar looked puzzled.

"If your relationship with your brother is so strained," said Ahlund, "then your request for these soldiers to call you *brother* was ironic at best and ominous at worst."

Gunnar's gaze went distant for a moment. Finally, he laughed.

"Dammit," he said. "Can't do anything right. This is why I was never cut out for this sort of thing. Unworthy just like you. . . . Maybe tomorrow is our chance to fix that."

CHAPTER 102

Justin was dragged through an arched doorway in the side of the stone structure. The soldiers shoved him in and backed away. Inside, it looked even more like a coliseum, with terraced walls built in a bowl-shaped amphitheater design. But instead of theater seating, the terraces were lined with rows of rectangular stone boxes. Nearby, one of the boxes was broken, and a pile of debris lay where it had spilled from inside.

Yellowed bones protruded the hard earth. Human skulls with soil-filled eye sockets rested side-by-side.

Tombs, Justin thought. *Hundreds of them.*

Each of the sarcophagi lining the walls was an ossuary large enough to hold a dozen or more bodies. Several others had also been broken open, probably by grave-robbers, and the disassembled skeletons lay scattered upon the ramparts. Flowering grasses peeked through ribcages and pelvises. This was no coliseum. It was a necropolis—a city of the dead.

Out of the shadows on the other side of the amphitheater stepped the incongruous, eight-and-a-half-foot-tall frame of Lisaac. The voulge was strapped to his back, its giant, cleaver-like blade sticking up above his shoulders. Justin felt the urge to be insolent, but the way that man stood there, impossibly huge, staring at him with those sunken eyes, turned Justin's tongue to lead.

"You are becoming one of them," Lisaac said. "A cythraul. Even I did not know they could transform living flesh into one of their own. Remarkable."

Justin looked at his arm. It looked like the limb of a burned corpse, yet it was strong and within his command. Despite being quite narrow, it was heavy as iron, and his shoulder ached with the effort of carrying it.

"It is a gift," said Lisaac, "from Avagad himself."

Avagad, thought Justin.

Justin balled his left hand into a fist, feeling the painful tug at his wrist of flesh against non-flesh.

Behind Lisaac, a shadow crawled across the upper lip of the coliseum bowl. It came slinking down into the amphitheater. Another followed it. And another. Justin took an involuntary step back as dozens of lanky silhouettes came pouring over the tops of the coliseum walls. They climbed down into the interior. They hopped across the lids of tombs and skittered over the stone surfaces, kicking loose the skulls of the dead.

It was finally happening. The coblyns were attacking.

CHAPTER 103

Amid the rubble of Gaius, campfires flickered beneath the moonlight. Dozens of tents and lean-tos had been pitched against the ruins. The water shimmered like the flexing sheen of precious metal. And bobbing in the inlet were precisely one hundred black sails.

Atop an outcropping a mile away, Ahlund, Gunnar, Zechariah, Hook, and Olorus took turns with a spyglass.

"I thought Drexel said several hundred ships," Olorus said.

"He either overestimated," said Gunnar, "or some have since departed. Either way, it's good news for a change."

Hook signed, *"They could be stationed in open waters, out of view."*

"I can't help but wonder," said Zechariah, "if Justin and Leah are down there."

"Perhaps," said Olorus. "Or might the missing ships have ferried them away? What I mean is, are we too late?"

Ahlund had been wondering the same thing, but he wouldn't have dared say it. It was a poisonous thought that could not be allowed to take root.

"Tomorrow, we will know," Ahlund said. He nodded at Olorus and Hook. "Or tonight, should you come across some evidence." The plan was for the two of them to slip in, alone, and sabotage as much as they could get their hands on before dawn.

"Drexel was wrong about the number of ships," signed Hook. *"What if he was also wrong about these people not being Mythaeans? Maybe it really is Gunnar's brother launching an invasion. If that is the case, we are fighting the wrong enemy, and Leah and Justin could be anywhere."*

"Are any of you familiar with the Demon Wars?" asked Zechariah.

Hook signed, *"You refer to ancient eastern mythology."*

"What sort of tall tale you got for us this time, old man?" said Gunnar. "Parable? Fairytale? Ghost story—?"

"Fairytale!" snarled Zechariah.

The men looked at him in surprise, for he was suddenly brimming with anger. He swore nastily in an old language that probably only Ahlund could understand.

"How I tire of coddling you thickheaded cretins!" said Zechariah. "The truth of my words is confirmed time and time again, yet you still think *I* am the doddering fool? Idiots! All of you! How have you not yet found the humility to keep your blessed mouths shut? If I am forced to stomach your stupidity another minute, I shall do you all a favor and use the hand I have left to bash your feeble brains in."

Ahlund had to stifle his satisfaction at the others' stupefied expressions. No one said—or signed—a word.

Zechariah cleared his throat. "You've all heard stories of the Ancient Elleneans. Long ago, they lived in harmony across the entirety of the Oikoumene. It is said that they were so in tune with aurym that it gave them indefinite lifespans, great wisdom, and uncanny strength. My own people, the Brethren, knew only a fraction of the lost knowledge of the Ancients. The Elleneans were humans as they were meant to be. But they were not alone on this planet. An inhuman race invaded their lands. The Elleneans fought back, but, over the centuries, demons overran and conquered the Oikoumene. In the end, no safe haven remained. The Elleneans were defeated. Humans were driven to the brink of extinction, and demonkind enslaved the remnant. For two thousand years, the demons reigned as overlords, and the human race grew weak and pitiful under their masters' whips. Mankind deteriorated. Their innate connection with aurym was severed. Strength faded. Lifespans became short—and diseased. And the wisdom of the Ancients was lost.

"Yet here we are today. And how? Because humanity rose up, led by a single hero wielding aurym power the likes of which the world had never known. It was said that this hero, called *ethoul*, had come from another realm beyond the Oikoumene, much like the demons themselves. But this was no demon. The 'fallen angel' led the first human rebellions and began a war that drove the demons back across the Great Ocean. And although the angel perished in the fighting, humanity was ultimately able to reclaim the Oikoumene.

"Our species was freed from the captivity of demon armies because of one fallen angel. Perhaps the rumors of the ethoul's aurym abilities have been exaggerated over time—mythologized to godly proportions—but the legend of the fallen angel still has the potential to inspire and influence. To unite armadas, armies, and allies as unlikely as us."

Having said his peace, Zechariah stuck his chin out defiantly and nodded once for emphasis.

"Well," said Olorus, smiling, "now that granddad has put us all in our places, I believe it's time Hook and I be off."

Zechariah looked annoyed for a moment but only grinned and shook his head, muttering, "Oh, aurym help us. . . ."

"You sure you two don't want some help?" Gunnar asked the Nolians.

"Anyone tagging along would just slow us down," said Olorus. "We'll stash our equipment just outside camp, slip in, cause some trouble, and be waiting for the rest of you come first light."

Ahlund shook hands with Hook, who nodded. When he offered his hand to Olorus, the lieutenant grabbed it strongly and squeezed, his hairy forearm bulging.

"When next we meet," said Olorus, "it will be in the glory of battle."

"Give them hell," said Ahlund.

"I'll give it to them twice!" said Olorus. His reply was so quick that Ahlund got the impression he had been told as much—and had given the same response—many times in the past.

Olorus turned to face Gunnar. "No doubt our Guardian will fight with his flaming sword, but I am curious, Gunnar. Do you plan to call your brothers and sisters into battle with you, the leaves and the flowers? Will you grow the forest up around us for cover? Infect the enemy with a bout of hay fever? Call on the pine cones to launch themselves like siege missiles?"

Gunnar smiled and gripped Olorus's shoulder. "I'm afraid my talents are only useful on a smaller scale." He patted a satchel strapped to his belt. "But, if all else fails, perhaps I can attract some honeybees."

"Ah, the gardener's secret weapon!" said Olorus. "How unfortunate that the rest of us will have to make do with lowly swords, shields, and spears."

"Stay alive, gentlemen," said Gunnar.

Hook signed, *"You, too."*

The Nolian soldiers turned to leave, but Olorus promptly fell and hit the ground with a startled grunt. Looking around confusedly, he found his feet stuck in a wad of tall grass that had inexplicably knotted itself around his ankles, tying him in place.

The lieutenant laughed, vowing, "You'll get yours, gardener!"

Olorus extricated himself from the grass, and he and Hook snuck down the hillside toward Gaius. Ahlund watched them go, wondering if he would ever see them again.

CHAPTER 104

Justin looked at Lisaac in alarm as the coblyns advanced. But the big man seemed unconcerned as they closed in, hissing, growling, crying, and hooting. Maybe he couldn't hear them.

Then Lisaac raised a hand and said, "Stay back."

The coblyns stopped.

It took Justin a moment to register what had happened. He could hear the coblyns breathing. He could smell their putrid stench. Up close, he could see that their upper and lower jaws had pairs of eye teeth that overlapped the lips. Their faces reminded him of a jack-o'-lantern his family had once forgotten about on their back porch. For weeks after Halloween, it had sat there, undisturbed, and when Justin had stumbled upon it in mid-December half-covered in snow, it was shrunken and pruney and black—its simple, grim expression caving in on itself and the decaying meat so rotted-out that you could push your finger right through it.

Some of the coblyns sat crouched like gargoyles upon the tombs. Their pruned faces, like that old pumpkin, looked like the flesh could have been pushed in with one good shove. Others paced back and forth like dogs at the ends of short leashes, but they came no closer.

"They're . . . listening to you?" breathed Justin.

Lisaac pointed to a coblyn perched on the lid of a broken sarcophagus and said, "You. Dispose of yourself."

The coblyn reached down and plucked an ancient skull from the pile at its feet. It raised the skull, swung its gangly arm upward, and smashed itself in the face.

The coblyn reeled back from the blow and struck again. And again. And again. Black blood sprayed with each impact. It fell to its knees, but still, it kept hitting itself. Shards of bone shattered from the skull. Finally, it raised its arm for another strike, trembled, and fell. Its body tumbled down the terraced wall, pitched forward, and hit the courtyard with a thud. Dark, watery fluid oozed from the cavity where its face had been. It twitched once, then lay still.

"Their obedience," said Lisaac, "is unfailing."

Justin could hardly speak. "I thought that—"

"That they were mindless beasts?" Lisaac shook his giant head, making a *tsk-tsk* sound with his tongue. "Hardly. Coblyns, the Lesser Demons, were bred to be footmen. They are motivated by two things. Loyalty and hunger. And they are inherently obedient to their generals: the cythraul.

"Coblyns are not unintelligent; they simply lack discretion. They will live like animals unless told otherwise. That is how they have lived in the Oikoumene for ages—ever since the High Demons were driven out and forced to leave their footmen behind to dwell in the dark places and to hunt by night. Without leadership, coblyns are ruled only by their hunger. But at the command of their masters, they will become soldiers once again. Their lives mean nothing to them. They will eagerly give up their existence if a cythraul commands it. They obey me, now, only because the cythraul commanded them to do so.

"Once ordered into battle, a coblyn will never stop. It will never falter. It will never pause to rest. It will fight until it dies on its feet from exhaustion. Human soldiers will retreat when outmatched. Coblyns have no concept of retreat. Human armies require food and water, and the longer they fight, the more resources they need. Coblyn armies require no provisions. They gather their sustenance by feeding on the corpses of those they defeat. The longer they fight, the stronger they become."

"Coblyn armies?" said Justin.

Lisaac's mouth twitched with a grin. He swept a hand toward the whining, baying coblyns around them. "We collected these and many more from the Drekwood. There are probably millions in the dark places of this continent, living and spawning in the wilderness like animals for untold ages, eagerly awaiting the return of their cythraul masters to give them their marching orders."

"Who the hell are you?" said Justin. It was all he could think to ask.

"Before Avagad contacted me, my men and I were simple raiders, pillaging Darvellian trade caravans in southern Athacea," said Lisaac. "I was already a servant of daemyn. I worshipped the black aurym in my homeland in the jungles of Ythia. But on the day Avagad came into my mind to call me to a greater cause . . . that was when everything changed. It was the day my devotion to daemyn took on true meaning. Now, my men and I serve alongside cythraul, collecting coblyns for Avagad's war machine. Just imagine how many others, like me, are carrying out his orders across the Oikoumene even as we speak." One of Lisaac's dinnerplate-sized hands closed into a fist. "With hordes of coblyns heeding the call of cythraul generals, Avagad will soon command an army no human force will be able to stand against."

"But you are human," said Justin. "How could you side with these things?"

"This is the dusk of the old world," Lisaac said. "A new age is beginning. One in which mankind and demonkind will become one. Glorious daemyn will flood the world, and all will worship the dark god of the flaming sword."

"The god of what?" said Justin.

Lisaac took a deep breath and set his shoulders back as if basking in the splendor of it all. "You will know him even better than I do," he said, "soon enough."

"I am not who Avagad thinks I am," Justin said.

"That is a cowardly deception," said Lisaac.

"No. I'm telling you, I'm not—"

"Do not insult my intelligence," Lisaac cut in. "I felt your arrival in this world. So did Avagad, the cythraul, and many others. What better standard-bearer to usher in the age of demons than a fallen angel? Angels and demons brought together in a divine alliance. Look at your arm—proof that what Avagad cannot gain through diplomacy, he will take by force. This is your first step toward understanding the mysteries of daemyn. I have been tasked to serve as your first teacher. You can be a willing student, or you can be a slave turned by the cythraul fully and forever robbed of your free will. The choice, to me, seems clear."

Lisaac extended a hand toward Justin.

"Join us, Justin."

Justin looked at his arm. Shaking with nerves, hardly able to believe what he was about to do, he raised his demon arm and reached for Lisaac's awaiting hand.

CHAPTER 105

Morning sunlight streamed over the top of the coliseum. Lisaac smiled at Justin's outstretched hand.

Justin reached up with the other hand, grabbed his own pinky finger, and snapped it backward with a pop-*crunch*. He bit his lip to stifle a scream and almost fell to his knees from the pain.

Slowly, the smile faded from Lisaac's face.

Justin sucked in a breath through his grinding teeth. His pinky hung lopsided, broken backward at the base.

"What . . . are you doing?" said Lisaac.

"Just saving you the trouble, Tiny," said Justin. "You think threats and torture and pain are enough to manipulate me?" He grabbed his ring finger. "Join you? I would sooner break every bone in my body my—*self*!"

He yanked back, hard. The ring finger was stronger and didn't break as easily, but with steady pressure, it weakened and finally gave. The second knuckle popped, and the rest of the finger bent backward like a lever. Justin cried out. When he could catch his breath again, he squared his shoulders, sneered at Lisaac, and said, "Think you can do better?"

The coblyns in the coliseum had begun to rile at Justin's display, but Lisaac raised a hand to restore them to order.

"You, Justin, are a fool," said Lisaac, "but you will be a valuable asset, once that iron will has been broken."

Lisaac reached over his back and unhooked something. He swung his arm, and an object flew toward Justin and landed at his feet. It was a sheathed sword.

But it was not just any sword, Justin realized. The crossguard had forward-sloping quillons, giving it a distinctive *Y* shape that Justin would have recognized anywhere. It was the heavy, two-hander claymore he had found in the caves under the Shifting Mountains.

"My sword," said Justin.

"You attempt to goad me into taking action against you," said Lisaac. "Very well. Take up arms and defend yourself. Your first lesson will be to be careful what you wish for."

Justin picked his sword up off the ground. But instead of defending himself, he pulled the weapon from the sheath and pressed the blade against his own neck.

"Big mistake," Justin said.

Lisaac's face dropped. He seemed too frightened to move.

"Break me? Turn me?" said Justin. "You need me alive for all that. If I'm really as important as you say I am, I can only imagine what Avagad will do when he finds out you let me die."

Several seconds passed, and neither man moved. The coblyns on the terraced formations babbled and squawked excitedly in voices that sounded like children's laughter played at half-speed. They seemed to sense the tension between the two men.

Justin could almost see the oversized gears turning in Lisaac's head, but finally, the big man said, "And can you imagine what we'll do to that dainty princess when you're gone?"

A steely fist gripped Justin's heart, and he felt his confidence shrivel up and fade. His own life would be a small price to pay to stop Lisaac and the rest of these people. Leah's life, however. That was another matter. She would probably want him to do what was best for everyone—not just for her. He didn't want to put her in danger, but he also didn't want this madness to continue any longer. He remembered the house, destroyed outside the walls of the Shifting Mountains by a cythraul's blast, people screaming, all because of him. As long as the cythraul, Lisaac, Avagad, and others like them thought he was a fallen angel, innocent people were going to keep getting hurt. If the cythraul turned him, how many people would suffer?

Maybe dying right now is for the best, thought Justin. *Maybe Leah can find a way to escape and rally the others with news of what happened here.*

He had been bluffing about the torture, of course. Enough of it would inevitably break him. He just wanted the pain to be over—he wanted it all to be over. He was never going to see home again, anyway, so what was the point?

Do it, he thought. *Just a little slip of the wrist is all it takes. No more fear. No more pain.*

Lisaac watched Justin, and Justin watched him right back. The coblyns were babbling louder than ever.

It'll be so easy. And then it's all over. Why not? End this madness now. Just do it. Do it. Come on. Do it. . . !

"Do it."

Justin blinked in confusion. He could have sworn he had heard that last one.

"Do it. Do it."

The thought was strangely overwhelming. It became a chant ringing through his head: "Do it. Do it." The tone changed with each repetition. At first, it sounded like himself. Then it became the voice of his father scolding him. Now, it sounded like his mother encouraging him: "Do it! Do it!"

Justin clutched the sword's hilt with both hands. He flexed his fingers, tightening his grip. The chant was growing in volume and number, joined by the voices of his teachers, friends, classmates, and other voices that sounded familiar but he couldn't quite identify—bit players in his life he had long forgotten about. Everyone had shown up for the party. "Do it," they were all saying. "Do it."

Attempting to stall for time, Justin tried to remove the sword from his throat and realized . . . he couldn't.

The voices converged. The many became one. A single, guttural tone snarled, deep and fiery: "DO . . . *IT*."

Cold panic gripped Justin. He tried to open his fingers, but they were frozen in place around the sword's handle. He tried again to pull the sword away from him. The muscles in his good arm stood up with the effort, but the sword remained pressed to his neck.

Justin moved his head back, trying to put some distance between himself and the stubborn weight of the sword. If he couldn't move the sword, he could at least move his neck away from it.

But the sword followed him, closing the gap.

Justin gasped as cold steel dug into the fleshy part of his neck between his jaw and his Adam's apple. He wasn't holding the sword anymore; he was holding it back.

Something else, some invisible force, was pushing it toward him.

PART IX

MADRIGAL

CHAPTER 106

Justin's hands shook with the effort of pushing back against whatever was pushing his weapon toward him. The pressure was so great that he realized if he let up at all, the blade would push right through him.

He took a step backward, but it didn't help. The sword stayed pressed against his throat. He tried again to let go, but his hands were locked down tight. It almost felt as if something was wrapping around his fingers. Something invisible. Holding his hands to the hilt. Making it impossible to let go. All he could do was struggle against the weapon's unexplainable urge to travel along its intended path—into his neck.

Suddenly, he felt a strange tightening. A sensation like invisible fingers adjusting their grip, closing more tightly on Justin's hands.

The pressure increased.

Justin's lungs burned. He could barely draw breath against the sharp metal pushing against his windpipe. It was so much stronger, whatever this thing was, and it was steadily wearing him down. Overpowering him. He dared not turn his head to the right or to the left even a fraction of an inch, lest the movement give the sharpened edge purchase and open his skin. He felt sweat dripping down his neck—at least, he hoped it was sweat.

The invisible hands tightened their grip again, and for a second, Justin thought he could see the shadows of long, dark fingers—too many fingers for human hands.

Daemyn! he realized.

The voice spoke again—this time not in his head, but from outside. Though he could not see the speaker, the point of origin was only inches from his face. He felt hot, sulfuric breath douse his ear as it said in an off-key choir, "FINISH . . . THIS."

Justin heard a whimper and realized it was his own. His arms felt like rubber. A minute ago, killing himself had somehow seemed selfless and noble. Only now did he realize his mistake: Killing himself was exactly what this darkness wanted.

It was too strong. The hands of daemyn were controlling him, driving the sharpened steel into his throat. A sliver of pain shot through Justin's neck as blade broke the skin, and Justin did the only thing he could think to do. He shouted, "*Help*!"

At once, the sword shifted. The blade trembled and began to move away from Justin's neck. He opened his eyes to see who had come to his aid, but no one was there. At least, no one he could see. He still appeared to be standing alone. He could still feel daemyn's viselike grip trying to force the weapon into his neck, but instead, the blade was being moved steadily away from him.

He looked down. Perhaps it was some illusion, some trick of the rising sun, but a glowing light seemed to be playing across his fingers. A *third* set of hands, he realized, had closed around the shadowed ones. And they were guiding the sword away from his neck.

Aurym!

The sword eased farther from his throat. He saw a tiny ribbon of his own blood clinging to the blade. The dark choir screamed furiously in defeat, and the sword suddenly turned to dead weight in Justin's hands.

Justin let go. The sword fell to the ground. He stood, panting, looking dumbly at the weapon. The opposing forces—the shadowed hands and the glowing ones—were gone, as if they had never been there at all.

Across the necropolis, Lisaac was watching Justin. He looked hesitant. Or nervous.

Justin put a hand to his neck, and his palm came away smeared with sticky, red drops. Not a lot; the cut was only skin deep, fortunately. But much farther, and. . . .

I almost did it, thought Justin. His hands began to tremble. *I almost did it.*

What had first entered his mind as a thought—a mere idea—had welcomed in something much more powerful and terrible. Daemyn had slipped in, in the guise of his own self-righteous intentions. The dark voice had nearly convinced him to go through with it. When that hadn't worked, the shadowed hands had tried to physically impose their will on him, and all his strength had not been enough to stop it.

Daemyn, a force he hadn't even believed in, had almost killed him. And aurym, something he'd been even less sure of, had saved him.

Justin knelt and picked his sword back up, looking at his blood on the blade. He drew a tight grip on the hilt, forcing his hands to stop trembling.

I still might die today, thought Justin, not with fear but with acceptance of the fact. *But not like that.*

He planted his feet on the packed earth of the courtyard. His arms were weary, but he raised the sword in a defensive position, the way Zechariah had taught him, ignoring the pain in his broken fingers, and narrowed his eyes at Lisaac.

Lisaac pulled the cleaver-headed voulge from his back and spun it in a masterful flourish. The haft rotated like a windmill's blades, producing whooshing noises in the air as it whirled. Then he leveled it at Justin, and he smiled. The coblyns cackled gleefully.

Justin looked up at the ramparts of the stone coliseum. A lingering shred of naiveté still believed that his friends would come to the rescue. A blast of volcanic fire would come searing over the walls, and Ahlund would rush in. Justin in time, Zechariah would plunge into the coblyns, sword spinning and hacking off limbs. And Olorus and Hook would loose their spears as Gunnar and Leah rushed the courtyard to join the fray.

But the moment passed, and no such miracle occurred. There were only coblyns. And Lisaac. And dead bones in tombs. Justin was alone.

No, he thought, feeling a warm glow within. *Not alone. . . . Never alone.*

With speed defying his ungainly size, Lisaac charged. The blade of the voulge dragged in the dirt behind him like a ship's rudder. He spun in a full circle, lifting his weapon in a horizontal arc at Justin like a scythe to ripe, golden wheat.

Justin only had time to recoil a step before the impact. His feet left the ground. His center of gravity did an illogical circle in the air, and he landed elbows-first in the dirt and rolled across the ground. His sword landed beside him.

The morning sky above Justin swayed like the horizon on an ocean voyage. Had he been cut in half? Was he dying?

Lisaac stomped toward him. Justin shot to his feet and rolled. He grabbed his sword and came up at the ready. He looked down at his body. His ribs were on fire, but he saw no sign of injury on his bare chest or stomach. No blood except some scrapes where his elbows had hit the ground. Lisaac gave a gap-toothed smile and patted the blunt, bladeless end of his voulge. Rather than cleaving Justin in two, he had hit him with the nonlethal side. Still, it was a small miracle that Justin was standing. Even with the blunt end, a strike like that could have shattered bone.

No thinking about how much it hurt, rang Zechariah's words in Justin's head. *If you get hit, get back up and fight. Remember how he did it and don't let it happen again.*

Instead of waiting for the next attack, Justin tightened his grip on his sword and sprinted at Lisaac. The big man only watched.

Justin spun his sword, feinted high, turned, and cut low, aiming for Lisaac's thigh. Before the strike could land, the haft of the voulge rapped against Justin's forearm, knocking the sword from his hands. In the same instant, Lisaac's plate-armored knee drove into Justin's chest. Multiple ribs popped.

Justin shouted in alarm and pain, but his cry was cut short. A massive hand grabbed him by the throat, picked him up bodily from the earth, carried him up in a wide arc, and slammed him down onto his back. What little wind was left in his lungs was firmly knocked out. Broken ribs stabbed at him from the inside. He reached for his sword on the ground—

A massive boot came down and pinned his right arm against the ground. His fingertips brushed the pommel of his sword in the grass, but he couldn't reach it. Coblyns screeched and howled around him.

"Your pretty healer can mend broken fingers," said Lisaac over him. The big man positioned the sharpened edge of the voulge's cleaver-blade to let it hang suspended above Justin's pinned hand. "I am curious to see if she can reattach them."

Through clenched teeth, Justin wheezed in panic as he watched the blade drop.

CHAPTER 107

Ahlund, Gunnar, and Zechariah stood on the outcropping overlooking Gaius with five hundred Hartlan soldiers assembled in ranks behind them. Down in the ruins, people shouted at one another as they rushed from their tents, some hopping on one leg while still trying to pull up their pants. Several of the black-sailed ships docked on the shoreline were on fire, and men on the decks threw buckets of water into the flames.

Other ships drifted aimlessly away, unmanned, their mooring lines cut. Men waded out through the water trying to catch them.

"Well done, Nolians," Gunnar mumbled.

Ahlund was tempted to agree. Olorus and Hook had held up their end of the bargain. Now, the mayhem in the enemy camp was intensifying as the rising sun revealed the white sails of the Hartlan fleet. Fifty ships sailing for Gaius. When Drexel's ships were in position, Ahlund, Gunnar, Zechariah, and the five hundred Hartlans would descend the hill and charge the ruins. Thus far, all was proceeding according to plan except for one thing.

Ahlund exchanged a look with Zechariah. His face said it all. He felt it, too.

Cythraul.

Not since that first attack on the Gravelands had Ahlund felt the presence of the daemyn monsters quite so strongly. Even battling a cythraul face-to-face in the Drekwood had not felt like this. There were several of them, and they were close.

The Hartlan fleet drew nearer. The lead ships fanned outward into a funnel-shaped attack pattern as they neared the inlet. Archers were assembled on their decks. Of the hundred enemy ships at Gaius, less than a quarter of them had yet managed to mount a defense. One of the sabotaged ships was now completely engulfed in flames, pouring thick, black smoke from the portholes as it tipped precariously and began to sink. Its men abandoned ship into the surf.

To Ahlund's surprise, dozens of other ships still sat beached along the shoreline unmanned. Olorus and Hook had done a fine job, but Ahlund did not think it was possible that they could have incapacitated the entire crews of so many ships. The only explanation: There were too few men at Gaius to have manned them to begin with, even before the sabotage.

The enemy force was smaller than they had anticipated. And judging by their slow, ineffectual response to being attacked, they were poorly trained. Gunnar, apparently coming to the same conclusions, raised his fist in triumph as if the battle had already been won.

"We outnumber them!" he shouted. "Now we crush the dogs beneath our boots! Cut them down! Stomp these invaders out of existence!"

A cheer went up among the Hartlans. They beat their shields with their swords.

Gunnar shot Ahlund a grin.

On the inlet, the first ships to meet slid against one another, hull-to-hull. Tethering hooks were thrown, fastening the ships together. Arrows rained down, and humans on both sides dropped dead or wounded. Hartlan foot soldiers boarded the opposing ship, and with swords, halberds, and axes, they hacked at the enemy sailors. From Ahlund's vantage point, the bloody theater of war was eerily silent. The scene repeated itself across the inlet. Hulls slammed. Weapons clashed. Bodies tumbled into the roiling surf.

"It's time," said Zechariah.

Gunnar pulled his cutlass from its scabbard and raised it high. "Charge!" he cried.

Gunnar leaped from the outcropping and sprinted down the hill. Zechariah shouted with fury and followed, and Ahlund drew his sword and ran after. Behind them, the five hundred Hartlan soldiers stormed screaming down the hillside.

Down the hill and across the wooded plain they charged. As they emerged from the trees, Ahlund saw the enemy perimeter: a paltry force of archers and guards who only now realized their exposed rear was being attacked. Officers shouted, trying to redirect their inept forces, but there couldn't have been more than one hundred defenders. Child's play.

Five hundred yards from the encampment, the Hartlan army split as planned. Zechariah took half to the left; Gunnar and Ahlund, with Pool, Borris, and Samuel close on their heels, took the other half to the right. The five hundred soldiers diverged like a branching river. The enemies scrambled to adjust their defenses.

Three hundred yards from camp, Zechariah's forces were arcing wide while Gunnar and Ahlund's platoon drove straight forward. Ahlund could see the entirety of Gaius, now: scattered rubble, half-standing stone buildings, and white and black sails mingling on the water beyond.

At two hundred yards, arrows began to fall. There were dull thuds as they hit the ground and sickening smacks when they struck true. Heroic war cries turned to screams of pain and death. To inspire his followers and frighten his foes, Ahlund raised his sword high and let the blade spit trails of fire into the air as he ran.

One hundred yards away, and Ahlund was eyeing up his first kill: an officer who had posted himself just a little too close to the front lines and was shouting orders at his soldiers—if these people could be called soldiers at all. They wore no armor and were hardly armed. Ahlund could almost see the whites of the officer's eyes. But something at the corner of his vision suddenly reined in his full attention.

Out at sea, a Hartlan ship was going down. And crawling all over its decks, like parasites overrunning a host, were innumerable black figures. Leathery creatures the size of children tore open the bodies of Hartlan soldiers and sailors to rip out and devour their innards even as they slipped beneath the sea.

"Coblyns!" Ahlund shouted.

The warning had hardly left his lips when the cargo hold of one of the beached ships along the shoreline—one of the vessels he had assumed were unmanned—burst open from the inside.

A ten-foot-tall, bone-armored monster ducked out of the cargo hold and stepped into the light. A singular, jagged horn extended from its forehead, and in its hand was a giant, wickedly curved scimitar.

Ahlund gritted his teeth. He had sensed the presence of cythraul, but he had not expected them to be this close.

The cythraul raised its behemoth sword high in the air and unleashed a demonic roar that rose up and shattered the din. In response, cargo hold doors up and down the beach were thrown open from the inside. Rampaging hordes of coblyns spilled forth from the bellies of the ships. They poured out onto the beach—creatures beyond count, shadowing the sands in a wave of black like spilled tar. Hundreds, perhaps thousands of them. Hopping, knuckle-walking, crawling, and sprinting through the ruins of Gaius. As a single, cohesive unit, they ran toward the advancing Hartlan army.

They are charging. . . . Ahlund realized. *At the cythraul's command!*

CHAPTER 108

The change in the Hartlans was palpable. Their charge slowed. War cries faded to silence. Confidence and enthusiasm withered.

A small force of the enemy defenders broke from the camp and charged at the Hartlans. Gunnar, who had not slowed, was the first into battle. He thrust his cutlass downward between a man's shoulder and collarbone. At the same moment, Ahlund swung his sword at his intended target, pouring liquid fire over the unlucky officer. Infantry barreled in behind him, and the armies met in a bloody tumult. Some came shield-first, battering so fiercely that enemies were knocked off their feet to be run through where they lay. Others came blade-first, splitting flesh and bone.

On the other side of the battle, Zechariah and his soldiers charged into the lesser-defended portion of camp with deadly success. The old man clutched his sword—blade pointed downward—in his off hand. The buckler-shield was strapped to the forearm of his missing hand. He ducked a pike-thrust and swiped upward, severing a soldier's head. A jet of blood streamed skyward in his wake. Guards were driven back. Archers toppled from their posts. All across the battlefield, the untrained enemy soldiers fell to the superiority of the Hartlans.

But it wasn't soldiers Ahlund was worried about.

It did not take long for Gunnar and Ahlund to reach their rendezvous point, the stone ruins of a large building with enough cover to serve as a command post. Ahlund sliced a lingering enemy soldier across the chest, kicked him to the ground, then ducked behind a pile of stone blocks beside Gunnar. His bodyguards, Pool, Borris, and Samuel, were with him, and the surrounding infantry hurried to set up defenses.

"What the hell is going on?" Gunnar yelled, looking over the fortifications. "There are coblyns coming out of those ships!"

On the shoreline, the cythraul stood bellowing strange words. Hundreds of coblyns were still spilling from the guts of the ships, though none had yet reached the Hartlan attackers.

"They're obeying the cythraul's commands," said Ahlund.

"This was not part of the plan!" said Gunnar.

A soldier standing guard beside Gunnar twisted painfully and went down with an arrow stuck through his midsection. Pool, Borris, and Samuel encircled their captain, looking frantically for the source of the shot. Turning, Ahlund spotted a bastion of enemy archers posted atop a stone tower. Bowstrings twanged, and several more arrows rained down.

Then Olorus and Hook suddenly emerged behind the enemy archers at the top of the tower, driving dagger and spear into their exposed backs. The rest of the archers turned to face the Nolians but were quickly overpowered and went down. The last archer took a wild swing at Olorus who ducked it and kicked the man squarely in the chest, sending him plummeting from the tower.

Olorus looked down and offered a neighborly salute toward Gunnar and Ahlund at the command post. Ahlund replied by signaling ahead at the coblyns. Olorus nodded. He and Hook procured bows and quivers from the fallen archers and began firing at enemy soldiers and coblyns alike.

Hartlans clashed with enemies in the streets of Gaius. But to Ahlund's surprise and relief, the coblyn horde had stopped charging. They were holding their position, apparently waiting for their master's command. Some seemed to be crawling on top of one another, several bodies deep, awaiting the cythraul's command and trampling and crushing many of their fellows beneath their churning, collective mass.

"The plan was to drive them to the sea," Gunnar shouted. He pointed at the coblyns. "We can't drive *that* back!"

Ahlund said nothing. On the inlet, half a dozen Hartlan vessels were now sinking, with coblyns swarming their decks like maggots on carcasses. Drexel's fleet had switched tactics out of necessity. To avoid being overrun, they kept their distance, circling around the enemy ships to fire with arrows, spears, and flaming darts. But that was taking time. They were supposed to have landed by now, to bring reinforcements to the fight on the ground.

But even if they could, Ahlund thought. *What chance do they have against a cythraul? A single daemyn blast could destroy an entire ship.*

The choice was clear. Retreat was the only option.

"Ahlund!" came a voice on the wind.

About a hundred yards away, Zechariah and his platoon had made it to their designated waypoint. Shields, axes, spears, and swords rose and fell all around him, but Ahlund could still see the old man's frantic gestures. He was pointing not ahead, at the coblyn horde, but behind them—back toward the hillside they had charged down just minutes ago.

Ahlund turned. Something was moving in the woods beneath the hill. He saw a tree fall forward. Stepping over it came the massive, black form of a cythraul. It swung a giant axe indiscriminately, felling another tree. Another cythraul stepped up behind it. And behind that one, a third.

"Definitely *not* part of the damn plan!" Gunnar shouted.

As the three cythraul came forward, pushing over trees as if they were fragile reeds, the little hope left in Ahlund evaporated. It felt almost comical now, to think he had ever believed they held the upper hand here.

The cythraul on the beach roared. The coblyn army charged.

Across the sands of Gaius they stampeded: a thousand mindless animals, against a few hundred soldiers. Zechariah and his platoon pushed across the battlefield, reuniting the two prongs of the Hartlan infantry at Ahlund's position. Zechariah's beard, buckler, and robes were painted in bright red splatters. The old man approached Ahlund and Gunnar but didn't say a word. Ahead, the coblyns were closing the distance. Behind, the three cythraul were only about two hundred yards away. One of them clutched a battleaxe with a blade the size of a wagon wheel. Another wielded a rusty scythe, and the third dragged along a sword with a blade longer and thicker than Ahlund's entire body.

Ahlund looked at Zechariah, then at Gunnar.

"If I am to die," Ahlund said, "then I shall die well."

Without waiting to see who, if any, would follow, Ahlund hurdled the stone barricade and ran toward the beach. The stinking, black wall of coblyns rushed at him like high tide.

Ahlund produced a wide arc of sweeping, billowing flames, burning a clutch of coblyns alive and dousing the surrounding horde in a deadly conflagration. He charged headlong into the bulk of them, hacking, stabbing, cutting—trailing whirlwinds of fire in his wake.

CHAPTER 109

Atop the stone ramparts, coblyns were climbing up over the ledge faster than Olorus and Hook could kill them. Detached arms still clung to the stone where they'd been hewn at the shoulders.

One overzealous coblyn suddenly swung over the edge, landed atop Olorus's back, and tore at him with its claws. Hook tossed his knife at it. The attacker slouched and fell from Olorus's back with the blade buried in its skull, but in the same moment, Hook's leg was pulled out from under him. He toppled over the side.

"Hook!" Olorus yelled.

He rushed to the edge. Hook dangled over the side, holding the elbow of a severed arm whose claws, gripping the stone even in death, were all that kept him from plummeting into the churning horde below.

Olorus ignored the claws digging into him from behind—tearing the soft tissues of his legs and back—as he leaned over the edge, grabbed Hook, and pulled him up.

Olorus turned. Roaring with rage, he seized one of the coblyns clawing at him, lifted it bodily, and snapped its spine over his knee. Hook kicked another over the side of the platform.

A dissonant, roaring noise rose up above the mayhem of the war zone, and Olorus looked up in time to see a cythraul's daemyn attack—a comet of black energy—rocketing directly at him.

"A glorious way to die," decided Olorus.

The ball of daemyn hit the structure and exploded. The floor beneath Olorus's feet split and dropped out from beneath him. The tower collapsed in on itself. Coblyns were still attacking Olorus as he fell. He and Hook continued to fight, even as they rode the shattered stone blocks downward, toward the epicenter of the explosion.

CHAPTER 110

Ahlund and Gunnar fought back-to-back while Zechariah, Pool, Borris, and Samuel did their best just to survive. Every coblyn cut down was replaced by two more climbing over it to launch themselves upon sword and shield.

As the coblyn army attacked from the front, the three cythraul launched daemyn attacks from the rear. With every blast, a dozen or more soldiers were eaten alive by darkness. After only a few minutes of assault by the cythraul, less than half of the original five hundred Hartlans remained.

Ahlund was drenched in sweat and blood. The coblyns just kept coming, and his arms were growing weary from the sheer volume of the work—hacking and slashing without end. A blast of daemyn landed so close that he could smell the burned flesh of its victims as they were snuffed from existence. The shock wave knocked him off his feet, and it took great effort to rise again. He summoned his aurym and deliberately set fire to a nearby mound of coblyn corpses, creating a curtain of flames to shroud his position.

Mind, body, and spirit, Ahlund silently chanted.

Claws grabbed at him from every side. He cleaved through one coblyn's chest and issued a blast of flame at a dozen more, but another attached itself to his side with razor-sharp claws. Talons wedged between the plates at his forearm, puncturing the flesh. He felt blood begin to flow. He shook the creature loose and crushed its skull beneath his boot. A Hartlan soldier beside him, a chunk already bitten out of his neck, was pulled to the ground and torn open. The legless torso of a halved coblyn squirmed hungrily toward the frenzy.

A coblyn jumped atop Gunnar's shoulders and groped for his throat. A Hartlan soldier caught it through the midsection with his sword, but saving Gunnar left himself exposed, and he disappeared beneath slashing claws and gnashing teeth.

Claws. Teeth. It was all Ahlund could see. Claws. Teeth. Daemyn. . . . And blood.

With mind, body, and spirit, Ahlund thought as more claws punctured his skin, more blood flowed, and the roar of battle dulled into serene silence, *I commit my soul to the Beyond.*

CHAPTER 111

It was out of pure reflex—stupid, imprudent instinct—that Justin foolishly reached his left arm over to try to shield his right hand from Lisaac's falling blade.

He felt the impact of the blade against his arm. But that was all he felt, just impact. No pain.

Realizing he had shut his eyes against the impending mutilation, Justin opened them. The great cleaver blade of Lisaac's voulge sat suspended against his blackened, stone-hard demon arm. While Lisaac's mouth was still hanging open in surprise, Justin pulled his right arm free, grabbed his sword, and drove it into Lisaac's ankle. The blade bit bone, and the giant stumbled backward, growling angrily.

Despite the pain of his broken ribs, Justin rolled sideways and got to his feet. Lisaac stooped to examine his ankle. Blood dribbled over the grass.

Justin looked at his blackened demon arm. Lisaac's blade had come down with the force of a guillotine. Yet Justin's demon arm was still in one piece. The only sign of damage was a sliver of a nick on the surface of the bony material. It looked like a single, ineffectual hatchet-strike against a great tree trunk.

Justin flexed the fingers at the end of his demon arm and couldn't help but grin. Didn't even hurt.

Lisaac swung the voulge over his head. "*Back!*" he bellowed.

Coblyns skittered back up the sarcophagi-studded structure. Justin hadn't noticed their advance until now. It seemed that while the humans had been fighting, they had been inching closer. They were like dogs; obedient, yes, but patient? No.

At Lisaac's command, the coblyns retreated to a safe distance. They growled and snarled, fangs bared, hopping up and down like apes.

Lisaac attacked again. The injury to his ankle slowed him down, but he was still deadly quick. He swung his voulge in a wide arc—too wide for Justin to evade it. Just as before, the blunt end was aimed to swat him across the courtyard. But this time, Lisaac was angry. Angry enough to do real damage. Maybe even kill him.

Justin did the only thing he could think of. He jumped toward Lisaac, into the attack. The voulge still hit him. That much was unavoidable. But moving inward placed him closer to the fulcrum of the attack, just above Lisaac's wrists, where less force could be put into the swing.

The pole of the voulge slammed across his shoulders like a baseball bat. His teeth rattled with the impact, but he held his ground. Lisaac, agitated at being so closely entangled with Justin, tried to shake the boy, but Justin wrapped one arm around the voulge and held tight.

Justin could smell Lisaac's sweat and his fetid breath. He swung his sword and chopped at the big man's chest. Justin's blade hit true, but it rapped harmlessly against

Lisaac's plate armor. He hacked at the voulge instead, but the pole was as thick as a log. His blade bounced off, gouging only a tiny wedge in the haft.

Justin hardly knew what was happening as he was suddenly lifted from the ground by the pole-end of the voulge and tossed. He lost his sword somewhere in midair and hit the ground knees-first. He extended his hands to try to soften his landing, but the pressure against his crooked fingers made him cry out. Broken ribs jabbed at his insides.

It took multiple attempts to gain his feet. Then he rushed to his sword. He tripped and landed in front of it, gasping for air.

"You do not give up," said Lisaac from behind him. "That can be good. But only if it does not get you killed. It is foolish to fight an opponent you cannot defeat. If you die, it is all for nothing. If you survive, even if you must surrender to your enemy, you can defeat him later. Learn his ways. Bide your time until more favorable conditions. Kill him then."

"Surviving is overrated anyway," said Justin. He picked up his sword and turned to face Lisaac.

"That strong-willed streak is going to get you into trouble," said Lisaac, examining the chunk that Justin had taken out of the haft of his voulge. "We'll see how insolent you are once the cythraul turn you fully, when your will is no longer your own and your friends are at our mercy. Then you will know the meaning of power. You will torture that old man to death just to please Avagad. You'll slice open the belly of that Guardian and present him as a feast to the coblyns. . . ."

But Justin wasn't listening. Something else was going on that demanded his full attention—something inside him.

He should have been angered by Lisaac's words, but, for some reason, all his anger had suddenly disappeared. In its wake was something he had not felt in ages: tranquility. The strangest sense of peace was rising up from within his chest. It washed over him, purging him of anger, fear, and doubt. It was serenity. It was understanding. It was an awareness that bordered on omniscience—as if he were somehow outside himself watching a scene unfold, with comprehension greater than that of its players. It was sudden and certain knowledge beyond doubt.

Knowledge that he could kill Lisaac.

CHAPTER 112

Justin did not understand how he knew this, but it was a truth so indisputable that it somehow required no explanation. In a way, he had never been so sure of anything in his life.

Part of him wished it wasn't true; to comprehend what he himself was capable of was terrible knowledge. But a threshold had been crossed. This truth could not be unlearned or forgotten. The Justin who had lived without the knowledge of his own potential would never exist again.

"... And you will burn those soldiers alive," Lisaac was saying. "And finally, after she has watched it all, that delicate little princess—"

"Let us go," said Justin.

Lisaac's mouth split open in a gap-toothed smile. "What?" he said.

"Leah and I," said Justin. "Let us go."

"You are begging me for mercy so soon?" said Lisaac.

"No," Justin said. "I'm commanding you."

Lisaac's smile only sharpened. His pitted eyes shone with delight. In the constant twilight of the Drekwood, this giant man had seemed like a monster. But now, in the full light of morning, he was even worse. The sun revealed him for what he really was. A thing worse than a monster. A human given in to monstrous deeds.

"You are not a captive anymore, Justin," Lisaac said. "You are my student now. We are allies. And we are both—"

"Let us go," Justin repeated. "I don't want to hurt you."

Lisaac erupted with laughter. Huge guffaws echoed through the necropolis. The coblyns joined in, hooting and chattering as if they understood the joke.

Justin sighed. He did not want to take a life, but there appeared to be little choice. He lowered his sword. He tightened his grip on the hilt, and the a'thri'ik shards forged in the blade lit up bright green.

Lisaac stopped laughing.

Justin let the knowledge flow through him. His blade glowed. The green light became dazzling. It intensified as he absorbed and perpetuated peaceful understanding that was beyond him. He let it course through his body, through his arms, through his hands, and into the sword. The blade became an obelisk of starlight glittering with green sparks.

"Enough!" Lisaac bellowed, shielding his eyes from the sword. His voice was brimming with rage, but there was also a measure of fear—almost panic. "You think you know power? I will show you true power! This ends now!"

Raising the voulge above his head, the giant charged.

Justin's heart was a ball of fire in his chest. His veins seemed to flow with acid. Lisaac barreled toward him with his weapon raised for the kill, and Justin lifted his glowing sword high over his head and said, "I'm sorry."

The sword bloomed green as he swung it downward like a hammer to the anvil. The air split open, and a blast of emerald light exploded from the blade.

A rush of wind tore wildly at Justin's hair. A sound like thunder pulsed against his eardrums.

The emerald blast sizzled outward in a blinding arc. It rent the earth like a spade. Green sparks crackled along the perimeter as it sped toward Lisaac. He had time only to drop his voulge and raise his hands in futile defense before the blinding arc of energy hit him. For a moment, his giant silhouette was visible within the emerald brilliance. The roar of the energy drowned out any last sounds he might have made. Within a zero-gravity supernova, his silhouette floated, stretched, warped, contorted, and then drifted away from itself, dividing into quartered sections. The sections split into thick slabs, which fragmenting into nuggets, then puzzle pieces, then specks, then a fine mist that spread and faded until even the mist was overtaken and disappeared entirely within the light.

A shock wave rippled outward, flattening the grass and sending debris flying. Justin was knocked back a step. But the arc of energy did not stop. It traveled the length of the courtyard and hit the side of the coliseum. The edifice jolted. Stone ramparts at the center disintegrated while those at the periphery turned to flowing, molten rock. Chunks of the structure as large as houses broke from their foundations and rolled, half melted, into the forest. Tombs spewed skulls, ribs, and rubble. Coblyns caught within the blast dissolved into nothing.

Justin raised an arm to shield himself from flying stone and bone. He dove sidelong as the airborne lid of a sarcophagus came cartwheeling across the courtyard. And still, the green energy arc kept going. After cutting through the necropolis walls like an axe through kindling, it traveled into the forest beyond. Fully grown pines were uprooted. Others burst aflame for an instant, then blackened like spent matchsticks.

When the blast finally dissipated, spreading and fading into an aurora borealis above the forest, Justin felt like he was waking from a dream. The a'thri'ik shards forged into his sword faded from brilliant green back to their normal color, until the sword he had found under the mountains was indistinguishable from any ordinary steel.

Like the light of the aurstones, the peace—the serene understanding that had consumed him a few moments ago—also faded. Its luster was paling, and as the dust settled, Justin could not believe what he had done. Nothing in the path of the aurym blast remained. The ground was split open like a tectonic fissure through the earth, and a giant bite had been taken out of the amphitheater, leaving a gaping hole in ruins that had stood strong for hundreds or thousands of years.

Beyond the necropolis, the forest was clear-cut. Not even the topsoil remained. Several smoldering trees in the distance were still in the process of falling. They hit the ground with muted crashes.

A jagged crater marked the spot where Lisaac had been vaporized. Not a crumb of him remained.

Justin looked around for the coblyns. The aurym blast had killed many of them, but the rest they were nowhere to be found.

Then he heard the screams.

CHAPTER 113

Instantly, Ahlund was deaf and blind.

It felt like a lightning bolt had struck the inside of his head, engulfing his vision in white light, filling his ears with a sharp ringing. Death had come to meet him. For so many years, he had chased it, unafraid to face it—welcoming it. Now that it was finally upon him, he realized how unnecessary it had been to so diligently seek a host that welcomes all comers eventually.

At the end of everything, he almost wished he had more time. But time was gone, now. The light would take him, and he would ride at last to commune with his ancestors before judgment, for good or for ill.

Something like rolling thunder was shaking his bones, and he awed at the fact that he still had bones in this realm beyond the world. There was a cleansing fire in his head, and all he could see was light, and the ringing in his ears grew thicker and less distinct until all he could hear was a shattering, humming echo.

But his feet were still touching solid ground. And his hand was still clutching his sword. The light receded. The sound faded. The physical world reappeared around him as if a great fog had been lifted all at once, and Ahlund suddenly realized he was not dead but standing stock-still and defenseless in the middle of a crowded battlefield. Yet he was unharmed. Because his adversaries were *also* all standing still, locked in place by some unseen force.

Like him, the coblyns stood frozen, their heads pointed skyward. Their shining, beady eyes darted back and forth as if looking for something they could not see, and their slitted, lizard-like nostrils expanded and contracted. The Hartlan soldiers, unaffected, were taking the strange opportunity to cut down as many dumbfounded coblyns as they could. Ahlund's ears still did not work; the scene unfolded silently.

Beside Ahlund, Gunnar was on his knees, holding his forehead and blinking his single eye as if fighting a debilitating headache. Zechariah, his robes coated with blood, black and red alike, stood staring into the distance. He looked like he was listening to a song he had not heard in a long time.

"What . . . is happening?" Ahlund said.

Zechariah turned to look at him, and although Ahlund could not hear him through the echo in his ears, he could read the old man's lips as he said, "Justin."

A bellowing, otherworldly roar from the cythraul on the beach brought Ahlund's hearing back. It snapped the coblyns out of their stupor. The Hartlans had slain as many as possible in their immediate vicinity, but more now began to close in.

Ahlund shook his head to clear the remaining fog. He grabbed Gunnar, pulled him to his feet, and shook him roughly, but the admiral's eye rolled dazedly in his head. As the coblyns resumed the fight in earnest, Ahlund practically carried Gunnar behind the cover of a short, stone wall and threw him to safety. Zechariah joined them, shortly followed by Pool, Borris, and Samuel.

"Hold this position!" Ahlund screamed to the soldiers around him. He grabbed Gunnar and shook him again.

"What in the name of bloody—?" said Gunnar. He finally managed to focus on Ahlund. "What happened? It was like sensory overload. I couldn't even—"

"It was Justin calling on his power," Zechariah said. "The boy did it."

"You mean he. . . ?" Gunnar said.

But Gunnar didn't finish his thought. His gaze had gone distant, watching something on the battlefield behind them. Ahlund turned. The three cythraul that had been approaching from behind were turning their backs. They were walking away, leaving the battlefield.

Zechariah frowned deeply, looking sick. "They felt it, too," he said. "They're going after him."

CHAPTER 114

Ahlund heard a noise nearby. He saw a coblyn thrown violently aside by an unseen assailant. Another went spinning to the ground, its neck broken by the swing of a shield. Pushing through the battle, killing with calculated intensity, came Olorus Antony and Hook Bard.

The two men stepped up to join the others. Both bled from many wounds, Olorus in particular. A gash across his temple had painted half his face red like warpaint.

"Was that what I think it was?" said Olorus without introduction. "Aurym?"

"You felt it, too?" Ahlund said.

"I thought I heard something," Olorus said. "A noise like distant thunder. But when the coblyns froze up, we took the opportunity to make our way back here, and—"

"It was Justin," Ahlund said. "It came from somewhere west of here, and I think those three cythraul are on the trail as we speak."

"Then we have to go after them," Olorus said. "With any luck, Leah is with Justin. They won't stand a chance against those things!"

"We can't!" said Gunnar. "If we leave Drexel and the fleet without support now, a lot of good people are going to die."

"Look around you!" Olorus shouted. "There are hardly any good people left to die! Will staying here change that? Call a retreat! Pull our people back to the woods so we can follow after those things!"

Ahlund's mind was racing. The three cythraul were already out of view in the forest. Whatever Justin had done, the ripples of his spent energy had drawn their full attention, and it wouldn't take them long to find him. He turned to face the Gaius harbor.

On the water, Drexel's fleet was still slowly but surely pressing inward, maneuvering around the sinking or flaming bulks of defeated vessels.

The cythraul on the beach roared commands at the coblyns.

"We stay," decided Ahlund. "By drawing those cythraul away, Justin gave us a chance to win this."

"Win?" Olorus said.

"Our people are too overworked for a retreat," said Ahlund. "Even as they ran, they would be pulled down and preyed upon to the last."

"If we are too overworked to retreat," said Olorus, "then surely we are too overworked to kill an army one thousand enemies strong!"

"We don't have to kill a thousand enemies," said Ahlund. "We only need to kill one."

He pointed ahead, toward the mouth of the inlet, at the bone-armored cythraul with the single, pointed horn on its head like a black spire.

"*That* thing?" blurted Gunnar.

"I have only seen coblyns behave as soldiers while under the command of a cythraul," said Ahlund. "Maybe if we kill it, their assault will fail. Against an army, we don't stand a chance—but against a disorganized herd of animals? Maybe."

"Cut off the head, and the body will follow," said Zechariah. "Are you sure about this, Ahlund?"

Ahlund knew what Zechariah was really asking. His question was not whether Ahlund was sure his plan would work; it was a question of whether their efforts should be spent here, instead of assisting Justin.

Maybe I am wrong, thought Ahlund. *Maybe it would be better to split up. Some of us can go after Justin while the others stay here and fight.*

In the middle of his reasoning, a proverb of the Ru'Onorath suddenly entered Ahlund's mind, one he had partially shared with Justin on the road north of Lonn. He looked at the men around him.

"Fear is a wolf," he said, "and the coward and the fool are its prey. . . . But the righteous man is a lion! Wolves cannot harm him! The last time we fought one of these things, it took every one of us to kill it. We can do it again, but I will need all of you. We'll assemble the troops and charge—split the horde in two and hit their general with a full assault."

Ahlund took turns locking eyes with each man.

"If we allow fear to govern our actions today, the enemy wins no matter the outcome," he said. "Be lions! Charge with me!"

Zechariah stroked his blood-streaked beard thoughtfully. "Few can say they have killed a High Demon," he said. "To kill a second . . . will be glorious."

Olorus and Hook exchanged glances, then nodded. "Let us drive this scum into the sea!" said Olorus.

Gunnar turned to Pool, Borris, and Samuel. "What do you say, boys? For Vick?"

"Aye!"

As Gunnar and his bodyguards spread the word among the soldiers, Ahlund looked back toward the forest where the three cythraul had disappeared.

"Hang on, Justin," he said.

CHAPTER 115

Justin had almost reached the doorway when several men ran through, pursued by a group of coblyns. A few bled from scratches and gashes clawed across their backs or stomachs. With Lisaac dead, Justin realized, the coblyns were no longer obedient henchmen. They were ravenous beasts, and friend and foe alike were fair game.

The men fled past Justin, but the coblyns pursuing them suddenly stopped in their tracks. They sniffed at the air and looked at Justin, then bared their fangs, and began to circle him. Beady eyes watched him from snarling, drooling faces. They inched forward cautiously, as if waiting to see what he would do. They understood that he was dangerous. They had fled the coliseum after his display of power, but now, they were testing him.

The deductive reasoning of these creatures, Justin decided, had been vastly underestimated.

A painful scream outside the necropolis made Justin grit his teeth.

Leah's still out there, he thought. He looked at his sword in his hands. *Okay. You did it once. Do it again!*

Justin took a deep breath. He reached out for the energy. He focused on the peace and knowledge, beckoning it to flow through him, through his hands, into his weapon. With a mighty war cry, he raised his sword and swung it at the coblyns.

Nothing happened.

"Crap," said Justin.

The coblyns screeched and attacked.

Justin's first strike was pure instinct. He swung his sword clumsily but managed an effectual strike, lopping off the first coblyn's head. Black blood shot skyward. The next one changed, and he drove his sword into its sternum. Another pounced before he could pull the blade free, and he raised his blackened left arm to defend against it. The coblyn's teeth shattered against the stony chitin of Justin's demon arm. He used the moment to pull his sword free and split the coblyn's skull. He elbowed the next one in the face, and its neck snapped.

Justin sprinted through the necropolis archway toward camp. He nearly collided with a soldier who fell down in front of him, blood spitting from his torn neck. A coblyn pounced and pushed its claws into the man's stomach. Justin quickly killed the coblyn and turned to the man on the ground, intending to help him to his feet, but the man did not move.

All around, the screams of the dying filled the morning air. Swords clashed against claws and teeth. Soldiers slew coblyns by the dozens, but they were outnumbered at least five to one. No matter how many of the beasts fell, it seemed to do nothing to dissuade the rest. The creatures knew no restraint. They attacked not to kill, but to maim and disable so as to feast on living innards for as long as their prey could cling to life. Men went down with grievous wounds. Soldiers trailing viscera tried to crawl away as groping, tearing claws pulled them back. Red and black blood mingled and flowed over the gravesites.

"Leah!" he shouted as he raced through the chaos. "L—!"

A shadow with substance tackled Justin. He hit the ground with the thing on top of him. Claws slashed his bare chest, drawing blood and startling him with flaring pain.

Intestines hung from the coblyn's teeth as its jaws snapped inches from Justin's face. He knocked it back, then drove his sword through its mouth and out the back of its skull. Kicking the creature's corpse away, he rolled to his feet.

"Leah!" he yelled as he ran. Fear of finding her hollowed-out body among the corpses filled him with cold dread.

"Justin!"

Justin sprinted toward the voice. At last, he spotted her standing with her back to a campfire. In one hand, she wielded a short-handled hatchet. In the other, a burning torch. Coblyns circled around her. One lunged at her, and she swung the torch to ward it back. It retreated just in time to be cut down from behind by Justin's blade.

Justin felt a searing pain in his side and turned to find a coblyn clinging to him, its claws hooked in his skin.

So fast!

He tried to throw the creature off of him, but it tightened its grip, puncturing even deeper into his flesh and making him cry out in pain.

Leah raised her hatchet and bashed the coblyn's skull in. The thing went limp and fell from Justin's side.

Justin and Leah took up positions in front of the campfire, standing back-to-back, warding off the circling predators.

"Thanks," Justin said. "You all right?"

"Am I all right?" said Leah. "Look at yourself."

Justin was trying not to.

"Lisaac's dead," he said. "Long story. The short version is that the coblyns obeyed him, and now that he's dead, they're going crazy. We should get out of here."

Leah nodded, then tossed her torch over the coblyns' heads. The creatures watched its course, and Leah turned and jumped over the campfire, running the opposite direction. Justin followed. A few coblyns chased after them. Justin cut one down, and the others soon abandoned the chase in favor of easier game.

As the two of them raced into the woods, Justin hazarded a fleeting glance at the carnage. Men being pulled down and ripped open, eaten alive. He recalled his wish, just days before, that these men would die, and it made him sick. Now, he wished he could save them. Or at least, as Ahlund had once done for a badly injured boy on the Gravelands, put them out of their misery. Instead, all he could do was run and pray for their sake that it would all be over soon.

A bone-chilling boom rose up over the trees. It was a noise Justin had heard enough times by now to recognize as the roar of a cythraul. Leah kept moving, and so did he.

When a second roar came floating over the treetops, Justin felt something he had not felt in days. Pain in his left arm. His demon arm burned, seemingly from the inside out. He gritted his teeth, trying to ignore the pain.

They reached a stream and began wading across. He was knee-deep in the water when another cythraul roar shook him. Suddenly, the pain in his arm was beyond control. His vision blurred. Thick, black spots like drops of ink on a page appeared before his eyes and seeped across his vision. He tried to keep moving, but his legs were numb. He tumbled forward.

"Leah!" he yelled with the last of his strength.

His knees hit the stony riverbed. His sight telescoped to blackness as his head went under the water. There was fire in his arm, but the last thing he felt was water in his throat.

CHAPTER 116

"You again," said Justin.

Avagad smiled. "You didn't think I would just forget about you."

The tower room was exactly as Justin remembered it. Avagad stood before him, tall and straight-backed in his ceremonial armor of white, crimson, and silver. The diamonds on his crown shimmered.

By now, Justin understood that only his mind, not his body, was in this place—wherever or whatever this place was. As such, it did not surprise him to see that his left arm was fully human again, with flesh and muscles. Nor did it surprise him that he was wearing comfortable clothing rather than the rags of a prisoner.

"My arm," said Justin. "You had it changed so you could establish a connection with me more easily."

"That's part of it," said Avagad, "but it is also a sample of things to come. You will be turned fully, but there is still more I require of you—things that can only be accomplished while you are still in your human form—before you become a cythwraith."

"Cyth-wraith?" said Justin.

"You have much to learn, my boy," said Avagad. "I *had* a tutor arranged to teach you the basics."

"Sorry about that," said Justin.

Avagad shrugged. "The world is an emptier place for Lisaac's loss, quite literally, but it's no matter. I found his intellect to be fairly adequate, but he clearly had a critical lapse of judgment when he underestimated you. I admit, I also underestimated you, Justin. Rest assured, I will not do it again. But I digress.

"Using your aurym power against Lisaac was . . . unwise. I am not the only one searching for you, Justin. There are others. Some with far less savory intentions than my own. Most simply intend to enslave you. Others want to test their abilities against a fallen angel. At least one wants to cut you open for study. And another, I have learned, wishes to devour your soul like a coblyn to gain your power. Completely illogical. Putting aside their various intentions, they share something in common. All are converging on you as I speak. When you used your power, you alerted them to your precise location."

"Then I'll have to deal with them," said Justin.

"The same way you dealt with Lisaac?" Avagad said. "My, my. You drown a rat, and suddenly you do not fear wolves."

Justin hesitated. "What do you mean?"

Avagad stroked his chin and sighed heavily through his nostrils, as if something weighed heavily on his conscience. "Your future is painted in blood, Justin," he said. "Nothing can change that, now that you have ascended. Powerful enemies are coming your way. But you need not face them alone. That is why I have contacted you again. To propose an agreement."

"I won't make any agreement with you," said Justin. "I've seen what you're doing out there. Enslaving. Torturing. Making deals with demons."

Avagad titled his head. "It seems Lisaac shared more information with you than I would have preferred. His intellect may not have been as adequate than I thought. Maybe I should commend you for eliminating him."

Avagad paused, but this time, Justin said nothing. Everything the man said seemed to be aimed at evoking a response. Maybe it was better not to answer.

"You should never turn down an agreement before you've heard the offer," said Avagad. "In this case, I can offer you something no one else has. The truth."

He turned his back to Justin and strode across the room toward the globe—the one that had ripped apart the last time Justin had been here. Beside it was a small table, and on the table sat a book. Avagad stopped in front of the table and placed his hand on the book.

"Deceit can be a powerful weapon," Avagad said. "There is only one thing I have found to be more effective." He patted the book with his fingers almost lovingly, then walked across the room, putting distance between himself and the table. "See for yourself."

Justin stayed where he was. He didn't know the rules of this place. What if the book was endowed with some sort of power?

"No tricks," said Avagad as if reading his mind. "Just an ordinary book. The only way it can harm you is with the knowledge it contains."

Justin approached the table, watching Avagad closely. He picked up the book. It was old and worn, bound in ancient, unmarked leather. Some of the stiff parchment pages hung out, barely clinging to the binding. The first few pages were blank, and they creaked as he flipped through them. A few pages in, Justin's eyes went wide. The book contained lines upon lines of handwriting. English handwriting. It was the first time since arriving in the Oikoumene that he had seen recognizable letters.

> *As I begin this volume, I can't help but think back to my earlier writings, when I was still convinced this was all a nightmare or a fantasy. For a while, I thought it was purgatory, and at times, it has come close to a kind of hell. Back then, all I wanted was to return to Earth. I spent a long time thinking it was all a dream, praying I would wake up. I wondered if I had gone insane and was trapped in my imagination. Eventually, I realized that this place was real. As real as Earth itself. If I hadn't come to that realization, I surely never would have discovered that there is a way home.*

CHAPTER 117

Justin's hands were shaking as he turned the page. His eyes raced over the sentences.

> *Why do I write this? I think it is to help maintain my sanity, because even after I accepted my reality, my fate was not so easy to reconcile. Often, I wondered if I would ever see my family again. Was I destined to die here, in this alternate world so far from my home that the distance could not be measured in miles?*
>
> *I don't know how I got here, and I certainly never expected to become the man I am today. I never would have thought, in my lifetime, that I would need to raise a weapon to defend myself . . . let alone to take so many lives.*
>
> *I may have discovered the way home, but leaving is no easy matter. Every day, I wake up and wonder, is my time in this world of swords, shields, magic, and monsters finally nearing its end?*
>
> *Will I ever see my family again? Or will I die here, farther from home than any map can measure?*
>
> *Over time, I have begun unconsciously referring to this world as "Antichthon." It is based on an ancient Greek theory I remember from school. The great thinkers of that time believed that Earth orbited a "central fire" in the middle of the universe, but they reasoned that this cosmic mechanism would be off-kilter unless it had some other object to balance the scale: a counterbalance, with a mass equal to that of Earth,*

orbiting the central fire at the same rate of speed and along the same orbital path. An object that would never be visible from Earth because it was always on the opposite side of the sun, at the extreme opposite end of the orbital pattern. This hypothetical planetary body was referred to as the Counter-Earth. Antichthon.

(Note: The theory holds no water, of course, but "Antichthon" seemed an appropriate nickname for this world.)

Initially, I thought Antichthon might be Earth. The lack of modern technology led me to believe I was in the distant past, yet nothing I encountered seemed to match up with human history as I knew it. Perhaps Antichthon was Earth in the distant future, after civilization's fall. But the world's geography was so vastly alien that I had to concede that this wasn't possible, either. A day is not quite a day, and a year is not quite a year, implying geophysical processes different than Earth. But worst of all were the double moons. Oh, how many nights I lay awake and cursed those moons amid the alien constellations!

Antichthon and Earth are different planets, but based on recent developments, I believe the two worlds exist not across vast distances, but rather, ALONGSIDE each other. The way one paper map might lie on top of another, unconnected, despite their closeness of proximity. The Keys of the Ancients seem to allow certain people to move between the maps, momentarily bridging the gap between worlds. And only the bizarre and unique aurym capabilities of an ethoul, or "Fallen Angel," can power the Keys to open the door. I, for one, never meant to take the path less traveled by. Yet it seems only I can take it.

The people's legends speak of others like me from long ago, and the similarities between these worlds seem evidence enough that humans from Earth have influenced this place. For instance, one of the languages they speak in the western Oikoumene is nearly identical to English. I remember reading a study in linguistics indicating that when two populations who speak the same language become isolated from one another, it takes very little time for changes in vocabulary and speech patterns to arise. New words are adopted and old ones abandoned, even in a consistent environment, at a rapid pace. If a community becomes truly isolated, speech patterns can change so quickly that in as little as 100 years, a member of the isolated community would be nearly unintelligible to someone from the original population. How could it be, then, that I am able to communicate with people who appear to have developed separately from Earth?

Consider the reckoning of a mile—a measurement used both on Earth and on Antichthon. On Earth, "mile" comes from an ancient Roman unit of distance measuring an estimated 1,000 steps (derived from the Latin, "mille," meaning "thousand"). So why, in a world where there was no Latin, and certainly no Roman Empire, would a "mile" be used to measure distance?

Such extrapolations can be done with nearly every word in the English language. The development of any language is dependent on the cultural and historical influences of its geographical place of origin. There is no explanation for why any form of English would be spoken here unless someone brought it with them from Earth.

My arrival in this place was certainly none of my own doing. But I am grateful that I was able to decipher the mystery of the Keys of the Ancients. Without the Keys, I never would have been able to return home. Nor would I have been able to come back to Antichthon again. But, of course, by now, I have come to understand that traveling between the worlds comes at a terrible price—

Without warning, the book was wrenched from Justin's grasp. Justin jumped back in surprise. Avagad stood less than a foot away from him, though Justin had neither seen nor heard his approach.

There was a malicious sort of boredom in Avagad's eyes as he turned and walked away with the book.

"Where did that thing come from?" Justin asked.

Avagad crossed the tower floor. He stopped before one of the large windows and stood gazing out into the sky with the book in his hands.

"A sect of monks once claimed this book was sacred," said Avagad. "They called it the Book of Unfinished Dreams."

"Who wrote it?" asked Justin. "Why do you have it?"

"One question at a time, please," said Avagad. "The monks claimed that this book was written by the hand of a deity. The words of a fallen angel. To answer your second question, I have it because I wanted it."

"That part about Keys opening doorways," said Justin. "Is it true?"

Avagad turned to face Justin. He said nothing.

"Answer me," Justin said.

"I wouldn't know what you are talking about, Justin," said Avagad, "because in five thousand years, no one has been able to translate the language written in this book."

Justin bit his tongue.

"Yet you can, I see," said Avagad. He raised an eyebrow. "Keys and doorways? Interesting. I wonder what else you might learn from this book if you had the time to read it from cover to cover."

Justin swallowed hard.

"The monks from whom I relieved this book considered it to be quite holy," said Avagad. "But to the rest of the world, it is only a tattered, dusty old tome containing an indecipherable dead language—scribbles, for all anyone knows. It is essentially worthless."

Avagad held the book up in one hand. With his other hand, he flexed his fingers, and a ball of swirling, purple fire appeared in his palm. He held the book over the fire, so close that smoke immediately curled from the edges of the loose pages.

Justin stepped forward, reaching for the book. In response, the violet flames grew higher, licking the binding. Justin quickly stepped back, and the fire likewise retreated.

"As I said, Justin," said Avagad. "There is only one weapon more effective than a lie. A well-aimed truth." He raised his eyebrows. "Admittedly, it was a bit of a gamble. I wasn't even certain you would be able to read this book. I am delighted to see that you can. And equally delighted that you learned so much from it so quickly." The fire in Avagad's palm climbed upward. "What irreplaceable knowledge must lie within these pages."

"Don't. . . ." said Justin. He tried not to let it sound like a plea.

It was in my hands, he thought, watching the book's corners blacken in the flames. *Keys of the Ancients. Devices that can bridge the gap between worlds but at a terrible price. But how, and at what price—why didn't I turn to the last page?*

"And so, we return to my proposed agreement," said Avagad. He seemed unconcerned that the book was succumbing to the purple flames in his hand. "Now that you know what I've brought to the table, perhaps you would like to reconsider. It occurs to me that any answers you might gain from this book will disappear if it is destroyed. And clearly, I have not manipulated the contents in any way, because I cannot read the words. And, come to think of it. . . . Oh, dear. It's getting quite warm."

"Get on with it," Justin said. "Get to the point!"

Avagad's brow sharpened into a scowl. "You don't seem to realize who you're dealing with, Justin. If you were anyone else, you would be de-fleshed and quartered for that sort of disrespect."

Justin said nothing.

"We both have achievable desires," said Avagad. "It is only logical that we help one another. Even as I speak, your friends are losing a battle against my forces in Athacea. And that's only a small fraction of my war machine. As for you, your evasion of Lisaac's forces will give you only a momentary respite. My cythraul and their coblyn armies will find you. No matter where you go, they will follow. The way I see it, you have two choices. You can condemn yourself, and your friends, to a lifetime of pain, suffering, and anguish." Avagad let the fire go out and presented the charred book enticingly. "Or we can work together. I'll call off my attack this very second. Perhaps your friends are still alive and will be allowed to go free. In addition, this book will be yours, along with a legion of librarians and scholars to help you unravel its mysteries. All this, I will give to you. In return, I ask for only one thing."

Justin was afraid to ask but said, "What?"

"One year."

"Huh?" said Justin.

"One year as a commander in my army."

"I'm not a soldier," said Justin.

"Of course you aren't," Avagad said. "And I would never ask you to be. Your friends are the ones who want war. All I want is peace. The people of the Oikoumene should be united, not torn apart. Together, we can achieve this. I don't expect you to devote your life to my cause. Just a single year. Your role will only be symbolic, and after that, you will be free to leave and do as you see fit—I give you my word. Why, with the secrets of this book, you might even find a way home."

As Avagad spoke, Justin realized the tower had begun to melt around him. The colors ran together like sidewalk chalk in the rain. The connection was being broken again.

"I take your silence to mean you need time," said Avagad. "Very well. Autumn is almost upon us. I'll give you until the break of winter. One season for you to make your decision. In the meantime, my forces will continue to hunt you. If they capture you and deliver you to me, the deal is off and your servitude will be unconditional. And if you refuse my offer, it will not be my forces coming after you. I will do it personally."

Avagad paused and sighed.

"I would prefer the deal, if I'm being honest," Avagad said, "but the choice is yours. A good king uses diplomacy when he can but never hesitates to resort to force when he must. So, I'll warn you now: If you shun my peace offering, I cannot be held responsible for what happens to you or your friends. I am skilled at diplomacy. But I am lord and master of war."

Justin started to step forward and say something but found he was moving in slow motion, as if the air had turned to mud. The words died in his throat.

"Make your choice," said Avagad, his voice stretching out to long, deep tones. "But remember. I hardly expect you to fight a war. Your friends, however. That is exactly . . . what *they* will . . . expect . . . from . . . you."

CHAPTER 118

A heavy line of Hartlan defenders did their best to keep the coblyns back as Ahlund and Gunnar assembled the rest of the soldiers into an attack pattern. Olorus and Hook took point in a wedge-shaped formation with Ahlund, Gunnar, Zechariah, Pool, Borris, and Samuel at the center.

An arrow suddenly struck the face of a Hartlan soldier—a young woman—positioned beside Ahlund. It tore the skin from her cheek, deflecting off bone. She recoiled, blood flowing down her face, then straightened up and retook her position, ignoring it. Looking in the direction of the shot, Ahlund realized that across the battlefield, the human element of the enemy, who had withdrawn upon the coblyns' arrival, had now gathered on the hillside ruins with bows and were raining arrows down on the Hartlans.

Ahlund sneered. *Cowards*, he thought. *What sort of human joins forces with demons?*

No matter how valiantly the Hartlans fought, staying here would mean a gradual defeat as their numbers were chipped away. Their only hope was to attack the cythraul head-on.

The great creature paced back and forth along the beach, bellowing demonic roars. The mossy tangles of a black beard hung from its face. It consistently divided its attention between roaring orders at the coblyn horde onshore and launching daemyn attacks at the approaching Hartlan fleet. The long, pike-like horn atop its skinless skull made it easy, even from a distance, to tell which direction the creature was facing.

Ahlund saw the horn turn seaward, its attention momentarily diverted toward the fleet. Now was their chance.

"Charge!" Ahlund screamed.

The Hartlan defenders parted. Olorus and Hook raised their shields and charged up the middle, into the coblyns. The rest of the soldiers sprinted behind, keeping a tight, rigid, wedge-shaped formation. Anyone with a shield kept it raised as they ran. Like a human battering ram, the Hartlans plowed through the coblyn horde, into the black heart of the fray.

Swiping, slashing claws were everywhere. Enemies bounced off shields or were knocked down and trampled. A few Hartlans on the perimeter were caught by grasping hands and disappeared into the murderous, hungry blackness. But finally, Olorus and Hook burst free of the coblyns' rear lines. The Hartlan infantry followed their charge, emerging on the beach.

Immediately, the Hartlans scattered, shifting from a tight cluster to a wide dispersal to limit their susceptibility to the cythraul's daemyn blasts. The Nolians rolled to either side. Ahlund dove and came up running. Zechariah raced along a tangent while Gunnar followed. Some Hartlans sprinted forward over the sands, and others turned to defend against the coblyn ranks.

The cythraul's first daemyn blast carried away five Hartlan soldiers and at least thirty coblyns. The explosion at the center of the impact zone blew a crater in the earth, and veins of indigo electricity danced across the ground, turning sand to glass and flesh to ash.

Ahlund sprinted at the cythraul. He could see its glowing, empty eye sockets, its dagger-like teeth, the rusted notches in its scimitar. And as Zechariah, Gunnar, Olorus, Hook, and a strike force of two dozen Hartlans formed a wide semicircle to swoop in on the monster from all sides, the cythraul turned its gaze directly on Ahlund. It raised its hand, creating a singularity of darkness within its palm.

"Fire!" Ahlund yelled.

Olorus and Hook raised their bows and loosed an arrow apiece, hitting the cythraul's legs. With a flourish, Gunnar raised his hands, and the leafy growths clinging to the arrows' shafts burst to life.

Vines grew rapidly, wrapping around the monster's legs. Roots burrowed into the sand. Zechariah circled wide, approaching from the rear as Ahlund called on aurym and stabbed at the air. A billowing cloud of white-hot fire shot from Ahlund's sword and hit the shrubbery growing at the monster's feet, setting it ablaze. Samuel, Pool, and Borris tossed pouches of seeds into the flames, and as each hit true, Gunnar channeled his power into them, growing them from seedlings to full size in seconds, and increasing the thickness and the strength of the aurym-fueled foliage steadily encasing the monster's lower half.

As Gunnar's plants grew, Ahlund's inferno spread. All the while, every Hartlan with a bow fired arrows at the monsters. Others threw spears, knives, or whatever was handy. The cythraul's body became a pincushion of projectiles. Its legs were rooted into the ground by Gunnar's vines. Fire danced across its bone-armored exoskeleton.

The cythraul roared in surprise and anger. Ahlund could not be sure how much true damage they were inflicting, but the cythraul was surprised enough by the coordination of the attack, at least, that it still had not unleashed the daemyn singularity in its palm.

Finally, Zechariah reached his mark. Having circled around behind as the rest attacked, he now jumped. His aurym-fueled agility carried him through the air. He landed blade-first, driving his sword into the exposed back of the monster's neck.

The cythraul visibly buckled under Zechariah's blade, its roar stifled in shock.

Crouched atop the cythraul's shoulders with one arm wrapped tightly around its pointed horn, Zechariah yanked on his sword to pull it the rest of the way through the cythraul's neck—as he had done to behead the cythraul in the Drekwood.

The cythraul threw one arm back with a roar of renewed rage. An elbow wider than Zechariah's head struck the old man squarely in the face. Zechariah fell like a rag doll.

"*No!*" Ahlund shouted.

Zechariah flopped limply to the ground. The cythraul—with Zechariah's blade still stuck halfway through its neck and black ichor pouring from the wound like a waterfall—turned and pointed its hand at Zechariah. The daemyn swirled and crackled with purple lightning in the monster's palm as it grew to a deadly zenith. Zechariah stirred. He looked up, set his jaw, and faced it.

Ahlund stoked his sword with more aurym power than he had ever attempted before. The heat from his own weapon hurt his face and his hands as he sprinted forward, the blinding white blade trailing blue spectral trails. With a savage war cry, Ahlund leaped forward and swung his sword downward at the cythraul's wrist.

The point of impact exploded in a combination of energies.

CHAPTER 119

A blast of fire-wreathed daemyn hit Ahlund like a mallet, lifting him off his feet. His body tumbled through the air. The ground switched places with the horizon several times before he crashed down in the sand with his neck bent awkwardly under the full weight of his body, causing a bolt of pain to shoot down his spine.

Though his ears were ringing and something within him was certainly broken, Ahlund managed to get to his feet. Zechariah was still alive, limping up the beach. The cythraul had dropped its scimitar and was clutching the stump where its other hand had been a moment before. Black blood shot from its wrist in streams and splashed across the sand.

Ahlund tried to light his sword to hit the cythraul with another attack while it was stunned, but for the first time in his life, his power failed him. All he could produce was a feeble wreath of smoke from the blade. The effort alone made his head swim, and he fell to one knee. The energy he had expended in his last attack had been too much.

He looked around. The Hartlans couldn't hold the coblyns back much longer. Olorus and Hook had been forced to stop firing at the cythraul and take up their shields, falling back to help reinforce a weak point in the Hartlan defenses. The Hartlan strike force that had charged with them on the beach still fired arrows and threw projectiles, but many were out of ammunition.

The cythraul let go of its bleeding wrist, roared in anger, and used its good hand to rip and tear at the burning vines holding it in place. Its beard was a mass of flames, but it seemed not to notice. With a quick jerk, it pulled one foot out of the sand, lifting a chunk of the ground up with it.

"Ahlund!" Gunnar shouted.

Sweat trickled down Gunnar's face. The veins in his forearms bulged with the continued effort of calling on his power.

"I can't . . . hold it!" he yelled.

The cythraul ripped its other foot free and stepped forward. Ahlund tried to stand, but his sword was too heavy. Olorus and Hook, stuck holding back the coblyns, could only watch the cythraul pull free of its lashings and advance.

Suddenly, a Hartlan soldier threw his bow to the sand. Drawing his sword and raising it high, he screamed, "For Hartla!" And he charged.

"Wait—don't!" Gunnar called.

But it was no use. The man was running at the cythraul.

The rest of the Hartlan strike force followed his example and charged at the cythraul to engage the beast in close quarters. Several were carried off at once by a single swing of the monster's massive fist. The others swarmed and drove sharpened steel into the monster's stomach, legs, chest, and lower back—any weak spot they could find.

The cythraul roared in frustration. It swung its good arm at the attackers, but those who were batted down only stood back up to attack again if they could. Some were burned by Ahlund's fire. One man was crushed beneath a stomp of the cythraul's giant foot. But the rest fought on.

Black blood soon flowed from wounds uncountable. Hartlan soldiers climbed up the monster's back to attack its shoulders and neck. Zechariah's sword was still stuck there, and one man reached it, stood on the creature's shoulders, and stomped on the hilt, driving it deeper. The cythraul summoned its daemyn power but flailed awkwardly as it attempted to unleash the attack. The blast sailed wide and hit nothing but nearby ruins.

Ahlund blinked. To his astonishment, the cythraul was slowing.

Its roar sounded halfhearted. The glow of its eyes was growing dim. It wavered on its feet, then dropped to one knee.

The Hartlans saw their chance and took it. With the cythraul on one knee, they pounced and began hacking at the exposed neck. Their swords rose and fell repeatedly, chopping at the neck like hatchets. Every soldier was coated in black blood by the time they struck spinal cord. And then, with a snap-*crack*, the neck gave way.

The head flopped unnaturally to one side. The weight of the skull tore the rest of the soft tissues loose. The cythraul's last roar was a choked gargle as the head dropped from the shoulders and rolled across the sand.

"Hartla!" the soldiers screamed, thrusting their dripping blades skyward.

Zechariah, bloody and bedraggled, managed to raise his good hand in victory along with the rest. Gunnar fell to his knees, spent. Ahlund, still on one knee, thought back to his conversation with Justin: *Bright light casts deep shadows*, rang the Ru'Onorath proverb in his head. He had recited it to Justin, but he had not really believed it at the time. Nor had he shared the second half of the proverb: *Yet in full view, its glory is brighter than the sun.*

The Hartlans drew back as the bone-armored body fell, twisting unnaturally. Defying gravity, the body began collapsing inward. Soft matter ripped from exoskeletal plates like tender meat off the bone. With crunching, shattering force, the skeleton folded in on itself and exploded. A few soldiers too close to the blast zone were knocked to the ground by the shock wave. Then the remnants of the body disintegrated to dust and drifted away on the wind.

In an instant, the coblyns broke ranks, and Ahlund realized he had been right. With the cythraul gone, the coblyns were animals again. They continued to attack the humans, but now they also turned on each other. They climbed the ruins, and humans who had been the demons' allies moments before were pulled down and torn to pieces.

The Hartlan lines strengthened. The coblyns' lack of focus made them easier to overpower, but their numbers were still too many. Of the original five hundred Hartlans, Ahlund estimated only one hundred remained, and they were weary and wounded and trapped between the sea and a herd of carnivores.

"Retreat!" Ahlund heard Gunnar shouting. "To the ship! Go, go, *go*!"

Ahlund turned to see Gunnar pointing at a beached enemy ship. The cargo hold many coblyns had earlier emerged from still hung open.

Pool, Borris, and Samuel led the way. Olorus and Hook grabbed Zechariah's wounded body from the sand and half-led, half-carried him to the ship. The Hartlan lines fell back in a full retreat.

Ahlund tried to run, but he couldn't feel his body. Soldiers sprinted past him. The horde would be close behind, but he was on the brink of unconsciousness. He managed to get one leg up but couldn't support his weight. He fell face-first into the sand. Ahead, he saw Olorus and Hook had helped Zechariah into the ship and were now firing arrows at the pursuing coblyns as soldiers prepped the ship. They didn't see him.

Ahlund heard the snarling, roaring multitude behind him. In spite of everything, he held tightly to the hilt of his sword. His blade, ever his ally in life, would be his comrade in death. Hands grabbed him. But instead of being torn limb from limb, Ahlund was hauled to his feet.

Gunnar lifted Ahlund up, supported him by the underarms, and dragged him down the beach. But the cargo hold was too far away. Ahlund's weary mind flashed back to the Gravelands, to the sight of the open gate, the cythraul pursuing him from behind, and the knowledge that he would not make it there in time. Only by sacrificing himself could the rest be saved.

Gunnar tripped, and they both hit the ground. Gunnar scrambled to his feet, but Ahlund could only lie there.

"Leave me," Ahlund said.

Gunnar's arms slipped beneath him. "Like . . . *hell*!" Gunnar groaned.

Ahlund felt himself being lifted from the ground. His body was thrown over Gunnar's shoulders. Everything was moving—he was being carried. The world went dark. It was all over.

But, no. It was not the black veil of death devouring his mortal sight. It was the shadow of a roof over his head. He was inside the ship's cargo hold.

Ahlund fell roughly to the floorboards. He heard shouting and a great thud as the cargo hold door slammed shut, followed by the scratching and pounding of coblyns hurling their bodies against it.

"All's aboard!" Borris shouted up the hatch.

"We're off!" someone replied.

Somewhere above, sails were unfurled. Ahlund felt the ship moving. He heard Olorus shouting in triumph on the deck above. The pounding of the coblyns against the door faded, turned to faint splashing, and then disappeared altogether.

Ahlund lay there, hardly moving, hardly breathing, his mind, body, and spirit so weak that he felt like an empty husk of himself. He turned to one side and saw Zechariah also lying on the ground. The old man was panting heavily. Dried blood covered his face, beard, and robes.

To Ahlund's other side sat Gunnar. The man was significantly smaller than Ahlund, yet he had thrown him over his shoulders and carried him aboard the ship like a lamb. The three men silently acknowledged one another.

A bloodied Hartlan soldier stepped forward and placed a hand on Gunnar's shoulder.

"Brother," the soldier said.

Gunnar looked at him, confused.

"Brother," said someone else from the other side of the hold.

"Brother!" Borris cried.

"Brother! Brother!" several soldiers shouted.

Dozens more joined in the chant. It grew in volume and fervor. Soon, it migrated from the cargo hold to the deck above, until the whole Hartlan infantry had taken up the cry. The entire ship reverberated with the chant.

Gunnar's mustache lifted in a smirk.

CHAPTER 120

"What they will. . . ."

"Justin."

"Expect. . . ."

"Justin!"

"From—"

A hand slapped Justin across the face. He looked up to see the frantic, dirt-smeared face of Leah Anavion leaning over him as he lay on the ground.

"How long was I—?" Justin mumbled.

"A couple of minutes," Leah said. "We have to move!"

Justin looked around. He was on the rocky bank of the small creek where he'd fallen. His boots were still underwater, but Leah had dragged him the rest of the way out. His sword lay on the rocks beside him. The burning sensation in his arm was gone, but within his heart and mind was a crushing, shadowy miasma. He knew by now what that meant.

"A cythraul is close," said Justin. "Follow me."

Pushing himself to his feet, Justin groaned from pain all over his body. Swollen, backward fingers throbbed with every heartbeat. Dried blood clung to his bare chest where the four-fingered hand of a coblyn had left its mark.

The deafening roar of a cythraul erupted from somewhere upstream. Justin picked up his sword, and they hurried along the bank, downstream.

The trees grew denser, shadowing the forest and turning the world into a gray-on-gray palette. Justin did not have the strength to run, but he tried his best to hurry, clutching his side and moving in a sort of hobbled jog. All the while, he thought about the tower, the man with the crown . . . and the book.

Unlike his previous encounters with Avagad, this recent visit was quite vivid in his memory. He remembered the words in the book. Keys that unlocked a doorway home. And he remembered the proposal. The book—and his friends' safety—in exchange for one year of service in Avagad's army.

Just one year, Justin thought.

There could be answers in that book. Answers that could lead him home. Maybe if he read more of the book, he could return home before the year was even up. Maybe he could take the agreement as a bluff and make it home before Avagad was any the wiser.

Another cythraul roar blasted across the sky, this time much closer.

Justin tripped over a rock and fell to his knees. Leah turned back and helped him up. Just standing caused him to cry out involuntarily in pain as his broken ribs stabbed at his side.

"Let me heal you," said Leah.

"Leah," he said through gritted teeth. "You're a ruler. Isn't it true that sometimes you have to make hard decisions?"

"Of course," she said, only half listening. "Do you want me to heal—?"

"And sometimes," Justin continued, looking at the ground, "you have to make sacrifices for the good of everyone else, right? Even if that sacrifice is yourself?"

Leah grabbed Justin roughly by the wrist, and he looked at her in shock. There was a severe, almost disgusted look on her face.

"Stop it, Justin," she said. "Don't even say you're thinking of giving up."

"If it will give you the chance to escape—" Justin said, but he was cut off.

"That has got to be the most selfish thing I've ever heard," said Leah.

"*Selfish*?" Justin said.

"You wouldn't be doing me or anyone else any favors by giving in to these monsters," Leah snapped. "Are you that frightened? You would rather give up than fight? Don't call that a sacrifice. You ought to be ashamed."

In spite of Leah's biting rebuke, Justin actually found himself grinning. "Very tactful, princess."

"Well, it's true," she said.

Justin sighed. Back at the cemetery, he had almost made a huge mistake. Nobody had told him how tricky this enemy could be.

"Daemyn is all around me," said Justin. "It's fogging my mind, trying to make me slip up. The worst part is, it doesn't even try to defeat you; it just sneaks in and makes you think you've already lost."

"We have not lost," Leah said. "You can't give in. We need you. . . . I need you. I know you didn't choose all this, but, well, neither did I."

Justin, still kneeling on the muddy bank, looked at Leah and realized she was right. Giving in, even if it did save her, would be a betrayal, because. . . .

Because she believes in me.

“Enough talking,” said Leah. “Let’s move.”

Justin stared down at the clear, running water in the creek. Then he closed his eyes, realizing what he had to do.

“Do you need help?” Leah asked.

Justin stood and hefted his heavy sword up to rest it on his shoulder. He found a nice log lying on the creek’s bank, walked over to it, and sat down.

Leah’s eyes went wide. “What are you doing?”

“Waiting,” Justin said.

“No, you are not,” she said. “Get up. It could get here any minute.”

“I’m not running anymore, Leah,” Justin said.

“We just talked about this! What good is it if you give up?”

“I’m not giving up,” said Justin. “There’s a time to run, and there’s a time to fight. And I’m sick of running.”

“But it’s a cythraul! How can you fight one of those things?”

Justin squeezed the grip of his sword. “The same way I fought Lisaac.”

Leah didn’t say anything. It was difficult to read her face. She was frustrated, but there was something else there, too. Maybe a little pride. Maybe she was so baffled by his actions that she could find no words. Or maybe she thought he was such a fool that it was pointless to argue. Whatever her thoughts were, she left them unspoken. She simply approached Justin and took him by the hand. Justin looked at her.

“This is going to hurt,” she said.

Before Justin could reply, Leah’s aurym flowed strongly into his hand, and his finger bones shifted back into position. He gritted his teeth and shut his eyes, flinching in pain and surprise when his backward ring finger popped into place.

When it was finished, he flexed his fingers and let out a breath. “Man, that sucks,” he said.

“Your ribs?” she said.

He hesitated, then nodded. She held a hand over his stomach and slid his broken ribs back into place. This was even worse, and the pain made him gasp a few times despite his resolve. There was a warming sensation as she knitted the bones together, securing the breaks. Then she closed a few of the cuts on his chest.

She paused, looking at his blackened demon arm. “I wish I could fix that,” she said.

“If there’s a way, I bet you’ll figure it out,” said Justin. “You’d better go. Find somewhere to hide, and please stay there. Don’t come out until it’s over, no matter what happens.”

“We could still make it,” she said, gripping his good arm. “You don’t have to do this.”

“I think I do,” he said. “Go, Leah.”

She squeezed his arm, then turned and jogged across the shallow creek. Justin watched her slip into a narrow crevice between a large rock and a tree trunk and duck out of sight.

Justin closed his eyes. Several minutes went by. He waited, listening to the creek.

The cythraul he had sensed roared. It sounded close. Then a second one, even closer, answered the call. So. There were two of them. That . . . complicated things.

Justin heard the stomping of giant feet and the crashing and snapping of trees being pushed over.

Mind, body, spirit, he thought, clutching the sword in both hands as he waited. His eyes were closed, but he could feel the green glow of his sword's blade as his aurym flowed through it.

PART X

FALLEN ANGEL

CHAPTER 121

A tree fell. Giant footsteps shook the ground.

The footsteps approached Justin. Then they stopped.

With his eyes still closed, Justin could feel the cythraul standing over him. He heard the deep, windy rush of its breathing. With every breath, its exoskeletal, bone-armor plating shifted against itself, producing dirty, grinding sounds.

Justin felt his aurym flowing through the a'thri'ik shards in the blade of his sword. Aurym was goodness. But this thing, this cythraul, this creature powered by daemyn. . . . Not until now did Justin fully understand the difference between the two forms of spirit energy. They were not two sides of the same energy. One was not the opposite of the other. Aurym and daemyn were distinct and wholly unrelated entities. One could not *be* where the other *was*. The disparity between them was greater than the difference between fire and water, hot and cold, or life and death; it was more like the difference between existence and nonexistence.

Justin cringed at the feeling of the cythraul looming over him and the volatile energies that powered it. Daemyn was greater than evil. It was the festering womb in which evil was conceived. And here, standing before Justin, was one of its bastard spawn.

Justin focused on the knowledge flowing through him. Aurym had told him he could kill Lisaac. But this time, the outcome was not assured. The possibility of failure and death did not, however, detract from the peace within Justin. The outcome was at once foreordained and also within his capacity to influence. Win or lose, he was playing his role, walking his path.

Justin opened his eyes. The cythraul, a ten-foot-tall monster armored with black bone plates, stood within spitting distance of him. A set of curled horns jutted from its forehead. A sharp, bony ridge crested its brow. Its shoulders were uncommonly broad, even for a cythraul, and clutched in its hand was a huge scythe. Justin recognized this creature. It was the cythraul that had touched him. It was the one that had turned his arm.

Justin heard more crashing coming from a different direction. He turned and looked. The second cythraul he had heard was pushing through the forest to join the first.

And a third cythraul was walking alongside it.

As Justin watched, the third cythraul punched through a nearby tree trunk as if it were made of tin foil. Crude rags covered the monsters' lower bodies. Boots covered their feet. Other than that, they wore no clothes or armor, only jagged, bone exoskeletons. Their heads were sharp, fleshless skulls. Between their dagger-like teeth, poisonous, yellow vapor vented with every breath. Their empty, glowing eye sockets flickered with unseen energies emanating from somewhere within their terrible bodies.

Smaller, shadowy forms slipped along through the undergrowth as they came, and Justin realized coblyns were slinking along at the cythraul's heels like dogs. There must have been dozens of them.

The two new arrivals took up positions behind the first cythraul. The coblyns skittered eagerly around their feet.

Justin noticed that certain characteristics varied between the cythraul. One of the newcomers had a great, hooked jaw bristled with a white-streaked beard, and resting over its shoulder was a massive, double-bladed battleaxe. The other newcomer was taller, approaching twelve feet instead of ten, with jagged barbs protruding from the elbow-plates of its arms like the horns of an armored insect. It used both hands to grip its sword—if it could be called a sword. The weapon was a giant slab of sharp metal as long as the monster's body, as wide as a cafeteria table, and half a foot thick. The hilt appeared to simply be a portion of the metal the cythraul had folded and crushed to fit within its hands.

The first cythraul—the one that had transformed Justin's arm—raised one of its hands and pointed across the creek, exactly where Leah was hiding.

Justin's heart sank.

The cythraul barked an earth-shaking, guttural command in another language. The coblyns took off, snarling and cackling as they raced toward Leah's hiding place. As they waded across the creek, Justin swung his sword in a wide, wild arc. Aurym flowed. The air split open.

A blast of green energy erupted from his blade and cut through the forest, hitting the coblyns. It sliced through the land, boiled the creek water, uprooted trees, and sent large rocks rolling through the woods. Any coblyns caught within the blast were disintegrated. Those along the periphery were doused in green, napalm-like flames that ate at their bodies until they fell over, dead.

When the smoke and steam cleared, the creek flowed over a newly formed waterfall, down into the fissure in the ground. Trees sizzled with green fire. Not a single coblyn remained. All had been killed in a single swing of Justin's sword.

The scythe-wielding cythraul seemed to smile with its lipless mouth. It pointed at Justin and opened its dagger-toothed maw.

"YOU . . . BELONG . . . TO AVAGAD."

The cythraul's halting speech sounded like the grinding of stone wheels. When the sharp teeth clicked together between words, it was like the smashing of boulders.

"JOIN US . . ." it said, "AND YOU SHALL BECOME . . . OUR UNDYING ALLY."

Justin sneered. "Never."

The monster spun its scythe in a flourish. "THEN YOU . . . SHALL BE . . . OUR ETERNAL *SLAVE*!"

Before Justin knew what was happening, a black vortex of daemyn came flying in his direction. It hit the ground in front of him with a deafening, seismic explosion, and he found himself instantly airborne, riding a chunk of dislodged earth.

The jarring, unexpected impact of Justin's body striking the upper limbs of a tree knocked his sword from his grasp. He flew wildly through the canopy and crashed through branches for what felt like a long time before he finally slammed down onto the ground.

Dirt, branches, and rocks came crashing down. Within seconds, he was buried beneath the debris, blocking out the sun. It felt as if a building had collapsed on him.

Justin shook his head, trying to regain his bearings. His body was pinned down, but nothing felt as if it had been badly broken. He heard a cythraul approaching, and he wedged both hands under a large limb across his chest and pushed as hard as he could, groaning with the effort. Finally, he got his feet under it and kicked it aside. He scrambled to dig through rocks and dirt. He pulled himself the rest of the way out and quickly spotted his sword. It had fallen straight down and stuck upright in the ground.

Ignoring the approaching cythraul, Justin ran and yanked his sword from the ground. At his touch, the blade turned a blinding green. He screamed in fury as he turned and swung his sword, emitting a blast of emerald aurym energy.

The blast arced through the air. It seemed to hit the horned cythraul squarely across the upper body. But the explosion that should have followed never came. The roar was swallowed up in penetrating silence.

Justin watched in astonishment as his aurym blast slowed to a halt, swirled in place, and then began to shrink. The green light dimmed. It spun inward into the center of a whirlpool, diminishing until it was only a tiny dot of light—within the cythraul's palm. Then the cythraul closed its hand into a fist, and the light disappeared altogether, sucked into the singularity.

The cythraul flexed its fingers, looked at Justin, and laughed at him.

Just like that, the bottom dropped out. Everything Justin had been feeling seconds before—the peace, the wisdom, the calm understanding—was gone, snuffed out as easily as his aurym within the cythraul's palm. The glow of his sword was fading.

"No . . ." said Justin.

As panic seized Justin, his weapon darkened completely, until it was nothing but a piece of metal. The three cythraul roared in what was either delight or bloodlust. Just for fun, the bearded one swung its battleaxe, chopping a tree in half with a single blow. Their nightmarish voices echoed through the forest as they came for him. The one in front bellowed, "THE ANGEL . . . *FALLS*!"

"Come on, come on," Justin pleaded, shaking his sword with both hands, trying desperately to bring it back to life. "You can do this. Come on."

He tried to imagine aurym returning and brightening the blade, tried to remember the feeling that had opened the gateway to access the power. The nearest cythraul stomped threateningly at him and took delight in the way he almost fell backward in fright.

"Come *on*!" Justin cried, squeezing the sword's hilt. But it was like trying to force color into the gauge stone. It was impossible again. The power had left him.

The tall, sword-wielding cythraul swept its arm sideways, casually tossing a ball of daemyn at Justin. He tried to dive out of the way, but the ground erupted, and he sailed through the air again. He managed to hold on to his sword this time but landed hard on his back in the shallows of the creek. The wind was knocked out of him on impact. Heavy stones rained down, peppering his body, cutting and breaking his skin.

He set his jaw, trying to keep his chin from quivering. He couldn't help thinking about what Avagad had said—about how Justin thought he could kill wolves just because he had drowned a rat. Justin could not even count on death as a reprieve. What awaited him was a fate worse than death: transformation into a demon. In the meantime, these monsters were having fun toying with him.

A thought passed through Justin's head.

When the power was with you, you acted bravely. But even a coward can be brave when the odds are for him.

The thought came fully formed—not as individually spoken words, but as a complete and unabridged concept. Justin listened, unsure whether he was thinking it, or if it was coming from somewhere else.

Act bravely now, Justin. Even in death, be brave. Think and understand beyond the fear.

Leah, thought Justin. *If nothing else, maybe I can distract the cythraul and give her an opportunity to get away.*

The thought gave new strength to his body. Using his sword as a cane, Justin pushed himself up. Blood trickled over his eyelids from a cut on his forehead, and he had to wipe it away to see properly. One of the cythraul raised a bone-armored hand. A ball of daemyn again appeared in its palm. And again, Justin knew, it would not be a killing blow. He would be caught in the resulting shock wave and thrown through the air, batted around like a mouse caught between house cats. Killing him was not their intention. He could not fight them, but perhaps he could take some of the control away from them.

The cythraul let loose its daemyn, and Justin acted. Just as he had done to Lisaac, he decided to do the last thing his enemy would expect: He charged forward and jumped straight into the line of the oncoming blast.

CHAPTER 122

Ahlund's eyes snapped open. He felt echoes in his mind. Echoes of a powerful battle. Aurym and daemyn clashing with deadly force. He could almost see it, like the afterimage of the sun behind his eyelids.

He lay with his head against the floorboards, staring at the cargo hold ceiling, feeling the ship rock in the surf as it drifted out to sea. It felt like he had just closed his eyes, but someone was shouting in alarm, "Cap'n! Cap'n!"

"What is it?" Gunnar said.

Pool was standing halfway up the stairs to the deck. "There's. . . . You better have a look at this, cap'n."

Gunnar and Zechariah got to their feet. Forcing his muscles to obey, Ahlund somehow managed to stand as well. Gunnar came to his side and supported him by one arm. Zechariah took the other, and they climbed the stairs together and emerged on the deck of their confiscated ship.

The sun was blinding. The ocean breeze tousled Ahlund's matted hair. The sails of their new ship were black, but the orange and white flag of Hartla had been run up the main mast.

Drexel's white-sailed fleet surrounded them. Of Drexel's fifty ships, only about two-thirds remained. The rest had been taken down by daemyn blasts or overrun with boarding coblyns. Gaius was several hundred yards behind them. Corpses—human and demon alike—littered the ruins. Coblyns still wandered in small groups, gradually dispersing into the surrounding woods. Reverting to their natural form, they fled the daylight and sought the shadows. Ahlund hardly dared estimate how many soldiers had been lost back there. They had paid a heavy toll, but the battle had been won.

And then Ahlund saw it. Out across the sea, the northeastern horizon was black. It looked as if the ocean had turned to tar.

"What in blazes?" said Olorus.

It took Ahlund a moment to realize what he was seeing. Black sails. Belonging to black ships beyond count.

"It's the rest of the black fleet," Gunnar said flatly.

"Five hundred ships strong, at least," someone said from behind them.

Ahlund turned. It was Drexel. He had boarded their ship, evidently to convene with Gunnar. Black blood splattered across his hat and an open wound on his forehead testified to his contribution to the fighting. He stroked his beard and gazed out at the horizon. "Hard to tell from here," he added, "but we know from prior run-ins that it could be as many as one thousand. And the wind is with them."

The survivors of Gaius stared at the black sails. Ahlund said nothing. He felt nothing. Their hard-fought victory had prolonged their lives for a few minutes at best.

"Admirals?" came a voice from above.

Ahlund looked up. A lone Hartlan sailor stood in the crow's nest, watching the sea with a spyglass.

"What is it?" Drexel said.

The lookout said nothing. Ahlund wondered if the size of the black fleet had her stunned beyond words. But then Ahlund noticed where she was looking. Not at the enemy to the northeast at all but to the far west.

"Well?" Drexel barked when his patience had run its course, but still, the woman said nothing.

"Sailor," said Gunnar gently.

She looked down.

"Tell us what you see," said Gunnar.

"A fleet," said the lookout.

"We see it!" Drexel shouted, annoyed.

"No, sir," the lookout said. "Not the black fleet. Another fleet. With gold banners. And blue. And crimson."

Drexel's brow furrowed. "Gold, blue, and crimson?"

"Syleau, Winhold, and Arillion," said Gunnar. "Mythaean states."

"And allies of Hartla!" said Drexel, his face lighting up. "Responding to our couriers! They have come to our aid!"

Now, Ahlund could see the sails materializing on the western horizon.

"They just keep coming!" shouted the lookout, still gazing through her spyglass. "So many of them—and they're sailing at the black fleet!"

"Someone get me a spyglass!" Drexel shouted. "Man your battle stations, all of you! Send word to the other ships! This fight isn't over! If we can commandeer a few more of those empty ships onshore, we can bolster our—"

But Drexel was interrupted by wild shouting from the crow's nest. It took a moment before the lookout's exclamations could be understood. "The black fleet has turned about!" she was crying, her voice cracking with excitement. "The black fleet has turned about!"

"Turned about?" said Drexel.

"Yes, sir!" said the lookout. "They're retreating!"

"*Victory*!" Olorus bellowed.

Olorus's cry set in motion a collective shout across the ship. Soon, it seemed the whole fleet was cheering with one voice.

Ahlund turned toward shore, looking at the thickly wooded hills behind the beaches of Gaius.

Hang on, Justin, he thought. *Stay alive just a little longer.*

CHAPTER 123

Sliding on his knees toward the oncoming ball of concentrated blackness, Justin raised his left arm like a shield. He did not know if what he was about to do would work or not, but there was nothing left to lose now.

The daemyn collided with his arm. He felt a slam of impact. The earth shook beneath him.

But the blast did not explode. Instead, the black cloud of daemyn hung suspended in midair before his arm. Then it warped, spun, folded in on itself, and shrank. The world around Justin became a torrent of swirling wind and chaos for a moment. Then all faded away to silence as the daemyn blast disappeared entirely—absorbed into a singularity in Justin's blackened, chitinous, demon arm.

Justin stood, unharmed. He looked at the three cythraul. They had stopped walking and were frozen in place, watching him. Facial expressions were difficult to read on fleshless skulls, but Justin thought they looked almost shocked. He grinned and flexed his fingers.

The monsters advanced on Justin, no longer laughing. They were done playing.

Justin wondered what awaited him once they turned him fully. Would his mind be gone? Or would he remember himself? Would he be a prisoner in his own body, robbed of his free will, forced to watch himself obey the commands of Avagad and these creatures?

And if it happened now, would he remember where Leah was hiding?

"The princess will be first," Avagad had said. "I will make you look her in the eye as she begs you for mercy while you pull out her heart and feast on royal flesh—"

"No!" Justin shouted.

Leaping forward, he swung his sword in two quick slashes through the air. The blade exploded with green light. Twin arcs of blinding, emerald energy shot through the forest.

The bearded cythraul wasn't quick enough. The first arc cut him diagonally from hip to shoulder. The second arc collided with full force against his chest and exploded, shredding his torso. The other two cythraul recoiled, shielding themselves from the aurym energy as their comrade was shredded into flaming pieces.

The horned cythraul charged and swung its scythe. Burning pain cut through Justin's thigh. His leg buckled, suddenly unable to support his weight.

Justin fell, shocked by the pain in his leg. He tried to swing his sword, but the cythraul's giant boot kicked his hand. He had a momentary glimpse of his sword, kicked from his grasp, spinning through the air to land in some weeds.

Justin hit the ground with a small splash. At first, he thought he had fallen into the creek. Then he realized it was a pool of his own blood.

He looked down. His leg was still attached, but the scythe had cut him to the bone in a horizontal slice across his upper right thigh. The muscle had been cleanly severed. His hands shook uncontrollably as he clutched at the gash, trying to push together two hunks of flesh that should have been connected.

As the two remaining cythraul watched the remnants of their brother's body implode, Justin gave up trying to stop the bleeding. He lay down on his chest and used his elbows to drag himself, inch by inch, toward the place where his sword had landed in the tall grass.

The horned cythraul stepped forward, wedged its foot under Justin, and flipped him over onto his back. The boot came down, stamping on Justin's chest and pinning him to the ground. Hundreds of pounds of pressure drove all the breath from his lungs, making even a scream of pain impossible. The cythraul knelt over him.

Justin felt cold. So cold. His teeth chattered. He could only watch in silent agony as the monster's horned head leaned down and down and down, getting ever closer to his face, until he was eye-to-empty-eye with it. He must have been no more than six inches away from the cythraul's face. He felt heat radiating from eye sockets as big as dinner plates. He smelled its poisonous breath. The great mouth opened, daggers parting to reveal a black chasm so wide that it could have bitten his head off at the shoulders. It raised its hand and reached for him.

Even in death, Justin, something told him, *act bravely. Be brave, but not of your own bravery. Be wise, but not of your own wisdom. Be strong, but not of your own strength.*

Justin closed his eyes. Fear, panic, and struggle would not serve him in death or whatever fate awaited him. Instead, he felt peace, courage, wisdom, and strength. He nestled against the feelings like a child in its mother's arms. He understood, now, that these feelings were not his own—they never had been. They had always been outside of himself, ready to welcome him in whenever he needed them. If only he had not tried so hard, maybe he could have found them with more consistency over the course of this brief life. Maybe he could have found peace, or even brought peace to others.

Everything will be all right, he heard someone say. It sounded like his mother. And for the first time in a long time, he believed it.

But he also knew something else: a piece of knowledge that came to him unexpectedly, but that was unquestionably true. Somehow he knew, even without seeing, that his sword was not in the weeds where it had fallen. No—it was in the air right now. It was sailing toward him. He did not know how he knew this or how it had happened. Leah had done it, maybe. Snuck from her hiding place, retrieved it, and thrown it his way in an act of desperation. All he knew was that it was coming toward him, and if he wanted it, he only had to reach out his hand and take it.

Eyes still closed, Justin reached out with his hand. The hilt of his sword landed in his palm.

Justin closed his fingers around the sword's hilt and opened his eyes. One day, he would meet his end. One day, he would find peace.

That day would have to wait.

Justin drove his sword upward between the cythraul's roaring jaws. With a splitting crack, the blade punctured the roof of the cythraul's mouth, lanced through its head, and burst out the top of its skull. The roar stopped. The cythraul made a gagging sound.

Justin tightened his grip on his sword. He called on peace, courage, wisdom, and strength. They did not exist *in* him; they were outside of him and existed *through* him. They flowed through Justin, through his hands, into the sword. When the combined energy met the aurstones in the blade, aurym power manifested solidly—like a surge of molten metal.

The cythraul's head was ripped from the shoulders. Black blood spewed from the neck. For a moment, Justin saw a headless body struggling to hold its ground, still trying to reach for Justin against the energy cascading from his sword. Then the hand clutching the scythe flew off and went spinning skyward. The other arm dissolved off the bone. A leg tore away below the knee. Ribs became visible through a disintegrating torso. The body levitated as gaping holes ate through muscles, flesh, and exoskeleton.

In a flaming, emerald explosion, the cythraul expanded, split, and vaporized. A wave of energy pulsed like a ripple from the epicenter. A circular lightning bolt expanding outward, mowing down trees. The third cythraul tried to raise its hands in defense, but the wave hit it just above the waist and cut cleanly through its bone armor. Its top half and bottom half fell in opposite directions, spilling slimy piles of black viscera. It reached desperately for its own innards, trying to pull them in, but electrical indigo energy danced across its body. The glowing eyes went dark, and the body disintegrated.

A moment passed. Debris rained down. Not far from Justin, an object came spinning down out of the sky and stuck into the forest floor with a thud. It was an enormous scythe, with one bony hand still clutching the handle. And then all was silent.

Justin let the sword fall from his grasp. His chest heaved in fierce repetition. Blood flowed freely from his leg. He couldn't move. He could hardly think. The forest canopy, which had been thick just minutes before, had been decimated by his aurym blast, and the sun beat down on him. He closed his eyes.

"You are full of surprises, Justin."

Justin smiled without looking. "Low . . . expectations," he breathed.

When he opened his eyes, Leah was limping into his field of vision. She clutched her side, and there were burn marks on her shirt.

"You're hurt," Justin said in alarm. "What happened?"

"It's not bad," she said.

"Let me see," he said.

Leah removed her hand. Blood dribbled down her hip. A strangely shaped burn had scorched her on one side from her waist to her ribs.

"It could have been worse," she said. "I managed to get out of the way, mostly."

"From what. . . ?" Justin started to ask but trailed off as he realized the answer. "It was me, wasn't it?"

Leah didn't say anything.

"I hurt you," said Justin.

"I'm all right," she said.

"I could have killed you."

"I told you it's not bad," she said. "I'm a healer, I should know. Yours, on the other hand, is . . . bad."

Leah kneeled over him and placed her hand over the bone-deep cut in his leg, but he pushed her hand away.

"Do yours first," he said.

"You've lost too much blood—"

"Leah," he said. "Do yours first. Please."

For a moment, her hard eyes were unyielding, as usual. Then, without a word, she held her hand over the wound on her side and closed her eyes. Justin watched the flesh crawl and melt together. It left an off-white blot of ugly, rutted scar tissue.

"I wish that scar was somewhere I could see it," said Justin.

"What does that mean?" said Leah as she began treating his leg.

"So I wouldn't forget," said Justin. "So I would be reminded that I almost killed a friend." He closed his eyes and gasped against the pain of the aurym-healing process. He dared not watch whatever she was doing. "Saving my life almost cost you yours. Look at what I did here. This kind of power is dangerous."

Leah was quiet as she worked, and Justin kept his eyes closed.

"Something can be dangerous without being bad," Leah said. "It's all in how you use it. You used it to save us."

"Save us?" said Justin. "All I did was buy us a little time. There are more of them out there. And if we don't—"

With his eyes closed, Justin didn't even see it coming. His only warning was the warmth of her face a split second before her lips pressed against his.

A moment passed that was more than a moment. When their lips parted, Justin opened his eyes. She was looking down at him. He had never noticed the tiny, gold flecks in the green of her irises before. He opened his mouth to say something, but Leah cut him off.

"Justin," she said. "For once in your life, shut up."

While Leah healed a cut on Justin's forehead, he lay back, rested his head on her lap, and fell asleep. He did not dream.

CHAPTER 124

The ship's dark hull and black sails seemed almost to absorb the afternoon sunlight beating down on the Raedittean Sea. Initially, a Hartlan flag had been placed atop its mast. But Gunnar had ordered that it be taken down and replaced with a different one: the flag he had worn as a bandana, bearing the emblem of a sword with ivy wrapped around the blade. He had dubbed this new vessel the *Gryphon II*.

Several hours had passed since the Battle of Gaius. The black fleet had retreated eastward to parts unknown, and Admiral Drexel and the combined fleets of Hartla, Syleau, Winhold, and Arillion had sailed to Hartla to hold council. Meanwhile, the *Gryphon II*, with a detachment of soldiers and sailors, led a small escort of ships northwest to skirt the coasts of Athacea.

Gunnar, Olorus, Hook, Zechariah, and Ahlund surrounded the ship's wheel. Samuel did the steering.

"You're sure it came from this direction?" asked Olorus.

"Positive," said Zechariah.

Ahlund left his assurances unspoken. A powerful battle had taken place somewhere in this direction. Even from miles away, the sensation had been overwhelming: thunderous spiritual forces, culminating in one final blast—a detonation of aurym that was orders of magnitude greater than that which had halted combat at Gaius. Was it possible that the helpless boy from the Gravelands who had not been able to stay on his steed could really wield such power?

"Cap'n!" shouted Borris from the crow's nest. "Er—I mean, admiral! I see someone!"

"Where, Captain Borris?" Gunnar shouted up the mast.

"Over there at—*Captain* Borris?" Borris said, flabbergasted.

"I'm buildin' a new fleet, lad," said Gunnar. "Ye'll all be captains, and I'll not be takin' no for an answer! Now report, cap'n! What do you see?"

Borris positively beamed. He smiled crookedly because of his scar as he trained his spyglass on the Athacean coastline. "Two people!" he shouted. "Comin' out of the woods near yonder creek!"

Ahlund put a hand to his eyes against the sun. Sure enough, on the shoreline ahead, two figures walked along the creek, leaning against one another for support.

"Set course, Captain Samuel," Gunnar said. "And prepare the dinghy, Captain Pool."

Samuel and Pool, as they complied, looked at least if not more thrilled than Borris.

"Now, I know what you're going to say, Olorus," Gunnar announced. "You want to be a captain too. But I'm afraid it wouldn't be fitting. In Nolia, I am told, a lieutenant of the High Guard holds more esteem than a ship captain. As eager as I'm sure you are to serve under me, I'd hate to see a man of your stature be demoted—"

"It's the boy and the princess!" Borris shouted from the crow's nest.

"The princess?" Olorus shouted up the mast. "You're sure?"

Borris smiled and nodded. "It's her!"

"She's alive!" Olorus yelled. He grabbed Hook by the arms and grinned like a madman, repeating, "She's alive! She's alive!" Hook, in spite of himself, was doing his share of mad grinning, too.

By now, Justin and Leah were waving at the ship.

"The fallen angel lives," Ahlund whispered to the old man beside him.

"It's either a miracle or a curse," Zechariah whispered back.

Ahlund looked at him.

"Now," said Zechariah, "we have to decide what to do with him."

CHAPTER 125

Upon seeing the sinister-looking black ship, Justin and Leah nearly fled back into the woods. Luckily, Leah noticed the familiar flag flying on its mast.

A lifeboat met them at the shoreline, manned by Pool and a few sailors, and Justin and Leah rode it over the surf. Leah had done everything she could to heal Justin's wounds, but the trauma had taken its toll. His injuries throbbed. His head ached. He was weak from blood loss and shivered despite the relative warmth of the air. He was grateful when someone threw a blanket over his bare shoulders.

Lines were dropped as they pulled up alongside the black ship, and the lifeboat was hoisted up. As soon as they reached the level of the main deck, Leah was snatched bodily from the boat by the bear-hugging arms of Olorus Antony. Leah returned the hug and laughed. The lieutenant was crying tears of joy.

When he finally put Leah down, Olorus gave Justin the same treatment, picking him up and hauling him out of the boat as if he weighed no more than the princess. All around them, people were celebrating the reunion. Justin finally freed himself from Olorus and did his best to hide how badly the greeting hurt. Hook, standing quietly beside Olorus, simply shook Justin's hand.

As Justin was ushered through the crowd, he found himself looking around and taking a mental head count. Pool had rowed them to the ship. Olorus and Hook had greeted them. He saw Gunnar and Samuel not far from him, and at the back of the crowd stood Zechariah and Ahlund. Only Vick, the fourth member of Gunnar's crew, seemed to be missing. Justin felt strange. He knew he should be happy to see them but found that he had to force a smile.

Gunnar stepped forward to greet him. "Wasn't sure we'd be seein' you again, lad," he said.

"Same here," said Justin. He gestured up at the black sails of the ship. "Where'd all this come from?"

"Amazing what you can do with a couple Drekwood trees, and a little elbow grease, ain't it?" Gunnar said. He slapped Justin on the shoulder and winked.

"Didn't you say you built the *Gryphon* out of Drekwood trees, too?" said Justin.

"I may have exercised some creative license in the telling of that tale," said Gunnar. "The *Gryphon*. The truth is . . . my uncle gave it to me."

Justin cocked an eyebrow.

"You see why I spiced up the story," Gunnar said.

It seemed like just about everyone had shaken Justin's hand or given him a pat on the back by the time he made it to Zechariah and Ahlund. For a moment, the two men just stood looking at him—Zechariah as if addressing a troublesome youngster, and Ahlund with the same face he always wore. Then Justin grinned and said, "Boy, have I got a story for you guys."

For the first time since Justin had met him, Ahlund Sims smiled.

Someone put a hand on Justin's good shoulder. He turned to find Leah standing behind him. She was holding his sword. He had left it in the dinghy.

"Don't forget this," she said.

"Oh, yeah," said Justin, taking it. "Thanks."

Leah crossed the ship to rejoin Olorus and Hook. Justin watched her go.

"The cat's eye sword—of course!" Zechariah said with a smile. "With a'thri'ik aurstones forged in the blade. So that is how you called on aurym. I should have known! That type of aurstone is rather rare, and the talent to use it is rarer still. It is fortunate you are one of the few who can."

"A lot of dumb luck," said Justin. But his eyes went distant as he said it. He knew, full well, that luck had nothing to do with anything that had happened.

Ahlund's smile changed to a look of concern. He grabbed the blanket draped over Justin's shoulders and lifted it, exposing the black, rock-hard arm.

"What happened, Justin?" breathed Zechariah, wearing a look of horror.

Justin leaned in. "I'll explain everything," he whispered, "but we're not safe here. I don't know how many cythraul Avagad has in this area at the moment, or. . . ."

But Justin trailed off at the look that flashed across Zechariah's face: a mix of surprise and recognition.

"You know him," said Justin.

Zechariah chewed on his tongue. It looked like he was about to answer when Justin was grabbed from behind and forcibly spun around. It was Olorus, shoving a bottle of something into his hand.

"A drink to your health, my boy!" Olorus called out, and he raised a second bottle and shouted for all to hear, "Here's to Justin Holmes! For saving the princess of Nolia—and all our sorry arses!"

"Here, here!" came the shout of sailors all across the ship.

Justin raised the bottle and pretended to take a drink. Sailors cheered. Justin turned around to face Zechariah and Ahlund again, but the look of surprise and recognition on Zechariah's face was gone, replaced by what Justin took to be a phony smile.

"We can *talk* later!" said Zechariah. He stole the bottle from Justin's hand, took several quick gulps, and smacked his lips. "For now, let us celebrate!"

Pool had taken to dancing about the ship, playing a tune with his flute. Sailors started dancing. Others clapped or stomped their feet in time. Justin tried to continue speaking with Zechariah, but the old man pushed through the crowd in the opposite direction, as if something else demanded his attention. When Justin turned back to speak to Ahlund, he found that the tall mercenary had wandered off to speak with Leah.

Justin stood alone, feeling troubled.

As the black ship set sail, people came to speak with Justin. They handed him more bottles to drink from. They toasted to his health, though most did not seem to know the details of how he had "saved" them—and neither did he, but it apparently had something to do with coblyns.

Justin tried politely to join in the merrymaking, but he didn't feel much like celebrating. He felt bad about it, but as he looked around at all the dancing and singing, he couldn't help but think that all these people were very ignorant. If they knew what he knew, they wouldn't be celebrating.

He tried to put on a happy face anyway, for their benefit, but he couldn't.

CHAPTER 126

Upon arriving in Hartla, Justin found himself part of a citywide celebration. News had spread of the victory at Gaius. Olorus had been keen to half-drunkenly describe the battle to Justin, along with the events leading up to it, in vivid detail. He skipped many explanatory points in his excitement, leaving Justin a bit unclear on the hows and the whys, but when it came to the blood and gore of battle itself, the lieutenant was a regular wordsmith.

Hartla's harbor was filled with sails and colored banners, plus one larger set of black sails belonging to the *Gryphon II.* The people spoke of a demon army, a black fleet, and the return of Admiral Gunnar Erix Nimbus. They spoke of a member of the immortal Brethren, a fire-wielding Guardian, a Nolian princess, her faithful soldiers, and five hundred brave Hartlan soldiers, of whom less than one hundred had survived. As for those who had charged the cythraul and dealt it a killing blow on the beach, they had gained immediate hero status.

Justin and the others were whisked from the *Gryphon II* directly to an infirmary. The healers were baffled by Justin's arm and, like Leah, could do nothing for it. From there, he was sent to a bathhouse for his first washing in a very long time. He was given a set of clothing: light leather armor, a formal toga, and an orange cape. It was, he was told, the traditional garb of a Hartlan military officer.

A new sheath was found to fit Justin's cat's eye sword, and he quite liked how bold it looked strapped to his back, with the hilt sticking up above his shoulder. The only problem was that the Hartlan toga left his mutilated demon arm clearly visible. Seeing how disturbed most people were by the sight of it, Justin asked if it could be covered in something. The attendants agreed, and they wrapped it from shoulder to wrist in black satin. The result looked decorative instead of shocking.

Soon, Justin was marching toward the royal palace surrounded by his friends and the Hartlans who had charged the cythraul at Gaius. The streets were lined with people, and Hartla's towering buildings, constructed right into the sandstone cliffs, were a sight to behold. But Justin hardly noticed the scenery. He could barely take his eyes off Leah walking beside him. He had never seen her in anything other than dirty traveling clothes. Now, she was in a flowing blue dress, with her dark hair hanging past her bare shoulders. Justin found himself in awe of how stunningly beautiful she was.

Entering the palace, Justin was hit with the cheers of thousands. The pungent aroma of wine filled the air. The hall was filled to bursting, not only with Hartlans but with captains and officers of the ally colonies who had come to their aid during the battle.

The recognized heroes stood before the rulers of Hartla seated on their twin thrones. For several minutes, Count Wulder Von Morix tried to quiet the crowd. He eventually gave up and just started speaking.

". . . A great day in the history of the Mythaean race," he was saying when the people finally quieted enough to hear him. "A few brave souls stood against overwhelming odds to run an enemy out of our lands." He gestured to the Hartlan soldiers. "You men and women have earned places of honor in these halls and will forever be remembered as defenders of your homeland. Henceforth, you will each go by the title of Demon-slayer! For your bravery, you will be granted. . . ."

Justin's attention wandered. Ahlund stood beside him, dressed in the same military regalia as Justin. Olorus, Hook, Pool, Borris, and Samuel were similarly outfitted. Zechariah, however, had been content with a clean set of robes, black, plain, and undecorated. One of the sleeves, however, was empty.

Justin looked at the empty sleeve and shivered. It had taken him a while to notice the old man's missing hand. He had been horrified to learn *he* was responsible.

"It wasn't your fault," Ahlund whispered beside him, as if reading Justin's mind.

Justin hung his head. "If I had been stronger—"

"You were stronger than anyone could have asked of you," Ahlund said.

Justin smiled a little. He had a feeling that was about as close as Ahlund Sims came to giving a compliment.

"And you, brave men and women," bellowed Drexel Von Morix, addressing Gunnar and the rest. "Fate brought you to us in a desperate hour. The renowned admiral of Eppex, Gunnar Erix Nimbus, seemingly back from the dead!"

At the front of the procession, Gunnar bowed. He was dressed royally, complete with a new admiral's hat with a grand white feather stuck in the top. He had one hand tucked cockily in his belt.

"And with him," continued Drexel, "came a Ru'Onorath Guardian, two Nolian soldiers searching for their abducted princess, and a man claiming to be one of the mythical, immortal Brethren. A madder story, I could not have imagined!"

Laughter rippled through the crowd.

"But I personally witnessed their bravery and their power," continued Drexel. "As we fought on the sea, they fought on land against an army of monsters. And through it all, they not only triumphed, driving a dark and evil enemy from Hartla's borders, but reclaimed the fair lady on top of it all!"

Cheers rose up throughout the palace hall. Olorus put his hands together and pumped them triumphantly in the air for all to see. Leah curtsied, causing Justin to do a double take at the girl he knew better with a sword in her hand and healing a blood-coated wound.

When the commotion died down, Count Wulder said, "You good men and women have not only done us a service in arms, but you helped bring together the forces of three of our strongest sister colonies. Syleau, Winhold, and Arillion!" Upon speaking each name, he paused to let their assembled sons and daughters throw up corresponding cheers. "Today marks the forging of a powerful new Mythaean Alliance, and the dawn of a new era for our great Thalassocracy. We are honored to call you allies and friends of all true-blooded Mythaeans!"

Cheers erupted. At a signal from the count, music began to play. Wineskins were dispersed, and food was served.

As the others began to mingle, Justin hung back, quite uncomfortable with it all. He watched his friends from a distance as they exchanged pleasantries with anyone who managed to gain an audience with them. To Justin, it all felt like compensation for a loss. The demons had been driven back for now, but at what cost? Of the five hundred Hartlans who had marched on Gaius, *four hundred* were dead. And who knew how many others had died on the ships that had been overrun by coblyns? While celebrations ensued in the rulers' palace, how many families were mourning the loss of a father, a mother, a son, a daughter, a sister, a brother?

And how many more will die, thought Justin, *when Avagad's armies return?*

Justin was pretending to admire the palace architecture when Leah came to stand beside him. She placed a hand on his shoulder and leaned in to speak in his ear so she could be heard over the crowd.

"They didn't even mention you!" she said.

Justin blinked in surprise. He thought it over for a moment, then laughed when he realized she was right.

"If they only understood what you did," she said.

"I couldn't have done it without you," Justin said. "Speaking of which, I never got to thank you for throwing me my sword back there."

"For what?" she said, cupping her hand to her ear.

"For throwing me my sword," he repeated, leaning in a little closer to be heard above the commotion.

Leah turned to look him in the eye. Her face spelled confusion.

"I didn't throw you anything," she said.

Justin found himself speechless, partially out of surprise at her words, but mostly at how close their faces suddenly were. Her hand was still on his shoulder. Her neck smelled like flowers.

Someone called Leah's name, and she turned. It was some dignitary wanting to toast her health. Leah turned back to Justin a moment, gave him a playful, closed-fisted jab—

touching her knuckles against his jaw and pushing only firmly enough to turn his head a bit. She backed away, smiling, and disappeared into the crowd.

Justin ran his hand over the black satin covering his demon arm. Somewhere deep within, a tingle sizzled through the bone.

Justin backed through the crowd, retreated into a rear corner of the room, and finally, escaped down an adjoining hallway.

CHAPTER 127

Keys of the Ancients, thought Justin. *Keys.*

He could still hear the echoes of the Hartlans' drunken revelry as he sat on the floor in an abandoned hallway, his back against the wall, staring at his sword sitting in his lap. A solitary torch in a sconce on the wall above him lit his surroundings. He thought about Avagad. He thought about his friends. But most of all, he thought about the book. How he wished he could have had more time with that book, to learn the secret of the keys that could, supposedly, open the way to Earth.

One year, he thought. *One year in Avagad's service in exchange for the book. . . . Keys.*

"Hiding!"

Justin looked up. He had not heard Zechariah's approach. Shadows fell thickly from the folds of his robed silhouette, but heaviest of all was the shadow where his right hand should have been.

"If I didn't know any better," Zechariah said, "I'd say you were avoiding us."

"I can't celebrate," said Justin. "Not knowing what I know."

Zechariah stepped fully into the torchlight. "Sounds like you need a drink more than anyone. I'm afraid knowledge can be one of the greatest burdens of a life well-lived. A recurring challenge will be wearing a brave face in spite of it. I wish I could say it gets easier."

"The cythraul are collecting coblyns from all over the world," Justin said. "Avagad is behind the whole thing. He's got these people who are serving him. They're building an army—"

"I know, I know," Zechariah said.

"So you do know Avagad," said Justin.

Zechariah hesitated. "I do, though I have not heard his name in many long years. I wish I had known from the start that he was the one behind all this." He looked hard at Justin. "He connected with you, didn't he?"

Justin nodded.

"And he did that to your arm?"

Justin said nothing.

"I'm sorry, Justin," said Zechariah. "You should not have had to face him alone. No one should. But, in hindsight, I would not change the way things happened even if I could." He raised his right arm, indicating the missing hand. "Not even this. The tribulations you faced were better than any lessons I could have taught you. You discovered your aurym power, and it led to a great victory over the enemy."

"You were trying to get me to discover that power all along, weren't you?" said Justin.

Zechariah shrugged sheepishly.

"So, what happens now?" Justin said. "What happens after this party's over?"

Zechariah studied him, stroking his long, white beard. "Justin, I am deeply sorry you did not find your way home. I can only imagine what you must be feeling. But you have friends here. And those friends know the truth of what happened today. The echoes of your aurym power interrupted the fighting at Gaius and drew away three of the four cythraul from the battlefield. If that hadn't happened, we would not have stood a chance. The only reason anyone survived—the only reason there is hope left in this world tonight—is you."

Zechariah walked across the lighted circle to kneel beside Justin. He placed his good hand on Justin's head.

"Your friends know," he said, and he ruffled Justin's hair, thoroughly messing it up. "And we're damn proud of you."

As Zechariah stood back up, Justin smiled in spite of himself and ran a hand over his hair, trying to fix it. Zechariah turned and walked back the same way he came.

"Why didn't you tell me?" asked Justin. "About the aurym power I was supposed to have?"

Without turning around, Zechariah called back, as he disappeared into the shadows, "And have it go to your head, Master Holmes? As if that willful streak of yours needed encouraged!"

And with that, Justin was alone again.

Keys, he thought. *Keys. . . .*

Key.

Something about the word suddenly struck Justin as odd. Well, not odd, exactly, but familiar.

A nugget of a memory wiggled its way to the surface of the gray matter between Justin's ears. It was something Zechariah had told him, just before they had made their violent first acquaintance with Olorus and Hook while riding up into the Shifting Mountains.

"This little rock," Zechariah had told him, on that distant mountain trail, "is what the Ancients called *y'thri'ra*, which means, in the common tongue, 'keystone.' Among aurym-users, it is better known as a 'gauge.'"

"Impossible," said Justin.

Justin looked down the hallway, but Zechariah was gone. Justin reached into his pocket and found the tiny pebble. He had been carrying the gauge ever since Ahlund had given it to him on the road north of Lonn. Not even as a prisoner had he been without it. Looking at the dull, quartz-like little rock, he thought back to the strange wording in the Book of Unfinished Dreams.

I believe the two worlds exist not across vast distances but alongside each other. The way one paper map might lay on top of another. . . . The Keys of the Ancients seem to allow certain people to move between the maps, momentarily bridging the gap between worlds. And only the bizarre and unique aurym capabilities of an ethoul, or "Fallen Angel," can power the Keys to open the door.

Justin held the gauge, the keystone, in the palm of his hand, staring at it. How hard he had tried to light this little amulet, and each time to no avail. He had never been able to make it glow. Not until his battle with Lisaac, when the presence of evil had made the need intense, had he been able to draw on aurym at all.

If I use it now, thought Justin, *and feed aurym through it, will it take me home?*

Yes, came the answer from somewhere outside himself. *It will.*

Justin stood. He removed the orange cape from over his toga and armor, and he let it fall to the floor. He slid his cat's eye sword into the sheath on his back.

With the gauge in his hand, he opened his palm until his fingers were stretched flat. He felt peace, knowledge, and understanding flowing through him. He let the power surge through his arm, into his hand, and through the stone. It had glowed blue in Zechariah's hand in the caves. Under Ahlund's influence, it had produced an intense orange light. But now, the bright spot that appeared in the stone's center was green as jade.

The light grew, expanding outward like a dilating pupil, until the entirety of the stone was encompassed in green radiance. It grew, and soon a swirling, verdant nebula was expanding and contracting in Justin's hand. Green shadows danced across the palace hallway. He was doing it. He was making it glow, just like Ahlund and Zechariah had done.

But there was a second form, he realized, beyond this elementary manifestation. He could push it further, to something more.

Taking a deep breath, Justin flexed his hand, curling his fingertips upward and feeding his power through each finger to converge on the stone.

The light crackled and sparked. The gauge floated off his hand and hung levitating over his palm. The light grew so bright that it encompassed all vision. With it came a loud humming noise, like the sound of many winged creatures taking flight at once.

The humming reached a crescendo. The green nebula became a galaxy, and the visible incarnation of Justin's power seemed to be all that existed.

CHAPTER 128

Gradually, Justin withdrew his aurym from the stone. The light faded, but the brightness had taken its toll; even after the light of his aurym devolved into a speck and disappeared within the gauge stone, his vision was momentarily impaired.

But he didn't need sight to notice the changes. There was noise. So much noise everywhere. Some came from close by, some from far away, but it was constant and inescapable.

And it was cold. His Hartlan toga provided little protection from the snow that fell on him and lay several inches deep around his feet, covering the flat, hard surface on which he stood.

The dissonant noise around him began to take on individual forms: distant vehicles, the hum of electrical heating units, and the whispering roar of a plane somewhere high overhead, miles away. In front of him were rectangles of bright, electric light in familiar patterns.

"My house," he heard himself say.

The flat, hard surface he stood on was his driveway. The rectangles of light were the lighted windows of his living room. And that darkened one above. It was the second-story window of his bedroom.

"Home," he said.

Never had so simple a word carried such profound meaning to Justin.

After everything he'd been through—all the death, the danger, the darkness, the sorrow, the pain—here he was, in a place where safety was not only tangible but downright likely, and very nearly assured if you played your cards right. Here, a violent death in bloody combat was about as far removed from everyday life as the moon in the sky—the single moon in the sky.

Nothing had changed. The house looked the same. The truck was in the driveway, and there were Christmas lights on every home, up and down the street.

But why were there Christmas lights? Justin had been gone for weeks. Even Jeff Emerson next door—a man who was devout about purging decorations the very day after Christmas—still had twinkling strands hanging from his gutters.

Turning, Justin saw his Uncle Paul's SUV parked in the driveway. Was it still Christmas Day? The same day as the day he'd left? Had it all really just been a dream?

Justin looked down at his arm wrapped in black satin. He rapped his knuckles against it. Hard as stone.

"Definitely not a dream," he said.

The weeks he had experienced since leaving seemed not to have passed on Earth. Time must have moved differently between the worlds. But none of that mattered anymore. He was home. He could go in his own house, climb the stairs to his own room, and go to sleep in his own bed.

My bed! he thought as he looked up at his darkened bedroom window. *I never thought I would miss my bed so much.*

No more sleeping on the hard ground! Or on cold cave floors. Or in enemy encampments, waiting to be tortured. He was safe. He was home. Everything was finally back to normal, just as he'd hoped for ever since waking up in that terrible place. Finally, things were right.

So, why wasn't he happy?

He looked at the dining room window and realized there were people inside, seated at the table. At the head of the table was the bald head of Grandpa Holmes. Uncle Paul sat beside him. There were two more places set, but both were empty. One for his father, of course, and the other for him. It seemed time *had* passed here, but not enough for his father to not set a place for him at Christmas dinner. There was something supremely comforting about returning home to find the table still set for him.

Still, he must have been missing for several hours by now. They were probably worried. If he was careful enough, he might be able to sneak in, slip up to his room to change into something normal—something that would hide his arm—and take his place at the table. "Sorry," he would say. "Ran over to a friend's house to spread some Christmas cheer. Forgot my phone and lost track of time. . . ."

And then what?

Life would go on as usual, just as it always had. Things would be back to normal, and everything would be fine. No more sword fights. No more demons. No more danger. No more war.

"But not for them," whispered Justin. "Not for Leah. Not for Ahlund or Zechariah. Not for any of my friends. Only for me."

But this is what you wanted! his inner self screamed. *You're finally home. You don't have to worry about that stuff anymore. All you have to worry about is doing your homework, finishing high school with some decent grades, and. . . .*

In the window, the half-height silhouette of Justin's father rolled by in his wheelchair. Sandy blonde hair, so much like his own. Glasses perched atop a nose that was too big for his face. An infectious smile. Three plates balanced precariously on one arm. Ben sat each plate down on the table in succession, then rolled to his place. Justin sniffed the air and could smell the food from here. He could almost feel the warmth of the house. He thought of the softness of his pillow, in his bed, in *his* room, in his home. The guilt of leaving his new friends behind was giving him second thoughts, but he knew, once he walked through that door, any lingering doubts would be erased. He would be back home, and he would never want to leave his comfortable, ordinary life ever again.

And yet, a tiny voice within—a voice that, by now, he had learned not to ignore—spoke up.

You are not meant for an ordinary life.

"I can't stay here, can I?" he said, and he knew the answer.

He could almost hear Leah's voice saying, *You are full of surprises, Justin.*

"I keep surprising myself, too," he whispered.

Opening his hand, he looked at the gauge, the Key of the Ancients, and stared at its dull center. He let his power flow, just a bit, and saw the way it reacted: a little, green spark like the bioluminescence of a firefly on a summer night.

He looked at the dining room window again, and he shivered against the cold.

"I have to go back," he whispered, as if his father might somehow hear him from out here. "I know you need me, but right now, they need me more. Someday, I will come back here. For good."

He felt a lump forming in his throat.

"I'm sorry for leaving. I'm sorry for the pain it will cause you. I wish I could explain. But if I walk through that door right now, I don't think I'll have the strength to finish the task entrusted to me. If I go in there even for a minute, to tell you where I've been and where I'm going, I'll never leave. So I can't. Someday, I'll explain everything, and I'll ask your forgiveness. But right now, I can't."

Justin curled his fingers, willing his aurym into the stone. He covered it with his opposite hand to hide the burning light. He looked into the dining room window of the house on Main Street Extension one last time. Tears blurred his vision. The light was turning his world into a tapestry of green on green. His aurym had nearly consumed him when his father's head turned to look out the window. Their eyes met.

Grandpa and Uncle Paul were oblivious. They neither saw Justin outside nor noticed Justin's father watching something out the window.

A curious look came to the face of Ben Holmes. And then he did the last thing Justin would have expected. He smiled. He adjusted his glasses, and he smiled.

Justin's lip quivered, and he had to clench his teeth to keep his resolve. He raised a hand and waved. Ben Holmes nodded to his son.

"I'm sorry," Justin said. "Everything will be all right. I promise. Goodbye."

The light became everything, and Earth disappeared.

CHAPTER 129

He pushed open the front door with one hand. His calloused palms worked the metal rungs to propel the chair out into the bitter cold. Twin, parallel trails in the freshly fallen snow marked his course down the concrete ramp and into the driveway. Dinner was over, and inside, he could hear the clinking of plates as his brother scraped them clean for the dishwasher.

A few more pushes and he had reached the center of the driveway. Here, he stopped.

The snow was coming down hard. So hard it had almost blotted out the tracks in front of him. But as he leaned forward, rested his elbows on his knees, and adjusted his glasses, he could see them: inexplicable footprints, in the center of the driveway, without a single track leading to or from, as if someone had been dropped there right out of thin air.

Benjamin Holmes arched his neck and looked up into the night sky, letting the snowflakes hit his face. They stuck in his five o'clock shadow and clung to his glasses. He closed his eyes, focusing on the warm, humming, all-knowing energy of aurym.

"You found your way back home," Ben said to no one. "Only to leave again."

Dimples formed in Ben's cheeks as he smiled. "I always knew you would be braver than me."

He looked down again. The footprints were already nearly erased. He gave the vague outlines one last look, painting the picture in his mind's eye, then turned his chair around and pushed his way back toward the front door.

He stopped before the ramp and glanced back over his shoulder.

"I wonder," he whispered. "Did you figure it out yourself? Or did you find my book?"

He considered.

"I hope someday your journey brings you back home again," Ben said. He ran a hand over his lap, feeling the fleshless leg beneath the fabric of his pants, hard as bone-plated armor. "Until then, good luck out there, Justin. Do your best. And don't look back."

Justin returns to the Oikoumene in

THE FALLEN AENEID

Go to **www.thefallenodyssey.com/freesequel** to read the sequel for free.

A Message from the Author

Dear Reader,

First off, thanks for reading. I'm not sure what else to say right now, honestly, which is kind of an embarrassing spot to be in when words are you work. . . .

I suppose I'll start by stating the obvious: If you're reading this, you have either (a) just finished reading *The Fallen Odyssey*, the first book in a three-book series, or (b) skipped ahead to read the last page before actually finishing the book (which is total anarchy—go back and read it through properly, you barbarian).

If you belong to the above-mentioned group (a), I hope this book isn't the worst thing you've ever read. If it *is* the worst thing you've ever read, I am a bit baffled as to how you got here; to read 140,000 words of a story you dislike makes you either a glutton for punishment or some sort of compulsive completionist. Either way, you brought this misery on yourself. But thanks for reading anyway (and don't forget to recycle).

If you did like the book, however, then as a small token of my gratitude for sticking with me through these pages, I would like to give you the sequel, *The Fallen Aeneid*, for free. In an ideal world, I would be able to mail a free paperback copy to you and anyone else who wanted one, but that just can't be done.* Instead, I can do the next-best thing. I can send you an ebook copy right now—this minute, in fact. If you go to the following web address, the book will arrive in your email inbox instantly. Just go to: **www.thefallenodyssey.com/freesequel**.

Three more quick things, and then I'll say so long for a while. First off, if you're interested in a signed paperback copy of *The Fallen Odyssey* for you or for someone else, go to **www.thefallenodyssey.com/reserve-your-paperback**. Second, because I'm a big believer in the value of getting young adults and teenagers to read more, young readers are welcomed to a free ebook copy of *The Fallen Odyssey* suitable for reading on phones and/or various devices. Just go to **www.thefallenodyssey.com/readerdeal**. (Reminder: Keep things age appropriate. Over the age of thirteen is probably best.**)

And third, if you got five minutes or more of enjoyment out of this book, please take five minutes to leave a review on Amazon. If you got less than five minutes of enjoyment out of this book, consider yourself off the hook.***

Thank you for joining me on this adventure.
Ever journey on.

—Corey

* It's tempting to try sending paperbacks if only to become a regular at my local post office. "Corey!" the somehow-always-angry-looking ladies behind the counter would shout in unison as I walked in.
** The author does hereby absolve himself of any liability for children having nightmares about monsters, demons, mutilated hands, transformed limbs, scorpion-spiders, ad nauseam.
*** Also, I'm sorry.

ABOUT THE AUTHOR

COREY MCCULLOUGH is an independent copy editor, proofreader, ghostwriter, and author. He lives in western Pennsylvania with his amazing wife Vanessa and their two beautiful daughters. His favorite pastimes are reading, writing, playing video games, spending time with his best friend (Vanessa), and, most of all, being a dad.

Instagram @cbenmcc
thefallenodyssey.com
facebook.com/mcculloughwrites
facebook.com/thefallenodyssey
mcculloughauthor@gmail.com
cbmcediting.com

Made in the USA
Columbia, SC
26 June 2020